A HAUNTED MAN

STUART NEILD

DRAGOON PUBLISHING LTD

First published in 2004 by e-booksonline (UK) Ltd

This edition (second) published in 2006 by
DRAGOON PUBLISHING LTD

ISBN 0-9553413-0-2

Cover design and typeset by Design Office, Alsager, Cheshire

Printed and bound in the United Kingdom by
ER Design & Print, Alsager, Cheshire

DRAGOON PUBLISHING LTD
Dane Mill Business Centre
Broadhurst Lane
Congleton
Cheshire CW12 1LA
United Kingdom

www.dragoonpublishing.co.uk

Author's notes

There is no better place to start a thing than at the beginning, so at the beginning we will indeed start. Boag-Munroe was a character I created way back in 1988 in a short story I wrote for Fear magazine. The magazine folded and the story didn't get published. A second Boag-Munroe story was written for the old Pan horror books, and that didn't get to see the light of published print either. Somewhere along the line these stories got lost and to be honest, in their original form, they're probably best left that way. I came up with a third story, or rather a play, a mish-mash of the first two stories combined in the early 1990s. This was duly considered by BBC Radio Four as the first in a series of Boag-Munroe plays. Once more the project bit the dust. Over ten years later, Boag-Munroe project number four lies in your very grasp. It's been a long way, baby.

The Boag-Munroe from back then was a lot older than this present-day one. Maybe that Boag-Munroe lives in some different parallel universe to the one in this book? Maybe this more youthful Boag-Munroe will grow into the creaky old codger in those old defunct stories? Who can tell? The one thing I can say is that this book would not be here today if it were not for a select group of people who have backed me and had faith in me over the years. Top of the list are my parents. Without their help and support, a lot of other things (myself included) wouldn't have seen the light of day, least of all this book. Joking aside, I really do owe them all my love and thanks. They are good people and not enough good people are recognised and thanked in this world. This book is dedicated to you, Mum and Dad. Thank you both.

Other thanks go out to my agent who also happens to be my wife, Sharon; to my three children, James, Jessica and Charlotte; and to my good friends, Rick Wilson, Mike Lightfoot, Mark Gibson and James Cook.

I hope they and you enjoy this book and other Boag-Munroe adventures to come.

And remember, ghosts do exist. I should know. I've seen…

Stuart Neild
The Witching Hour, 6th June 2004

PROLOGUE: THE PAST

She didn't have a care in the world. She should have done, on account of what was happening to her; but for now, for some reason, she felt more interested than frightened. The fear factor had passed away after a month, leaving her with only wonderment and anticipation.

She turned to look at the clock face, which was illuminated by the soft September moonlight that filtered through the slight gap in the curtains and into her bedroom. Eleven thirty. Another fifteen minutes and he would arrive. He… whoever *he* was.

Instinct forced her to jump out of bed. She checked that the catch on her bedroom door was locked, likewise her window. Now, feeling a little easier, she jumped back under the sheets. This had become the same routine over the past couple of months. A series of checking doors, windows, then waiting, then checking again and waiting and yet more waiting. Then at eleven forty-five, like clockwork, he would arrive.

About three weeks previously she had sneaked her boyfriend into her bedroom; not an unusual thing for a teenager to do, but this wasn't for entertainment purposes. Her boyfriend had a vested interest in these types of things. He… *it*, hadn't turned up that night though. It was as if *it* knew.

In the early stages she'd had numerous girlfriends stay over. But each time someone spent the night, *it* didn't show up. It was no wonder she wasn't believed. But she believed. She'd seen all the proof she needed and a whole lot more.

Eleven thirty-five. She was ready and settled, awaiting the night's outcome. The room and the house were 'at one' and silent; there was not even a murmur from either her parents' or little brother's rooms. They were all heavy sleepers and were not interested in the slightest at what they saw as a sixteen-year-old girl's flights of fantasy.

Eleven forty. Now she could hear a sound. It was an old cliché, but the noise of her heartbeat swam up from her body and swelled into her ears.

Eleven forty-three. The time was almost upon her. The temperature dropped. Now there would be no escape, even if she was afraid.

Eleven forty-five. The curtain billowed although the window was tightly shut. She pulled the blankets up, close to her chin and watched intently. The white light appeared first as it had on all the other nights. Within seconds the outline of a small boy appeared within it. A few seconds more and the outline was filled in. The boy in the light was dressed in a fashion straight from the Second World War era, complete with gas mask at his side.

She smiled softly. "Hello."

There was no answer from him.

"It's nice to see you again." She greeted him like an old friend.

His mouth opened, conversing, but no sound emitted from it, like watching television with the mute button on. He looked afraid; perhaps that was why she felt calm in his unusual presence. Then he was gone. Twelve o'clock and he vanished as always, leaving her lying in her bed, pondering her next move for the following night.

Little did she realise that she would soon be dead.

CHAPTER ONE: THE PRESENT

"Arthur!" the girls shouted at the red-faced boy.

He hurried on as quickly as possible, away from the female huddle standing on the street corner, half embarrassed that they'd acknowledged him and half with the sound of his own name. Nobody was called Arthur in this day and age, no more than anyone was called Cyril or Mavis.

The sight and sounds of the females passed and he drew a sigh of relief. They were two years older than his ten years of age but the fact that they were females, and at high school to boot, made the age gap seem light years apart.

He was late now, by at least an hour. He was definitely in trouble. He'd been at a friend's house playing the latest console games. That was where the complications started. It was a friend who shouldn't have been a friend, at least in his mother's eyes. The friend in question, although only Arthur's age and a fellow classmate, was also a convicted thief and general all-out rogue, hence the fact that he always had a great collection of the latest and best games, on account of his rich pickings. And rich picking it had been tonight indeed. Three top games had been unleashed for Arthur's approval. It was no wonder he was late and in a panic that his cover story would surely be blown. He had said he would be with a more savoury friend, but surely his mother had rang that friend by now, to challenge Arthur's no-show homecoming. In fact she could be ringing at that very moment.

Whatever the moment, it didn't matter. He would be found out.

He raced through Northwich town centre, pausing at the top of the subway. The bypass was unusually busy for the time of night, but it was coming up to Christmas, so he took the challenge and raced into the grim underground passage. The smell of stale urine was as vicious as the coldness of being below ground, surrounded by concrete corridor. Drab yellow lights lit the way and within seconds his subway adventure was over and he was heading across Chinkers football field, through the masses of dog foul that the under-nine's football team had been sliding about in half an hour earlier.

He finally ran out of breath, by the graveyard of all places. He didn't dare look to the left and through the metal railings to the churchyard. The news was full of children going missing, but it wasn't the thought of some stranger taking him hostage, or even murdering him, that scared him. It was the thought of seeing a ghost that filled him full of dread. That, and what his mother would do to him when he got home.

He fought for his breath and mounted enough of a challenge to get it back before breaking into a jog, past Roker Park, and onto the final straight.

They say most disasters happen near home. He might have only been on the earth for a decade, but Arthur's young ears had picked up that phrase from somewhere and his brain had stored the information, only to release it now, just as he heard other breathing, just as heavy as his own, coming up from behind.

He didn't dare turn round.

He pushed himself forward.

There was never anyone about by the park at this time. The streets were deserted as always and the few houses around were unlit and empty-looking. He shouldn't have taken the shortcut. In his head, he could hear his mother shouting at him. He could almost hear her sobbing for real as the panting behind became more furious, and the footsteps became louder. His mother had not wanted him to go out tonight, not with all the missing children trouble. She'd conceded because his brother, although four years older, had gone out camping over night in a nearby field with friends. Now Arthur found himself telling himself what he'd told his mother: that the child snatchings had happened far away.

So who was it closing in on him?

He raced past the vandalised phone box on the street corner, and onto his home patch. Normally the Danefields council estate was full of young children playing out at unholy hours, but not tonight. Curtains were tightly closed, doors locked shut.

Arthur could hear it, whoever or whatever it was, still coming behind him. He thought of stopping and banging on a front door. If he did, would anyone answer? Would whatever was after him catch him?

Arthur didn't dare stop. Home was nearly in sight, even though no living creature could be seen.

He was nearly there.

Arthur felt his heart sink as his stitch began to penetrate his pain barrier. He felt his head go dizzy. With a blur, he hit the ground.

The jogger passed by and, with him, so did Arthur's fear, only to be followed by embarrassment. He picked himself up and brushed himself down, and within a second he was on course and racing round the corner to home.

The mass of police cars and general activity outside Arthur's house, hit him with the realisation that his mum had rung the police and reported him missing. Now he almost wished he was. Shamefully, he made his way up the path, stepping through a huddle of neighbours. His mum was waiting, tearful, at the door.

"Arthur. Your brother is missing."

The words drilled into his brain and stayed there, wriggling about, causing him great discomfort as the reality of them set in. His elder brother was missing? Soon other sentences embedded into his skull. They told the full story. When his brother had gone camping, he'd had a row with one of his friends and stormed off home. Of course, kids being kids, nobody checked if he'd got home safely. Home hadn't panicked because he was supposedly out with friends, all of them safe in numbers. But Arthur's brother's number had been subtracted. Now he was a different number: a missing number. He was number three to go missing in the past three weeks.

PC Graham Pratt stood like a spare part. Not the kind of spare part that someone might find a use for in the not-too-distant future, more of a discarded one and liable to be left that way. The police hotshots had been called in and were buzzing all over the place. He sniffed with distaste. He'd never liked the Danefields council estate. It was full of cheeky kids, the sort that took the mick to the hilt and got away with it to the max. You couldn't even so much as throw them an icy glance, or they'd have their social worker onto you.

A little bit of humanity ignited a tiny piece of guilt in Pratt's soul – it was a missing child after all. A moment later, and the guilt had flickered out of life as quickly as it had flickered in. One less to give him abuse or any of the other crap he had to put up with, he thought, whilst on guard outside the council house, now the buzz of all the activity. The hotshots don't have to put up with this, he sneered, as someone shouted "Pig!" at him. The hotshots just get all the good bits. They come and go as if they're in an episode of a television cop show. They don't have to stand in the freezing cold for hours on end, guarding the crime scene.

Damn it, this isn't even the crime scene. This is a case of standing outside a council house, warding off unnecessary visitors, or rather nosey bastards. No doubt the papers will arrive soon. He hated reporters more than kids and hotshots combined. Blood-sucking leeches, that's all they are, he thought. Plus they get paid about a million-times more than I do, and what for? A bit of gossip?

He sniffed, feeling he was coming down with a cold. His body ached and creaked. He was twenty-eight years old but felt like fifty. A hotshot passed him by and gave him a dirty look, while a teenager shouted abuse in the distance. Graham Pratt hated his life and all the hassle that went with it.

CHAPTER TWO

The face was pure evil. Mary knew it even before she saw it. She knew he wanted to kill her, even before she'd heard him walking slowly up the gravel-filled path that led to her front door. She knew it was the man her parents had warned her about, even before he'd knocked so loudly and menacingly on the front door. When the knock finally rang out, in and around her ears, she dived for safety at the back of the settee. She would hide there, for now, but it was a poor comparison to the safety of her parents. Why had they left her all alone, when they knew about the man? It was them who had warned her of him, her own father especially and constantly: "Be a good girl and do as your dad says or the nasty man will take you away for good."

She hunched up into a ball, not daring to peek round the settee, fearing to gaze at the large glass living-room window that would easily betray her.

Another knock rang out. What if the door wasn't locked? What if he broke in anyway? If he was as bad as her dad had said, he'd think nothing of breaking into a house to get to his victim.

The knocking finally stopped. Silence reigned supreme. But somehow, the silence was worse. She took a deep breath. Was he still there, silently waiting? She would have to look sooner or later.

Gingerly, she tipped her head round the corner of the settee. To her absolute horror he stood in full view at the window. His face was a total blur, no features, no eyes or mouth, just an evil blankness.

But she knew he had seen her. She knew he was looking at her, and now that she had given herself away, she knew he was going to kill her.

Mary Edwards often reminisced both reluctantly and darkly about her former nightmares. Even now, twenty years since the nightmare had haunted her, helpless in her sleep, she went back to it as a curious, conscious afterthought. At least now, like the bad memory it was, she could send it back to the darkest recess of her mind.

She'd had the luxury of looking back a lot just recently, about various events in her life, since the recent break up from her husband. The lack of belongings and small flat she now resided in, gave her a lot of time to think about things. At least she still had her son, Andrew, fast asleep in the next room. He may have been only ten, the same age as her when she had suffered those terrible nightmares, but he was a great comfort to her, and probably had more intelligent conversation in him than her soon-to-be-ex-husband.

Gently, she opened the bedroom door and gazed at the angelic sight of her son, illuminated by his night-light. He'd been restless for the past two nights. Something she put down to the recent events of the split. Still, he was sound asleep now; she was thankful enough for that.

The doorbell rang. She wasn't expecting anyone, especially at this time of night, but she raced out of the room and towards the front door of her flat, before the bell rang again and destroyed her son's precious sleep.

"Thought I'd just nip round to see how you were."

Before Mary could even reply, she looked on with mild surprise as the petite blonde squeezed past her and began to make herself at home in her living room.

"Don't mind me!" Mary's surprise was sliding off and sarcasm seeping in.

"I won't." The blonde tossed her hair back and sprawled outright, relaxing on the settee. "I've brought wine," she exclaimed, brandishing the bottle in her outstretched arm.

Mary eyed the bottle. "So I can see."

"I thought it would help us wind down."

"Us?" Mary asked.

"Well you've had enough stress over the last couple of months, and I've just split up with my boyfriend."

Mary looked unsurprised at the revelation. "But Sue – you always split up with your boyfriend on a Friday night."

Sue smiled, "But tonight is Saturday. That alone must tell you the seriousness of the matter."

"But you've only been with him for three months."

Sue rolled her eyes and sighed. "Yes, yes, I know. And you'd been with John for twelve years."

Mary looked a little guilty; she knew that it must have seemed like she wasn't bothering about her best friend's problems. And, after all, Sue had always listened to her problems, and there had been a lot of those lately. She took the bottle from Sue and examined it.

Sue winked. "Red wine, your favourite."

"You mean *your* favourite."

"Never turn your nose up at a free drink."

Sue noticed the small sniffling figure of Andrew, appearing silently behind Mary. "I think we've got company. How are you doing, little man?"

"Andrew, what are you doing up?" Mary pushed the bottle aside. "I'll have to get him settled again, Sue. You start without me, I won't be more than a couple of minutes."

Mary gently shut the bedroom door behind her and sat on the edge of the bed where her son was sitting with his head bowed.

"What's the matter, Andrew?"

"I'm not tired."

"Don't be silly. You'll make yourself ill."

"I'm scared."

"What of?"

"The man."

Mary looked concerned. "What man?"

"The man with no face. He stares through the window at me." Andrew grew hysterical. "I know he's bad. I know he wants to get me." He became a sobbing wreck, crying into the comfort of his mother's arms.

Sue held up the nearly empty bottle triumphantly. "Whatever took you so long? It didn't take me long."

"So I see." Mary sounded distant.

"What's up? More problems in single-mother land?"

"Let's just call it a night."

"Are you kicking me out? I've been waiting here over an hour."

"Don't make it sound like that. I can do without the whole guilt trip thing laid on me right now."

Sue jumped up to her feet. "It's OK." She sounded sharp. "Here, keep the bottle and what's left in it. That's what friends are for after all."

"Don't be like that, Sue."

Sue, worse for the wear from the drink, scrambled to the door. "Have a nice night."

She slammed the door shut behind her. Normally, Mary would have given chase and coaxed her back. Sue's life had been so littered with such volatile moments that Mary was used to them and didn't take offence at Sue's many outbursts. But Mary had other concerns now; much more pressing concerns. Her son had told her something, something she hadn't wanted to hear, something she had feared to hear. He was having nightmares, the same nightmares about the same man. The same nightmares she'd had all those years ago and told no one about, ever. Not a living soul.

Mary silently crept into her son's room. His night-light still illuminated his troubled, but sleeping features. She pulled up an uncomfortable chair and sat beside him, trying to make herself as settled as best she could. She knew she wouldn't get a wink of sleep tonight so it was a waste of time trying.

The night drifted on. He did not murmur.

Mary looked on, looking like the very essence of tranquillity watching over her son. But in her head, she was in complete turmoil.

CHAPTER THREE

The midnight wind forced its way mercilessly through the trees of Marbury Country Park, bending all but the strongest of them in its wake. The giant iron gates that sat beside the lonely road lay wide, like open arms, inviting rather than deterring, the purpose they had once fulfilled. They were redundant now. The great house no longer stood, so they had nothing else to guard but hundreds of years worth of memories. In between the deep woodland at either side, the grounds were still well kept, on account of the area now being a nature reserve. The lawns were neatly trimmed, with signposts dotted about, giving visitors a short burst of history about the area, house and its legends.

Just inside the gates stood a party of five. They were all alone, separated from the rest of humanity, miles from any living thing on the lonely landscape.

A red-faced, highly overweight, excitable-looking man called Nigel seemed to be the leader. He had the face and the figure of a sixty-five year old, the zest of a twenty year old, but was in fact thirty-five years old and counting.

Next in line was the strange bird-like figure of Jason. As he spoke his head jerked forward, almost accusingly, like a scrawny pigeon pecking at seed. Nerd-style thick glasses and a crop of spiky hair crowned his thin head. It portrayed a kind of rebel look the rest of his persona didn't have, making him look like a train-spotter on acid.

Seated in a wheelchair was Hannah, a woman who was proud to admit her eighty years of age. Her face was beaming. At the back of her eyes you could almost see her chuckling that she was outwitting death. Her face was ecstatically red where the wind was slapping her cheeks.

The other two were a male and a female, the male about seventeen and the female slightly younger. Neither had any distinct features to boast of or be embarrassed about, but the girl, whether she would admit it or not, obviously had a hankering for the boy.

"We'll have to split up." Jason's words, but not exactly those the group wanted to hear.

"I don't think it's wise," Nigel offered.

"We've no other choice. The others haven't turned up so it's down to us five, or else this has been a waste of time and effort."

"I don't feel easy about it," Nigel protested again.

"You've not suddenly become afraid of the ghosts we chase, have you?" goaded Jason.

Hannah spun round in her wheelchair to face Jason dead centre: "It's not the dead he's afraid of; it's the living."

"The missing children?" Jason sneered. "Well, we're not children."

"No… but others in this group aren't exactly adults," Nigel volleyed back.

Hannah chipped in: "Don't be offended, Jason. He's talking in age, not mental terms."

Jason stood smouldering.

"Bradley's just seventeen and Emily only had her sixteenth birthday two weeks ago," Nigel stated calmly.

"The children that are missing aren't that old, hence the term 'children'," Jason spat.

Nigel walked close to Jason in a slightly intimidating manner, or at least as intimidating as he could possibly manage. "From five to fourteen. And who's to say he won't be thinking of adding a sixteen or seventeen year old to his collection?"

"Or a thirty-two year old who has always lived with his mother and father," added Hannah.

Jason backed away, slightly flustered. "We don't even know they're dead."

"They're dead all right." Hannah's voice had a ring to its tone that made the words sound as equally true as they sounded horrific.

Nigel looked darkly. "Whatever, it's not our concern. And I'd like to keep it like that."

The two youngest members of the group thrust themselves forward. They had obviously picked up on things that hadn't been meant for their ears. The boy spoke: "It's all right. I can look after myself."

The girl breathed into life: "Me too. Just as added safety though, I could tag along with Bradley?"

Bradley looked down at her with something definitely the opposite of her look of admiration.

"Take the lake lookout then," Jason ordered before anyone could offer any support or objection.

Bradley and Emily left straight away; Emily trailing Bradley's large strides as he disappeared into the darkness of the trees. Nigel headed to more woods in the opposite direction. Jason paused for a second in thought.

"I'll be fine here. You run along." Hannah smiled at Jason.

"I'm just trying to find my notes," Jason replied nervously.

"It was your idea to split up. Not scared, are you?" Hannah asked.

Jason grunted an insult under his breath, too quiet for human ears, and then vanished into yet more trees straight ahead. Hannah pulled her blanket up closer and sat waiting. Little did she or any of the group realise they were being watched by a figure in black from a distance.

"It's a nice view." Emily looked at Bradley, admiring him more than the view of the lake that spread in front of them. A couple of unoccupied rowing boats bobbed on the water; otherwise, everything else was still.

"We're not here for the view. I thought we were here for the ghost." Bradley always kept Emily at arm's length.

She gazed back at the lake, a little taken aback. She'd waited a long time to get so close.

"It's your first time, isn't it?" Bradley asked.

"Pardon?" She looked even more taken aback.

"Field work."

For a few seconds she looked lost, hurt even. Then she slipped back into simply looking up at him like a lost puppy dog.

Bradley scratched at his chin. "My dad's friend saw her. She came up from the lake just there, right in front of us. He was night fishing. My dad had been with him, but had to head off early. So there was my dad's friend, sat alone on his fishing basket, on a night, let's say, like this."

Emily visibly gulped.

"At first it was the air that changed, it went colder, much colder, and he knew something was coming." He paused, admiring his handiwork in Emily's uneasy face. "But by the time the realisation had set in, she was there, rising up from the lake. Of course by this time he couldn't move."

She lapped up every word in a trance. "Why not?"

"Fear. He was paralysed with it. Have you ever been that afraid?"

She spoke nervously, afraid to be heard: "No."

"She appeared out of the water at the very point her body had been thrown in. The white shrouded figure of the Marbury lady."

Emily cottoned on to what Bradley was doing and stood up to him with some false bravado. "You're not scaring me, if that's what you think."

"I'm only telling the truth. That's what we're doing here, isn't it? Proving things, finding out the truth?" He carried on trying to find chinks in her fragile armour.

"You do know the full story of the Marbury lady, of course?"

"Of course!" She threw her answer back.

"How she was supposedly an Egyptian princess who was murdered by her husband when he found out she had a lover. A lover she would meet via a secret tunnel running under the grounds. The tunnel's gone now. Or rather nobody knows where it is. It might even run under here."

She crossed her arms and shot him one of those looks her mother always gave her father, when she was displeased. "Are you telling me this for your benefit or mine?"

Bradley backed off. "Look, I'm only messing about."

She turned away from him, silent. She'd caught that trick off her mother too.

"Come on, Emily. Don't go funny on me."

She smiled at him forgivingly.

He, in turn, went back to tormenting: "Of course, there have been other murders around here. There was one only about sixteen or so years ago. It might have been less. Some girl got…"

"Yes, I know!" she screamed, cutting him off mid-sentence.

He smiled, "You *are* scared."

"No I'm not."
"Good, because I've just remembered something I left back at base."
"Base?"
"Yes, by the gates. I won't be long."
"Bradley!" She said it with a mixture of anger and fear.
Bradley ran headlong into the darkness, leaving her alone. Apart, that is, from the black-clad figure neither she, nor the others had seen. A figure that was moving closer.
She heard a twig snap. She spun round. "Bradley?"
The wind whistled. The trees and the darkness closed in on her, as did the figure. She didn't dare speak; she felt the atmosphere go cold, very cold. She wanted to follow Bradley, head back to where the others might be, but she was frozen. Was it the same fear that had frozen Bradley's dad's friend to the same spot?
A sudden splash. Something had sounded out in the lake. Emily focussed her eyes out onto the water. It was still. She backed away from the lake, not taking her eyes from it; she didn't even dare take her eyes off it to run, not even when the white figure rose up from the lake in front of her.
A black leather glove clasped her mouth before she could let a scream depart from her lips. The arms that pulled her away from the apparition were gentle yet strong.
A voice whispered in her ear: "It's not real." The hand stayed firm, stifling any sign of a scream. "It's your boyfriend playing a trick, trying to scare you. It's just a white sheet being hauled up on a fishing line."
The hand let go.
She spun round to face the darkly dressed figure that had held her.
Her first thought was how handsome he was. The second thought was the danger she felt she might be in.
"It's OK. I'm not going to hurt you. I'm just not letting him have the satisfaction of scaring you."
Why did she trust him? She searched for an answer in her head. He seemed handsome, gallant and charming. But didn't the Devil have all the best tunes?
He took her gently by the hand and led her towards the figure hovering over the lake. He thrust his arm up high. She heard a snapping sound and the ghost, or rather the white sheet, fell lifelessly into the lake.
"Who the hell are you?" Bradley sprang up from behind a bush.
"Someone," the figure answered, not giving anything away.
"Someone?" Bradley asked angrily.
"Someone who's not too impressed with your little trick," the figure answered emotionlessly yet again.
"And what business is it of yours?" Bradley roared up to the figure, trying to be intimidating.

The figure didn't flinch and spoke softly: "You may be able to scare little girls. But I think you'll find grown men a little harder."

Bradley visibly shook with frustrated temper.

The figure turned to Emily: "If you'll excuse me, I must press on."

After a few seconds pausing and staring at one another, Bradley and Emily took chase after the figure. They finally caught sight of him approaching an astounded-looking Nigel.

"What?" Nigel sounded as astounded as he looked. "It's you!"

The figure smiled, "Of course it's me. I arrived about an hour ago."

"But I wasn't expecting you."

"It's a surprise."

Nigel wasn't any less astounded as time went on. "It's been ten years!"

"It's even more of a surprise then. Anyway, you look like you've seen a ghost, and I'm tired. I'll be at the old place... I've got the key. I just thought I'd drop by to let you know I'm back, old friend."

Nigel was open-mouthed. "Of course."

"After all, it's only manners. I'll see you in the morning then."

The figure left, striding into the distance and darkness, its long black leather coat billowing.

Nigel stood amazed.

Bradley and Emily finally got to Nigel.

"Who the hell was that?" asked Bradley.

Nigel turned to him, still perplexed. "That," he paused, "was Professor Boag-Munroe."

The walk from Marbury Park, on the outskirts of Northwich, to Victoria Road in the centre was long but not too taxing for Boag-Munroe. The night air, although cold, was refreshing, and seeing old and familiar sights mixed with new, made interesting night-time viewing.

Victoria Road itself looked exactly the same as it did ten years ago, when the professor had left it far behind. A massive row of Victorian terraced houses, resplendent with red crumbling brickwork, and bulging bay-windowed fronts.

Boag-Munroe felt for a familiar key in his pocket. Just feeling it, knowing it was going to be used again, sent a shimmering feeling of history through his bones.

With one decisive push, he swung the door open. More familiar feelings washed over him. Happiness tinged with sadness. All those memories.

He made his way down the long narrow hall, through the dining room, and into the living room, sitting down on the same settee he'd left behind all those years ago. It was dustier and a little less sturdy, but still standing the test of time.

The past began to overwhelm him. Perhaps he shouldn't have come back?

Boag-Munroe paused in thought, thinking about re-exploring the rest of the house. He bit his lip, smiled… and left the building.

"We might as well call it a night." Nigel looked tired.

Jason was stomping around Marbury Park, unable to control his anger. "An extremely valid scientific experiment ruined by some clown!"

Nigel had listened to Jason's tirade long enough. "That clown, as you call him, is the reason this society has what it does have. Who else would supply funding? Would you, Jason? Could you?"

"Jason's right," Bradley's still-bruised ego butted in, "he spoiled everything."

Nigel smiled sarcastically. "Like you did with your childish practical joke on Emily? Or was that part of the scientific experiment?"

"Bradley didn't mean it." Emily stood by the boy who she wanted to be her man.

"No *of course* he didn't." Nigel was still in sarcasm mode.

"What was he doing up here anyway?" Jason blurted.

Nigel shrugged his shoulders. "It's a free country. Who knows?" He could see he was getting nowhere with this particular lynch mob, so gave it up as a bad job and walked away, leaving them cursing among themselves. He made his way towards the ever-smiling face of Hannah.

"It's been an interesting night," roared Hannah over the wind.

"Interesting?"

"Yes, your friend turning up like that out of the blue. Or should I say, out of the darkness?"

"He's like that. You never know what he's going to do next. Or when and where he's going to appear, or disappear for that matter."

"What is it, ten years since he left for America?"

"It's about that."

"So why has he come back?"

"I don't know. I've been renting his old house out for him since he left. As you know, he gives the rent from it to the society. It's been unoccupied for the past four months though."

"And how did he know you would be here at Marbury?"

"I've no idea. He just seems to know. He's always been like that, without care or explanation."

Hannah powered her electric wheelchair in the direction of the van in which they'd travelled to Marbury Park.

"The return of Professor James R. Boag-Munroe," she laughed. "I think I'd better hang on to my wheelchair. I've got a feeling the ride is going to get a bit more exiting, if not faster and bumpier from now on."

At this point another figure in black descended on the group.

"What do you lot think you're playing at?" PC Graham Pratt had appeared from nowhere, better than any ghost ever could.

There was some mumbling and nervous fumbling. Only Nigel and Hannah stood firm. The rest of the gathering seemed to melt into the darkness.

"We're on a ghost hunt," explained Nigel.

"Really?" Pratt replied with more sarcasm than enthusiasm. "Fancy that."

"We're the Northwich Supernatural Research Society, NSRS, for short," added Hannah.

Pratt nodded smugly. "I'm Police Constable Pratt, that's PC Pratt for short, and seeing as we're being short, I'll be short and sweet. Why don't you crazies bugger off, before I book you all for loitering?" Pratt had tried to think of some other group who used the initials NSRS, so as to hit them with copyright infringement, but he couldn't, so he didn't, and loitering seemed the next best thing to ruin the party.

They moved without any more hesitation. Pratt felt the warm feeling of a job well done. He often had a sniff around Marbury to catch out courting couples. If he wasn't having any fun, why should anyone else?

He watched them round up their things and move off into the distance. Weirdos. He hated weirdoes. Ghost hunting society, he scoffed to himself, but then realising he was alone he began to feel a little uneasy. He headed back to his car.

It was a strange sensation for Nigel, feeling both tired and yet wide-awake with wonderment. He was tired because of his night's work at Marbury, but in wide-awake wonderment of the sudden and unannounced return of Boag-Munroe. Alone, after dropping the rest of his makeshift team home at this unearthly hour, he headed the van onto Castle Street and up Castle Hill, past the myriad of takeaways that made the small village of Castle, the capital of Northwich's bachelor and divorcee population.

Nigel turned the van into Beeston Street, past the church, and within a couple of minutes was parking it, bumper to bumper, into the only parking space left, ten doors down from his own house.

Nigel turned the key and entered the house, not bothering to turn on the light, and walked into a shapeless mass of darkness.

"You took your time." A familiar voice cut through the darkness, nearly making Nigel jump out of his skin.

"How the hell did you...?"

"You know better than to ask a question like that of me."

"Never a straight answer is it, James?"

"Never give away your tricks and secrets."

"Surely you've built up enough of both over the years, to give a few away?"

"Never surrender a trick, or secret. Not one. You pull one brick out; the rest will only come tumbling down."

An uneasy silence followed.

"Why have you come back like this? Are you in trouble?"

Boag-Munroe smiled, "No more than usual." He noticed Nigel wasn't amused. "I needed a break. I'd been in the States for a long time. What is it they say… Maybe too long? At any rate, I landed back in England a week ago."

"A week ago?"

"Yes. I wanted to see some friends. Then, as everybody does in the end, I came home."

"Something doesn't add up. Why would you leave America so suddenly?"

"Because, believe it or not, the call to home is in us all, like a homing beacon if you like. I was born and bred in Northwich. All right, it might not be the most appetising of places, but it's still in my blood. So I thought I'd take a little holiday."

Nigel stretched a leg. "It's a nice speech, but whether you're afraid to give away any of your secrets or not, I've known you long enough to know, it doesn't quite ring true."

Another silence, this time stretching longer.

Nigel finally broke it, realising he couldn't match Boag-Munroe's steely gaze. "It's good to have you back, old friend."

Boag-Munroe gave a slight pause, and then smiled, "It's good to be back."

Nigel smiled, but deep down he wished he knew what secret his friend was keeping from him, for his unexpected return.

Even deeper down, Boag-Munroe wished he knew too.

CHAPTER FOUR

Mary felt like death. She had managed to sleep for all of five minutes before having to get Andrew ready for school. She rang in work sick, promising herself that as soon as she dropped Andrew off at school, she would grab a few hours of sleep.

All night she had watched over him, thinking at best, worrying at worst, and being mystified at least. How could it be possible for her son to have the same dream that had plagued her at the same age, twenty years ago? Especially as she had told no one even the slightest detail of what had gone on in her head?

It had been a hellish trip for her, suffering the torment of it in silence. Her mother had always been unapproachable. And her father...

She cut her thoughts off. No point dwelling in the past. It might all be coincidence. Andrew might sleep soundly tonight, and at peace.

But what if he was? What if he was to witness that faceless figure of evil like she had for that long period of time?

She recalled the figure. After weeks of fear, it finally formed a face, night by night, bit by bit.

She pushed her thoughts away again.

She'd recognised the face.

Mary brought herself back to the present, shaking.

"Andrew, come on! You're going to be late." Andrew was late for school.

The adrenaline of rushing to get her son to school had eaten into Mary's energy reserves. Now she found herself at an all-time-low of tiredness. The effort to reach the top of the stairs to her flat was annoying and even unpleasant, like a feat of endurance, akin to scaling Mount Everest. She'd almost forgotten what it was like to have such a sleepless and energy-sapping night. Now that lifeless feeling she'd had all those years ago had come back with such a vengeance.

"Hello there."

The words came from behind Mary, as she wavered her key over her flat's door lock. She turned with what little energy she had left to see her neighbour from along the hall.

"Hi." Mary's greeting was weak, but as polite as she could possibly manage.

She struggled with her key.

"You look tired." The neighbour, a mass of black greasy hair, spots, yellow teeth and always an unwavering smell of vinegar, closed in on her.

"I saw you," he stuttered, "earlier on," he stuttered some more, "with your son."

"Did you?" Mary asked. Her patience was running out with her key, the lock, and the neighbour. She noticed the drool dripping from the bottom lip of the short, unhygienic-looking youth, who was now moving even closer.

"Yes, I did see you," he persisted.

"Right." It was the only polite answer she could think of as he moved even closer.

"Must dash." She stabbed her key into the lock and in one swift movement, had opened the door and shot herself through, into the open space of her flat.

She slammed the door shut behind her. "Not a full bag of shopping, that one," she said to herself as she got her breath back.

She sat down, phone in hand, jabbing at its illuminated digits. "You can't choose your neighbours, but at least you can choose your friends."

An electronic voice answered.

"Hello Sue."

The electronic voice garbled.

"You're still talking to me then?"

More garbled sounds.

"Look, I'm sorry about last night. I was just a bit stressed out. You know how it is."

Silence on the line.

"Sue?" Mary inquired.

The garbled voice returned. Mary looked relieved.

The garbled chatter continued.

"No, I'm not at work. I've had the day off."

There was more electronic gibberish down the line.

"No, I won't feel up to it tonight."

The electronic voice went up a few pitches.

"No, I'm not being funny."

Up a couple more pitches.

"Don't be like that."

Silence on the line, followed by the sound of being cut-off.

Mary shrugged her shoulders, not looking too bothered, and tossed the phone to one side.

"Lunatic neighbours and touchy friends. You got it all, babes. Welcome to single-life city," she said to herself, before sprawling out on the settee to embrace sleep.

She was late.

Mary bolted up from her slumber. Without thought, she sprinted to the door, stopping only to reach out for her car keys.

"Hello again." The weird neighbour was waiting outside her door, on the landing.

Mary was in no mood for small talk. She brushed past him, but he followed.

"You look like you're in a hurry."

"Really?" She couldn't help the sarcasm.

"Are you late to pick your son up? Normally, you've left by now."

She turned on him in an anger she couldn't conceal. "Are you watching me?"

"I don't... understand," he stuttered.

Mary wasn't interested. "Because if I were you I wouldn't bother. There's nothing interesting to see."

She stormed off, leaving the strange youth still as foul smelling and dirty-looking as earlier, but now also bewildered.

She would never get to the school on time, not now. The traffic was chock-a-block in Congleton and she had to get to Macclesfield in three minutes. She wished she could have avoided Clayton bypass, as did all the others stuck in the traffic jam, which always seemed to blight this part of the town at this time of day. The car crawled another centimetre before coming to yet another standstill at Rood Hill traffic lights. It was an agonising wait, but the traffic at this time and first thing in the morning was always the same in Congleton. It was even beginning to give her second thoughts about moving to the town. It had seemed like a good idea at the time. She was still close to her home town of Macclesfield, so Andrew didn't have to change schools, but she also had enough distance that she wasn't constantly bumping into her ex-husband. And her best friend, Sue, lived in Congleton. And whatever, the flat was only a temporary measure while the wounds took their time to heal.

Time ticked on. She wasn't going to make it on time.

The nightmare came back into her head.

She was late for Andrew.

She pushed the nightmare aside. At the same time she also pushed away her pride. As the traffic juddered to a halt once more, she reached for her mobile phone.

"Hello John. Could you pick Andrew up from school? Round about now?"

The male voice was cold and to the point: "It's not my day to have him."

"I know that."

"Plus there's the small matter of me being at work."

"I know that as well."

"If you can't cope with the situation…?"

Mary snapped back, "The thing is, something's cropped up and I'm stuck in a traffic jam. Will you pick our son up from school?"

The phone went dead.

"Bastard!" she hissed before slamming her palm on the dashboard.

Both Mary and the car sat fuming.

An obnoxious tinkling tune that she'd thought cute at the time of buying her phone bounced irritably around the car's acoustics.

"Hello!" she barked down the phone.

"I'll pick him up and take him back to our place. Or rather *my* place."

The phone went down before she could add anything to the conversation.

Our place? My place? It had been her home once. She couldn't understand why her ex, John, was turning the knife. If she'd wanted to be a bitch, she'd no need to have left. She could have just kicked him out. That's what Sue had suggested. She'd done it to enough blokes in her time.

Luckily for John, Mary wasn't Sue.

The traffic began to flow a little easier, although now she wished it would slow back down. She wasn't relishing the fact she'd have to see John. She didn't need a face-to-face, not right now.

Mary turned and spoke into her mobile as she reached the familiar cu-de-sac. "Listen, John, I'm parked up the road. I can see the house. Just let Andrew walk to the car."

"What are you on about?"

"I don't want a scene."

"Grow up."

"John, please."

The phone went dead. John wasn't good at many things in life, but if phone slamming had been an international sport, he'd be the world champion by now. In fact, some of Mary's friends, excellent phone slammers themselves, were quite envious and even mystified that a man should possess such a cherished woman's talent.

"Here we go again," Mary sighed to herself as John approached the car with Andrew trailing behind.

John tapped on the car window, which Mary duly wound down.

John stood silent. He'd made the first move; now he was waiting for Mary to make hers.

"What do you want, John?"

"I want us to be civil to one another."

"It's a nice thought, but I don't think it will work."

"Is that all you've got to say?"

She bit her lip. "No. When push comes to shove, I'd like us to both be civil, for Andrew's sake."

"Good." He nodded. "That's that then."

Andrew reached the car. "Hiya, Mum." He said the words with a tinge of sadness that worried Mary. Didn't he want to be parted from his father? Did he love John more than her?

"You do realise I've had to take time off work. This has cost me half a day."

"I appreciate that, John, and I'm sorry. It's just one of those things."

"That's what you put everything down to, one of those things."

A message alert sounded out on Mary's phone as Andrew climbed into the back of the car.

"I suppose that's him ringing you now."

"Bye, John." Mary's answer was short, sharp, and to the point.

She looked down at the message flashing on her mobile screen.

It was him.

The traffic back into Congleton hadn't been that bad, which was just as well, as there was a fog dropping along with the night. She was glad to get back into her flat and even more pleased that her neighbour hadn't been hanging around to greet her. She settled Andrew down to his tea and then stared at the text message her mobile presented her. "WHERE ARE YOU?" it boldly asked, in even bolder letters.

As if she would tell.

The knock on the door signalled a series of questions in Mary's mind. Who was it? What did they want?

Mary edged to the door hesitantly, and opened it with slow caution.

She seemed startled by the short figure that stood in the passage outside.

The little man spoke. "I'm the caretaker, remember?"

"I remember." She bid him entry. "The damp patch in the kitchen."

He smiled and, carrying a bag of tools nearly as big as he was, vanished into the kitchen.

"All done." The caretaker reappeared.

"That was quick!" Mary was surprised.

"It was just a washer that had come a little loose."

"So that's that then?"

"Yes." The caretaker seemed reluctant to leave. "My brother owns this building." He sounded proud and seemed to grow in stature.

"Oh, really?" a not too particularly interested Mary replied.

"Yes. He bought this place a good ten years ago and did it up. I helped him a lot. I used to live here myself, on this floor, down the hall. Now my eldest son lives there."

The unhygienic creep from down the hall. Mary shivered. The little man in her flat, standing before her, had played a massive part in creating the '*it*', who lived down the hallway. Now she just wanted to get him and his bag of tools, which he probably used for murdering people, out of her home.

"Fancy that," were the only two words she could muster.

"Have you met him yet? He's a bit scruffy-looking, dopey even. Lazy as well. He needs a good kick up the arse."

She didn't reply. She couldn't think of anything to say.

"He's a bit taller than me. But then again, who isn't?" he laughed.

Mary felt obliged to join in, so she forced out a laugh as uncomfortable as the situation. Her laugh, forced or not, faded quickly. "Yes, I've met him. Lovely lad."

The caretaker's laugh came to an unnatural and abrupt halt. "I'd better be off. If there's anything else that crops up, you know the number."

He left as suddenly and abruptly as his laugh had abated.

Mary wandered into the kitchen to check his handiwork. It didn't look so handy. What had been a trickle of water on the floor was now turning into a flood. She looked at the number for the caretaker and then, tossing it aside, reached for the emergency book to find a proper plumber.

It was at this precise moment her mobile vibrated into life.

It was a text message.

It read plain and simple: "I KNOW WHERE YOU ARE."

CHAPTER FIVE

Northwich train station had seen better days. The yellowing bricks from the Victorian age were still in evidence, but so was the mindless graffiti and vandalism from more recent times. Most local people knew that every now and again, a big tidying-up process would commence, but within days of it finishing, the station would be back to normal. You always faced a losing battle with kids when the law is too lenient with them.

"Why are we waiting here?" Boag-Munroe moaned.

Nigel turned to Boag-Munroe. "Because the van has broke down. We've no other way of getting there at such short notice."

Boag-Munroe walked further up the platform. He cut a lonely figure as the wind flowed under his long leather coat, making it rise up like a cloak around him.

He wasn't the man Nigel once knew.

An assortment of litter danced around Nigel's feet, following him wherever he moved, making him look like the Pied Piper of unwanted rubbish.

"Your friend seems a little distant," whispered Hannah.

"Jet lag," whispered Nigel back.

The rest of the group stood in their own little huddles. As usual, Emily followed Bradley around like a bad smell. Jason stood, sour-faced as ever, with an equally sour-faced Mrs Ruth, who, seconds earlier, had been giving everyone a detailed description of her IBS.

Mrs Ruth loved to talk in initials, so in a way, it only seemed right that if she was going to suffer from a complaint, it would be irritable bowel syndrome. In the fact that the overweight and overbearing, middle-aged woman was a pain in the arse, there also seemed to be some poetic justice.

She must really have been suffering with her IBS; her face was looking so sour it seemed as if she was sucking in both of her shiny cheeks, while squeezing a fresh lemon with her tonsils. She was always called Mrs Ruth on account of nobody knowing her first name; nobody had taken the trouble to have that long of a conversation with her to find it out. She had a very abrupt manner, a fetish for calling everyone 'love', and an even bigger fetish of talking down to people. She professed to be a medium, so at least she did have someone to speak to, although she had to be in one of her trances to do so. When in a trance she spoke under the moniker of Chief Little Running Big Horn, her Indian spiritual guide who took over her body on her séance shindigs.

"Hey, Big Steve! Not looking good for City, is it?" Alan Gentle shouted up at a man passing over the station bridge. The man, looking startled, nodded. He looked distinctly like he wanted nothing to do with Alan Gentle, and hurriedly carried on making his way home from work. This was understandable because Alan was somewhat loud to listen to, and even louder to look at. He wore a garish purple, green and yellow shell suit, with red, rotten trainers. He was quite large in body, if not in mind, and on his head sat an unruly mop of jet-black hair. On top of this sat a black baseball cap, and sprouting out the side of it was a radio aerial. To those in the know, Alan Gentle had a small radio concealed in his cap so he could hear the football results any time or any place. To those not in the know, when he strode through the town with his aerial erect, he either looked like an escaped crazy, or a visiting Martian. What made it worse was his perfect clone standing next to him, smaller in size but the same in looks, clothes and aerial fetishes – Tony Gentle, the younger and smaller of the Gentle brothers. There was thought to be a third Gentle sibling, but no one had seen or heard him, just rumours of his existence in the terraced house they all lived in with their ninety-eight year old mother.

The train blustered into the station. Boag-Munroe felt as though his legs were tired and heavy, even though the walk to meet the rest of the group had been short because the station was on his doorstep, or at least at the top of Victoria Road where he had returned to reside. He felt distant from the human race. Perhaps he had spent too long concerning himself with things he shouldn't have been? Sometimes the dead should be left well alone.

Boag-Munroe relaxed into a dusty seat. The service running from Manchester, through Northwich, to Chester wasn't the cleanest, fastest or smoothest, but it did the job, even if the train was rarely on time. Nigel had told him they were lucky it hadn't been cancelled without explanation, which was what often happened at unmanned stations.

Boag-Munroe eyed his companions. He was messing with the dead again. What the hell was he doing? Coming along for the ride with his friend, that was what he was doing. This trip was important to Nigel. It was the least Boag-Munroe could do.

Chester railway station was bleak and sooty, and the coldest railway station Boag-Munroe had ever had the displeasure of sampling. Though, as unpleasant as it was, he still felt a strange sensation of nostalgia, which reminded him of when he was young, on those cold nights with his parents, at bonfires and night-time Christmas shopping; a time when there was always that promise of a warm home to go back to.

He seemed a little sad at these thoughts. His home wasn't that warm and he was here for the rest of the night at any rate.

The whole night was a publicity stunt for the local radio station. They would be broadcasting live while several invited groups, investigators of the paranormal, held a ghost watch along various points of the city walls. The whole exercise was to be transmitted live, with a phone poll deciding which group should fill the radio station's paranormal slot on a full-time basis.

Nigel wanted that slot. Boag-Munroe knew that. He also knew his friend deserved his fifteen minutes of fame.

"Now what?" Jason flapped about, moaning about the lack of taxis outside the station. Lack, as in adding up to none.

"It's a bloody long walk to those walls." Alan Gentle grinned as if he felt at home in the disarray.

Hannah looked worried. "I hope my wheelchair battery holds out. I wouldn't want to get left behind in a big city."

"It's Chester city," hurled Jason, "not Dodge city. We're hardly going to leave you for dead." Before whispering under his breath, "As tempting as that may seem."

"It's a bloody long walk to those walls," repeated Alan Gentle.

Everybody turned to Nigel, looking for some guidance. He sighed. "We'd best make a move. No point us standing around here getting cold."

They all made a move. Everyone except Boag-Munroe. He was already on his way, leaving the rest trailing behind.

Hannah's wheelchair broke down. Or rather her battery died. Boag-Munroe caught this out of the corner of his eye but, as the rest of the group were behind him, he kept walking as if he'd seen nothing, only giving a wry smile to himself as the others took turns pushing the old woman firstly down and then up the subway and along the road towards the outside radio broadcast at the walls.

The outside broadcast unit consisted of a van situated under the clock bridge in the city centre. The city centre itself was dead, apart from the odd huddle of would-be ghost hunters. Nigel went over to the organisers who acknowledged him straight away.

Boag-Munroe turned to Jason. "So what are we looking for?"

Jason looked horrified at such a question.

Boag-Munroe carried on, obviously enjoying winding Jason up: "I mean, I know we're here for the ghosts, but any in particular?"

"Roman soldiers have been spotted along the walls for years," Jason retorted in anger.

"Well that's not something you see every day," quipped Boag-Munroe. He winked at Hannah who in turn chuckled and winked back.

"Hello."

Boag-Munroe turned to the unfamiliar female voice. Before him stood a stunning example of womanhood. At least that's what his inner voice told him. Tall, tanned and slim, her piercing eyes seemed to reach into his soul, pluck it out of his body, and then replace it back where she'd found it, all in the blink of a long black eyelash.

"I'm Eloise."

Boag-Munroe smiled, "I'm sure you are." The line sounded corny, but it was the first thing that came into his head because he had been taken so off-guard. "I take it you're not a tourist?"

"No, I'm not a tourist," Eloise smouldered. "Let's just say I have an interest in things that go bump in the night."

"Would you care for a walk along the walls?" Boag-Munroe asked.

"I'd love to."

Jason looked and sounded horrified. "You can't just wander about as you please! This is a scientific experiment, for the radio."

Boag-Munroe turned to catch a glimpse of the Gentle brothers playing Eye Spy. "For the radio, you say? That's OK then. They won't see a thing."

Returning from the radio van, Nigel witnessed Boag-Munroe taking off with his mystery female companion. Perhaps Boag-Munroe hadn't changed that much after all?

"Are you always this cool with the ladies, Professor Boag-Munroe? Or should I call you James?" Eloise teased.

"I've been called worse."

"Of course, from what I've heard, most of the girls you talk to are, how shall I put it, not exactly the life and soul of the party. More just the soul."

"Next you'll be telling me you're a fan. I take it you've read a couple of my books?"

"I've read all twenty."

"I thought they were quite hard to get hold of in this country?"

"I ordered them from America and I'd quite like them to be signed by the author sometime."

"I'm sure I could oblige, sometime."

"Good. Tomorrow night it is." She handed him a piece of paper. "Here's the time and directions."

"Forward, aren't we?"

She began to walk on ahead, grinning broadly. Boag-Munroe didn't give chase. It had never been his style, and he wasn't about to start now.

"And anyway, how did you know I was going to be here in the first place?" he shouted after her.

"Word gets around." She strode off, leaving Boag-Munroe to return to Nigel and the group.

"Losing your touch?" Nigel quipped.

"No, just regaining it a little," Boag-Munroe retorted.

"I thought you'd cut back on the women?"

"You make it sound like cutting back on cigarettes."

Nigel smiled, "You have women like a chain-smoker puffs on cigarettes."

"Not any more. I'm a lot older now."

"Thirty-five isn't old."
"I never said it was. Just old*er*."
"So what was that?" Nigel asked.
"What?"
"What you were just doing."
"It's called keeping your hand in."
Boag-Munroe grinned so broadly that Nigel couldn't help grinning back.
While Boag-Munroe and Nigel joked for the moment, others were standing shell-shocked. Around the outside radio broadcast no one was grinning. News was just filtering through that another child had gone missing, and it was on their very doorstep; from the very city they were transmitting from.

PC Graham Pratt was exhausted. It was one o'clock in the morning. He should have been home at eleven, but work had dictated otherwise. Work always dictated. It was no wonder the divorce rates where so high in the police force. Not that he was married or had a girlfriend. Either too tired or at work all the time.

He flicked the radio on and slumped onto the settee. Music blared through the paper thin walls.

It was no use complaining. It was a young single mum, no doubt entertaining one of her many boyfriends. It was a necessary evil Pratt had learned to live with, albeit through gritted teeth. The one complaint he had made had backfired on him. Or rather she'd counter-complained about him.

Apparently it didn't look good for a local policeman to complain about a single mother. Pratt's superiors hadn't been impressed. Not much did impress them. Pratt despised his superiors as much as he despised the girl next door. He despised them as much as his long, unsociable working hours. In fact, he despised the police force period. He'd given up everything for it; moved away from home, left all his family and friends. And for what? The company of a crackling radio that he used as an attempt to drown out the hysterical laughter of the girl next door. It was always the same whenever she entertained one of her male friends.

Then something from the broadcast caught his attention. He caught the word 'Northwich'; something to do with ghost hunters. He remembered the loony tunes he'd pulled up at Marbury Park previously. He remembered his hatred for most things, if not all thing. Then he fell into a deep sleep.

CHAPTER SIX

A scream. Andrew's scream.

Mary bolted to his bedroom to find him sobbing into his pillow. She felt an all-too-familiar feeling overcome her.

"Andrew? What's happened?"

"Nothing," he sniffled.

"You don't scream for nothing."

He wasn't forthcoming with any more information.

"Is it because your father and I argued today?" she asked.

He didn't answer.

"I'll take that as a yes then."

Andrew stirred. "I don't want to talk about it."

She held out her hand to stroke his hair, but he quickly pushed her away. He'd had the nightmare. She could sense it.

"Fine. I'll let you go back to sleep."

"No!" He lunged at her leg in an effort to stop her.

She sat and held him, until something like a peaceful sleep found him once more.

"Why are we going to the market?" Andrew obviously didn't want to go out.

"I need to get a new sim card for my phone." Mary answered as honestly as she thought she could.

"Why?"

"Because I want to change my number."

"Is that so Dad can't get in touch?"

"No. I'll give him the new number."

Andrew paused in thought. "Why do you want a new number then?"

"Because…" Mary couldn't think of anything else.

"Because?" Andrew pushed the question.

Mary became flustered. "Because that's what I want. A new number."

There was a silence.

"Is it because of those funny text messages you get?" the boy asked innocently.

There was a longer silence.

"What text messages?"

Andrew turned away. He spoke softly: "I know you don't want to talk about it."

Mary pondered for a moment. "We all have things that we don't want to talk about, but maybe we should."

Andrew paused. "When are we going to see Dad again?"

She smiled, "You can see him soon."

"Can I see him today?" Andrew's eyes lit up.

How could she resist? "You can see him today." Mary smiled on the outside, but felt sick within.

Mary didn't feel comfortable leaving Andrew with his father. She knew very well that he wouldn't do anything to harm his son; it was just the nightmare business. Though perhaps he wouldn't suffer the nightmares with John?

Perhaps he was going to suffer something worse?

Perhaps it was a warning?

Her nightmare.

The fact kept hitting her back in the face, time and time again.

It was best that she spent some time away. She had to know how it would affect Andrew, for the better or for the worse. The night out with Sue around the pubs in Congleton was a distraction, and a necessary one, although she kept her mobile phone close at all times. Sue had wanted to go on to a club, but Mary was having none of it. The evening ended at Mary's flat.

"Where's your weirdo neighbour tonight?" Sue flung herself down into a handy chair.

"Don't say his name or the devil might appear."

"Which devil? You've got so many sitting on your shoulder."

The words were said in jest, but they sent an icy shiver through Mary. "It's no laughing matter."

"You could always go back to John."

"I'd rather not," Mary replied flatly. "In fact, I'm not sure he would have me back."

"And if he would?"

Mary looked sad. "I wouldn't go."

"So that's that then."

It may have been the worry, or it may have been the drink, but Mary found herself breaking down.

"Hey! Why the tears?" Sue rushed to comfort her.

"It's just that everything's so messed up."

"Don't worry. It's like the song says… 'You will survive'."

"Do you think so?"

"I know so."

"Sometimes I'm not so sure."

"Well, you should be sure. It's the only way to be."

"I know. It's just that everything's got on top."

"Don't worry. I know how it is."

"I've been getting some weird text messages."

"Tell me more."

"The one-night stand."

"You should have given him my number, honey. I'd have sorted him out."

"I've sorted him. I've changed my sim card. I've got a new number."

"Sounds sensible."

Mary got even more upset.

Sue put her arm around her. "Don't waste your tears. All you need is a regular good night out, once a week. John would love to look after Andrew; it wouldn't be a problem."

The thought of ending up like Sue sent Mary over the edge. As much as she liked her friend, Sue's lifestyle wasn't for her. In a split second, all Mary's troubles and worries merged into one bottleneck of a problem. Then the words tumbled out before she could acknowledge them, never mind think about them.

"Andrew's been having nightmares."

"Has he been wetting the bed? I'm told a lot of kids of his age who witness a break-up do."

"No," she shook her head and her tears aside, "he's having the exact same nightmare I had twenty years ago."

Sue looked dumbstruck. After a while, when she realised Mary was serious, Sue managed a single word: "Oh."

CHAPTER SEVEN

PC Pratt had turned up at work early of his own accord. The radio he'd fallen asleep to had finally woken him up with the news that another child had gone missing. He'd rushed into work under the premise that the early bird caught the worm; the worm in this case being some interesting duties, instead of the drivel he'd been assigned recently.

It wasn't to be the case.

The hotshots were still in evidence, although many had moved on to Chester. What was worse, he'd been handed one of the worst assignments he thought possible. He had to visit the local schools, one after another, and give a talk to the kids about safety, and what to do if a stranger approached them. He had never felt so unimportant in his life. A serial child-snatcher had struck in his area and all his bosses saw him fit for was nothing short of public safety announcements. Life was neither brilliant, nor exciting. But at his lowest ebb, in front of a rabid bunch of high-school students, PC Pratt remembered what information his radio had imparted to him the night before. Something about a ghost hunt at Chester, and the word 'Northwich'. Putting two and two together, he could only think of one group of loonies that fitted the bill in his mind. And in his mind he'd already decided to keep a very close eye on them.

Warrington, by its own admission, might not have been a city, but it certainly acted like one. A would-be city, with a young, boisterous and teeming nightlife.

As soon as Boag-Munroe stepped off the bus at Golden Gate Square, he found himself swamped by scantily-clad women, and men, visibly freezing to death in their thin shirt sleeves. He pondered for a second why women were the more hot-blooded and unaffected by the cold; then dismissed it like so many other stray thoughts he had.

Boag-Munroe stood at the designated meeting place, in the middle of the pub area, where people weaved in and out constantly. Wherever he looked there was a sea of partying people.

Then the sea parted, and the most scantily-clad beauty of the night presented herself before him.

"Hello again," she smiled.

Boag-Munroe nodded approvingly at Eloise's sleek tanned figure and dress. She was wearing a mere flimsy white affair that didn't leave much to the imagination, but a lot to temptation. She clicked one of her black high heels down, as if to get his attention onto her face and away from her body.

He smiled, "Where's the party?"

When Eloise flung her arms and head back, her dark raven hair shimmered down her bare back. "It's all around."

Boag-Munroe raised a quizzical eyebrow.
"Are you coming?" Eloise was impatient.
She led the way until they both became lost in the crowd.
"So what do you think?"
"Wonderful." There was something obviously sarcastic in Boag-Munroe's manner and tone.
The pub was large, and packed with people, getting more so with every passing second. His senses were being attacked. The loud music, the smell of expensive cigarettes, cheap perfume, and strong drink assailed every sense.
Boag-Munroe shouted into Eloise's ear, "Do you come here often?"
Eloise was impervious to his sarcasm. "I like to let myself go now and then." She grabbed his hand and pulled him further into the heaving throng of people.
As soon as they came out the other side they found themselves in a small space with a yellow door. In big red letters on the door were the words 'Staff Only.'
Eloise opened the door and yanked Boag-Munroe into the blackness behind it.
"Where are we going?" he asked.
"Follow me."
"I take it the party is over?" he asked, while following her through a dark corridor and up an even darker stairway.
She looked quite solemn as she stood with her hand wavering over another door. "No. The party has just begun."
She pushed the door open and out of it poured the most electric of atmospheres. Boag-Munroe felt the hairs on the back of his neck stand on end as he entered what looked like a giant ruined church.
"What is this place?" He managed the sentence, before hearing the door click and lock behind him, leaving him without vision and in some confusion.
He pulled at the door.
It was locked.
He turned to confront what pieces of the former place of worship he could see with the aid of slithers of moonlight perforating the smashed brickwork. It all seemed so massive and unexpected, like walking into another world. Another world where he didn't feel welcome.
Then he heard the voices, whispering at first, then slowly building up, until they were almost deafening. He could hear them loudly, but not clearly, anything but clearly; no matter how loud they got, they still seemed to be whispering, or chanting perhaps? It sounded like a thousand voices attacking him from every nook, cranny and corner of this once-hallowed place.
Then silence. Silence, black and cold.
The door opened. Eloise stood ,there expressionless.
"Follow me," she ordered.

"Where to?" he asked calmly as if nothing had happened.

"Just do it." Her voice had a sense of urgency.

Boag-Munroe raised an eyebrow for the second time that night. "I'm fine as I am. I think I'll just wait here for a second. I'm more at home with the spirits up here than with those served downstairs. I've had a lot of experience of this kind of atmosphere. Maybe too much. Sometimes it dulls the senses."

"Fine," she snapped. She began to close the door, but Boag-Munroe forced it back open with the palm of his hand. He was not in the mood for any more games.

"I think I'll leave the door open, let some fresh air in…" he paused, "if you don't mind?"

Eloise didn't reply but merely turned and headed back down the stairs.

Boag-Munroe followed, overtaking and blocking her path before she could re-enter pub land.

She looked up at him apologetically. "We had to know."

"We?"

Eloise corrected herself quickly. "*I* had to know. Consider it a test."

"And did I pass the test?"

"With flying colours." She seemed a little jealous.

"Maybe you'd like to take the test?"

"No." Her reply was sudden and firm.

"I thought as much. You were scared. You wouldn't enter that place… whatever it was." His face began to look a little more serious. "But you were more than willing to lead me."

"I said I had to know."

"You said *we* had to know."

Eloise began to lose her temper. "I told you, *I* needed to know."

"Needed to know what?"

Eloise pulled herself away from him... then lurched forward, kissing him passionately on the lips.

"You have something a lot of men don't have."

Boag-Munroe looked startled. "I don't know whether to take that as a compliment or not."

"Take it as a compliment. You're the kind of man who a woman like me could fall for."

"And what kind of woman are you?"

"Your kind."

She kissed him again, leaving him more dazed at this experience than the one upstairs.

She slipped gently through the door back into the pub. Boag-Munroe quickly followed but she had disappeared into the heaving mass. He knew trying to follow her was futile. If a girl like her didn't want to be found, then she wouldn't be. Instead, he stood at the bar patiently waiting to be served.

As the local nightclubs opened their doors, the pub dwellers filtered out at a steady pace, in search of even later nightlife. Boag-Munroe expected this; in fact he had waited for it.

He ordered another whisky from a blonde barmaid and tried some idle chat.

"What's the deal with upstairs?"

She looked confused for a second. "What do you mean?"

"I'm told you have a former place of worship upstairs."

"The old church? I can't stand the place. The owners of this place were supposed to be turning it into a nightclub. It was gonna be a gold mine. They were going to call it 'The Church'."

"Original. So what happened?"

"Planning permission fell through. Me, I keep away from the place. It's as haunted as hell."

Boag-Munroe pretended to look surprised. "Haunted?"

"Yeah, as in ghosts."

"I see."

"We hear all kinds down here when we're locking up at night."

"What like?"

She went off to serve a customer then returned to Boag-Munroe.

"Voices and bangings."

"Voices and bangings? And what do these voices say?"

"I dunno. None of us ever stay around to listen to them. We just lock up and go. And we never go upstairs to that place."

"Is this gentleman bothering you?" A bouncer appeared at Boag-Munroe's shoulder.

Boag-Munroe decided to answer for her. "No, we were just talking about the ghosts upstairs."

The bouncer pressed forward, towards an unflinching Boag-Munroe. "Are you being funny?"

"No, why? Should I be?"

The bouncer pushed his face so close that Boag-Munroe had to turn away.

"You do realise that in this day and age you can easily buy products to help dental hygiene?" Boag-Munroe insulted him off the cuff.

Enraged, the bouncer threw a fist. Boag-Munroe blocked it before sending his elbow into the bouncer's nose, bringing him down to the floor in a bloodied heap.

"Hope you learn to live with your ghosts. I've had to live with mine." Boag-Munroe threw the words at the barmaid as he strode over the bouncer towards the exit.

The other bouncers who'd caught a glimpse of what had happened dashed out to tackle Boag-Munroe, but he had gone; vanished into the crowd, as if he'd never been there in the first place.

The nerves Nigel had on the way to the radio station were astounding. On a scale of one to ten, they were eleven and rising. He was still astounded that the group had won the station's 'ghost-hunting' competition in Chester.

Jason merely sat beside him, pecking at Nigel as he drove.

"We should charge for membership."

Nigel ignored him.

Jason carried on: "A nominal fee, but a fee nevertheless."

"And who would we get to pay this fee?"

"The members."

"As in us?"

"It's just a nominal fee and if we play our cards right with this radio slot, membership could explode."

"Spontaneous combustion perhaps?" Nigel had had enough of Jason's droning. He switched the radio on in an effort to drive out the monotonous voice.

"Are you listening to me?" Jason sounded more like a nagging wife with every passing second.

"I always drive better with the radio on loud. It helps me concentrate."

"But do you have to have it on *so* loud?"

"I've a lot of things on my mind at the moment. I need the extra concentration stimulus." Nigel turned the radio up even louder.

The radio, no matter what station, appeared to be all news and no music. It seemed normal broadcasting had been brought to a standstill, because of the missing children crisis. Everywhere was understandably full of it: newspapers, television. Everybody's conversation seemed to focus on it. There were no leads, no suspects, and hope for the victims and their families was beginning to run out. With the fourth missing child, the country had come to a virtual standstill. The world itself waited with baited breath for any new developments. What brought things home to Nigel was how close to events he had been. He hadn't paid much attention to the first two missing kids. They'd been from the London area, so to someone who didn't travel further than a twenty-mile radius of home, London seemed a million miles away. But the others, one from his home town and now one from the nearby city of Chester, were just too close.

There was also the coincidence: the fact that Nigel and the others had been in the city centre just after the girl's disappearance. It was a coincidence he'd have rather not think about.

"Small, isn't it?" sniped Jason as they entered the radio station reception.

"What were you expecting?" It was funny, but Nigel was now finding Jason's presence rather calming. The more he bitched and moaned, the more it took Nigel's mind off his nervousness. It came as surprising to him, how the feeling of wanting to strangle someone, can help you overcome anxiety.

"Hi guys. How's it hanging?" The DJ, who had been with them at the ghost watch night at Chester, greeted them.

"Just fine," quivered Nigel, his hatred for Jason waning and his nervousness returning.

"That's cool," the DJ beamed.

Jason stood silently. Mr laid-back, lover-man DJ, repulsed him. So much so that he made his contempt obvious in wincing facial movements.

"So it's just the two of you then?" the DJ asked.

"Well, it looks like it." Jason's answer had all the finesse of a pickaxe to the back of the skull.

"Fine." The DJ became even more laid-back. "Only it's just..." he paused in cool thought, "it's just that… I don't know how to put it, but there's only room for one more in the studio upstairs. One guest on the show, as it were. Something to do with fire regulations." He turned to Jason. "You don't mind waiting down here, do you? There's a coffee machine over there."

Jason looked in horror at the drinks dispensing machine, his proposed companion for the evening. Nigel whispered in his ear: "I've got some change if you need it?"

"Well, I won't," Jason snapped.

The DJ and Nigel left Jason and the coffee machine to become acquainted.

Nigel sank deeply into his plush, black leather seat in the studio. He tried his best not to wriggle, to avoid the leather making embarrassing sounds, but it was hard not to.

"Is that true about the regulations?"

The DJ grinned, "Of course." He carried on grinning. It was a grin that said it all.

"Are you cool?"

"Pardon?" Nigel looked confused.

"Relaxed? Chilled out?"

"I'm fine." Nigel relaxed, only to find he was going red at the embarrassing noises that his chair was making.

"Good. The show starts in seven. Minutes that is. I think we'll start the phone-in early, if you're up to it?"

An unsure Nigel nodded, "Yes, brilliant."

"It's always best to hit the ground running. Jump in at the deep end as it were."

"Righty-ho," said Nigel, still nodding.

"So you know the procedure. I'll introduce you, ask a few questions, and then we'll open the callers' lines up."

Nigel began to sweat profusely. "Right."

The DJ took note of the perspiration. He began to make an effort to divert Nigel's mind away from the worry of his radio debut.

"It's madness about those missing kids isn't it?"

"What?" Nigel was miles away.

"The missing children. God knows what's happened to them. It's giving the press a field day."

Nigel didn't answer. He simply sweated some more.

"Sorry, that came out a bit cold. But you can't help wondering what's happened to them. No signs of a struggle, snatchings all over the country, and not a trace of them or any clues. I've never known the like before. I don't think anyone has. What's your theory?"

"I don't know," Nigel stuttered. He didn't want to be reminded. It made him even more nervous than his present situation. It was just too much reality.

"Right, countdown is progressing, nearly show time."

Nigel quivered and prayed he didn't pass out with radio fright.

Boag-Munroe sipped gently at his whisky and coke. He had just returned from Warrington and was getting settled to listen to Nigel's graveyard shift broadcast. He put his feet up and relaxed. From the radio in the corner, Nigel sounded far from relaxed. Stuttering answers followed every other question; the questions in-between were just met with silence. Boag-Munroe cringed in sympathy at Nigel's ordeal. He wanted to turn the radio off but felt a loyalty to share his friend's torture. Then the caller rang in who was to change Boag-Munroe's perspective of the phone-in programme. He now listened intently to every single word.

Boag-Munroe was waiting for Nigel as he parked up outside the house. Nigel knew he would be somewhere about. He knew what had happened tonight would have sparked his interest. And when something like that happened to such an extent, it sent a shiver down Nigel's spine.

CHAPTER EIGHT

"And then he did what?" Mrs Ruth was hanging on to Jason's every word.

"Left me downstairs. I mean, am I, or am I not a representative of this group?" Jason made it seem like the crime of the century.

"It's just not on, love, is it?" Mrs Ruth fuelled the flames even more.

"Don't you think we're getting carried away a little?" Hannah hoped to inject a bit of common sense into the proceedings.

"I'm sorry, love, but I agree with Jason totally. Nigel hasn't treated us fairly. We won the radio broadcast fixture as a team, and he doesn't even give us a second thought." Mrs Ruth obviously wasn't going to let go.

"And Nigel is, and always has been, the team leader. He was running the show years before any of us turned up." Hannah, equally, wasn't going to let things lie and was determined to have her say. After all, this week's meeting was being held in Hannah's bungalow, so she was determined not to back down on her own ground.

"And where is our leader now?" Mrs Ruth hit back.

Hannah didn't have an answer. "He's never let us down before, and you yourself missed the Marbury expedition."

"IBS, love. I was suffering. And at least I took the time to ring you on my MP."

"What?" Hannah looked perplexed.

"Mobile phone, love."

Jason came in for the kill: "It's all gone to his head."

"I hardly think one night of talking on the radio is going to put him on the celebrity A-list," Hannah fought back with a last gasp.

Mrs Ruth saw another opening: "And then there's this Boag-Munroe character. I'm well-read, as you all know..."

"And if we didn't, you'd let us know," Hannah hit back.

Mrs Ruth pretended not to hear, "...But I don't remember coming across any of his books."

"He's arrogant," Jason added.

"Who?" Hannah asked.

"Boag-Munroe, of course!" Jason snapped.

Hannah turned on Jason. "You didn't like him from the off."

"First impressions count, love." Mrs Ruth stepped in yet again.

Hannah was beginning to feel like a pack of wolves was closing in on her.

"Yeah, I don't like this professor guy." Bradley added his twopenn'orth.

Emily and the Gentle brothers remained silent in their respective corners. Emily was happy just looking at Bradley, and the Gentle brothers were happy enough, just looking at nothing in particular.

"I propose we should have a leadership challenge," Mrs Ruth interjected.

"I think you've been watching too many political debates on telly," Hannah gasped, now rapidly running out of breath.

Jason shot up in the air. "I second that proposal."

Hannah's stomach lurched, disheartened with all the talk of mutiny. The night hadn't started well, and she had a funny feeling it was going to get worse.

"How's he been?" Mary hovered at the front door of her former home.

"Fine." John's answer was simple and with no frills. He stood at the door like a soldier on sentry duty.

Mary couldn't understand why he was being so defensive; this was the last house she wanted to go into. It had taken her long enough to escape, so why would she want to break back in?

"Did he sleep well?"

"Well enough."

Simple answers. Cold answers. He just wasn't willing to share anything with her anymore, not even harmless information.

Andrew appeared behind his father. "Hiya Mum."

"Are you ready?"

"He's been ready for over an hour. You're late," John snapped.

"Hangover," Mary said apologetically.

"Really?" John didn't sound impressed.

A stony silence ensued.

"Do you want a coffee?" A hint of warmth crept into John's voice.

"No, I'm fine." Mary tried not to sound cold, but it came out like an icy blast anyway.

"When can I see Andrew again?" There was still some warmth in John's voice, but signs of a northerly breeze were definitely floating in.

"Soon." She didn't know what else to say. She'd had enough of making promises she couldn't keep, so now she was taking no chances.

"Are you seeing someone else?" The question came out of the blue but in such a mild and innocent manner, it struck Mary into a temporary state of surprise.

She found the words: "No, I'm not."

John handed her Andrew's sleep-over bag.

"It's just that I'd rather hear it from you than from someone else."

"That's fair enough." She managed to find the right level of sympathy in her voice.

Mary and Andrew moved away, leaving John alone. From his window, he watched them drive off. He continued to watch even when the road was empty.

She'd hurt him, like no one or no thing had ever done before, intentionally or not. The pain was still deep inside, eating away at him. He wanted to hurt her back, or at least make her share his pain. Wouldn't that have been fair?

They'd shared everything else.

There was one way; just one sure-fire way of hitting back. He didn't want to use it but his options were running out. She'd looked radiant. He'd felt like death.

He stood for a moment more at the window, staring into emptiness. Then he picked up the phone to make the call that would put his desperate plan into action.

CHAPTER NINE

Andrew raced around the edge of Astbury Mere with an energy Mary hadn't seen in him for a long time.

"He's looking well." Sue commented on Andrew's abundance of energy. Sue had also noticed the improvement since Andrew's time with his father. She snatched the lead of the sausage dog she was walking round the lake. She yanked it so hard it nearly tore the dog out of its skin. The dog vainly looked up at her, asking in almost human terms, what was that for?

Sue liked to be acknowledged as the boss constantly; and if she wasn't, she'd think nothing of tugging on someone's lead as a little reminder. It had to be said that Sue was a creature of habit, and one of those habits was putting her foot in it, in the wrong place and at wrong time, every time.

"I rang a radio station about your problem."

"Excuse me?" Mary looked as surprised as the near-strangled sausage dog had.

"Just some late-night radio show that I listen to. Sad, isn't it?"

"Sad? Please explain what you've done?" A look of horror crept over Mary's face.

"Nothing much. I just rang this radio phone-in and told them about your problems."

"My problems?" Mary looked so angry that, if she'd had a sausage dog, she wouldn't just be yanking its lead, but swinging it over her head.

"You rang a radio phone-in and discussed my problems?"

Sue was unaffected as always. "Yes."

"Why not discuss your own problems? You've got enough," snapped Mary.

"But it's not me having the nightmares."

"No, it's my son."

"Whatever. It's weird shit and these guys deal in weird shit."

"What guys?"

"The guys from the radio show. They're coming to see you tomorrow night."

Andrew threw a stone into the lake. It made a loud splash. Mary wanted to throw Sue in after it.

The ripples on the water faded. Mary looked round. "Andrew?"

Andrew was nowhere to be seen.

"Andrew?" There was panic in Mary's voice. A panic Sue picked up on.

"Calm down, he's over here."

Sue looked behind a bench, but Andrew wasn't there.

"He's hiding behind that bush," Sue offered.

Mary raced to it, but once again, no Andrew.

"He's just hiding. Kids do it all the time."

"And just recently kids go missing all the time." Mary was beginning to sound frantic.

The mere was beginning to look a very lonely place. It was winter after all. The summer days, when families took their children and dogs for leisurely walks around the water's edge, were distant memories. The surrounding trees were bare like skeletons. There weren't many places to hide. There wasn't even another living soul about, apart from Mary, Sue and the sausage dog.

"He's gone." Mary burst into tears of fear. "I should have taken notice. The dreams. They were warnings."

"Boo!" Andrew appeared from nowhere.

Mary's tears ceased. She grabbed him by the arm and slapped him as hard as she could, across the backside.

He looked up at her; hurt and hatred mixed in his eyes.

"You're big enough to know not to run off. Especially when you know about those children," Mary scolded.

"What did you hit me for?" Although Mary had already offered the reason, Andrew had already rejected it as soon as it had rolled off her lips.

"Because I did."

"Dad wouldn't hit me."

"No, he wouldn't, would he," she retorted.

"I'd rather be with my dad."

The words cut her like a knife.

"I wish I could live with Dad, instead of with you in that stupid little flat."

The words cut deeper. If Andrew had been a sausage dog, Sue would have strangled him herself.

"I don't have nightmares with Dad. Just with you."

The air hung heavy around everyone.

Mary handed Andrew's sleep-over bag to John, along with another two bags filled to the brim.

"This should last him a good few days."

John shook his head in bewilderment. "What's all this about?"

"He wants to be with his father. That isn't a problem, is it?"

"No." John had yet to regain a normal train of thought.

"I'll ring you tomorrow to see how you're both getting on." Mary left John juggling the three bags, looking down at his son.

He stood there thinking about his son. He also thought about Mary and what the phone call he'd made would do to her.

The four children were quite comfortable in their spacious surroundings. Every luxury had been provided for them. Anything they wanted, if not here at their grasp, was at their beck and call with a simple request to their friendly captor. They may have been prisoners, but they were VIP prisoners.

For the younger ones in the group, it had been made to look like an adventure; a big game. For the older ones it was a chance to make money. Lots of it.

Sometimes their thoughts did wander into thinking what their loved ones must be going through with their disappearance. Other times they wondered what kind of reception they'd get on their homecoming, and whether they'd get into much trouble for their part in the proceedings.

But kids though they may be, they knew offers like this didn't come along every day, or at all in a normal person's life.

The eldest of the group sat counting his money. "I'm gonna buy a car. A Porsche," he said to the second oldest.

"You can't drive," he replied wearily. They'd had the same conversation for the last two days.

"I don't need to be able to drive." He waved cash in the air. "I'll get a chauffeur. We're all made for life, do you realise that?"

The second oldest sat presiding over his hoard of money. "I suppose we are." There was a tinge of sadness in his voice, which betrayed the fact he suspected it wasn't all going to be plain-sailing.

If truth were told, he didn't think it was going to be plain-sailing at all.

Nigel didn't feel like answering the door. He hadn't felt like answering the phone, and had indeed been able to ignore its call even though it had been ringing constantly. In fact, he'd not fancied doing anything, except for hiding away. The only reason he was heading to the door now was that the knocking was so persistent. In the back of his mind he could imagine his friends and neighbours ringing the police, and them knocking his door down, because everyone thought he was dead. Everyone except Boag-Munroe, of course. He knew Nigel better than that.

Imagine Nigel's surprise when he opened the door and it was the police.

"Good evening, sir." PC Pratt glared down at Nigel, who was clothed in the most unfashionable brown dressing gown possible.

Good evening," Nigel managed to answer back, although he suspected that the unfolding situation was going to be anything but good.

"Would you mind if I came in, sir?"

Nigel had recognised PC Pratt straight away. "If it's about the other night at Marbury…?"

"As a matter of fact it is," Pratt cut in. "I just need to ask you a few questions about your little group: what you get up to, members' names and the like."

"If you're so interested, why not come to one of the meetings?" Boag-Munroe appeared from behind the officer in the open doorway. "I think they're still held weekly aren't they, Nigel?"

"Yes." Nigel nodded quite lamely.

Pratt spun round. "And you might be?"

"Professor Boag-Munroe."

Pratt paused for thought. "Very nice. And what are you a professor of?"

"This and that. But more that than this."

Pratt bit his lip and retained his cool. "I take it, sir, you belong to this ghost-hunting group?"

"That's a bit of a grey area. I mean... I was one of the three originals, the leaders of the group if you like. But that was a long time ago."

"So what are you now?"

"I'm not entirely sure."

Pratt lost his cool. "You do realise there is such a thing as wasting police time?"

"And equally, therefore, there must be such a thing as wasting the public's precious time."

Pratt was astounded. "I beg your pardon?"

Boag-Munroe was used to astounding people, so he carried on with his own line of questioning. "And what enquiries would these be anyway?"

"I'm not at liberty to say."

"Then my friend and I are not at liberty to answer. So if you wouldn't mind, we're very busy people..."

PC Pratt's head was in such a spin he hadn't realised he was being escorted out and the door was being shut on him, until it had happened. He stayed on the Beeston Street pavement for a minute, trying to come to terms with what had just happened. When he couldn't, it just gave him the resolve to dig into matters even further and deeper.

Nigel turned to Boag-Munroe: "Did you have to upset that copper like that?"

"Not really. But we both know I have problems with people in authority, and anyway, he seemed to be doing a good enough job of upsetting you. Mind you, that isn't exactly difficult."

"What's that supposed to mean?"

"It means you've been hiding in here ever since you went on the radio. As it happens, I think I've left you stewing for long enough. We've work to do."

"Excuse me?"

"Of course I'll excuse you. We're old friends after all. And by the way, the dressing gown – it doesn't do anything for you."

Nigel stood firm. "I'm not doing this."

"Doing what?"

"I'm tired."

"You've slept for about two days."

"Maybe I need two more," Nigel fought back.

"Maybe you do." Boag-Munroe could see he was getting nowhere, and left without further ado.

Close by, PC Pratt was watching.

CHAPTER TEN

The door to the Gentle household slid open by the tiniest of fractions and then halted. From behind the slight crack, Alan Gentle's features appeared, or at least some of them did.

"Hello?" Alan whispered from behind the door.

"It's Alan, isn't it? Remember me?" Eloise was going to lean forward provocatively, but Alan's restricted vision made that play redundant.

"No," he said in a panic.

"From the ghost night at Chester."

The recollection of Chester came back to him, but he still sounded uneasy. There was football on the television. He wasn't used to strange girls turning up on his doorstep, especially one that looked like a model. "What do you want?"

"To come in would be a nice start."

"You can't." Alan Gentle's panic heightened.

"Why ever not? I won't bite. I just need to talk to you about a mutual friend."

"Eh?"

"Professor Boag-Munroe."

Alan Gentle seemed relieved at this. "Oh, him?"

"Yes, him."

The door opened a fraction more.

"What about him?"

Eloise smiled. She wasn't going to talk on the doorstep and wasn't leaving until she got her way.

Alan hesitated. "You'd better come in then."

The sacred door opened a few more inches, just enough for Eloise to squeeze through. It closed behind her with an almighty thud.

"Nice place you've got here." She didn't mean it, but it was something to say. The living room was a shrine to dolls. There were boy dolls, girl dolls, dolls in boxes, dolls out of boxes, dolls of all shapes and sizes.

Eloise pushed a heap of them to one side, and sat down in the space she'd made. There must have been thousands of the damn things, strewn everywhere. It was less of a house and more a scrapyard of dolls. She peered around at the sea of miniature plastic figures that glared back at her. Perhaps graveyard would have been a better description; she noted that a lot weren't in the best condition. They were lucky if they weren't missing the odd eye, hand or other such limb. The disability of these dolls seemed to give the scene an even more grotesque look.

Tony Gentle scuttled into the room, shot a horrified look at Eloise, then at Alan, and scuttled back out.

"We're collectors." Alan seemed half proud, half apologetic.

Eloise nodded at the unbelievable mess of plastic all around her. "You don't say?"

Alan hovered over another doll-clad seat opposite Eloise. However, he decided not to disturb the dolls on it and perched on the chair's arm instead.

Eloise realised she wasn't going to be offered any creature comforts, such as a drink or decent conversation. She decided to push on with the matter in hand. "I suppose you're wondering what I'm doing here?"

Alan Gentle merely scratched his head. Somehow it felt naked without the cap and aerial on top.

"I'll get down to business." She tried her best to look tempting, but reclining into a pile of plastic toys didn't really add to the ambience.

"I'm looking for a friend."

"Who is it? The professor?"

"No. When I said I was looking for a friend, I was thinking more along the lines of someone I could confide in... Someone like you. Do you think you're up to the job?"

Alan looked bewildered. "I don't know."

"I just need you to do me a favour."

Alan slid off the arm of his chair, flattening a pile of soldiers. He stood up. "Like what?"

"Nothing too taxing." Eloise seemed to smoulder even more. "You know the professor and I are seeing one another?"

"I think... I mean I don't know..." Alan stuttered.

"That's right. You took the words right out of my mouth. I don't know where I stand with him properly. He's just so elusive. That's where you come in."

"Me?" Alan's panic seemed to be growing again.

"That's right, hot stuff. You." Eloise stood and crossed the room as sleekly as she could, whilst navigating the dolls that were carpeting the otherwise-bare floorboards. She stood next to Alan. "I want you to be my inside man."

Alan recoiled in shock. "You what?"

"I want you to keep an eye on the good professor for me. I want to know his every move."

"What for?"

"I need to know that I'm the only woman in his life. You see, I've had a lot of bad experiences in my life." She tugged playfully on one of the curls on Alan's head. "I've been used by men before. It isn't nice. Tell me, Alan, have you ever been used and abused?"

Alan looked jolted. "Not by men."

Eloise ripped a piece of Alan's hair out in frustration.

"Ouch!" he screamed.

She was getting sick of his stupidity. "I think you know what I mean."

"What's going on here? I'm not having any of that." An ancient-looking woman lurched into the room. Her speed was amazing considering her obvious advanced years.

"And you might be?" Eloise was as cool as a cucumber.

"I'm his mother. Now get out of my house."

Eloise might have been as cool as a cucumber, but if Alan's mother had had a cucumber close to hand, she would have used it in the most offensive manner possible on Eloise, such was her rage.

"I know what you are – a bloody whore!" The strength of the old woman matched her speed, and within a couple of swift movements, she was bundling Eloise out of the house.

"And don't come back, you dirty little bitch."

The door slammed shut.

"So much for feminine charm," Eloise muttered as she slid into her car.

It was only a short drive to Leftwich estate where Eloise would put Plan B into action. She passed some shops where a group of kids with the intelligence of amoebas sat shouting abuse at any passer-by. She could tell it must have been a regular occurrence, as nobody took any notice. She parked up near to a shop. She needed some cigarettes; the stress had finally got to her. She didn't like this part of her work, but it was necessary. Still, she felt it was beneath her.

"Fancy a bit of this, love?" The words came from a nine year old grabbing at his crotch.

Eloise smiled at him, half in sarcasm, and half in pity.

She entered the shop, and quickly emerged again, cigarettes in hand.

"Fancy some of this?" A youth of about seventeen copied the previous child's action.

The way Eloise grabbed him tightly by the crotch brought tears to his eyes.

"Yes, I do fancy some of that." She twisted, and then let go. She lit up and drove off round the corner. She crawled the car along Belgrave Road, and searched for the correct number.

Bingo. She found it.

A simple tap on the door was all it took for an elderly, plump woman to answer.

"Is Jason in?"

The plump woman smiled, "He's in his room. I'll just get him."

Jason came to the door. He needed little or no persuading to let Eloise in.

Across the road, in her bungalow, Hannah was watching intently. She'd been watching the dimly lit road for the past two hours. It had been the usual trouble – local kids throwing mud at windows and other bits of minor vandalism – that had prompted this spying action from her. Fed up with being a victim, over the last few nights she'd become a one-woman neighbourhood watch. It took her mind off things, helped her to focus on doing something positive with the remainder of her life. That was the reason she had joined the group in the first place. She'd always been interested in ghosts; so, seeing an advert in the local paper, she thought it might be fun. At eighty years old, she figured she couldn't have many more years left in this world, so she might as well have a gander at what it might be like in the next. Plus, it got her out of the house. Chasing the ghosts outside stopped her from being haunted with the ones that sat inside with her, on cold lonely nights. Her husband – in her eyes, the finest man who'd ever lived – had died five year previously. Most of her fiends had passed on, if not to the other side, then to the next best thing: God's waiting room, otherwise known as old people's homes. So in a way, as daft as it might seem and although she'd never admit it, Hannah was glad of the odd bit of agro. And after all, there wasn't much that life could throw at her which could surprise her.

However, the scene she had watched of Eloise entering Jason's house was not something she had been expecting. But so interested she was at this prospect; she carried on with her surveillance more intently than ever. Hannah could sniff out a rat a mile off. Now she could sniff two rats. And they weren't a million miles away.

CHAPTER ELEVEN

Alan Gentle was up at six o'clock, as usual. He had things to do today. After the excitement of the stranger the night before, it was back to some form of normality.

He left the house at eight. He had a job to do. Not that he'd ever had a proper job; rather errands to run, lots of them, mostly for his mother, but some now, for Professor Boag-Munroe. The very latest computer hardware was top of the list, along with an expensive mini cassette recorder. Exact models and which shops he could purchase them were written down. The professor had covered every detail. Paper, filing equipment and blank cassettes came next. On his mother's list sat sprouts, potatoes, beans and a cucumber. At least he wasn't likely to get his mother's list mixed up with the professor's.

The walk from Alan's home in Barnton to Northwich town centre was a bind, but Alan didn't like the bus. When alone, he always got the feeling he was being stared at, which he often was, on account of his attire. He felt the massive wad of notes the professor had entrusted to him. Two thousand pounds... plus twenty from his mum. This was probably Alan's finest moment.

Then he spotted Jason looming in the distance. What are the chances of that, he thought. There was always a downside to any moment. No matter how fine.

"Hello Alan. I thought I'd bump into you along here."

Alan looked at him suspiciously. It was too perky for the Jason he knew and who everybody hated.

"What do you want?"

"What do you mean? What do I want?" There was acid in his voice.

Alan felt easier.

"I stayed at a friend's house last night. That's why I'm here, now."

Alan began to feel uneasy again. It wasn't the obvious lie that disturbed him. It was why Jason would lie in the first place.

Alan clutched the notes tighter.

"So what do you know then?" A false grin plastered Jason's face. With him suffering from a heavy cold, his nose red and his pale skin whiter than white, he looked like a satanic clown.

"I don't know anything." Alan panicked. In his panic he spied the bus to town. He flagged it down.

"Where are you going?" shouted Jason as Alan jumped on the bus. "I haven't got any change for the bus."

Neither have I, thought Alan.

Alan was kicked off the bus a few yards down but it was enough of a head-start to escape from the advancing Jason.

Winter mornings in Northwich were always harsh. Boag-Munroe dragged himself from under his bed covers. His head was still full of the nightmares from the night before. As consciousness came, those nightmares faded away. Boag-Munroe was grateful for that. With a glass of coke, colder than the December air, he stood peering out of his tall bedroom window at the churchyard. Wherever he went, he couldn't escape the dead. He finished his drink peering down at the ruffled sheets. It was his bed; he'd have to lie on it.

Downstairs, some heat was found in front of an antiquated gas fire. The flames in it flickered in and out, without any recognisable shape or form, just like the memories in Boag-Munroe's head. He still hadn't pieced together what had happened. He'd searched in vain to regain his memory, but massive chunks of it were still unaccounted for. He couldn't remember a thing about the past two to three weeks. One minute he was in America, the next back in Northwich at Marbury Park. He knew he could make a phone call to America, he had his agent's number, assorted friends, ex-lovers and people he worked with, but he held fire. Something inside made him like that. For some reason, strange as it may seem, he didn't know which of them to trust. Perhaps that was instrumental in his homecoming? He mulled the idea over. The more he pushed, the deeper the answers seemed to be embedded. He decided to leave well alone. He was sure it would all piece together. Until then he had other things to focus on.

"Will you stop pushing me on this?" Nigel was wild-eyed. "I wouldn't have come round if I'd known you were going to go on about it."

Boag-Munroe leaned back against his gas fire, silent.

The wildness left Nigel eyes. He now merely looked tired. "What am I saying? I knew you wouldn't let this go."

"I don't see what the problem is." Boag-Munroe looked genuinely confused.

"I just don't feel easy about it."

"What do you mean?"

"It's just a feeling," Nigel replied.

"Funny things those are, aren't they?"

"What?" This time, Nigel looked confused.

"Feelings," Boag-Munroe explained.

Nigel shook his head. "Do you really think you can help these people?"

"I don't promise anything."

"This is about people's lives."

Boag-Munroe drew a deep breath. "We both know that. And we both know the penalty for ignoring a warning."

"Who's to say that this is a warning?"

Boag-Munroe stood firm.

Nigel looked sad. "And if it is a warning, it doesn't mean to say we can do anything."

"No it doesn't." Boag-Munroe turned his back on Nigel.

"James?"

"Yes?"

"I don't think I could stand to see it happen again."

"Can you just stand idly by, though?" Boag-Munroe asked, as he turned back to face Nigel. "In all honesty I think not. I know the type of person you are. It will come back to haunt you, and watching it unfold would be worse than the guilt of doing nothing." He paused, "We can make a difference. I'm sure of it."

"You still think about her, don't you?"

Boag-Munroe gave a sad little smile. "I'm sure we both do."

"We weren't to know." Nigel held his head that bit lower.

"Not back then. But now it's different."

"It wasn't our fault was it?"

"No it wasn't." Boag-Munroe sounded like the epitome of truth. But, to his own ears, his words sounded completely hollow.

Mary thought she might now sleep better without having to watch over Andrew all night. It just wasn't the case though. She couldn't switch off. She counted the minutes until they turned into hours. Yet another night had lapsed without sleep.

Daylight filtered in now. She'd have to get up for work soon. It hardly seemed worth going to bed in the first place for what comfort she'd had.

She wondered how Andrew was; what he was doing.

Mary resisted the temptation to use the phone. She wasn't going to give John the satisfaction.

She pushed her face down hard into the pillow. For some silly reason she found comfort in this act. She stayed very still, listening to her own hypnotic heartbeat.

After a while she sat up with a start. She felt disoriented. She made her way downstairs, not even bothering to dress. She didn't know what urge was driving her, but it was there and powering her on.

She stopped in her tracks at the front door, her hand wavering over the lock.

A loud knock on the door. She recoiled. The muscles working her voice box wanted to ask who it was, but her consciousness smothered them out. She remained silent.

Another loud knock. She stood naked, shivering.

Who is it? The words formed in her brain but still didn't emerge from her mouth. A sense of danger overcame her. She had the impression it wasn't a good idea to open the door, or even let anyone know she was there.

She held her breath and tried to muffle the sound of her own heartbeat.

The heavy knocking returned, much more persistently. It carried on and on, seeming never to end. She clasped her hands to her ears as the noise grew.

The silence that ensued when the knocking stopped was worse.

She stood waiting for a sound, any sound. None came, nothing except the sound of birds outside. She calmed down a little and approached the window. Looking out, and downward, she saw him standing there, as bold as brass. She bit her lip in horror and sank to her knees, pulling her horrified eyes away from the man in the street.

Finally she found the courage to look again.

He was gone.

Outside, the birds had stopped singing.

CHAPTER TWELVE

John couldn't face the thought of breakfast. He couldn't face the thought of any food passing his lips. He knew his stomach would reject it straight away; such was the turmoil he was in. Across the table his son munched happily away at his cereal. He was oblivious to what his father had done out of spite. John would have liked to keep it that way but knew these things had a way of coming out. Perhaps he could get away with it; maybe nothing would come of it. John allowed himself to dream.

His son shovelled some more cereal into his mouth and crunched hard.

There was no way he could get away with it. He'd started off a chain of events he could now only watch helplessly.

He turned to look at the phone. He was waiting for it to ring and let him know something had happened. He began to sweat like the madman he felt he was becoming.

"What's the matter, Dad?" enquired Andrew in between a mouthful of cereal.

"Nothing. Why do you ask that?"

Andrew started to mess with his breakfast, swirling it around the dish with his spoon. "I don't know."

John was grateful for the end of the terrible crunching sound. "There must be a reason. People only say or do things, because they have a reason."

Andrew silently stood up and left the table. He went and sat in the living room and watched television.

John wiped the perspiration from his brow. He followed his son but didn't pursue any kind of answer from him. Andrew didn't need to say or do anything. He had no reason to. No reason at all.

Mary hauled herself into the steaming hot bath. The water was too hot, maybe even boiling. It stung and reddened her normally pale skin. The water lapped at her body; the pain of it sharpened her dulled senses. She needed to be sharp, that was the effect she wanted. She wanted answers, answers to what was happening to herself and Andrew. Was she going mad? Was she driving him mad as well? She didn't know how to deal with the situation; everything was spiralling out of control, and fast.

The steam from the bath glided up, down and around her like a misty roller coaster, twisting and turning, over and under. That was exactly how Mary felt. It was all a giant roller coaster with no brakes and she was running out of track at a rapid rate. Sooner or later she was going to come off the tracks.

Maybe she already had?

What was happening wasn't real. It couldn't be.

A loud rapping sound. The front door.

Mary spluttered out off the bath as red as a lobster. She grabbed the nearest towel and headed for the cold air near the front door.

She waited.

Another set of raps.

"Mary? Are you in or what?" It was Sue.

Mary opened the door.

"You've turned you mobile off."

"What?"

"I've been trying to ring you?"

A confused Mary reached for her mobile. "Damn! The battery's run down."

"So, are you going to get dressed or what? A fine figure you might have, babe, but things like that don't do it for me," Sue smiled.

Mary didn't appreciate the joke. "What do you want?"

"Charming. You don't answer my phone calls, leave me standing at the door. Finally when you do answer, you expose yourself to me. Then you insult me. Nice."

"I'm not in the mood for it, Sue."

"No, you never are. Anyway, about tonight…"

"There isn't going to be any tonight."

"So you're not going to meet this guy then? A guy that might, just *might*, be able to help you."

"There are enough cranks in my life without adding any more to the rogues' gallery."

"You've gotta go. Just to see. I've arranged for you to meet him at..."

Mary snapped off Sue's sentence. "I'm not interested."

"Fine, just fine. I go to all this trouble. Make a fool of me, why don't you?"

"That's exactly what you're doing to me."

There was a silent stand-off. Letters dropped through the letterbox.

"Your post." Sue handed the mail to Mary.

"Thanks."

"Thanks for nothing." Sue did her usual disappearing act, with the aid of a slamming door.

Mary sat, post in hand, trying to find some vague sensations of normal life. She opened the first two letters: junk mail. She hovered over the third. The writing on the envelope was familiar, but not a welcome familiar. She opened it up, with a joint feeling of horror and anger.

The sender was the last person she expected or needed.

Sue's curiosity got the better of her yet again. She decided it was only a small white lie, pretending to be Mary, and meeting this Professor Boag-Munroe character. She didn't see any harm in it. After all, she might learn some useful information, which she could, in turn, pass on to her friend.

It had just turned noon when she reached the war monument in Sandbach.

The winter sun was beginning to have some effect, and was melting the hard frost that the morning chill had coated the ground with.

She looked at her watch. Was he late or was she early?

"Are you early or am I late?" Boag-Munroe appeared, smiling, from behind the monument. "It is Mary, I take it?"

"Yes," she sounded uneasy, "of course I am." Sue passed an approving eye over Boag-Munroe. He didn't look anything like she had envisaged. He was tall, dressed all in black, very handsome and charming, but with a streak of devilment behind his staring brown eyes. She noticed a big gold sovereign ring on his right hand. No wedding ring. She smiled.

"Shall we talk over a drink?"

"Of course." He waved her on.

The ring caught her eye again, hypnotically. She wondered how many other women he'd hypnotised with it in the past.

The quaint little pub was quiet, even though it was lunchtime. Sue was on her break; she had slipped out of work from around the corner to meet Boag-Munroe. Luckily her work mate, Mary, didn't ask where she was going. Sue didn't like lying… even though it came as second nature to her.

"So, you have a bit of a problem then?"

"I know, but I'm sure you can help."

"That depends. You see really, I need to talk to the organ grinder, not her monkey."

"You what?"

"I'm sorry if I sound blunt, but time could be of the essence. I need to speak to your friend, one to one."

Sue looked hurt. "Aren't I good enough?"

"I'm sure you're very good at the right time and place." Boag-Munroe's face was serious. "I know you're not Mary. Don't ask how, I just do. I need to speak to her and I need to speak to her soon."

"You certainly know how to woo a girl." Sue looked hurt.

"Maybe later." His seriousness faded. "Perhaps we should start again. I'm Professor Boag-Munroe, and you are?"

"Sue."

"I'm very pleased to meet you, Sue." He took her hand and shook it. He then carried on in the smoothest tone possible. "Now, Sue, to me it's quite obvious you are a resourceful, caring and very understanding person, especially to put yourself on the line like this for your friend."

Sue giggled. "It was nothing."

"But it was something. We got this far and I for one would like to take things a lot further."

She looked shocked but enthralled. "You would?"

"Of course. But now I need your help as well. I need to see your friend. Can you fix that for me?"

"Why is it so important to you?"
"Research. Plus I want to help. I like to give a little something back."
"Mary's worried out of her mind."
"That's understandable."
"Is it that serious?"
"It depends. It could all be something and nothing."
"But you don't think that, do you?"
Boag-Munroe was honest. "No, I don't."
"What if she won't meet you? I couldn't persuade her to come here today."
"Then you must make her. Her life or that of her son may depend on it."

CHAPTER THIRTEEN

The children couldn't help giggling. It was a normal enough reaction for kids in their early teens when seeing what they were seeing. They'd been told about it by other kids and heard about it on the whispering breath of passing strangers, but they hadn't quite believed it. They had to see for themselves. And seeing is believing.

Alderley Edge was known for its fair share of strange sights. Legends of Merlin, the wizard, and King Arthur, so it wasn't surprising that it attracted more than its normal quota of strange-looking people, but here, in front of them, was the proof. The wizard, if that's what you could call him, and you obviously could, because for all intents and purposes he was dressed like a wizard, was seated in the woods, a small fire by his side, quietly minding his business. The children watched him for a time, this thin little wizard, not doing anything much, apart from perching on a boulder, watching his fire fade in and out. At one stage, he devoured a whole pack of rich tea biscuits, which didn't seem a terribly wizard-like thing to do, and then took out a tea flask and swilled his food down. If they hadn't known better, they'd have said he was taking a tea break. Then he was up, back to work with a vengeance, waving his hands in the air, chanting, and doing a bit of a jig as if it were the most normal thing in the world.

After about an hour they were beginning to get bored. The wizard produced another packet of rich tea biscuits from thin air, which was a wizard-like thing to do, and after taking another swig from his flask, settled down for another tea break. He wasn't exactly the most exciting or productive of wizards.

The children finally got bored of watching. The giggles turned to yawns, so they moved on. They had at one point tried throwing bits of dirt down onto him and hit him with a barrage of name-calling in the hope that one of their number might get turned into a frog, or that the wizard might spontaneously combust in temper, but neither happened. They went off to tell their friends and family about the freak that they'd seen down near the caves.

It was a job. That's how he had looked at it. It was the only way to look at it to stop him from crawling up his own rectum and dying there with the sheer embarrassment of it all. Heaven knows he had starved enough for his art; it was about time his art gave something back to him, and at least with the embarrassment of this latest escapade came a bloody good pay cheque. It was at times like this he was glad he didn't have any family. God knows what any wife would think of him prancing around Alderley Edge pretending to be the reincarnation of Merlin. But still, it was a job, and an acting job. It wasn't Shakespeare and he wasn't exactly treading the boards but he was definitely living the part. And he was catching the attention of the public eye with his pretence. At first just the local newspaper and later, within a day or so, a Manchester paper, and now a television news show was interested. It was looking like a job well done. He was being paid to be in the limelight, and in turn it was sure to lead to other jobs. He sat back on his boulder He had enough provisions to last him a couple more hours.

"Hello," a polite-sounding voice called from behind.

He spun round, dropping an extremely tantalising chocolate digestive in the process.

"Is it Merlin?" the face belonging to the voice appeared. Clean-shaven and not looking more than a day out of high school. Journalists were getting younger, and so more prone to ask stupid questions.

"I'm Merlin." He could have kicked himself at the answer. He sounded not so much Merlin, more like a re-take on Spartacus.

"I've come to the right place then. I'm with the News."

Merlin looked around. He couldn't see any television cameras. "What kind of news?"

"Current affairs. It's on the telly."

Merlin smiled. He was a current affair now. He'd always wondered what it felt like to be one of those. "What can I do for you, young man?" he shouted back to the youth, who was now approaching ever closer, with his note pad and pen in hand.

"They've sent me down to ask a few questions."

"Fire away." Damn, he thought. Fire away? He was supposed to be Merlin the magical wizard. If he carried on like this, the only acting jobs he'd be getting on the small screen would be daytime tots television.

"Hello Merlin." The reporter waved his hand nervously as he got within touching distance. "It's just a few questions. Not too many. You don't have to turn me into a frog or anything."

With great effort, Merlin got himself into full wizard character. "I, Merlin, would not stoop to such petty wizardry over somebody so unimportant."

The reporter looked a little hurt that he wasn't important enough to be turned into a frog. "Oh, OK, that's all right then. Perhaps we can get started?"

Merlin nodded majestically.

"You are Merlin the wizard?"

"I am."

"*The* Merlin?"

"I am a reincarnation of Merlin, but for all intents and purposes I am he."

"Right. So your real name, if I've got it right, is Brian Boothroy?"

Merlin fumed. "That was the rebirth name my parents gave me."

"Right. And it was also the name used by you all through high school?"

Merlin boiled with anger. If he could have struck the little smarmy shit with a bolt of lightning then he would have. "Don't you want to know what I'm doing here?"

"I was just trying to get a little background first."

"I'm not interested in background. Everybody knows my background. I want to tell you what I'm here for."

"Right."

"Right it is," Merlin snapped. "The ghost of King Arthur has called me back to these caves, where my former human body was laid to rest all those years ago."

"OK."

"He has called me back for he intends to rise; he and his army, as they promised to do when England needed them."

"And does England need them?"

"According to King Arthur, yes, it does. That's why his ghost came to me. I am here to prepare."

"Prepare for what?"

"His coming."

"So when is he coming?"

Merlin could have strangled the upstart. "As soon as the man known as Professor James Boag-Munroe makes himself known to me."

The reporter sniffed, making his unimpressed feelings visibly known. "We'll get back to you." He hurried away to saner pastures.

Merlin sat with his biscuits, wondering when Boag-Munroe would make himself known.

Baby-sitting. He used to be a serious bodyguard, but now he had to get used to baby-sitting a bunch of kids. Kidnapped kids.

Kidnapped or not, it was still baby-sitting, and they were still a bunch of kids. To think he had worked his way up by being the bodyguard to various Z-list stars, up to E-list, D-, C-, B-, and then enough A-list stars to fill a small galaxy. This was to have been the ultimate – one of the biggest rock stars of them all; top of the A-list, or at least until another came along. And here he was baby-sitting the kids that the A-list star had kidnapped.

It had been a simple plan. An A-list star's life can be a boring one, especially a solo singer. Always on the road, always looking for new highs, always looking for new twists in life; anything to catapult him into the legend status league. Though the only status he was going to come under now was infamous. The money hadn't dried up but the hits were definitely slowing down to a trickle. It was one hell of a publicity stunt he was pulling off. If he managed to pull it off.

Sam Herbert, the bodyguard, was an integral part of pulling off the stunt. The A-list star, known as Red Leather, simply because he always wore red leather and had the surname Leather, had come to trust Sam implicitly. He knew Sam had a very unhealthy love of money, and seeing as Red had a very unhealthy amount of money, he surmised that Sam and he would attain the perfect working partnership. Sam was the only one of Red's team of three, full-time bodyguards to be entrusted with the secret. It meant Sam had to personally do everything when it came to the kids. Red just popped up every now and then to put their minds at rest and to get them to continue playing the game. Of course he gave them money, lots of it. After all, he was extremely wealthy and a famous person. That's why Sam was keeping his head down, doing as he was told. He was going to make a lot of money out of this situation. More than Red knew about. Sam had it all planned out. Every last detail.

The kids were all resting. It was quite tiring having every material object that you've ever wanted. The large set of wooden-panelled rooms, deep in Red's mansion, were among the most comfortable that ever existed. Computer games, DVDs, toys; all sorts of trinkets and treasures littered the rooms.

Desmond, the second oldest of the children was the most tired. He was tired of the rooms, of the ugly guard, Sam, peering in at them or being off-hand when they asked for something. He'd finally got sick of Red's fleeting visits, which had grown ever shorter. He wanted out; he just didn't dare admit it.

He glanced over to the door. Sam's menacing features appeared at the glass portal. He always seemed to know when someone was looking his way. For a few seconds their eyes fixed onto one another, boy versus man. Desmond pulled his gaze away. He retired back to his area of the spacious playroom-cum-prison. He thought about a lot of things. He thought about the situation he was in and he thought about the money, but most of all he thought about home on the Danefields council estate in Northwich.

CHAPTER FOURTEEN

"Why? Why did you do it?" Mary hammered on John's door.

"Just calm down," he shouted behind the safety of his living room window. "There's no need to cause a scene."

"Open this door now and give me back my son, you utter bastard."

"Just be reasonable, Mary. You said he could stop for a while."

She knelt down and picked up a loose house brick from the garden wall. "Let me in or I'll put the window in."

"Mary. Don't be daft."

She threw the brick.

John ducked.

The brick went sailing through the window leaving a large, gaping hole.

"You mad cow!" he screamed through the hole.

"Mad? You don't know the half of it," she screamed back. "Or perhaps you do and that's why you're staying in the house. *My* house."

"*My* house. You didn't want it. That's my window you broke."

"It'll be your neck next time." She paused in her anger. "Or would you rather it was your bank balance? I could hit you where it would really hurt."

He thought for a second, then opened the front door.

Mary grabbed him by the throat without a second thought. It was only when she saw the tears in Andrew's eyes did she let go.

She calmed herself. "Andrew, we're going home."

Andrew shook his head in a tear-stained defiance.

She grabbed him and hauled him out to the car, past John and the watching neighbours.

A draught blew through the gaping hole in the window. The neighbours behind twitching curtains looked through it. John watched his life seeping out of it.

"You look like you've had a good sleep."

Nigel's sarcasm was not lost on Boag-Munroe. "It was the humming in my head. It kept me awake."

"Don't worry, you're not going mad. They're filling the old salt mines in," Nigel explained.

"I never said I was going mad," Boag-Munroe mumbled to himself on his doorstep, listening to the droning sound of distant machinery. He paused for a second and then followed Nigel indoors.

"I've come for a reason." Nigel twitched. He always twitched when he had something to get off his chest. "Two reasons as a matter of fact."

"Go on," Boag-Munroe urged Nigel, before he disappeared entirely in a fit of nervous twitching.

"Hannah rang me this morning. It seems your female friend from Chester has been doing some checking up on you. Hannah spotted her calling at Jason's. She thought it a bit suspicious so she let me know."

"That's good of her." Boag-Munroe sounded distant.

"Also she informed me of what happened at the last meeting."

"You missed a meeting?" Boag-Munroe's ears pricked up at this revelation.

"There's talk of a leadership challenge." Nigel hung his head despondently.

"Let them talk. That's all they can do. I wouldn't worry about a bunch of freaks."

"And if a bunch of freaks don't think I'm fit to lead them, where do you think that leaves me?"

"Misunderstood, obviously. Why did you miss the meeting? It isn't like you."

"Mother is ill. Cancer. I thought I should let you know. She always liked you."

"You sound like you've given up on her."

"She's old, and I'm just being realistic."

"When were you or I ever realistic?"

Nigel smiled, but it soon faded from his lips.

"Get lost!" Mary shouted down the phone at Sue, before slamming the receiver down. She didn't need any of this now.

Andrew sat sobbing in the corner. A look of hatred pierced out from his eyes that he directed straight at his mother.

"Andrew, you can look at me all you like, it won't make a bit of difference." Mary couldn't contain her temper; even now she was taking it out on her son.

"I want to see my dad."

"Well you can't."

"You said I could stay there for a while."

"I have my reasons, Andrew. Just don't ask any more."

"You're just a bitch."

"What did you say?" The outburst took Mary aback. "You want to know the truth? The truth is your dad has done something very bad, something he's done out of spite, because he and I aren't together any more. He is the lowest of the low. He used something he'd been entrusted with. He used it against me – me that had given it to him in the first place." She got her breath back. "I never want to see him again and I never want you to see him again."

The last statement was enough to send Andrew hurtling tearfully to the safety of his room. A crumpled heap on his bed, he cried underneath a poster of Red Leather.

In the nearby town of Macclesfield, John was patching up his window and wishing he could patch up his life as easily. The cardboard and tape had done the temporary job. Now all he had to do was sit back and wait for the experts to fit a new window.

Most of his life seemed like the window: a patching-up job as best he could, and then having to sit back and wait for others. Perhaps it was best that way, out of his hands. Everything he did always seemed to go wrong anyway.

He thought about what he'd done to Mary, how he had betrayed her trust out of spite.

He felt his conscience pricking him, although it didn't last long. He looked at the window, and remembered how Mary had dragged his son away. He remembered all the good times. Now they'd been turned sour, tainted. He had nothing left except the house… with the smashed window.

The spite factor came muscling back in.

With his mind tired of dwelling on Nigel's problems, Boag-Munroe took some time out to look at his own predicament. For too long he had put off what he had to do, although it was only logical that he had to face the past, the recent past at any rate. If not to cure his paranoia, then to get some inkling of why his mind was missing the past weeks leading up to and including his homecoming.

He toyed with a card emblazoned with his agent's phone number but something was making him hesitate. Something unknown holding him back as it had done all this time. Now he knew he must push this something aside, unknown or otherwise, or else he would never get any further.

He dialled the number.

A familiar voice he hadn't heard for a while answered.

"Hello?"

"Dexter, it's me, James."

"James? Where the hell have you been?" The American voice sounded excited.

"Here and there."

"You gave me that same answer when you went missing in the Sahara Desert for two months." He paused, "You're not in the Sahara Desert now, are you?"

"No, I'm not. Far from it, in fact."

"So, where the hell are you then?"

Boag-Munroe didn't answer.

"You're back home in Northwich, England, aren't you?"

Still Boag-Munroe gave nothing away.

"You are," Dexter said knowingly.

"It doesn't matter where I am. What does matter is that I need your help."

"What kind of help? I'm just your agent, you're over there in England, and I'm in the States. What do you want me to do?"

"Just tell me what happened to me."

"What do you mean?" This time it was Dexter willing to give nothing away.

"Dexter, please." Boag-Munroe's voice was soft and sincere, but obviously stubborn enough not to budge from the matter.

Dexter held out a little longer, before giving in. "You had a nervous breakdown. You lost everything, and I'm not just talking about your mind."

Shocking as the news sounded, Boag-Munroe remained cool and firm. "How? When?"

"There was a scandal."

"What kind of scandal?"

Dexter wasn't quick enough imparting the information for Boag-Munroe.

"Look, we shouldn't be going into this over the phone. At any rate, you're obviously feeling a lot better now," reasoned Dexter.

Boag-Munroe wasn't going to be fobbed off. "Tell me."

Dexter cleared his throat. "You were on an investigation. I don't know the exact details but it was something to do with a new book. The investigation went wrong somehow."

"What do you mean, went wrong?"

"There were three of you. One of your team committed suicide, you had a nervous breakdown, and the final member of the group went totally mad. Whatever you three encountered, it was bad news for all concerned."

"What was the book about?"

"You wouldn't say exactly. Vague as always."

"I must have given you some information. You're my agent after all."

Dexter sighed. "*Was* your agent. I'm sorry, James. Like I said, you've lost everything. No publishing house will touch you now."

There was a long painful silence.

"Thank you, Dexter. You've been a great help." Boag-Munroe was as polite as ever.

"James, wait..."

The phone line went dead.

The phone call had been the last thing Dexter needed. He'd figured it would come sooner or later, but he would have much preferred the latter option. Boag-Munroe had put him in a difficult position. A real cliff-hanger of ethics.

Dexter huffed loudly and followed it up with a faint sigh. He liked Boag-Munroe. He'd known him a number of years and liked to think himself more as a friend than just a business associate. He'd even go so far as to label himself a good friend and, as Dexter didn't have many friends in his business, never mind good ones, it made matters worse.

But not so good a friend that he would sacrifice everything.

Dexter Pondsdexter had worked for everything he'd got, his business, his connections, his stature and standing. He wasn't about to lose it all.

He had to make a phone call.

Dexter hesitated over the phone for a second. It wasn't a hesitation of any consequence, just merely for his peace of mind. He didn't want to rush to impart the information. He did have some morals, or at least as many as a publishing agent could possibly have. He knew the consequences his action would have. But to hold on to what he knew, to even take that chance that it might be found out that he hadn't talked, was too much. Anybody could have been listening. Phone lines can be tapped and offices can be bugged. Especially by people in high places.

He had to clear himself.

Even if it would surely result in the death of Boag-Munroe.

CHAPTER FIFTEEN

"I hear you're not well," Boag-Munroe spoke softly to Nigel's mother.

She bade him sit down beside her, smiling through obvious pain.

"I take it Nigel doesn't know you're here?"

"No, but he wouldn't mind though, would he?"

"No, he wouldn't. He's a good boy and so are you."

Boag-Munroe laughed. "It's been a long time since I've been called a boy, or good for that matter."

"Then that's a shame. People obviously don't know the real you."

"Who does?" There was sadness in his eyes.

"I do, and so does Nigel. We both think it's good that you've come back."

"They do say a change is as good as a rest."

"And you look like you could do with both. Don't push yourself too hard; take that as good advice from a wise, but knackered, old woman."

"I will."

Her weak hand grabbed his, as strongly as she could muster. "You and Nigel, you always looked out for one another. You still will?"

He looked deep into her fading eyes. "We still will."

The fact that Boag-Munroe had managed to get most of the group out to a pub in Warrington, on a Thursday night, was a testament to his leadership skills. Nigel hadn't a clue how he'd done it but was quite happy to marvel at the fact. Indeed, he was astounded at the scene unravelling in front of him.

The Gentle brothers were both dressed in what looked like suits from a best-forgotten fifties era. The dull grey suits were complemented by glowing yellow dickey bows and the usual baseball caps with aerials, although for once not erected to full height. It was a fashion accessory no Gentle brother could be seen without. The bouncers stood no chance of keeping the Gentle brothers out. While more normal people had been turned away for various petty reasons, the ferocity of the bouncers' laughter at the Gentle brothers was enough to double the bouncers up, and render them helpless. The brothers Gentle passed unchallenged.

Boag-Munroe and Nigel also passed without dispute in the wake of the bouncers' near-hysterical laughter, but Jason was not so lucky. He had the type of face and scowling expression that could halt any laughter, no matter how uproarious. An iron bar-like arm blocked his path. "What do you think you're doing?" he spluttered at the bouncer, before nearly eating his own words.

The arm stayed steady and still. The look on the bouncer's face said it all. Jason meekly slipped away.

"This way," gestured Boag-Munroe to Nigel. He cut easily through the throng, as if parting the Red Sea.

Nigel merely bumped and squashed his way through, holding his breath as they passed through the staff-only door. He didn't fancy tallying with the bouncers. "We shouldn't be here."

"No shit, Sherlock?" quipped Boag-Munroe, sarcastically.

"Don't make light," Nigel quietly and nervously snapped back.

"I'm not, but take a look at this."

Nigel caught up with Boag-Munroe at the top of the stairs, just as Boag-Munroe swung open the door leading to the former church.

The atmosphere shook Nigel and he stood rigidly.

Boag-Munroe noted this. "I told you, didn't I? I knew it would take your breath away." He strolled to the middle of the room. "Don't worry, we won't be disturbed. At least, not by anything of this world."

"What about the others downstairs?"

"I'm sure they'll be able to find a taxi home."

"It seems cruel just using them as decoys."

"Cruel, but necessary nevertheless. Besides, it serves them right for challenging your leadership qualities. Anyway, they're all big boys and if truth be told, I'm sure they'll enjoy their play time."

Downstairs the big boys were indeed at play. The Gentle brothers with their strange mannerisms and even stranger attire had become the centre of attention. Alan Gentle was boogying away like he'd seen them do in films, much to the amusement of a bunch of young girls. His face lit up as they danced with him, rubbing against him for a laugh. At one point they began to mess with the aerial on his cap, going so far as to fully extend it at one point.

Tony Gentle stood, backed up against a wall, watching his brother's antics. You could almost see his thoughts on his face. He wanted the wall to swallow him up. As it was, he had to make do with going red-faced while some scantily-clad females pinched his posterior at regular, giggling intervals.

At this point, Bradley casually shot a glance over at what everyone was laughing at. He hadn't come with the group and hadn't even known they were coming. Unluckily for him, he just happened to be there with some friends. The coincidence wasn't staggering but it was enough to unsettle him when one of his friends shouted, "Is that them nutters that you know?"

Bradley went redder than Tony Gentle ever could. "No. Don't be soft." He hoped Emily didn't notice and spoil his lie. Though, to his surprise, she was no longer following him around like a lost puppy dog. She was getting plenty of attention herself: male attention. Bradley fumed. He'd only brought her so he could show off to his mates, how he could treat a woman mean and keep her keen.

Bradley's friend continued to taunt him at his lowest ebb: "That's them nutters that you know."

He wanted to die.

Nigel still hadn't got accustomed to the torch-lit darkness even after the hours had flown. He felt even more ill-at-ease to know all the pubs had emptied and that he and Boag-Munroe were truly alone.

Alone, in a vast, empty, cold and dead church.

"How did you find this place?" Nigel's whisper echoed round.

"You know me. I just seem to stumble on these finds. Or they stumble onto me. It depends how you look at it."

Nigel walked around in circles. Now it was the turn of his footsteps to echo in the shadows of the past.

"James, can you tell me one tiny, truthful and honest thing, without evading the question in any shape or form?"

"I should think so."

"Can you?" Nigel's tone was urgent.

"Yes."

"Are you losing your mind?"

Silence.

"No. I'm just trying to piece it back together."

Boag-Munroe produced a small tape player from out of his sleeve, in the manner a conjurer might pull out a bunch of flowers. "I think we can begin now." He stood in the middle of the room, bathed in Nigel's torchlight. "I'm Professor Boag-Munroe as I'm sure you already know."

Silence.

"Does anybody want to speak?"

Silence.

"Is there anything you have to tell us?"

Silence.

"I believe I was brought here for a reason. Do you know the reason?"

Silence.

"Do you know who brought me here?"

Silence.

"Is there any message you have for me to pass on?"

Silence.

A groan ran through the church. Nigel spun round, perspiration dotting his features, not knowing what the sound was, or where it had come from and he wasn't too sure that he wanted to find out.

Boag-Munroe remained calm and clear, focussed in the centre. The dead centre.

"I don't like this," Nigel whispered, but the surrounding silence amplified it.

"Your comments have been noted." Boag-Munroe turned his back on Nigel. "I'm going to leave the tape running. Feel free to speak at any time," he shouted to whatever unseen lurked.

Nigel wiped his brow.

Boag-Munroe crossed over to Nigel. "What is wrong with you?"

"Nothing," Nigel hissed.

Boag-Munroe put a reassuring hand on Nigel's shoulder. "Relax. The tape will do all the work for us now."

Ghost hunters? PC Pratt couldn't weigh it up, even though he'd had hours to mull it over while on his private stakeout. They hadn't looked much like ghost hunters when they'd spilled back out onto the Warrington streets worse for wear. He had been tempted to pull the nutters in the baseball caps but instead had decided to follow them. He was off duty and hadn't anything else to do. After the Gentle brothers had disembarked from their taxi, he sat outside their house, the engine of his car still running. He didn't wait long, just a little after some old woman had finished shouting and all the lights went off. At least he knew where another two of the loonies lived, he thought. He looked on that as a bonus while still perplexed where the others had vanished to. Still, he felt he was closing in. He was sure that, somehow, the group was tied up in the disappearances and he was going to make sure that he was the one to prove it.

Never had the feeling of a steering wheel between Nigel's fingers felt so good.

"That place was evil," Nigel moaned.

Boag-Munroe reclined back into the passenger seat. "Evil or misunderstood? Take your pick. It's all down to a question of personal taste and perspective."

"I've never felt anything like that atmosphere in there."

"That, my friend, was the atmosphere of a thousand lost souls. And probably another thousand who purposely didn't want to be found."

"It was horrible."

"More horrible for them than for you or me."

An uneasy silence held court for the rest of the way home.

It was six in the morning when they finally crossed the threshold of Boag-Munroe's abode. A tired Nigel followed an energetic Boag-Munroe, who was already feeding his tape into his newly delivered laptop computer system.

Both men waited for the tape's results. The playback on the computer picked up every hiss and crackle, using the special software Boag-Munroe had concocted. He listened intently. The tape seemed empty.

Nigel relaxed. "Nothing unusual there then."

Boag-Munroe's face gave away nothing. "So you say."

He replayed a section of the recording, a certain piece of static.

He amplified it.

Garbled words emitted from the speakers.

Nigel looked stunned. "It sounds like a male voice, saying four words. 'Mystery of the dead'."

Boag-Munroe shook his head. "Not quite. The four words in question, if you concentrate, are 'Ministry of the Dead'."

Mary wasn't sure which of them had screamed first, either Andrew or her; it didn't really matter. It was the early hours of the morning and both had been awakened from their deep sleep. Mary gasped for breath; Andrew, who had been sleeping safely by her side, did likewise. By the horror on his face she didn't need to ask him a single thing. She knew very well what had happened to him.

"It was him," Andrew sobbed.

"I know, baby." Mary drew her son towards her.

"I want my dad."

"It's OK, babe. Everything's going to be OK."

He began to cry uncontrollably.

"Now don't get upset." Stupid words. Tears were streaming down her face.

"He was here, walking about, outside the bedroom door. He was looking for me. He was going to kill me."

"Get up. We'll get dressed and then we're out of here."

Andrew didn't argue. He followed her, assembling his clothes in a hurry. "Where are we going? It's still dark."

"It doesn't matter where we're going. We're just going." She wasn't in the mood to give too many answers. Not when she herself had so many unanswered questions. The main and most frightening one being: Why had she experienced the exact same nightmare as her son, at exactly the same time?

Though now was not the time for getting the answers. She knew that. Now was the time for escape. Escape from an unseen and unnatural horror that she knew was closing in.

Sue turned up at Mary's flat at ten past eight in a highly positive mood. She was sure she could convince Mary that her plan of action was correct and that she should meet the ghost guys, or rather, one of them in particular. She was in such a positive mood, she didn't think anything of the door being wide open and unattended. She passed through it calling: "Mary? Are you in?"

Of course she must be in, leaving the door open like that. Then the silence hit her. She didn't call Mary's name again. But the sound of movement from Mary's bedroom got the better of her, and she crept over to the doorway, which stood ajar. She held her breath as she looked through at the unbelievable vision in front of her.

CHAPTER SIXTEEN

Dexter Pondsdexter swallowed hard. It was understandable; he was very nervous. He was waiting for the arrival of Carter Whitlowe, one of the most powerful, richest, and vicious men in New York. This was the man who'd had his former business partner fed into an industrial meat grinder. Of course, as nothing had been officially proved to implicate Whitlowe to the crime, he was still enjoying the high life. But even if his bloodied fingerprints hadn't been found at the crime scene, everyone knew the truth. Money talks… especially when you have enough to silence everyone.

Dexter Pondsdexter didn't want to be silenced. He could quite happily keep his mouth shut. He didn't want to be anything apart from Dexter Pondsdexter, successful agent and publisher. He definitely didn't want to upset Whitlowe. Dexter was a vegetarian. He didn't like meat. And he definitely didn't like meat grinders.

"Dexter?" Carter Whitlowe blew into Dexter's office like an undetected tornado.

Dexter's first thought was: 'Oh my God.' His second: 'Where's my secretary? Why wasn't she at her post, to give him a vital warning, to prepare and brace for the oncoming storm?' His third, more of a prayer: 'Please let me live. With all my limbs if possible.'

"I'm glad you've got something to report to me, Dexter."

"He's in Northwich." Dexter felt dreadful, no better than a little snitch, squealing to save his neck. Which indeed, he was.

Whitlowe didn't look impressed. "Yes, and we're in New York. So, where exactly in Northwich?"

"I don't know exactly. It's by no means a big place but it isn't small either. But he's definitely there."

Carter Whitlowe rubbed his chin. "That's all I need to know for now." He stopped. "I hope you're not bullshitting me, Pondsdexter. Bullshit sticks, bullshit smells. I can get bullshit anywhere, any place, so if I thought for one second..."

Dexter gasped, "The circle is closing in, don't you worry." He didn't quite know what circle he was alluding to, but it sounded good, and it might buy him a bit more time.

"Damn right it is. And you better watch that you don't get trapped in it."

Dexter had no intention of getting trapped into any circle. This rat was never cornered. This rat would leave the sinking ship before the first drop of water splashed out of place; before even the ship knew it was sinking.

"It's all going to plan," Dexter grovelled. "I said Boag-Munroe would get in touch and he did."

"He's definitely in Northwich, then?" Whitlowe barked, double checking. He didn't like to rip anyone's tongue out, unless he definitely knew they were lying.

"Well..." Dexter felt a moment of weakness.

"He either is or he isn't." Whitlowe pressed his face close to Pondsdexter.

"He is," Dexter squealed. He felt a sudden sickness growing in the pit of his stomach. He also felt the need to lie, to make him feel a bit better, even though he knew it would only be temporary, and he would probably feel worse for it afterwards. "I spoke to my contact an hour ago."

"Let me speak to him now."

"He's deep undercover." Dexter's voice rose higher with each word, as if some invisible force was strangling his testicles.

"Deeper than an hour ago?"

Dexter nodded. The more he lied, the more his lips trembled. He decided to keep them resolutely closed.

Boag-Munroe was focussed. He had commandeered Nigel and his vehicle to take him to Llangollen in Wales. He said that he had urgent business with an old friend. An old friend of Boag-Munroe's who Nigel had thought died years ago. It had something to do with this Ministry of the Dead business. Nigel had pieced that much together, but that was as far as it went. And as for Boag-Munroe, he remained as elusive on every situation as usual. Nigel decided to fish for more information as they headed for the home, or rather former home, of Leyton Blair.

"So, this Ministry of the Dead…?"

Boag-Munroe remained tight-lipped.

"What is it?"

"You tell me."

"You must have some idea. How's Leyton mixed up in all this? He must be a hundred and five if he's a day."

"He's eighty-five. Five years older than Hannah."

"Eighty-five, eh? What's he like up top?" Nigel pointed to his brain. "Is it all still working?"

"That's what we're going to find out now."

Nigel pulled the van up outside a set of large metal gates. He turned to a silent Boag-Munroe. "You should have rung, told them you were coming."

"The element of surprise is everything. Besides, they would never have answered."

"I wonder why?" Nigel rolled his eyes, while his tongue rolled out the sarcasm.

"I'll admit I was never their favourite person."

"Surely not?"

Boag-Munroe turned to Nigel, looking disgruntled.

Nigel carried on, prepared to disgruntle some more, "How do you know they've had Leyton put in a home anyway?"

"The grapevine."
"What grapevine? It's obviously a different to the one I use."
"Obviously."
"So why don't you use this grapevine to find out which home they've tucked him away in? Or doesn't the vine stretch out that far?"
Boag-Munroe shrugged off the remark.
By the time Nigel had locked the van, Boag-Munroe had scaled over the iron gates, and dropped to the other side of them.
"What are you doing?" shouted a horrified Nigel through the railings.
Boag-Munroe stopped and turned to him. "What does it look like I'm doing?" He turned back and carried on towards the house.
Nigel had no alternative but to clamber up, over and after him. He fell in an exhausted heap in the gravel. "Wait for me."
Boag-Munroe had already negotiated the long gravel drive and was hammering away at one of the immense doors to the country manor house.
Nigel finally reached his side. "I thought you said they don't like you?"
"They don't."
"So why are you hammering away like a mad man?"
"What do you expect me to do? Simply break in?"
"No."
"Anyway, how do you know what a mad man knocks like?"
"Just by watching you."
The door opened. A man who had all the manners and features of a weasel stood before them.
"Remember me?" Boag-Munroe's voice sounded like a block of cold, hard marble.
"Yes, I'm afraid I do," came the curt reply.
"May we come in?"
"Sadly, no. I hope you don't take this to be offensive, but it's hard not to be when you've caught me so off-guard. Needless to say, we weren't expecting you. I hope you understand?"
"Of course," replied Boag-Munroe.
"I hope you had a pleasant journey here. And I hope you have a pleasant journey back."
Boag-Munroe thrust out his leg to block the closing door. "I'm sure we will. When we're finished here." The tone in Boag-Munroe's voice developed into a chilling threat. "Where is he?"
"Where's who?"
"Your father."
"Wouldn't you like to know?"
Boag-Munroe grabbed the weasely-looking man by his throat.
"This is assault. I'll ring the police." The man stopped moaning and began gurgling as Boag-Munroe's grip tightened.

"I'm sure you will," the Professor replied calmly.
"You're killing me," he spluttered.
"Steady on." Nigel grabbed Boag-Munroe's arm without effect. The professor's grip didn't relax.
"Killing you? That's the whole idea, if you don't tell me what I want to know." Boag-Munroe let go of the wheezing man who slumped to the ground clutching the purple handprints on his throat.
"Green Acres Home for the Elderly. It's in the middle of Llangollen."
"Thank you. You've been most helpful," said Boag-Munroe, as if he'd just asked idly for traffic directions, rather than throttling a man half to death.

Nigel was in a panic. "What the hell did you do that for? What are you playing at?"
"I'm not playing at anything. I needed information and he had it."
"But did you have to do that? He might ring the police."
"I doubt it." Boag-Munroe carried on walking towards the car, his gaze unfazed.
"He could say it was attempted murder."
"He could. But then he might start worrying about other things. One being the fact that, if I'm being blamed for something, I might just go back and finish the job anyway."
Boag-Munroe scaled the gate in a second. "What are you waiting for?"
Nigel huffed and puffed and began his ascent.

Boag-Munroe was quite happy to stride idly around the picturesque Welsh town of Llangollen.
"Is this the right time for sight-seeing?" Nigel quizzed.
"What else would you rather do?" the professor enquired.
They stopped and stood peering over a bridge, down into the deep river below.
"I'd rather be getting over, whatever we should be getting over with," Nigel answered.
"And what's that?"
"What we came here for."
"We came to see Leyton."
"So why don't we just go and see him?" Nigel asked "You know where he is now."
"Because it's too early."
"Is there a waiting list? I thought he was in an old people's home."
"It isn't the right time."
"Well, when? It'll be dark soon enough."
"That'll still be too soon. We'll leave it a little bit later than that. About midnight. The witching hour has always been a particular favourite of mine."

"You've really lost the plot, haven't you?"

"No. I'm merely piecing it all together."

"You're thinking of breaking into an old folk's home, aren't you?"

"Not so much breaking in," he stressed the word 'breaking', "but there are ways and means."

"You can't just go and knock on a door, nice and civil can you? On no, that's not dramatic enough for you. You have to make a big entrance, crashing through a window or appearing from the shadows. Anyone would think you were starring in a movie."

"Who knows? They might make one about me, one day. I wonder who they'd get to play you?"

Nigel sat dejected on a bench. "You make me sick sometimes."

Boag-Munroe paused thoughtfully. "I've known you a long time, Nigel, and I can tell when something is preying on your mind, and it's not just about the leadership challenge for the group, because that's not going to even happen. And I don't think it's about your mother."

"Would you like me to congratulate you on being right again?" Nigel snapped. "It's about me, purely selfish it may seem, but that's how it is."

"What about you?"

"You got me that slot on the radio, didn't you? That's how we won the contract, because of you."

Boag-Munroe sat beside him. "I did a TV documentary with the head of the radio station, just before I left for the States."

"Got on well with her, did you?" There was a cold edge to Nigel's voice.

Boag-Munroe ignored the icy breeze, "Very well, in fact."

"So I'm finally making it on the back of you?"

"It's not what you know, it's who you know. I found that out years ago, when I met Leyton Blair as a matter of fact. Do you really think I would have been such a success, if it hadn't been for Leyton?"

"You'd have found a way."

"Maybe, maybe not. The show will happen for you. You must believe in it. Belief is everything."

"It was terrible."

"The worst."

"Thanks for the vote of confidence in me."

Boag-Munroe sighed, "I know exactly what I'm saying and doing."

A silence followed.

"And what are you doing?"

"What I've always done. Looking for answers." Boag-Munroe stood.

Nigel remained seated. "Sometimes I wonder what I'm doing. I know what I've done. Just about nothing. The highlights of my life have been a miserable failed book, seven years ago, and winning that radio slot that I messed up. And you got that for me in the first place."

"What are friends for?" Boag-Munroe caught Nigel's facial expression. Obviously it wasn't the glib answer he needed at this present time. "Look, they thought you'd be good and they still do. You're an expert. You've been the head of your own ghost hunting group for over twenty years."

"I remember when it was just the three of us, and we were all joint heads. Me, you and Deano."

"Better days? Is that what you're going to say?"

"Yes. I think they were."

"Don't be fooled. Younger days that's all. None of us had come up against anything back then. We were yet to have our dreams dashed."

"Not all of us have had them dashed." Nigel looked despondent.

"Yes, we did. That's the price we pay for getting older and wiser."

"I wonder what happened to Deano." Nigel seemed to perk up a little.

"Didn't you stay in touch?"

"For a while."

Boag-Munroe sighed. "That's what marriage does to you. It makes you disappear without trace."

"Do you remember when we used to wonder what we'd be doing in ten years time?" Nigel reminisced.

"We never guessed we'd be killing time, on a bench, by a river in Llangollen. Or at least I didn't guess that one."

"I wonder what we'll be doing in another ten."

"Who knows?" Boag-Munroe looked sad, "We're older and wiser, but still haven't got a clue. I've no idea who I am now, never mind who I'll be in ten years from now."

The professor stopped before he said any more. He'd said enough.

"Have you got an update for me, handsome?" Eloise was having fun teasing Jason, to the point of making his thick, black-rimmed glasses steam up.

Jason looked around the empty road. "Come in." He was worried that Hannah might be at her guard post across the road.

"I'm honoured."

The kitchen in which Jason tried concealing his visitor was stuffy and hot, but it was away from the gaze of Hannah's bungalow across the road.

"My parents are out."

"Are they?" The thought dawned on Eloise, that perhaps she'd teased Jason a little too far.

"Yes, at my older brother's. He's got a big house; supposedly the brains of the family, he's got more qualifications than have been invented and a job that earns him over two-hundred thousand a year. Still, I say he's a big-headed bastard. We don't get on." He came back to the job in hand. "At least we can talk better now. No one can hear us."

She held her breath.

"We went to Warrington the other night, to a pub. It was a scouting expedition."

Eloise breathed easier. "And what happened?"

"That's it, absolutely nothing. You see it was all Boag-Munroe's idea, something about us going undercover." He leaned forward. "Between you and me..." he stopped and lowered his voice, "I think Boag-Munroe is a fake."

"A fake, you say? In what way?" She tried to look concerned, but was losing all interest by the passing second.

"I think he's been deported from the States. I reckon they found out he wasn't writing those books. That he was stealing the ideas from people like me."

"Like you?"

"Yes. He joins an up-and-running ghost group, steals their ideas, and off he goes."

Eloise realised she was wasting her time with the likes of Jason and the Gentle brothers.

"Thank you," she smiled, trying to be as genuine-sounding as possible. "You've been a great help."

"So you'll look into this further then, and I'll keep an eye on things at my end?"

"Like I said, you've been a great help."

A quick walk round the corner, and Eloise slid into the back passenger seat of a large black car.

"Idiots, the lot of them," she hissed.

"So much for feminine charm," the driver commented.

"Shut it Jones!" Eloise snapped.

"The man's got a point," the man in the passenger seat added.

"Same goes for you, Smith."

"Perhaps we should handle things our way?" the driver offered as he started the engine.

Eloise closed her eyes and relaxed. "Perhaps you should."

"Twelve-thirty. Time to do my magic."

"Black or white?" Nigel laughed.

Boag-Munroe looked sly. "Depends on how I use it." He got out of the van. "Best keep the engine running. I might need a quick exit."

"So all of your magic is done with mirrors?"

"But, of course. How else?"

Nigel watched him disappear into the trees that surrounded the old folk's home, and hoped Boag-Munroe knew what he was doing. The one comforting thought was that he normally did.

The sight of Boag-Munroe stepping out silently from the darkest corner in your bedroom, would have been enough to give lesser men the age of Leyton Blair a fatal heart attack. But Leyton was well used to the ways of Boag-Munroe. And, as for dark corners, he'd had more than his fair share of exploring them in his time on earth.

"It's been a long time." Leyton spoke first.

"I know."

"You must excuse me if I don't get up."

Boag-Munroe moved closer. "How have you been keeping?"

"Not too bad apart from getting older. But as we both know, there are worse things out there than getting old."

Boag-Munroe hovered over the old man's bed.

"Why have you come?" Leyton croaked.

Silence.

Boag-Munroe finally spoke: "The Ministry of the Dead."

The old man spluttered a laugh. He then turned deadly serious. "Now why would you want to get mixed up with them?"

"What are they?"

"You know what they are. You didn't need to come here for me to tell you that. You've come across their type before on your travels," his expression grew darker, "and they will have certainly come across you."

"They don't miss a thing, I take it?"

The old man sighed, "No, they don't."

"Good for them." A grimace crossed Boag-Munroe's face.

The old man sat bolt upright. "You can spend a lot of your life chasing shadows as I have in my life. But in the end, if you do, the shadows may turn and end up chasing you."

Boag-Munroe paused, "It's been nice seeing you again."

He disappeared back into the shadows.

Nigel was beginning to panic. He could hear the sound of the burglar alarm in the old folk's home begin to ring like a crazed fire engine. It felt like the noise was forming a sonic hand, with a sonic finger pointing at him and the van he was sat in. He could almost hear the voices inside the alarm shouting: 'He's over here'.

The seconds passed; time slowed down. He wished he could stop it altogether. At least until Boag-Munroe put in an appearance.

Lights came on in the home, like a domino effect, first one light then another, lighting up the house like a feature display from Blackpool illuminations.

In the distance, competing with the nearby din, he heard the screech of police sirens.

Nigel caught sight of movement from the home's grounds.

Two burly male orderlies came rushing towards Nigel's van.

The police sirens grew louder.

Nigel forced the van into gear and wheel-spun it into motion, just as the orderlies were about to reach his door. He swung the vehicle into a dark side road by the house. As he did, a figure jumped down from a tree branch in front of him. He screeched to a halt. Boag-Munroe brushed himself down.

"Come on!" Nigel shouted in a fit of terror.

Boag-Munroe strode to the passenger side and calmly climbed in.

By this time the orderlies had gained ground and were almost in touching distance of the vehicle.

Nigel turned to Boag-Munroe. "I think your magic act is beginning to wear off."

The blue flashing lights of a police car appeared behind the orderlies.

"Put your foot down!" Boag-Munroe snapped.

Nigel didn't argue. He was in too deep now, deeper than he was used to in his normal life, but as deep as usual whenever Boag-Munroe turned up. Nigel shut out any memory of his normal self. He knew it was the only way to survive a police chase.

"Kill the engine and lights when I say." Although Boag-Munroe wasn't in the driving seat physically, he was in every other shape and form.

"We'll never get away," Nigel's last vestige of normality chipped in.

The road ahead twisted and turned. At any second Nigel could envisage them hurtling into the never-ending barrier of spiny-looking hedges, and warped-shaped trees. The cold night hit him as he realised Boag-Munroe had wound his window down, letting the wind rip in. A demonic smile played on Boag-Munroe's lips. He looked as though he was actually enjoying himself.

Nigel closed his eyes as he felt the steering wheel pull from his grip. He felt the van swing wildly to the left. He kept his eyes tightly shut as he braced himself for impact.

"Kill it!" Boag-Munroe shouted in his ear.

Nigel noted they had stopped and were now in a field, having ploughed through a gap in the hedge. Boag-Munroe's hand was on the steering wheel and his foot on the brake.

"I said kill the engine and lights."

Nigel did so.

They waited and listened in the darkness, as the sirens caught up, and then finally blazed past.

Boag-Munroe wound the window back up and then turned to Nigel, "I haven't lost my touch just yet, have I?"

CHAPTER SEVENTEEN

Night-time was always the worst time for Desmond, formerly of the Danefields council estate. He may not have been alone in sharing the large luxurious room with the others, but they weren't people he knew. Admittedly, he was getting to know them but they weren't his friends, his family. That's where they all should be now, back with their families. Red had promised they would be home soon and that he wasn't really keeping them prisoner, but Desmond wasn't sure. Especially so after their last meeting. Red wasn't showing the same interest in them as he had at first. Yes, he was still throwing money at them and with the promise of yet more to come. Amounts so fantastic that you couldn't even imagine... but the waiting was getting horrendous. He was bored. He couldn't understand why the others weren't. But that was him all over: a little different. A loner. He wanted to go home.

A flurry of activity occurred on the other side of the room. Red must have been reading his mind. As soon as he entered, the children flocked round. Of course Red lapped the attention up. He stood in the middle of them, glorying in playing the part of a false god.

As Red began to hand out expensive presents, much to the joy of his followers, Desmond began to realise that Red was a false god he no longer followed. If anything, he thought Red looked foolish, strutting about in his red leather jacket, clinging to the remainders of a youth long past.

"What's the matter, Desmond? Don't you like the present I've bought you?"

Red had caught him off-guard. Desmond shrugged his shoulders.

The singer said no more, merely patting Desmond on the head and walking away, back to the worshippers who still adored him.

Desmond cut a lonely figure on his bed in the corner.

Red finally got round to speaking to Sam alone. "I want you to keep an eye on Desmond."

"I keep an eye on all of them," replied Sam Herbert. "Twenty-four hours a day. That alone takes some doing."

There was a frosty silence between the two men.

Sam halted the silence: "If you think you can get somebody else to do your dirty work…"

"And if you think you can get the kind of money I'm promising you…"

There was another silence. Neither man said any more.

Red walked away.

Sleep didn't come easily to Red. He tossed and turned in his plush bedroom suite, wrapping the white silk bed covers over himself, in the manner of a makeshift shroud. It wasn't any event of the day in particular he was at unrest with, it was the fact that all events bothered him as soon as he was alone.

There were so many questions. What made matters worse was that he thought he had answers, thousands of them, but picking the right answer to the right question was impossible. The permutations were so many, that was why he had so much trouble sleeping.

He had to know he was doing the right thing.

Admittedly they'd guided him, the visions, he'd done everything they'd told him. But, to be honest, he had to question them, or at least his interpretation.

Could he have got it wrong?

Save the children. That had been the vision's message. What else could it have been?

He was well advanced in the process of doing what he thought to be right. He was bringing attention to the plight of the children. Left out in the cold, unsupervised, uncared for; waiting to be picked off by whatever predator took a fancy to them.

Not that he blamed the parents entirely. Once he'd been in their position, before the fruits of his musical talent had first flourished.

He was still paying for that mistake, and he knew he would do so for the rest of his days. He wouldn't have it any other way. At least it helped him a little, what he was doing now: guiding others, making them see. Shock tactics it may have been, but everybody was taking notice.

Sleep still evaded him. Perhaps because of the nightmares of people calling out to him, as they fell screaming into Hell's black pit. It was the children among these that disturbed him the most. He had to save them. He only hoped he was doing it the right way. He climbed out of bed. Prescription drugs lay within his reach. They were the only drugs he would allow near him now but he knew, only too well, the damage was already done. Prescription drugs or not, he needed their comfort. He took two pills in water and settled back, safe in the knowledge that now his nightmares wouldn't hurt as much.

The police were long gone. Boag-Munroe seemed very pleased with himself, almost to the point of gloating. Nigel was just glad that they'd escaped and that they were still breathing the fresh air of freedom, albeit only just.

Nigel's features furrowed.

"Don't worry. They won't find us." It seemed that Boag-Munroe was reading his mind.

"I'll just be glad to get back home."

"We're not going home."

"What?"

"Just drive. I'll give you directions."

Boag-Munroe, in his capacity as back-seat driver, led them into the dark country hills of Llangollen. The steep upwardly winding road was as dangerous as it was desolate. One wrong move and the van could have easily toppled over the narrow edge into nothingness. Nigel struggled with the steering wheel as the wind buffered the van's side, threatening to rip them from the hillside they were clinging on to.

"What the hell are we doing up here, James?"

"Compiling our thoughts."

"There's an eighty-miles-per-hour wind raging, we're hanging on to this path as best we can, and we've just escaped the police in the race of our lives, by the skin of our teeth. Can't we just compile our thoughts another time, somewhere else?" Nigel pleaded.

Boag-Munroe gestured for them to push on. Nigel knew that would be the case. Boag-Munroe was on the hunt. He wanted something from the hilltop they were heading for and nothing would stop him. Nigel dreaded what might be round the next corner. After a few more hugging of corners and near misses of going over the edge, they finally reached Boag-Munroe's prize.

"What's that?" Nigel stared in disbelief.

"A cottage," answered Boag-Munroe lightly. "A country cottage to be exact. Leyton's cottage. But don't worry, nobody will find us up here, only Leyton and I really know about it now. Well, perhaps 'shown an interest' would be better phrasing. Leyton bought it derelict years ago when we were doing some research."

"He didn't think of doing it up, then?"

Boag-Munroe approached the small ramshackle cottage with half its roof missing and bits of trees growing out of its smashed windows. "No. He didn't."

The inside of the cottage was no better than the exterior. Grey plastered walls, damp, and the odd bit of smashed and dirty furniture do not make a home.

"I think this should do us for the night. Who needs a five-star hotel, eh?"

"Exactly," Nigel answered, more than a little sarcastically. He began to look around, trying to find some scrap of comfort. "Why would Leyton Blair buy a tip like this? He's loaded."

"I told you. Research."

"Research into what?"

Boag-Munroe glided in close to Nigel and raised a knowing eyebrow, "I could tell you, but it might scare you."

"Grow up."

Boag-Munroe began to look about the place. He came to a halt when he saw the remains of a fire.

"I thought you said nobody really knows about this place," said Nigel as he too noted the signs of former life.

"They don't."

"I thought you said nobody was interested."

"They aren't."

"That mess doesn't look very old."

"A couple of weeks at most."

"So somebody has been here recently."

Boag-Munroe retrieved a piece of singed paper from the ashes. The words on it were hardly legible, but there was one thing about them he could discern. It was his own handwriting.

"What are you doing now?"

"Nothing." Boag-Munroe threw down the frail piece of lightly charred paper. A gust of wind picked it up. They both watched it, until it blew through the open door like a miniature magic carpet.

"Close it," Boag-Munroe ordered. His tone had taken a certain dark texture.

Nigel shut the door.

"You were going to tell me about this place. What research was Leyton doing here?"

"It's supposed to be haunted. A hundred years ago, a man whose wife died two years previous decided he'd had enough. His sister tried to stop him, but she was helpless. She locked herself and the man's two children in here, to protect them from him. He smashed through the door with an axe and killed them all. Then he killed himself by throwing himself off the edge of that spectacular drop on the way up here. Pleasant little story, isn't it?"

"If you like that sort of thing," Nigel answered uneasily.

There was an agitated look in Boag-Munroe's eyes and for a split uneasy second, Nigel could actually imagine Boag-Munroe running around with an axe, butchering all and sundry.

Boag-Munroe spoke: "Shall I start a fire then, or are we warm enough?"

"I'm fine for the moment." Nigel paused, "Did you come across anything in your research?"

"Stories."

"Go on."

"Well, the story goes that a few months after the murders, the vision of that night's events were played out in all their gory glory to anyone who dared to visit the cottage. Hence the place could never be inhabited. It became unwanted and forgotten. Leyton, coming from these parts, knew the story and one day he decided to purchase it."

The next question Nigel was almost a little too afraid to ask: "Did you and Leyton…" he stumbled, "Did you and Leyton see or experience anything in your research here, first-hand?"

Boag-Munroe smiled, "Now that would be telling."

A sudden thud echoed from the front door. The men stopped and stared at one another.

Nigel tried to speak, but fear choked him.

Five bursts of rapid thudding rocked the door.

"What is it?" screamed Nigel in terror as the thuds continued at a deafening pitch.

The door began to buckle.

Finally the thuds stopped.

The sound of Nigel hyperventilating filled the room.

Nigel looked at Boag-Munroe. Boag-Munroe looked at Nigel.

Boag-Munroe coughed into his hand and then strode over to the door. He paused.

Nigel's thoughts froze, encapsulated with unstoppable fear. No more movements were forthcoming from Boag-Munroe, making the agonising anticipation even worse.

"I can't take any more of this." Nigel stormed to the door. He swung it open.

There was no one and nothing there.

Nigel breathed a little easier when Boag-Munroe shut the door and bolted it.

"What was *that*?" asked Nigel, steadying his voice in the best makeshift manner he could.

Boag-Munroe's answer was as uncluttered and unruffled as his manner: "Ghosts."

CHAPTER EIGHTEEN

The air in Fleetwood was the same as it had always been: cold but fresh. It was a pleasant enough concoction and something Mary had been used to since her childhood. The sea breeze was strong enough to blow any cobwebs away… and Mary had plenty of those.

Andrew lay curled up asleep on the back seat as she wound down the car window to enjoy the familiar atmosphere. It took her back to childhood holidays when she had stayed at her Aunt Nelly's house in the middle of the quiet seaside town. She hadn't been back there for quite a while, but now seemed as good a time as any to return. The familiar shape of the tram shelter coming up on the horizon signalled the turning for Bloomfield Road, where her Aunt Nelly still lived. The colour of the shelter had turned from its familiar pea-green to a sickly yellow, but it was still an important land marker that signalled her arrival in a familiar and much-loved place.

Of course Andrew didn't like it. He hated Fleetwood; he found it boring. But with Blackpool just a handful of tram stops away, that wasn't too much of a problem. At any rate, to Mary it was a return to her childhood, or at least a happier part of it.

"Hello Aunt Nelly."

The frail old woman had answered the door after about ten minutes of knocking. It took another ten minutes for her to recognise Mary. Only then did she invite Mary and Andrew in.

"So how've you been keeping, Aunt Nelly?"

"Fine."

"I bet you've noticed how much Andrew has grown?"

"Yes."

"Have you been getting out much recently?"

"No."

Mary struggled to find a question for Aunt Nelly that might provoke more than one word.

"Have you seen much of old Fred?"

"No."

It obviously wasn't to be.

Teatime came round quickly. Mary had made the effort to stay indoors with Aunt Nelly, even though Andrew was pulling more and more fearsome faces by the second. It was only manners, Mary thought, to spend some time with her aunty; after all, they had dropped in on her at short notice. Andrew, however, didn't have time for manners; he wanted to hit the high life in Blackpool and had wanted to all day.

The smell of burning coal rose into Mary's nostrils. Mary considered herself lucky in that respect. Aunt Nelly was quite sparse with creature comforts, even necessary ones such as heating, so the fact that Mary could smell the five pieces of coal burning in the fireplace gave her hope that, if she hung around long enough, she might even start to feel some heat from them.

Like Aunt Nelly's dialogue, the fire began to die. Aunt Nelly huddled under a woolly blanket. Mary watched the final flame flicker. She thought of John.

She still had feelings for him.

The flame sprouted up with renewed vigour.

She thought about what he'd done.

The flame grew weaker again.

She thought about the good times.

The flame died.

She thought about John no more.

The bedroom was a fair size. Aunt Nelly's may have been a council house but all the rooms were generous in their proportions. As there were only two bedrooms, Mary had to share with Andrew, but she didn't mind. Tomorrow, they would have a look round Fleetwood market and maybe even have a jaunt to Blackpool. Who knows, perhaps Aunt Nelly would put an extra piece of coal on the fire, or come up with a two-word answer instead of one. Even Andrew had started to look a little perkier, having lost the scowl that had been a steadfast part of his features all day.

For the first time, Mary could relax. She lay back, happy in the ambience of the old fashioned, musty-smelling room. She pulled the bed covers up around them; the wooden floorboards gave out a faint creak as she did so, and then was silent.

A street light outside the window bathed the room in a relaxing yellow glow. The sound of the night's final tram rattled along the track, a mere stone's throw from their bedroom window. It seemed everything was going to bed for the night.

Sleep came easily to Mary and Andrew. Perhaps a little too easily. Aunt Nelly's house might have fallen quiet now, but an unknown icy breeze was making its way round the house.

It found what it was looking for in their bedroom. Mary felt the icy breeze cross her face. She pulled the covers up. The breeze passed and her sleep continued.

John was drunk. Very drunk. He'd gone to Congleton by bus to search for his wife. He didn't have a clue how he was going to get back home. He didn't even know how he was going to find her, which was probably why he had got himself drunk so quickly. It was the fifth pub he'd trawled through to no avail. He felt his head spin as he merely sipped at his pint in an effort to slow down. Too little, too late. It was the story of his life.

He stumbled a little, not a lot, but enough for a large scruffy gentleman to notice and tell him to "Take care". Normally, John would have agreed with this, but he was both pissed and pissed off. The scruffy guy turned his attention back to his group of friends, bragging something about his granddad having been the hardest man in Cheshire in his time. He stopped only to shout "Let's have another rock and roll record on the jukebox".

John slumped to a table.

The search was futile.

His life seemed futile.

The jukebox in the background played another rock and roll record.

The sight that had met Sue on stumbling into Mary's bedroom was still sending shivers down her spine, twenty-four hours later. It wasn't something that you got over that quickly. It just wasn't something that you witnessed every day. Of course Sue could chuckle over it now but, at the time, it was a case of the creepies big style. It wasn't something that you could call right, at least not right in the head. What she'd seen Mary's creepy neighbour doing to himself, over a pair of Mary's finest underwear, was definitely one for the mental photo album, but not to be dwelled on at tea time.

How should she break the news to Mary about what she'd seen in her flat? She didn't have a clue. She rolled it over in her mind. Hey, I caught your neighbour, the one that gave you the creeps, bashing his bishop over your smalls. It didn't sound right, but it was the only way to say it. At least the whole business had put a smile on the police officers' faces, who had carted him off to be questioned. Trouble was he was back in his flat now, just along the hall, and there was nothing Sue could do about it. There was probably not much Mary could do about it either.

Sue still couldn't believe her friend had disappeared without telling her. She didn't believe the police were investigating it or even taking it seriously. She understood they were stretched to their limits investigating the missing children, but Andrew was missing along with Mary and he was a child.

Sue examined her answering machine. No messages. She checked her mobile. No text messages, nothing. She tried Mary's mobile. It was turned off. She thought about Mary's flat being empty. She thought about the ghost hunters.

She thought, should she?

She didn't have to think for very long.

CHAPTER NINETEEN

John woke up. Waking up wasn't out of the ordinary, he did it all the time, but the surroundings he found himself waking up in were far from the ones he was accustomed to. John had no idea where he was or how he'd got there. He lifted himself up from the dirty, bare mattress he was lying on.

From somewhere below he could hear the voice of the King floating up from the floorboards. He steadied himself to escape from the stench-ridden confines he'd found himself in. He made his way downstairs, carefully treading so as not to fall down the gaping holes in the stairway itself.

Where the hell was he? He swore he'd never drink again.

John followed the voice of the King until he came to a shut door. He opened it tentatively.

The scruffy man from the pub the night before was sat beaming from underneath a large picture of his idol.

"Sleep well, did you?"

"Yes thanks," John stuttered nervously.

"Thought you might. I don't use that bedroom much. In fact I don't use any of my bedrooms. I sleep downstairs a lot. Not for any particular reasons. I just do."

John's head was spinning. He didn't understand the situation and he didn't understand the man. He wanted to offer something back verbally, but words failed him.

"You, my friend, look in need of a drink."

Half of John agreed; the other half wanted to be sick. It was no wonder he couldn't find words. He sat obediently in the chair that offered to him by the large gruff individual. As soon as he'd sat in it, he wished he hadn't. Because he had slumped down with some force, a dust cloud the size of a minor sandstorm rose up into his eyes, nose and throat. Everything cleared after a couple of minutes of spluttering, but the particles of dust that had lived on the chair were now caressing him all over. He stood up, but the dust and the vile smell of rotting flesh that came with it, seemed embedded in his clothes, hair and skin. He hoped this was just a very dirty house and not the home of some raving cannibal family.

"You, my friend," the dirty-looking man, a very possible cannibal, carried on, "look like a man on a mission."

"I am as a matter of fact," John managed to cough out, while checking there were no chainsaws or human carcasses hanging about. There wasn't; just some records from the fifties and sixties scattered about on the floor and some bird-watching magazines, stacked rather untidily in the corner.

"I'm on a mission too." The man raised a bottle before taking a deep swig of the liquid.

"I'm looking for my wife."

"You're looking for a wife? You don't want one, mate. They're nothing but trouble. My advice to you is to steer clear. I always have. Anyway, I'm blitzed."

"Pardon?"

"I'm blitzed. I've had a few. You know, like last night. That's why I gave you a lift here last night."

"Right." John hoped that's all he'd given him and not the bubonic plague.

"I mean I couldn't leave a fellow drinker out on the streets, now could I?"

John started eyeing up an exit. "No I don't suppose you could. Well, I have to be off now."

"No, don't say that. Have another drink. I'll tell you about the woman who broke my heart. I won't tell you her real name in case you meet her, so for arguments sake we'll call her Cindy."

"I don't mean to be rude but I really must fly."

The man looked hurt. "I don't believe this." He sounded hurt too.

John produced a picture of his wife. "This is her, my wife. You haven't seen her have you?"

"No, I haven't. And if she's your wife why don't you know where she lives?"

It was time for John to sound hurt now. "Because life's just not that fair or simple."

John put the photo away and left. He didn't turn back. He had a nasty feeling that he was at the crossroads. The council house he'd left had looked a lot like his own on the outside. The occupant on the inside looked nothing like John. For one, he was a lot older. But there was time, plenty of time.

Boag-Munroe suggested Nigel should go into town to pick up some provisions. Nigel wasn't entirely up for it but he couldn't really argue that much, because he'd been moaning constantly for the past five hours about the lack of food and other creature comforts. Nigel went reluctantly.

The fact that Boag-Munroe could hear footsteps encircling the isolated abandoned cottage did not signal the return of his companion, and he knew as much. The footsteps, heavy and a little older than he remembered, were instantly recognisable.

The handle on the cottage door twisted slowly. A creak of hinges as the door opened fully. Leyton Blair stood in the doorway, out of breath and looking a little worse for wear. He smiled, "You must excuse me for not knocking. If I'd spent that much energy, having already climbed up that hill, I would have fallen over, and at my age that's not a good thing. One never knows if one will get back up." He paused, "And, after all, this is my cottage."

"So to what do I owe this pleasure? Unfinished business? I take it you're not collecting rent."

"Unfinished business? Yes, if you like. One needs to tie up the loose ends, especially at my age." Leyton sat.

"So what are you doing in an old people's home?"

"Being old. That's my part in life's roll-call now. Still at least I didn't get old before my time."

"And what's that supposed to mean?"

"What was that? You asking a question? Perhaps the mentor can still teach his pupil something."

There was a silence.

"Perhaps you can. That is, I take it, why you came here?" the professor asked.

"And not without considerable effort I might add."

"It's nice to see you've still got some of the old defiance in you."

"I kept some in reserve. You should try the same or you might find yourself burnt out." Leyton pulled a whisky flask from inside his coat pocket. "Drink?"

Boag-Munroe hesitated then took the flask.

The old man reclined uncomfortably on a rotted and weathered wooden chair. "The Ministry of the Dead, eh?"

"What about them?"

"What about you, more like. They won't like you poking about into their affairs. Unless of course you're already their affair. How did you come across them?"

"EVP."

"Voices from the dead caught on tape. Electronic voice phenomena, ha!" Leyton slapped his thighs.

"I don't know what you find so funny."

"That's just it, I don't find any of it funny. You're in trouble. I can see that, even if you can't. So I advise you to leave the Ministry of the Dead well and truly alone, and they just might ignore you."

"And if they don't?"

The old man turned nasty. "This isn't a game, not any more. It's not just life and death, it's more than that."

Boag-Munroe remained unmoved. "How long have you known of this organisation?"

Leyton, calming down a little, mopped his brow and carried on, "Since I joined Voices."

"The group that were championing EVP?"

"Yes. The Ministry wanted to close Voices down."

"Why should they be interested in such a group, never mind threatened?"

"Because Voices as a collective was just too good. We had some of the finest mediums, scientists and even sceptics under one banner. We were breaking down barriers all the time. Barriers people didn't want us to go near, never mind break. We were doing what the Ministry of the Dead was set up to do, but we were doing it a damn sight better."

"Didn't Voices stop their work in the seventies?"

"Yes, when you were knee-high to a grasshopper. We were forced to do so by unsavoury means."

"So, I can take it the Ministry and its followers are quite fanatical?"

"No, just cold. As cold as steel and just as powerful."

"What else could one expect from a government organisation?"

"Government-funded to be exact..." Leyton corrected the professor, "if there is a difference."

"When were they formed?"

"Nobody knows. I do know a couple of members from Voices 'defected' to them, if that is the correct word to use. I also know that some who carried out a certain type of work for Voices had very strange deaths."

"Charming."

"Charming they're not. Ruthless they are."

"So tell me more," the professor urged Leyton. "That is why you came here, to tell me more?"

"What more do you want to know? What more do you need to know?"

"Always know your enemy. That's if they are an enemy."

"Forget about them, and just hope they forget about you."

"So you've told me already," Boag-Munroe's eyes narrowed, "what are you scared of?"

"Not for myself if that's what you think. For my children though, yes, I'm scared," he gritted his teeth, "the little bastards."

"Now who's being charming?"

"I've said enough. Whatever you've done, or are about to do; stop. I just hope they don't find out I've come here. I've put my neck on the line for you."

"That makes a change."

"I only hope it can make amends for things I've done in the past," Leyton paused, "or haven't done."

"This is all a little late in the day, isn't it?"

"That's the whole point – it isn't too late yet."

"Is this some kind of apology?" Boag-Munroe asked.

"Would you like blood?"

"You left me for dead."

"I'm sorry." Leyton stood.

"Don't mention it."

Leyton headed for the door. He paused and turned back to Boag-Munroe. "I hope things turn out OK for you."

Boag-Munroe nodded. "Thank you."

The old man left.

Boag-Munroe sat pondering his next move. He pondered for a long time. At least until he answered a call on his mobile phone. Then he pondered some more. He pondered until Nigel returned with the provisions. Nigel hadn't made it through the door before Boag-Munroe was ushering him back out. The professor had pondered enough. He'd had his calling. Now it was time they set to work.

Fleetwood pier was exactly the same as when she'd last seen it five years ago. In fact, Mary couldn't remember it changing in any shape or form over the past twenty-five years. There were even some of the old 'sit and ride' machines, which she'd sat in and rode as a little girl. Of course they were too unsophisticated for Andrew, as were most of the dusty machines that lay inside, but to Mary it was pure undiluted, nostalgic magic. Innocent times.

She dwelled on the word 'innocent' and a bitter taste formed in her mouth.

It was only eight in the morning and the pier and the machines were all shut down. Andrew was still recovering from the bumpy tram journey that had brought them to the front. It was only a short distance, but a short ride in a tram can throw the best of stomachs out of kilter. And Andrew didn't have the best of stomachs. That was something that Mary had passed on to her offspring. She thought about other things she'd passed on to him and suddenly the pier seemed a little darker and a lot creepier.

She tugged playfully at Andrew's arm, "Let's go for a walk along the front."

As they walked down the prom, the breeze hit them with full icy force. The pebbly beach was deserted, except for a fisherman digging for worms, and even he vanished after a time. Mary got a mental picture of him either falling down some endless pit he'd dug, or the worms revolting and dragging him underneath for pay-back time. She pushed the thoughts away. She was having more and more unpleasant ones so she didn't need to dwell on any in particular, not when another one would be along in a couple of minutes.

"It's cold," Andrew moaned as he caught a full blast of wind in the face.

"It's fresh and breezy," countered Mary.

They walked along the side of the beach.

"There's nothing to do here."

"The pier will be open soon."

"I don't want to go on the pier."

"Why not?"

"I want to go to Blackpool. They've got more piers, and a fair."

"There used to be a fair here."

"Where?"

Mary nodded at an empty car park to the side of them: "There."

Andrew was unimpressed. "There's nothing there now."

"I know. They knocked it down just after you were born."

"Great." The bitterness poured out of him.

"There used to be a little ladybird ride over there, some vintage cars on a track over there, and just there a small arcade."

"Terrific." Andrew's sarcasm was showing no signs of slowing down.

"Come on, I'll race you."

"Where to?"

She raced on ahead. "There's a crazy golf course up here."

Andrew followed.

After a few minutes of jogging that turned into a good ten-minute run, they found the crazy golf course closed and half vandalised in the sand dunes in the middle of nowhere. Andrew thought it strange even at his age that someone had chosen to build it here. No wonder it had gone out of business. Mary didn't seem to mind. She was thankful that neither of them had dreamed about the faceless man again. They had escaped to a more nostalgic world, in Mary's eyes. She remembered the crazy golf course from when she'd been a little girl, when a miniature railway had run beside it, until they closed it down because of kids throwing stones at it. The dusty sand that whistled up into their eyes made her feel like she was searching for lost tombs in Egypt, when it was in fact her own personal history they were unearthing.

She remembered how she'd played here with her father.

She went cold and wanted to leave.

"Let's go see if the pier's open now." Mary's tone of voice sounded urgent. The fun had dropped from her voice. "It's going to rain."

Andrew stayed put. "I thought we could have a look around. The place is wrecked already." He pulled up from the sand a mushroom-shaped house, with a hole in which the ball was supposed to go.

"Leave it." Mary didn't want the past disturbed any more. It felt too much like grave robbing.

Andrew threw the battered cement object back into the sand. He looked disappointed as his eyes rummaged over other crazy golf obstacles, which lay half hidden.

"Look at this." He began to dig out a yellow castle that was slumped on its side, deep in the sand.

"I said leave it!" Mary screeched.

This time Andrew stopped what he was doing.

Mary could see his face drop and felt guilty; he was only just getting back to something approaching normality.

"Come on, I'm going to take you somewhere." She grabbed his hand and he followed. "Aren't you going to ask where?"

"Where?"

"How does Blackpool grab you?"

Andrew shrugged his shoulders as if he wasn't bothered.

In truth, he wasn't bothered too much. He was just glad he'd been spared his usual nightmare.

PC Pratt couldn't think what he'd done wrong to warrant a summons to the Super's office. He sat as still as he could, doing his best not to perspire. It wasn't easy. As the Superintendent came in, Pratt stood to attention.

"It's OK Pratt, just relax. There are two gentlemen outside who want a little chat with you. Come in, gentlemen."

Jones and Smith, Eloise's two associates, entered the room.

"Right, gentlemen, I'll leave PC Pratt at your disposal." The Super left.

Jones sat in the Super's chair, Smith stood behind.

"We believe you've been showing a bit of an unnatural interest in the unnatural," Smith stated, rather than asked.

"Do you believe in ghosts?" Jones enquired.

"Well, don't," Smith added before Pratt could answer any questions.

"I think we've made ourselves clear." Jones stood.

Both men left the room. The Super re-entered and handed Pratt a sealed envelope.

"Sir?" Pratt looked bemused.

"It's a transfer. You leave today and start in your new position tomorrow. Don't worry about your belongings; we'll have them sent up to you. I have the rest of your duties covered, so all you have to do is catch the train to Dundee in two hours' time."

"Transfer? Dundee? Scotland?"

"Yes, PC Pratt. You've been promoted. Congratulations, Sergeant Pratt."

Pratt thought for a second. "I haven't even put in for my Sergeant's exam."

"Neither did I, Pratt, and look where I am. You've had the calling, now go."

Still dazed, Pratt stood up.

"But remember what the gentlemen said," the Super added. "We wouldn't want to see you lose those stripes and a higher wage packet as quickly and easily as you got them."

Sergeant Pratt was in time for his train and on it he left all thoughts of Northwich, England and ghosts behind him.

The day out at Blackpool had passed without incident. The fair wasn't open and the town seemed to be more geared up for Christmas shoppers, but Andrew had a pleasant enough time, so Mary enjoyed herself too. But going back to the cold darkness of Aunt Nelly's house was inevitable.

"Andrew's bought you a present, Aunt Nelly." Mary pushed Andrew into his Great Aunt's path. He handed her the present that his mum had bought, indulging in the pretence.

Aunt Nelly took the ornament. A multicoloured glass fish they'd bought from a £1 shop in Blackpool. It was the thought that counted, even if it was a very small afterthought.

"Thank you." A two-word statement from Aunt Nelly – things were looking up.

Aunt Nelly turned to Mary, "Have you seen anything of your mother recently?"

One step forward, two steps back.

"No, I haven't," Mary replied.

"I haven't either. I've not heard from her for a while. Is she keeping well?"

"I should think so."

"So, she's well then?"

Mary wished Aunt Nelly would return to her one-word answers, instead of these wordy questions.

"Yes, I think she is."

"Only I don't think she's ever been the same since she had that stroke. People are never the same are they, when they have a stroke?"

"No." Mary had fallen into the one-word trap herself.

"And what about you, Andrew, do you get to see much of your gran?"

Mary pulled him away before he could answer. "You'll have to excuse us, Aunt Nelly. I've just remembered something."

Mary ushered Andrew out of the house.

They caught a late tram and headed for Fleetwood pier.

"Are you sure it's going to be open now?"

"Of course it is," Mary answered. "It's only nine o'clock. You're lucky I'm letting you stay out so late."

"I'm tired," Andrew moaned as they walked up the deserted promenade front. In the near distance, the tall red life-buoys, bobbed up and down in the sea. They seemed to be watching Mary and Andrew's progress. The sea began to get choppy; the weather was beginning to turn. Splashes of rain assaulted them from every possible angle. A fishing boat, just about visible on the horizon, hurled about in the rapidly worsening storm. Soon Mary felt elements spit out everything they had at her and Andrew.

They ran past the little lighthouse on the prom to the safety of the pier. Andrew stopped them before they reached their destination. "Look!" he yelled, pointing at the end of the small pier.

"It can't be." Mary's words were laced with horror.

Looking over at them from the edge of the pier, the elements raging around him, stood the nightmare. The sea lashed its many watery tongues up the steel supports of the promenade, almost touching the overlooking figure with its ferocity. Mary wished it had swept him away and every memory of him.

"It's him, Mum!" Andrew screamed.

"Don't look, turn away."

Andrew buried his head into her side.

Mary wouldn't allow herself the same luxury as Andrew. She backtracked, never taking her eyes of the faceless figure for a moment. The figure itself didn't flinch for a second. Even when the whole of the heavens poured down upon it.

Finally, Mary ripped her gaze away. She prompted Andrew into a run and a policy of not looking back. Mary herself didn't look back now, as they passed the empty tram stop, along the closed-up novelty shop fronts, and headed through the darkened terraced streets, at the heart of Fleetwood.

A hundred different thoughts raced around Mary's head, each vying for its own space and airtime to be listened to. She pushed them all aside. She only had one objective now. They pressed on. Unable to keep up the pace, they stuttered to a halt near the famous Fleetwood market. Please let me see another living soul, she screamed inside herself, but her prayers were not answered. The rain lashed down even harder, stealing their energy and their breath away from them.

They managed to hit the town centre running. It was still isolated, but the promise of home was beginning to materialise.

Then Mary had an unnerving feeling. She had to turn round.

She fought it hard, holding on to Andrew even tighter as she propelled him in front of her. She had to turn round. An invisible force from inside her was goading her into doing so. She closed her eyes with grim determination; determined not to give in to the feeling. She opened her eyes and kept her path of vision straight ahead. The feeling and the goading stayed... and grew stronger as the street lights grew sparser. The feeling seemed to be nourishing itself on the darkness.

Or maybe it was finding nourishment in Mary's inner fear?

Mary's arm was almost yanked out of the socket by Andrew's sudden halt. She looked down at him, screaming in panic, "Andrew, what are you doing?" He stood staring at whatever Mary had been scared to confront. His eyes were glazed; his expression was of nothingness. Still Mary didn't dare turn round. She shook him. "Andrew, we have to move." Andrew stood still, transfixed. Mary couldn't help herself. She slowly joined Andrew into turning round.

There was nothing, just the thankful anti-climax of an empty street.

"Andrew!" She knelt down and shook him so hard that his head almost disappeared off his shoulders. "What did you see?"

He turned to her looking vague: "I didn't see anything."

The weather began to die down.

The green giant of a tram trundled up behind them. Mary was glad to grasp the change in her pocket to pay for the ride to take them the remainder of the journey home.

"I thought they'd stopped for the night."

She thought she'd feel better in the company of others, seated inside the juddering tram. But it was there she realised, no matter what, that she couldn't run and she definitely couldn't hide.

CHAPTER TWENTY

The road into Congleton from the direction of Northwich is long and winding. For a while, before you reach the residential areas, there is nothing but fields, hedgerows, trees and the odd farm. In the distance, but getting closer all the time, is an extremely large piece of ground rising up into the town's background skyline. It is for all intents and purposes a hill, but a large hill. A magnificent mound of earth that, reaching up into the sky, endeavours to pluck the clouds from where they lie around its peak, forming a fluffy crown on its head. No matter which way the road twists and turns, the view retains its status, always looking over the small town, acting almost as a guardian.

"What's that?" Boag-Munroe asked Nigel as they drove down the winding road towards the hill.

"What?" Nigel had been concentrating on the road.

Boag-Munroe pointed at the skyline: "That."

Nigel followed the direction Boag-Munroe was pointing, "That is known locally as the Cloud, for obvious reasons."

From behind them in the back of the van there was much moaning. Jason about not having enough space, Mrs Ruth about feeling sick; only the Gentle brothers were as good as gold. Boag-Munroe, to be honest, had wanted to keep it simple, just Nigel and himself. But Nigel had shown one of his rare moments of defiance and had insisted that they work as a team. Boag-Munroe had gone along with that for now but, when the shit really began to hit the fan, as he was sure it would, he reckoned he could make the others scarce.

The closer they got to the centre of town, the closer they got to the Cloud. Boag-Munroe noticed above and around it, the clouds weren't white, light or fluffy; they were dark and menacing. The Cloud itself looked down at Boag-Munroe like an angry giant. The skies above it were black.

There was a storm brewing.

Jones put his feet up on the car dashboard. "Not much to do at the moment, is there?"

Smith didn't reply, choosing instead to carry on munching his rather large cheeseburger.

Jones looked vexed. "Are you going deaf?"

Smith swallowed, "Not that I've noticed."

"Then why couldn't you answer me? It's rude not to answer. Anyone with any sense of manners knows that."

"It's also rude to speak with your mouth full."

Jones scowled, "I think we've worked together for too long."

"I know we have." Smith went back to his burger.

Jones watched him. He wished he'd bought himself one now. "I'm just waiting for a bit of action."

"It'll come."

"Don't tell me you've got the sight now!"

A radio crackled into life.

Jones swallowed his last piece of burger, "What did I tell you?"

Sue surveyed the motley crew in front of her. "You're just how I envisaged," she said.

Tony and Alan Gentle beamed at the remark; Nigel and Jason were content to look slightly embarrassed. Boag-Munroe for his part found a shadowy corner and skulked in it.

"It's nice to see you again." Sue pushed him even further into his corner. "These are your friends?"

"Yes." Boag-Munroe looked and sounded uncomfortable.

Mrs Ruth offered a handshake. "I hope we can be of service, love. I think we can."

"Pleased to meet you." Sue took the handshake with caution.

There was a calming before the storm as everywhere fell quiet.

"So now what do we do?" Sue asked.

"I can feel a trance coming over me." Mrs Ruth clasped her hand over her brow.

Boag-Munroe clasped his hand over his eyes in disbelief. "I think I'll just have a look round if that's OK?" He exited towards Mary's bedroom and a vision came into Sue's head of what she'd seen go on in that room, a few nights previously. Somehow she couldn't imagine Boag-Munroe doing anything like that.

"Something's definitely coming through." Mrs Ruth collapsed into a nearby chair.

"Hey up – she's off," Alan Gentle sniggered.

"Yes, I can definitely sense changing vibrations. As soon as I walked in I felt it calling out to me," Mrs Ruth persisted.

"I bet she did," Alan Gentle muffled a laugh as Jason stared daggers at him.

"I can feel myself going under." Mrs Ruth closed her eyes.

By this time, even Nigel was beginning to feel embarrassed by Mrs Ruth's amateur dramatics.

Sue was beginning to think she'd made a grave error. "What's she doing?"

"It's a trance. Can't you tell?" snapped Jason.

"Oh, right." Sue backed away realising she'd let the lunatics take over the asylum. "I'll just leave you to what you're doing and see what your friend's up to in the other room."

She found Boag-Munroe in the middle of Andrew's bedroom, deep in thought. Even though she had crept in silently, he knew she was there and he spoke without moving his gaze: "How's the sideshow doing in there?"

"Pardon?"

"The sideshow. The clowns are performing, I take it?" He turned to her. "Every circus, no matter how big or small, has to have its clowns."

"And that's how you see your colleagues? As clowns?" Sue sounded embarrassed for them.

"Would you have any faith in me if I saw them as anything more? Granted, my friend Nigel does know what he's talking about. That is if he let himself be heard above the rabble in there. It drags him down."

"I see."

"Don't get me wrong, they've got their uses. But those uses are best kept few and far between."

"That's a bit callous, isn't it?"

"If callous is what's needed for this situation then callous we shall be."

"So… Are you the ringmaster then?"

"I beg your pardon?"

"If they're your clowns and you're the head of the circus, you must be the ringmaster?"

"If the cap fits I suppose I'll have to wear it. Whether I want to or not."

Sue smiled, "So what are you looking for?"

"I haven't got a clue."

"You're honest. I'll give you that."

"Thank you."

"I thought you were supposed to be some kind of professor?"

Boag-Munroe decided to change the track of Sue's conversation to one he felt more comfortable with. "I can't see anything out of the ordinary."

"You should have been here a few days ago."

"Pardon?"

"Nothing. So… Is that it? Everything's fine?"

"Not necessarily. Sometimes you can pick these things up straight away; for others it takes time."

"Oh, are you a medium?"

He looked at her with such distaste he didn't really need to answer, and she knew not to ask again.

"I really need to talk to your friend, Mary."

"I told you, I don't know where she is."

"Yes, you do. I'm right here." Mary appeared in the doorway with Andrew peering behind.

CHAPTER TWENTY-ONE

"So what did you expect her to do with that lot in tow?" Boag-Munroe vented his anger.

"She could have been a *bit* grateful." Nigel tried, in the vain hope of some defence.

"What for? The cast of a freak show invading her home? Get real."

"I am being real."

"Are you? Your work is becoming a joke. They're making you a joke. The Gentle brothers, the world's hammiest medium, Mrs Ruth, the list could go on. They're all personalities, I'll give you that. But neither you nor I need personalities. This isn't a game, I keep telling you."

"Sorry I thought it was. I thought that was the whole point, that it is a game and we're the big game hunters, searching for the proof – proof of other things, other realms."

"You make it sound so glamorous." The sarcasm drooled from Boag-Munroe's lips.

"But it goes deeper than that with you, doesn't it. It's not just the glamour, it's not just the chase. With you, it's personal."

"Whatever you say." Boag-Munroe turned away and looked out of the van window. It was raining hard. They'd already dropped the others off. There wasn't anything else to do after Mary had hit the roof and thrown them out. Silence ruled.

"I still think she was ungrateful."

"Yes Nigel." Boag-Munroe sounded bored, but really he was frustrated.

Silence re-took its hold.

"I'll drop you back at yours," Nigel said, before sinking back into the murky swamp of silence.

"Thank you."

The rain began to come down harder. As they turned into Victoria Road, hailstones poured down, chipping away at the windscreen and nearly destroying all visibility. As they crawled through the weather, Boag-Munroe noticed a figure at the mouth of an alleyway. It looked like Eloise.

"Stop!" he screamed at Nigel who in turn slammed on the brakes.

Boag-Munroe leapt out of the van. Hit by rain and hammered by hail stones, he chased down the alley where the figure had vanished. She wasn't there. He stood, soaked through and bewildered. Slowly, he got back into the van.

"What the hell's up with you? Have you gone mad?" asked Nigel.

Boag-Munroe wiped the rain from his face. "It's a long story, but I don't know if I come out of it mad or not, or at least not yet."

"What do you mean?"

"Let's just say that, up to now, that bit has yet to be decided."

"James?"

"It's OK, I can walk from here." Boag-Munroe jumped out from the van. Walking off into the storm he cut a lonely figure.

"I don't believe it. It just beggars belief."

Sue stood like a scolded schoolgirl.

Mary carried on the scolding, "I know it's not much of a home but it's mine."

"I was trying to help."

"I'd hate to see you when you're hindering." Mary caught her breath before unleashing another outburst: "What about Andrew? Don't you think he's had enough to cope with recently, without having to walk in to that lot?"

"I did ask them to come, and you were very rude to them."

"That's why I was rude. I was allowed to be rude, because it's my home and I didn't invite them. Can you begin to imagine my shock at finding that lot in my home?"

"I've no need to imagine your shock. I saw it, and I was on the receiving end of it."

"I could kill you." Mary shook with anger, "And who was that mad woman?"

"I didn't get her name."

"You don't even know her name?" Mary looked even more horrified. "She told me she could talk to dead people. In my flat! Dead people in my flat. Can you believe that? I think she was imagining it, or at least making it all up. I wouldn't mind, but she wasn't even convincing."

"That doesn't matter. What does matter is she was there." Sue flipped. "It was help. I know it was pathetic, but it was the best I could do."

Mary bit her lip. As far as she was concerned, Sue's best wasn't good enough, but she had no one else to turn to. Mary calmed down.

"Sue?"

"Yes."

"Could you stay the night?"

Sue laughed. "I thought you'd never ask."

Sue was beginning to wish she hadn't agreed to the sleep over. Andrew's bed wasn't exactly comfortable and Sue wasn't used to sleeping in strange beds, at least, not alone. She dwindled away the dark hours thinking about everything that had happened in the flat. She wasn't sure about it being haunted, but it definitely attracted its fair share of strange visitors. She'd not exactly relished giving Mary the news about her neighbour, but at least it had distracted Mary's anger onto someone else, especially as the police had let him off with just a warning. Sue felt more nervous of that creep, than of creeping shadows or ghosts and ghouls.

Sue heard a thud. It wasn't a loud thud, but a thud in the middle of the night, without rhyme or reason, is enough to get anyone's attention.

The second thud held Sue's attention. She lay, holding her breath, listening. She lay waiting.

Nothing happened.

She wasn't sure what she was waiting for. She got up and went in search of something; the something she wasn't sure of.

She wandered into the living room. All was still. At least there was more light in the living room, either that, or her eyes were now becoming more accustomed to the darkness. By now her brain was also becoming more accustomed. It was asking questions. Where the hell had that thudding sound come from? It sounded to come from nearby, but she couldn't point a finger at its exact origins.

She heard something else.

Weeping?

A feeling of unnatural fear crept up from the base of Sue's spine, making its way slowly up her body, freezing every particle in her, bit by bit. She stayed still, listening.

The weeping was coming from Mary's room. It was low-pitched, like a muted radio crackling in the distance. But no matter how low, it was there.

She pushed forward, bracing herself for what she might see. She mentally ticked herself off. All the talk of ghosts was getting to her. Pull yourself together, Sue told herself without moving her lips.

She pushed open Mary's door.

Mary and Andrew were both sitting up in the bed, holding one another. Both were weeping. The bed itself looked like a life raft in a stormy sea. All around them furniture had been turned upside down and scattered around the bedroom.

Mary rocked back and to, snivelling through her words, "What's happening to us, Sue?"

Sue looked at the devastation around her. She didn't have an answer.

CHAPTER TWENTY-TWO

Mrs Ruth was quite surprised to answer her front door and find Jason waiting outside.

"Whatever is the matter, love? Don't you realise how late it is?"

"I've been thinking," he answered.

"Good for you, love. Do you want to come in, or do you want to carry on thinking in the cold?"

He followed her indoors.

"Take your shoes off, love. It's a new carpet."

He obeyed. He couldn't escape the fact that Mrs Ruth was a big woman, not in height, but in weight, and one with the face of a bulldog chewing a wasp. If it wasn't for the fact she thought she was better than everyone else, and for her dodgy stomach, she'd have made a great all-in wrestler. He wasn't ready to get on the wrong side of her.

"Now tell me what you've been thinking of, love," she said in some thick unrecognisable accent.

"I've been thinking about us."

"Settle down, love. I know I'm a very attractive woman but there's Mr Ruth to consider as well here. Just because nobody from round here has met him because he works away…"

"I'm talking about the leadership challenge."

"Oh, that?" She sounded disappointed.

"Yes, that. I think we should get it out in the open, officially. Just think – me and you, the dream ticket, leader and vice-leader."

"And which of us would be the leader and which the vice?" she barked.

"You'd be the leader, of course. The group would look up to someone like you."

"Of course."

"We need you. Look at what a mess tonight turned out to be. I'm not blaming Nigel entirely. He's got his good points."

"He has indeed."

"It's just that he doesn't make a good leader. And as for Boag-Munroe, the less said the better. I reckon he knew that woman would go off her head. He was trying to show us up so that he could look good."

"My thoughts exactly, love." Mrs Ruth humoured him. She was tired. "Anyway, I'll think about what you've said, love, I really will."

"You will?" Jason's eyes lit up.

"I will indeed."

"Then we can put it to the vote proper at the next meeting?"

"We'll talk again, love. You'd better leave now. Mr Ruth could come home at any time."

When alone, Mrs Ruth's unpleasant features mellowed. She didn't seem so hard; more lost than anything. There was a great feeling of sorrow about her that she usually kept hidden by her normally harsh, know-it-all exterior. If you can't be strong then at least look it. That was her motto. She looked at the clock on the mantelpiece. She didn't know what time Mr Ruth was coming home, or if he would come home tonight at all. And even if he did decide to, she wouldn't know what state he'd be in or what he'd do. The only time she'd have a clue was when he was there in the flesh, when it was too late.

At least he never touched her face. She thanked the Lord for that small mercy. When she sat down and thought about it, she didn't have much else to thank the Lord for. Her home, she told herself: that was the envy of most, as was her job. And then of course there was her stature in the community. She paused. Until, of course, the realisation hit her in the face, and then she'd have to find another job, home and community. She didn't like moving and for now she was settled in Northwich. Nobody really knew her, and those that did were the ones Mrs Ruth chose to know. They didn't ask any questions. She liked it that way. It was the way it had to be.

Pleased with his night's work, Jason scurried home, while Mrs Ruth sat down with a large box of chocolates.

Jason was nearly home, still somewhat distracted by daydreaming about his handiwork. A shadowy figure stepped out from the shadows in front of him.

"I've had enough of you." Icy breath dripped from the figure's lips.

Jason tripped back in fear, falling against an unlit lamp post as he did so. "Please don't hurt me," he snivelled.

The figure cast a long shadow over the grovelling Jason, as he fearfully tried to scramble on to his feet.

"The second thing I hate most in the world is a back-stabber. The thing I hate most of all in the world is a back-stabber who is trying to back-stab me or my friends." Boag-Munroe looked him in the eye with an unflinching calm menace, which Jason had never seen before, nor could have imagined.

"Please!"

"I don't want you to plead," growled Boag-Munroe. "I want you to understand."

"I do, yes," Jason nodded.

Boag-Munroe sniffed, pulled his collar up, and left Jason crawling around in the darkness trying to find his glasses and reclaim his dignity.

Nigel's house felt cold. The heating was on full blast but wasn't having any effect. Sadly the cold that Nigel was suffering was a very different one than the normal, physical kind. It was more mental, but still as effective in its torture nonetheless. He looked around at his belongings. Nigel was the type of person to hoard just about anything that meant the slightest thing to him. His small terraced home was untidy at the best of times, unhealthy at the worst. Of course he wasn't dirty, but having collected so many books, magazines, trinkets and the like, regular cleaning was a chore that he didn't get round to very often.

He didn't feel like cleaning at the moment, far from it.

He'd been broken into a couple of months previously. A few things had been stolen, nothing of much value: it was more that it had happened at all which affected him the most.

No matter how he tried to hoard things, lock them away safely, it always seemed there was someone or something waiting around the corner to steal them.

The clock read three in the morning.

Nigel wanted to sleep but couldn't. He'd ended up peering at old photo albums; ones he hadn't looked at for years. He felt a tear in his eye. Treasured memories lay in his lap, but the more he looked at them the more they hurt. It began to hurt too much.

He forced himself to look away and closed the album he'd been looking at. Although the pictures were still in his head; they haunted him. Everyone looked so much younger then. His mother, father, girlfriend and him. He wiped away a tear but felt another one instantly replace it. Everyone looked so alive.

He buried his head in his hands as a procession of tears streamed down.

An unsolicited phone call in the middle of the night is never a pleasant thing, even for Professor Boag-Munroe. He shook himself away from the jaws of sleep and answered the phone. An unanswered phone, and therefore an unknown caller, is worse than answering and getting whatever over with. The thought of: 'I should have answered that. Who was it? Was it important?' is even worse than trying to roll back into oblivious sleep.

"See what you've done, you bastard." The woman's voice was sudden, loud and violent. It gave the unnerving impression that it was going to jump out of the phone, take Boag-Munroe round the neck and throttle him.

"And how have you been keeping?" Boag-Munroe answered back.

"My father's dead because of you."

Boag-Munroe was stunned for a second, maybe even two.

"When's the funeral?"

The phone slammed down. What he'd said had been terribly cruel, admittedly, but for the moment, he couldn't think of anything else. He had, for once, been genuinely and completely shocked. He knew the hostile female voice on the other end of the phone. Not especially liked, but definitely known. It was the voice of Leyton Blair's daughter. And Leyton, it seemed, was dead.

Boag-Munroe brushed his hair back from his forehead. There were a lot of shadows in his bedroom, and as he knew only too well, sometimes shadows can be dangerous things.

Once he'd decided the danger had passed, he drifted back into uneasy sleep. But sleep didn't hold him. He sat bolt upright in bed. This time he'd been woken from his slumber not by bad news via the phone, but a nightmare – the most realistic one he'd ever had, a little too real for comfort. He could feel the flames around him, the black billowing smoke choking him. The feeling of being trapped. He'd felt helpless, and helpless was not a feeling Boag-Munroe liked.

Now conscious, he wiped the sweat from his brow. His eyes darted around the deserted room as if he was searching for some unseen assailant.

The shadows were closing in on him.

He slept no more.

CHAPTER TWENTY-THREE

The breakfast table was a frozen snapshot. No movement, an odd twitch of muscle, but that was it.

Sue, swallowing a final spoonful of cereal, managed to speak first: "So what do we do now?"

Mary put her hand to her brow.

Andrew sat staring at his untouched cereal.

"Some serious shit happened here last night. We have to do something… or are we just going to sit around all day and do nothing about it?" Sue persisted.

Andrew began to peck at his cornflakes as if to avoid the difficult question.

"We're not in any position to do anything." Mary sounded weary; she'd been in the front line of battle for too long.

Sue, however, was fresh to the fight: "Boag-Munroe can help. I know he can."

"I'm not letting those freaks anywhere near," Mary snapped. "God knows what they've done. They've made things even worse."

"Could things get any worse for you?"

Mary had to answer honestly: "Yes, I think they can."

Andrew finished his cornflakes and pushed his bowl away.

Mary decided that normality was what they needed. She sent Sue packing, and dropped Andrew off at school. She tidied the bedroom and rang work to tell them she'd be back tomorrow. She cleaned the rest of her flat.

The knock on the door came after two solid hours of work. Reminding herself of her new policy of normality, she only hesitated for a second, before overcoming her feelings of doom. She would be damned if she would be afraid of opening her own front door anymore.

"Hello again," Boag-Munroe greeted her. "I've come to apologise."

Before Mary knew it Boag-Munroe had glided into her living room.

"I think we got off on the wrong footing."

"What the hell do you...?"

"To help," he cut her short. "I only want to help. And you *do* need my help, whether you know it or not."

She was speechless as he paced around her living space.

"I need to know everything, every detail, however slight, good or bad."

She charged at him like a runaway train. "I'm not discussing anything with you!"

She halted in her tracks as her eyes met his unmovable gaze. She felt as though he was looking into her very soul. For some reason she was afraid of what he might see.

"I'm not impressed by people trying to turn my house into a sideshow," Mary reasoned.

"I can't say I blame you. But as it stands, they're gone and I'm here. And as I recall, I don't think I myself have ever been likened to a sideshow before, so we're pretty safe on that front," he smiled.

Mary calmed down but clung to the ice maiden routine. "Perhaps you'd be better off talking to my friend Sue?"

"I've already spoken to her in great detail. She has nothing more to offer me."

"Funny, that's what most men say after any amount of time in her company."

"You do realise you and your son could be in the greatest danger?"

Mary paused. She had to compose herself before she asked: "What kind of danger?"

"From what I've been able to establish from your friend, I would think that this apparition in your dream is not evil in itself but is simply a warning. But I think you've worked out that part yourself already."

"How can my son and I both dream the same dream about the same man?"

"You haven't spoken of your nightmares to him or anyone else?"

"No."

"So we have to establish the link. Obviously there's a biological one. But the crux of the matter is finding out what happened to you back then which could be happening to your son right now?"

Mary didn't answer. She didn't even want to toy with the idea, never mind speak on the subject. "I want you to leave now."

Boag-Munroe hesitated. "You've got my number if you need me. But before I go I'd like you to answer me a question."

"I don't want to answer any more stupid questions."

"Has there been any other activity, apart from the dreams?"

"I said I don't want to talk anymore. You've no place in my business or in my home."

"It's just a simple question."

"And I don't want to answer it; this has all gone too far as it is."

Boag-Munroe smiled, "That's OK. I think you have already answered my question." He left as quietly as he'd arrived.

Mary felt very alone.

To Nigel, guilt was like a piece of glass that dug itself a home in one's finger. For the most part there was no pain, but every now and again, when the finger was rubbed in a certain position, the glass would move and bite; bite hard.

Guilt was biting into Nigel now. He hadn't checked on his mother for days. She understood of course, or at least said she did, and Nigel had kept in regular contact over the phone, but it wasn't the same. He felt even guiltier as he set off to see his mother. He knew she would smile as he apologised for not visiting earlier, that she would hold his hand in that certain position so the glass of guilt would not bite. She was a good woman and for the most part he was a good son, visiting her every other day at least, and tending to her household needs.

He hadn't visited her for four whole days. He rubbed his hand over his steering wheel. The glass of guilt was biting hard.

"How are you, son?" she smiled.

How am I? More guilt. Nigel did his best to sweep it away. At least he was trying to make amends now. "I'm fine, Mother."

"Are you sure, Nigel?"

"I'm sure."

"You don't look fine. You've got the same look that you had when you used to soil your pants as a toddler. You knew you shouldn't do it but you did it anyway."

"Mother!"

"I take it you haven't been up to your old soiling tricks again, so what else is it?"

"Do you have to rake up the past and that part of it?"

"The past is what makes us, or at least makes our memories. More so at my age."

"Are you feeling all right, Mother?"

"No, it's more the matter of if *you're* feeling all right. And if not, why not?"

"You've lost me."

"Nigel, you go through life clinging on to so much guilt. I'm fine. Just because you've not checked in on me for a couple of days, it doesn't mean to say you're a bad son."

"Four days."

"Whatever. Don't worry about me, you just get out there and strut your stuff."

"Whatever you say, Mother. How are your legs?"

"Same as ever – bloody useless. If they weren't, do you think I'd be sitting in here so much?"

"I worry about you."

"Don't. If my legs were OK I wouldn't be worrying about you. I'd be too busy; I'd be up and running."

"Well, if you must know, that's exactly what I've been doing."

"Good for you." A sly grin crossed her lips. "I listened to your radio slot again last night."

Nigel could have cried. "No, don't say you taped it."

"Of course I taped it. But don't worry, you'll get better."

"Thanks for the vote of confidence."

"That's exactly what it is."

Nigel turned away. "Do you need me to get you anything from the shops?"

"Nothing any different than usual."

"Do you need any vacuuming doing?"

"The home help just left."

"Right." Nigel looked at his shoes.

"I'm glad you and James are up to your old tricks, living a bit."

"I know." Nigel seemed to want to avoid conversation by just agreeing to everything.

"I'm glad he came back. Things were left a little up in the air. The situation was... How can I put it? Glossed over, maybe? Even as the years passed, cracks were merely papered over. But at least those cracks can be filled in now. You've both been good friends to one another. Neither of you could help what happened."

"Listen, I've got to shoot off," Nigel interrupted.

She nodded knowingly. She'd more or less anticipated his reaction, but she had to get it off her chest anyway. In some respects she wished Nigel had been more like her than his father. A good man though he may have been, Nigel held a lot inside: any upset, any hurt, unlike his father who was quick tempered and only too willing to show his hurt. At least he'd got things off his chest.

Nigel had held his hurt in for a long time and, as much as she loved him, she couldn't do anything to help with the feelings that she knew still tore him apart inside.

As she was left alone, she looked around her empty bungalow, a little glassy eyed. She mumbled to herself: "Now you come to mention it, I could have done with some fresh milk."

Mary wasn't looking forward to darkness. She sat huddled up next to Andrew as Sue busied herself round the flat, cooking an extravagant meal.

Sue never cooked anything of any consequence unless she wanted to take her mind off something unpleasant. Tonight, she was preparing a four-course meal.

"Have you got any candles?" asked Sue without halting from her chores.

"Why? Are we expecting a power cut?" Mary said a little limply.

"No, but food always tastes better with the right presentation."

"And yours has to be presented with the lights out? I can't say it exactly bodes well."

Sue flung her an icy glance, which Mary deflected with a cold shoulder of her own.

"It'll be ready in five minutes. I've set the table."

Mary yawned. The red rings of tiredness and worry were now beginning to encircle her body, not just her eyes. Everywhere she looked seemed bloodshot. She didn't feel like eating, and had no appetite for Sue's meal, or even her conversation for that matter. Mary went along with it all the same. She didn't want to be alone, no matter what.

The meal passed uneventfully. The candles around the table withered down with the heat of time passing. Darkness and the cold took a heavy grip on proceedings.

"Shall I turn the fire on? It's freezing in here," Sue asked.

"You can do. The radiators are playing up again."

"Then get the caretaker to fix them. You pay your rent."

"The caretaker makes an even worse mess of things."

"You can't sit in a freezing flat," Sue protested.

"Turn the fire on then." Mary almost bit Sue's head off.

Sue switched on the fire and a slight warmth came from it. The three of them huddled around it.

"Why don't we put the lights on?" mused Sue.

"Because you wanted them off for the candles, remember? Your meal?"

"Yes, a meal I went to a lot of trouble cooking and not even a word of thanks."

"Thanks," Mary offered sarcastically.

Sue turned the lights on. "We might as well put the telly on as well."

"No, leave it," Mary stopped Sue in mid-flow.

"What are we supposed to do then? Just sit here waiting? And wait for what?"

"You tell me?"

Sue shook her head and picked up her handbag, "I'd better get off then."

"No… don't!" Mary sprung to attention, "We'll watch the telly if you like."

She turned the telly on and Sue put her handbag to one side and sat down.

The flickering images from the television showered the room.

"Not much on, is there?" sniffed Sue.

The television went blank.

"Great!" moaned Sue, "the meter's gone now."

"We're not on a meter. Besides the lights are still working."

Sue jabbed a finger at the on/off button on the television. "No, it's as dead as a dodo. It must be broken."

The lights went out, plunging them into darkness.

"Are you sure you're not on a pay-as-you-go electric meter?"

"How sure do you want me to be?" asked Mary, as she shambled about trying to relight the candles."

"I don't like this," whined Andrew.

"It's OK love; it's just a power cut," soothed Mary. "That or the caretaker from hell has cut the electric cables by accident while changing some bath taps."

"Ssshh!" Sue interrupted Mary. "What's that scratching? You've not got mice have you?"

"What scratching?"

"Listen."

Everybody listened intently in the candlelit room.

"I can't hear anything," Mary said.

"I can definitely hear scratching," Sue persisted.

"Why won't the lights come on?" Andrew moaned again.

"They will, just be patient," Mary whispered to him softly.

"There's definitely scratching." Sue's voice wasn't whispering.

"Will you keep it down? Andrew's a nervous wreck already. He doesn't need visions of a giant rat roaming around."

Mary stopped as she heard the scratching. It wasn't particularly loud, but it was there nonetheless. It was hard to pinpoint its exact location; it sounded as if it was coming from, not so much the floorboards, but the walls, or rather inside the walls.

"You can hear it, can't you?" Sue whispered to Mary.

Mary whispered back: "Yes, I can hear it."

The temperature in the room dropped even lower. The candles blew out. Andrew screamed as they plunged into total darkness.

"Nobody panic!" screamed a much-panicked Sue.

Mary grabbed Andrew and sighed with relief.

The scratching became more audible… and then stopped. The lights and television came on. Nobody said a word.

It was only when they turned and saw that two chairs had been neatly placed on top of the dinner table that anyone spoke.

"Mary? Can you see what I see?" gasped Sue.

"Yes."

"I take it you didn't put those chairs there?"

"No I didn't."

"That's all right then. At least I know I'm not going mad on my own."

The hard rap on the front door rang out through the room.

Sue looked apprehensive. "Do you want to get that, Mary? This is your flat after all."

The rapping sounded out again.

"It might go away," Sue offered.

Mary left Andrew on the settee, moved stealthily towards the door and unlocked it.

"Good evening!" Boag-Munroe noted their frightened faces and up-turned furniture, "I take it you weren't expecting me?"

CHAPTER TWENTY-FOUR

"He's dangerous." The nondescript-looking man stood up from behind his equally nondescript desk.

"We know that already," Eloise answered back. "The trouble is we don't know how dangerous or what kind of danger he is."

"Not yet at least."

"So what has been the whole point? What is the point in any of this?" Eloise asked.

"The point is that I am warning you, as a friend and as your superior."

"Do you really think I need the warning?"

He smiled, "No, but humour me. It makes me feel better. I feel as if I'm doing my job."

"Well… let me humour you a bit then. You're doing your job perfectly. Just like I'm doing mine."

"Confidence is a good thing, but so is common sense." His tone and his features darkened. He didn't look as nondescript anymore. "Personally, I think you rely on your instincts a little too much."

"You mean my gift?" she snapped back.

He retreated back to a position at his desk. "I think you know what I mean. We've talked about situations like this before. Your job was to keep track of Boag-Munroe but to keep your distance. Now he knows we're watching him."

"He knew anyway."

"Did he? I'm not so sure."

"Well I am."

"But that's not good enough. You should know that by now. You're not naive. You've been with us for four years. You should know this business inside out."

"But I don't know this business inside out. Nobody does, not even you."

A cruel smile slipped across his lips. "We've been here for a long time, watching, waiting. This project was entrusted to me and I intend to see it through."

"And for my part, so do I."

"Of course you do." He sounded patronising.

"Why did you call me here tonight?" Eloise could sense things weren't going her way.

He cleared his throat. "We're moving you on. You're needed elsewhere."

"Don't talk stupid. I was assigned this case and I intend to see it through."

"Yes, you were assigned, and then you saw fit to blatantly disobey every order, just so you could go off and follow your own instincts."

Eloise argued back: "Those instincts are why I'm here, along with others like me."

"You've been careless with the whole business of approaching your subject, introducing yourself to him so blatantly. And as for taking him to the church, it leaves a very bad taste in my mouth."

"We needed to find out more about him," she reasoned.

"You didn't find out anything we didn't already know. Just the opposite – he found out more about us. That alone put him directly on our trail. Us, the people that were supposed to be watching him. As for your pathetic attempts to infiltrate his circle of friends, I can only call it amateurish at best."

"I was handling the situation as I saw fit."

"My instructions were explicit: to monitor, not to make contact."

"I was in the field. I did what I thought was right."

"There's no argument. That's the way it is. The paperwork has already been completed. You leave for headquarters in the morning."

Eloise wanted to strangle him but held her true feelings back for the moment.

"I don't take any pleasure in this. I like you, Eloise. You're more respected in this organization than you think. Keep it that way. Please."

Eloise smiled, "I would like to say it's been a pleasure working with you, but it hasn't." She slammed the door behind her.

He waited a couple of minutes before pressing his intercom: "Jones? Has she gone?"

"She's gone," the electronic voiced rasped back.

"Good. Are you and Smith ready?"

"As always."

"Assign someone to keep an eye on her. I think it's time we brought Professor Boag-Munroe in."

"What are you doing here?" Mary barred the entrance to her flat from Boag-Munroe.

"Does it matter?" shouted Sue from inside the flat, "We need him."

Mary hesitated.

"Well, Mary?" Boag-Munroe left a meaningful pause, "Do you need me?"

Mary held her ground a few moments longer, before relenting and letting him pass.

He made his way over to the table with the two chairs stacked on top. He touched the out-of-place furniture gently before quickly withdrawing his hand.

"It looks like things are hotting up around here. These chairs are red hot." He backed away from them, "Not to worry, they'll cool down in a couple of minutes."

Everybody in the room gazed at Boag-Munroe.

"So what happened?" he asked.

Before anyone could answer, Nigel appeared at the door, helping Hannah into the room.

"This looks a cosy room," puffed Hannah.

Nigel was too busy puffing himself to pass any kind of comment.

"Remember what I said: divide and conquer," Boag-Munroe whispered to Nigel and Hannah.

Hannah was quick on the uptake and struck first: "You must be Andrew." She cornered the boy, almost falling over in the process. "I've heard a lot about you."

Boag-Munroe nudged Nigel into the direction of Sue, adding "And be careful, remember what I said. She's a man-eater."

Nigel bumbled his way forward to Sue with his eyes closed and a prayer ringing in his ears.

Boag-Munroe breathed into Mary's ear: "Shall we retire to the bedroom?"

Mary couldn't answer a question like that so she merely followed him.

Boag-Munroe closed the door behind them. "We may not have much time, so I need your undivided co-operation and attention."

Mary bowed her head. "I don't feel safe anymore."

Boag-Munroe took a deep breath. "Whether you're safe or not has yet to be established. What I do know is these things are happening for a reason... And that reason rotates around you and your son. Can you think who this man in your vision could possibly be? Can you fill in any of the blanks in his features?"

She held her head as if thought equalled pain. "I don't know. I get the feeling that it'll come to me, that whoever it is, that whoever wants to hurt us, it will be revealed, it's just that at the moment something's blocking it."

"It could be your subconscious that is blocking it. And as for everything being revealed, I'm sure it will but, by then, it might be too late. Whatever's waiting for you both in the future, it's coming closer with every passing second. Things are beginning to speed up. The furniture business for instance, that was actual matter being moved. This thing is a warning, a cry for help. The person it is trying to warn, trying to help, is you. Try to take notice of it."

"How can I not notice?"

"Don't run away from it. Let it in."

"But I don't understand."

"You must try to understand. You must remember what happened to you as a child. You must face it now as you did then. It's the only way to bring yours and Andrew's suffering to something approaching a satisfactory conclusion."

"I don't understand anything that's happening to us." She only just managed to hold the tears back.

"I call it the pain of saviour."

"Have I got to try to understand that as well?"

He spoke softer: "Imagine if you had a pain in your knee, you'd go to the doctor, especially if the pain was unbearable. The next thing, the doctor sends you for tests. The tests show a cancer. With a bit of luck the cancer has been caught early and can be sorted out before it can do any great damage. But if that knee hadn't hurt in the first place, there wouldn't have been any trip to the doctor, no tests, no help. The cancer would have grown, deadly and silent and you wouldn't stand a chance."

"Do I stand a chance now?"

Boag-Munroe turned away from her. "There are more things in heaven and hell and the in between than we can imagine, or ever could imagine."

"That's no kind of answer."

"We all stand a chance, especially when we know what we're up against. As it happens I think you now stand a very good chance. That is if you listen and learn."

"So what do I do now?"

"You tell me what happened to you when you were younger."

"I can't."

The temperature in the room dropped suddenly. It was the first sign of a ghost, but a very different type of ghost than the supernatural variety. This was a ghost from the past: Mary's past.

"You have to face it. This isn't just about you; it's about your son as well," Boag-Munroe urged her.

Mary's eyes glazed over. "His daughter… I was his daughter. That didn't matter to him though. My mum started to work nights, I was Andrew's age." Mary wiped away a tear. "I didn't say anything at first. I was just silent in my dread of it. When I finally did tell my mother she didn't want to believe it. She refused it. But I knew deep down she did believe it. She came off her night shifts not long afterwards. For a time I thought things might go back to normal, but they didn't. They couldn't. I hated him and I steadily began to hate her as well. He never came near me again, but I left home as soon as I could at sixteen in any case."

"Do they know where you live?"

"Dad's dead. Mum didn't know where I live, but she does now. Thanks to my estranged husband. He rang and told her, and that I wanted to see her. He thought he was getting back at me and he was I suppose. Trouble is he's getting back at Andrew as well. She's never seen him and I'd like it kept that way. Even though he's gone, I don't even want her near. She sent me a letter, but I binned it."

"At least we're getting somewhere now, hard as it might be."

"You think my past might be catching up with me, don't you?"

"It's definitely a theory. But which past? The long-dead and buried, or the more recent past?"

"You think my husband might want to hurt us?"

"It's an unpleasant thought but a necessary one to safeguard you both against."

Boag-Munroe could see the horror crawl all over Mary's face.

"I know John can be a bastard but..."

Boag-Munroe finished her sentence for her: "We mustn't jump to conclusions; we're just leafing through suspects. I'm sorry but for now that's how we must treat him. The same for any member of your family, especially your mother. Is there anything or anybody else I should know about?"

"A one-night stand got a bit stroppy. He'd texted me for a while, but I changed my mobile and he doesn't know where I live. He's from out of town, and anyhow he's one of those that's all talk."

"I'll be the judge of that. Who else?"

"There's the freak across the hall," she looked embarrassed. "He broke into my flat and..."

"And?"

"He did something over my underwear. I don't think I need to go into any more detail."

Boag-Munroe shrugged off her embarrassment. "It takes all sorts."

"The others will be wondering what we're up to."

"Don't worry. My team's more select this time – hand-picked by me."

"Best of a bad bunch, you mean?"

"I didn't say that," Boag-Munroe smiled. "I'm going to need to talk to your little boy. Is that OK with you?"

"I'm staying with him."

"I wasn't suggesting otherwise."

Mary fetched Andrew. He shuffled into the room with his head bowed.

"Hi, Andrew. I'm Professor Boag-Munroe. You've already met my assistants Nigel and Hannah?"

Andrew nodded his head.

"Do you know why we're here, Andrew?"

Andrew shrugged.

"We're here to help you out with the bad dreams. We're going to make them go away. But before we do, you're going to have to help us. Do you understand, Andrew?"

Andrew nodded.

"Is it the same man you see in your dreams all the time?"

Andrew nodded again.

"Have you seen him anywhere else apart from when you're asleep?"

"Yes."

"In this flat?"

"Yes, and outside."

"Where outside?"

"At Fleetwood. He was standing at the pier's edge in a storm. He was looking at us."

"Could you see his eyes?"

"No." Andrew's eyes bored into the floor.

"How did you know he was looking at you?"

Mary was about to speak, but Boag-Munroe stopped her, holding his finger to his lips.

Boag-Munroe spoke so softly it was almost a whisper: "Go on Andrew."

"I don't know. I could just tell."

"Like a feeling?"

"Yes."

"Can you feel the man's presence when you're awake?"

"Sometimes."

"Can you feel his presence now?"

"No."

"Thank you, Andrew. You've been very helpful. I think we can get things sorted out now. Tell me Andrew, are you any good at making tea or coffee?"

"No."

"That's just fine because I don't intend to drink it, but I'm sure my friends would like a drink."

"Go on, Andrew," Mary prompted him. "Sue will help you."

Alone again, Boag-Munroe turned to Mary: "Have you experienced things the same as Andrew?"

"Exactly the same. You can tell when he's near without seeing him. You know he's looking at you even though there are no eyes, no features, just a smooth face."

"But under the smooth face there are features and we must be able to see them if we're to know who the danger is."

A crashing sound emitted from the living room. Boag-Munroe and Mary dashed in to see what had happened.

"It's OK," said Hannah. "The lad just dropped a cup of coffee."

Sue and Nigel set about cleaning up. Andrew stood very still.

"What's the matter, Andrew? Why did you drop the coffee?" Boag-Munroe asked softly.

Mary answered for him, "Because he's arrived. He's here, now. I can feel..." she stopped, "*We* can feel him."

CHAPTER TWENTY-FIVE

The car pulled up silently opposite the block of flats. The two men inside were prepared to wait. They were used to it.

Smith turned to Jones: "Are they sure he's in there?"

Jones nodded. "Yes, they're sure, so I'm sure, and you should be sure."

"That's all right. Just checking," Smith replied tetchily.

"Well, I'm glad you're glad," Jones snapped back. "I'm just happy somebody's found a little happiness in this whole situation. Me, I'd rather not be sitting here waiting to go into whatever we're going into."

"The unknown. That's exactly what this guy is. All we know is that he's dangerous. It's not exactly a comforting thought is it? It's all that dumb bird's fault. They should never have given them the vote." Smith was at his most bitter.

"You ought to listen to yourself sometimes." Jones was equally barbed.

"I listen to myself all the time which is just as well because nobody else seems to do. I knew she was the wrong tail to put on him."

"And who made you Head of Operations?" Jones replied sarcastically.

"*I* made *myself* Head of Operations when she messed up so badly. Where will Lady Laceholes be then? I can tell you. She'll be messing up somewhere else," Smith snarled.

"I bet sometimes you wish you were back in the forces," Jones grimaced.

"No. They were beginning to overrun that as well."

"Who?"

"Women and the politically correct."

"You must breathe a sigh of relief then, knowing every morning when you wake up that you're the most politically incorrect man alive today," laughed Jones.

"Laugh all you like. But it's our bollocks on the line here. We've got to bring him in. How are we going to do that?" Smith sniped back.

"The usual methods," Jones shrugged.

"But this guy isn't meant to be the usual customer."

"It'll be fine."

"And if it's not fine?"

"Then you can blame it on the politically correct and women getting the vote."

Smith grunted, turning his head away and then back, as if he was going to get some sleep.

Jones jolted forward. "Something's happening."

Smith joined him in a little jolt forward of his own. "What?"

"Listen."

"To what?"

"Ssshhh!"

"Don't sshhh me."

Jones listened intently. Smith watched him even more intently.

Jones relaxed back: "It must be nearby traffic."

Smith rebuffed him with an annoyed glance and then sulked.

Jones let him sulk for a while longer before speaking again: "Boag-Munroe's in there with a group of others. There's about five or six of them."

"Are you getting the sight?" Smith looked horrified. "You *are* getting the sight, aren't you?"

"I'm only telling you what I've been told."

"Then how come I don't get told this?" Smith asked indignantly.

"Because you forget things and that's why people get fed up of telling you things; me included."

"Brilliant," Smith said sarcastically, "so this could be an all-night wait."

"There's something else though, a presence."

"What kind of presence?"

"They couldn't tell me. They could only sense its fear and frustration and advise us to be careful."

"Great, its lunatic time again. We need back up on this."

The back car door opened and Eloise's slim figure slid in behind them. "Your request is my command. And by the way, all hell's going to break loose in there."

"This isn't my idea of back-up," Smith spat.

"Relax," replied Eloise, "Boag-Munroe can handle it. If anything, he's provoking it on purpose. He wants answers and unlike you two patient gentlemen, he's not prepared to wait for them."

"You shouldn't be here," Smith frowned at her.

"But I am, so we might as well make the best of it."

The explosion of a glass window in the flat they were watching made them jump violently. Shards of glass rained down across the windscreen and the car bonnet.

"What the hell?" screamed Smith.

Eloise was smug. "Now what was it I said, boys? About all hell breaking loose?"

Andrew had buried his head into his mother's breast. Mary dragged him away from the now-gaping hole in her flat, where the living room window had been. A slight cut had opened itself up on Nigel's forehead. Hannah and Sue also had some tiny glass cuts dotted about their hands from when they had shielded their faces. Boag-Munroe was unharmed.

Boag-Munroe stood at the smashed window staring out. Every head in the room turned to him, waiting for him to say something profound.

"James?" Nigel spoke for all the others, "What happened?"

Boag-Munroe gave the smile of a man who knew exactly what had happened but wasn't going to let anyone else in on the secret, not just yet.

"Can you sense anything, Mary? When I say anything, I mean him, the man in your nightmares?"

"No. Not now," she shivered in shock, "but he was here."

"Before the window smashed?"

"Yes."

"Do you agree with your mother, Andrew?"

"Yes," Andrew mumbled from deep in her chest.

Boag-Munroe coughed, "Very good. Sue – why don't you take Andrew and put him to bed. I think he's had enough excitement for one night."

"I'm not leaving Andrew," Mary was quick to her son's rescue.

Boag-Munroe gave her a calming look. "Your friend will be with him and my friends will be here waiting just outside the door. He'll be quite safe, believe me."

"Safe? After what's just happened?" Mary could feel her temperature rising.

Boag-Munroe's temperature stayed at its normal cool-to-freezing-point self. "We need to talk again. Alone." Boag-Munroe's tone was polite but stern. Mary relented and followed Boag-Munroe into the bathroom as Hannah stood guard, while Nigel started to clean up the mess.

Alone with Mary, Boag-Munroe was still adamant: "We need to get to the heart of the beast. You have to confront your nightmare."

"I can't leave Andrew."

"I told you, you're not leaving Andrew. He is safe, as you both will be if you act quickly. You need to sleep, and while asleep you need to take notice of every single detail your inner mind conjures up. You need to find your nightmare in your mind's eye, track it down and keep it there."

"I don't understand."

"Do you ever wake up and see the shadows from your nightmares surrounding you?"

"I don't know," she stumbled.

"Well you must start to know. When you waken you must hold on to those shadows, hold them for as long as possible, make your conscious mind focus on them. You have to decipher what they are, what they mean. Only then will the features be filled in, and you'll know what danger lies ahead and who your enemy is."

"And what are you going to do?" Mary asked.

"All I can do is watch and wait."

"Is that it?" Mary made her disappointment known.

"This isn't an exact science. All I can do is guide you with the things I do know."

"And what *do* you know?"

"The window was a manifestation of frustration," explained Boag-Munroe. "Whatever is trying to warn you is getting desperate because you're not listening."

"What is trying to warn me? Is it a ghost?"

"It's not a ghost in the terms you're thinking. Think more along the lines of a poltergeist."

"An evil spirit?"

"No. An energy – an energy from inside you. You're gifted, a gift you passed to your son. Sometimes it happens that way. This is the inner you, warning the outer you that someone is trying to harm you. Just like someone tried to harm you all those years ago. And there's no way your inner self will settle, until it knows you're both safe. The same goes for Andrew's inner self."

"Or when it's too late and we can't be saved?"

Boag-Munroe turned away.

Nigel bolted in: "It's the police. And they want to speak to you, James."

Boag-Munroe thought for a second before entering the living room where Jones and Smith were waiting.

"You're as much plain-clothed policemen, as I'm the Archbishop of Canterbury," Boag-Munroe quipped as soon as they reached the pavement outside. They didn't answer. Boag-Munroe nevertheless allowed himself to be ushered by Jones and Smith to the waiting car.

Eloise wound her window down. "Good evening."

"We'd like you to come with us," said Jones.

"I'm sure you would," retorted Boag-Munroe, "and I would like to come. That's why I'm here, even though I'm a bit busy."

Boag-Munroe opened the car door and sat by Eloise on the back seat. "What is there left to say, except take me to your leader."

It didn't take Boag-Munroe long to deduce where they were heading. "Why are we going to Northwich?" he asked.

"Because we are." Eloise was the only one to give an answer, no matter how short it was.

"Is that where the Ministry of the Dead's head offices are? Or is it just a regional office?"

This time nobody was forthcoming with an answer.

"So what is it you and your superiors want to talk to me about?"

Again no answer.

The rest of the journey was silent. It stayed that way until they pulled into the drive of a large house, situated just past Leftwich estate, lying on one of the main road veins, London Road, that ran into Northwich.

"Shouldn't you have blindfolded me or something? I know where to find you now. Or is it a case of I'll just disappear into thin air when we're done? I'm sure an organisation like yours could organise that if need be."

Eloise's answer was cold, but had a certain ring of honesty about it: "Yes, we could."

Furniture in the house was sparse. Long wooden-panelled corridors with matching floorboards were in view and, as Boag-Munroe was led along them, he wondered if there were any actual rooms in the house at all. Finally he was led to something akin to a small waiting room. The party that had brought him promptly left. Boag-Munroe seated himself on a rickety wooden chair in a corner of the room. Seated in another corner, behind a desk, was what looked like a secretary. The woman, at least in her mid-sixties, carried on typing without even giving Boag-Munroe a glance.

"Nice night for it," Boag-Munroe called over to her.

Now she gifted him a solitary hawk-eyed glance over her small gold-rimmed glasses, before getting back to her ancient-looking typewriter and her work.

"It must be hard for you, working nights like this. I bet you don't get the chance to socialise much. Still, there must be some incentives. Is the pension plan any good?"

Not even a second glance.

"What's the pay like?"

The intercom on her desk buzzed and flashed. She pressed the button, which had the desired effect of letting a voice out of its electric prison.

"Send Professor Boag-Munroe in, Miss Cutts."

Miss Cutts nodded to a door opposite Boag-Munroe. Boag-Munroe entered another room through it. In that room sat a rather nondescript-looking man. He stood up from behind his desk and offered a handshake. "Welcome to the Ministry of the Dead."

CHAPTER TWENTY-SIX

The flat was silent. Mary and Andrew were sleeping side by side in her bed. Sue was getting her head down in Andrew's room. Hannah and Nigel stood a watchful guard; not knowing what they were watching for, or from which corner it would arrive.

"What do you think's happening?" Hannah asked.

"Who knows?" Nigel sounded worried.

"Have any of us got a clue about any of this? Do you know what we're meant to be doing here?"

"Observing, he said. And now I'd say we were holding the fort."

"And up to now we've observed exploding windows and him being arrested."

"He wasn't arrested," Nigel corrected. "He went with them to aid in their enquiries."

"Yes, he did," Hannah put her thoughts into words, "but don't you think it was a bit strange that they knew he was here? Why would the police be following him?"

"All kinds of reasons, but I've got a good idea," answered Nigel.

"You might as well tell me," said Hannah. "If it's interesting enough it might kill a bit of time."

Nigel explained: "He broke into an old people's home a couple of days ago in Llangollen."

Hannah looked horrified. "What for? What's he got against old people?"

"Nothing exactly, apart from the one he was paying an uninvited visit to. It was someone he had considered an old friend, somebody who had let him down badly."

"Remind me not to fall out with your friend," said Hannah, half jokingly.

Nigel turned to her, looking very serious. "He left James for dead. As far as Leyton Blair was concerned, as long as his scrawny neck was saved, that was it, job done. James had looked up to him. If the shoe had been on the other foot, he would have stayed to the bitter end."

"And you know that?" Hannah questioned.

"Believe me, I do." Nigel paused, "He saved my life one day. We were twelve years old and we were somewhere we shouldn't have been. We were investigating a haunted train tunnel of all things. I got my foot trapped in the train tracks, just like they do on the movies." He paused in a shudder. "And just like in the movies… along came a train." He paused again.

"Go on," Hannah ushered excitedly.

"We didn't stand a chance really, or at least I didn't. There were seven of us in all, and out of that seven, five bailed out straight away. That left just the two of us, James and me. The train was almost on us by the time he got my foot free. I could see it bearing down on us; I could feel it thundering down the track. I could almost feel the impact before it had happened. He was as unemotional as ever. He never even acknowledged the train, even though I had stopped breathing due to the oncoming horror. Of course, if he hadn't stayed so calm I wouldn't be here now to tell you this story. But that's James all over, calm and loyal to the end. It could have been his end as well as mine, and he knew it. It's easy to say 'putting one's life on the line.' James did for me as he has for others, including Leyton."

"Leyton?" Hannah obviously couldn't keep up.

"The man who he broke into the old people's home to see."

"He doesn't do things by halves does he, our good professor?"

"He never has and it's doubtful he ever will," Nigel agreed.

"And neither do the people that surrounded him or he comes up against," Hannah mused.

"What's that supposed to mean?"

"I don't think those two were police officers. They looked official enough, but looking and being are two different things."

"So who were they then?"

"I haven't a clue. And if anyone could hazard a guess that would have to be you. You're the only one he confides in," Hannah said, looking straight at Nigel.

"When you say 'confides', you must understand that the normal rational state of human mind doesn't come into play here," said Nigel. "Have you ever heard Boag-Munroe's concept of confiding? It's less confiding, more of a muddled box of cryptic clues."

"So what are you like at cryptic clues then?" asked Hannah.

"Not as good as I should be, after riding shotgun with him for as long as I have."

"So we'll have to wait until he gets back."

"I don't like the way you said that. It sounded like you slipped an invisible 'if' into that sentence. That's the kind of trick he does himself."

"I'm sure he'll be fine," Hannah tried to reassure.

"There you go again."

"What?"

"How you said that. That's him, word for word: saying one thing, meaning another. If they weren't police officers..." Nigel looked deflated, "I've let him down."

Hannah patted his shoulder. "When have you ever known James to not know what he's doing?"

Nigel paused. Then at last he saw the ray of hope: "Never."

"I thought as much. So that means we can relax a bit, doesn't it?"

Nigel ruffled his own hair with a sweeping hand, trying to clear out the cobwebs. "I suppose so." He still didn't sound too convinced.

"It's very important to him, isn't it? Helping this family?" pondered Hannah.

"There doesn't seem to be much middle ground with him. He's either just not interested, or up to his neck in it."

Andrew's bedroom door opened.

"I can't sleep. I'm going to make a brew, does anybody want one?" Sue asked.

Nigel and Hannah both declined. Sue disappeared into the kitchen and appeared a couple of seconds later.

"I couldn't be bothered. As soon as I turned the kettle on I felt sleepy, so I made do with water instead. Night." She disappeared again.

"Nice girl," grinned Hannah. "A girl like that would do you the world of good; put hairs on your chest."

"I'm sure she would." Nigel fell silent. "There was one girl once, a long time ago. She died. She was only sixteen. We'd been going out for about a year." He shuddered to a pause, "I loved her. I suppose it sounds silly, me saying something like that."

"No, it doesn't."

"But she was the one. I didn't know it so much at the time, but after she was gone and the years went by, I realised I hadn't got over her and wasn't ever going to. But there was more to it than that. She might have been a Juliet, but I've never been a Romeo and never could be. The really sad part is, I don't know if she ever really loved me. I know she cared for me and didn't want to hurt my feelings, but I could tell she wanted another. And he wanted her."

"If that's the case, why didn't they just run off together?"

A tear appeared in Nigel's eye. "Because, like I told you, she didn't want to hurt me. And the other person, well… the same goes for him."

Realisation dawned on Hannah: "Professor Boag-Munroe?"

"He was just James back then. Or Bogey. Some even used to call him the Bogeyman because of his interest in the supernatural. I think he quite liked that tag."

"So what happened to the girl? How did she die?" Hannah didn't really want to push the subject and upset Nigel any more than he was already showing, but she had to know.

"You would have heard about it. They don't talk about it now. She was murdered at Marbury, nineteen years ago."

"Oh, my dear child!"

"That's all she was really, just a child. And the warning signs were there, it's just that we didn't see them."

"What do you mean, Nigel, 'warning signs'?"

"For weeks up to her death, she'd seen an apparition of a small boy appearing in her bedroom. The boy had tried to speak, but she could hear no sounds, even though his silent lips continued to move. She tried to communicate with him but all to no avail. None of us believed her. Not that we thought she was a liar. I think we just thought it was her imagination. She wanted so badly to be part of our ghost hunting group, but we wouldn't let her. We were very strict on females in those days."

Hannah looked puzzled.

"None allowed. Sexist or what?" He swallowed a tear. "She still hung around with us though, a kind of unofficial member. We all used to hang out round Marbury back then, trying to catch sight of something out of the ordinary, but we wouldn't take her with us, not there. One night she camped out there with some girlfriends. An unexploded Second World War bomb went off. She was killed. Heaven knows what had disturbed the bomb. She was murdered by a ghost from the past."

"I remember. It was a terrible tragedy."

"James and I were supposed to be the great ghost hunters but we couldn't decipher the warning."

"How could you have known?"

"The clues were there, in the vision of the boy. Her old gran used to tell her stories of angels when she was younger. That everyone has one guarding him or her. When she had asked what they looked like, she'd told her they had the look of innocent little boys. That's what she saw, the apparition in her bedroom, a boy in clothes from the era of the Second World War. A boy who was trying to speak to her but couldn't be heard. It was a warning she couldn't hear in time. The bomb just went off; she didn't stand a chance."

"And you and James never forgave yourselves." The pieces fell into place for Hannah.

"That's why this case and other similar cases are so important to him. I think he views it as a penance."

"Is that how you see it?"

"I'm not sure how I see it."

Hannah watched the eyes of the man in front of her, a man who'd never had a girlfriend since his only love got killed. Somehow, she couldn't believe he didn't have his own penance, and conjectured he would be enslaved by it for the rest of his life.

"It's a nice place you've got here, if a little bare," Boag-Munroe gave a disinterested glance round the sparse-looking room.

The nondescript man smiled, "We like it this way. It's more practical. We clutter too much of our lives as it is. Anyway, let's dispense with the conversation and may I say how pleased I am to finally meet you." He briefly left the safety of his desk to greet Boag-Munroe with a warm handshake.

"Don't tell me… You've heard a lot about me?" Boag-Munroe accepted the handshake.

"Enough."

"And you are?"

He didn't answer.

"I don't suppose you've heard that much about us?" The nondescript smile began to look a little more humane.

"I've come across the odd rumour here and there."

"I'm sure you have. An organisation like ours can't exist for as long as we have without some whispers in certain quarters."

"But I'm sure you've been able to silence those quarters if need be?"

"If we've had to," the smile slid from his lips for a few brief seconds, "but please, Professor, forgive me. You are our guest. Would you permit me to fill you in on our work here, so as to heighten those whispers to the level of actual audible voices?"

Boag-Munroe smiled, "How can I resist? I'm almost a captive audience."

"Almost. But not quite. You can, in theory, walk out of here at any time you like."

"But in practice?"

"Now practice is a different matter altogether. It has to be put into motion before any of us knows the outcome."

Boag-Munroe let a glint of seriousness flash across his features. He could have played the double-meaning game all night long, but he had other matters pressing for his time at the moment.

"Why have you been monitoring me?"

The nondescript man sighed, as if he had been asked this same question more times than he cared to remember. "We monitor a lot of things. People, situations, it's nothing you should take personally. Especially as we've now decided to roll out the red carpet for you. First I have a question for you."

"Go ahead. I'm not going anywhere," Boag-Munroe calmly replied.

"You seem to be good at handing medicine out. What are you like at taking a taste of your own medicine?"

Boag-Munroe sat like a block of ice.

"The woman, Mary. You've been trying to help her and her son. I congratulate you on such an excellent cause to which you are devoting so much of your time. But may I ask, are there not causes closer to home, that you might be better devoting time and attention to?"

The block of ice spoke: "Such as?"

"Don't take this the wrong way, not even for a second." He paused, "Your own cause perhaps?"

A silence descended. Boag-Munroe became aware of a clock ticking in the room. It was a room like every other he'd so far encountered in the building: bare. Bare, that is, apart from the clock, one filing cabinet, two chairs and a desk at which his inquisitor sat.

"Please, you'll make my ego grow even larger," quipped Boag-Munroe.

The nondescript man smiled, "May I have the honour of showing you around and telling you more about our work?"

"I'd be delighted," Boag-Munroe answered.

"This is my office and I'm in charge of the operations in this area. A conclusion I'm sure you've already come to. Like all the best businesses, we have branches all over."

"I'm sure you do."

The nondescript man looked serious. "That's one thing you and I know very well – you can't be sure of anything."

He led Boag-Munroe out of the room, along seemingly endless corridors and through other blank rooms that were dotted here and there. None seemed of any consequence. Nothing he saw was of any interest. The building was just a shell, a temporary accommodation; everything indicated it. The tour finished back where it had started in the man's office.

"So you see," the nondescript man added, "we have nothing to hide."

Boag-Munroe nodded; unconsciously he held a finger to his lips, as if it was holding him back from saying what he really thought.

"At least not from you, Professor Boag-Munroe." The man paused, "We've been monitoring you for a while, for the simple reason that we believe you would be a valuable asset to the Ministry. And of course, the Ministry could be of great advantage to you."

He seated himself and motioned for Boag-Munroe to do the same. "We are a government-funded organisation, nicknamed Ministry of the Dead. A name we found so very adept that we stuck with it. Our staff includes psychics, sceptics, fortune-tellers, the ESP gifted, just about every shade of the out-of-the-ordinary you could imagine. You see we're like both sides of the coin, the dreamers, and those who specialise in looking at the facts in the cold light of day."

"So where do I fit in?"

"You are a rarity. You are both sides of the coin: the dreamer and the realist intertwined."

"And which side of the coin are you?"

He laughed, "That'll you have to find out for yourself. Will you join us?"

"Become a member of the Ministry of the Dead? It's quite an offer," Boag-Munroe paused, "but an offer I'm afraid I'm going have to turn down." He stood and offered his hand. "It's been a pleasure. Perhaps we can talk again some time in the future?"

The man shrugged, "Perhaps you should give yourself a little more time to decide? Yes?"

Boag-Munroe stood up, gave a sly smile and left.

The man was taken aback. Gathering his thoughts, he turned on his intercom, his hand trembling.

"Miss Cutts. See that Eloise is relieved of her duties immediately," he paused, "and indefinitely."

CHAPTER TWENTY-SEVEN

Both Hannah and Nigel had nodded off in their chairs. Everywhere was silent and still. It only served to make the scream all the more piercing. Nigel and Hannah shot up in unison and, if Hannah had been younger, they'd have arrived at the bedroom in unison too. As it was, Nigel got there first, while Hannah struggled to move, and then gave up. Nigel couldn't make out who had screamed, but it had been a blood-curdling one.

Sue entered the bedroom next, out of breath: "What happened?"

Nigel shook his head. "I haven't a clue."

Sue threw him a scolding glance. "You're supposed to be helping them."

Nigel backed away, at a complete loss for what to do. He left Sue comforting both Andrew and Mary, and went to join Hannah in the living room, where he felt a little more useful.

"What happened?" asked Hannah.

"You're the second person to ask me that in the last minute."

Somebody knocked on the front door.

"Great. That's probably the secret police again," hissed Nigel.

He opened the door, resigned that he might be letting yet more madness in.

"You look like you've seen a ghost." Boag-Munroe didn't wait for any reply. "Anything happened since I've been away?" He looked over at the broken window. "No more breakages to report?"

"Not yet," Nigel replied, still in shock.

"There's time yet. But what of our patients?"

Mary appeared at the door, silent and haggard.

It dawned on Boag-Munroe that all was not well. "What did you see?" he questioned urgently.

"What we always see," Mary sounded tired, but angry. "Him."

Even though she looked devastated, Boag-Munroe carried on questioning. He wasn't interested in emotions, just answers: "Did you recognise him? Any discernable features?"

She paused, keeping everyone in suspense: "No, but he was there."

"Where?" Boag-Munroe pushed her further.

"At the window, the smashed one."

He nodded. "From now things get a little rockier. A change of tactics is called for."

Mary didn't want to ask, but found she had to: "So what do we have to do now?"

"The opposite of what you have been doing. You don't sleep, at all."

"I would say you were crazy," Mary mopped her brow, "but at the moment, that doesn't sound so bad. The last thing I want is sleep. I've never been afraid of anything so much. Right now my life feels like a bad horror film."

"Like I said," Boag-Munroe continued, "it's going to get worse before it gets anywhere near better. Sleep deprivation is a terrible thing. In some countries it's still a valuable method of torture. But it's the only way we're going to flush out answers."

"How's it going to help?" Mary suddenly felt snappy again.

"You were wide awake when the window smashed," Boag-Munroe reasoned. "Perhaps that's what it wants. Or perhaps that's what it needs: for you to stay awake long enough, until you fall into a awareness dream state, a territory that goes with sleep deprivation."

Mary shook her head.

"You hadn't slept much when you saw the thing on the pier," Boag-Munroe pressed the point home.

"No, we hadn't," Mary had to quietly admit.

"Exactly. People who suffer from sleep deprivation are susceptible to all sorts of things: illusions, delusions, and things that might be real, but we can't explain. It's almost like going into a medium's trance. We need to make you susceptible."

"What about Andrew?" Mary asked worriedly.

"Andrew must stay awake as well, I'm afraid. Still, a few sleepless nights are better than an endless sleep, wouldn't you say?"

Mary left the room visibly upset at Boag-Munroe's final comment.

"That was a bit harsh, wasn't it," Nigel looked annoyed, "scaring her like that?"

"A necessary evil I'm afraid."

"And what about those police?" Hannah asked.

"An unnecessary distraction," the professor answered, indicating an end to this particular question and answer session.

Sue stormed in, not so much a bull in a china shop, but a bull that had seen red nonetheless. "Are you totally off this planet?"

Boag-Munroe stood his ground with a simple: "No. I don't think so."

"Do you know what I think?" Sue carried on, "I think I was crazy in the first place to let myself get dragged into this stuff, and now it's making a worse mess."

"You've heard the old adage: you can't make an omelette without breaking a few eggs?"

Sue gritted her teeth, "Those eggs you're talking about breaking are my friends. It's fine for you, they don't mean anything to you."

Boag-Munroe remained impassive. "You're right; they don't mean anything to me in personal terms. They're just a couple of people with a problem that I happen to think I can help with."

"More like you're using them as guinea pigs."

"That's a strong piece of wording. What would you rather I do, simply walk away, or maybe wave a magic wand and say everything will be fine?"

Sue stormed back to her friends, slamming the door behind her.

"How to win friends and influence people, by Professor James R Boag-Munroe," commented a sarcastic Nigel, gleefully. "Has a certain ring to it as a book title, don't you think?"

"I'll bear that in mind when I'm done here."

"I think you might already have had your swan song on this one, lad," Hannah said softly. "I don't think you're doing so well in the opinion polls at the moment."

"You don't say?" responded Boag-Munroe, not in the least bit interested. "Opinion polls have a habit of changing. We'll see what happens at nightfall."

Nightfall. It came with its usual sudden winter grace. The assembled group was still intact, but all were visibly tired by eight o clock for their own various reasons. All that is except for Boag-Munroe. Out of all of them, he had the most right to tiredness. He'd spent the whole of the night awake, being entertained by the Ministry of the Dead, but there wasn't even a flicker of stress or restlessness in his demeanour. Nigel worried that his friend was losing his humanness day by day. If truth be known and if Boag-Munroe had been asked, he himself would have admitted a little of his human side had been lost. Especially so on the day Nigel and he had lost so much together.

"Shall I make a cup of coffee?" yawned Sue.

"That'll be my fifth cup in the last half hour. I'm trying to stay awake, not burst my bladder," replied Mary.

Nigel and Hannah looked on as Andrew played on a games console. Boag-Munroe merely sat silently in the unlit background. There was an uneasy atmosphere.

Andrew, obviously frustrated, kicked his console aside and ran to his room. Mary stood but Boag-Munroe put a hand on her shoulder. "I'll talk to him." He followed Andrew into his room. Mary hesitated for a second then followed then both.

Andrew was face down on his bed. Boag-Munroe saw the poster of Red. "Nice poster."

Andrew hid his face even deeper into the comfort of his bed.

Boag-Munroe carried on, even though Mary was now standing behind him silently. "I know that one, Red Leather. When I say I know him, I mean personally know him, not wishing to name-drop or anything. We knew one another when we were younger. Nigel knows him as well, although as I remember they didn't get on too well. I suppose that's the same for all of us in life. We get on with some people and others we don't." He paused, "I'd like to think we could get on, Andrew. No matter what you may or may not think of me, I am trying to help."

Andrew's muffled voice rose from the bed: "I want to see my dad."

"All in good time. I'm sure your mum can arrange that soon enough when we're done."

"I want to see him now." There was an iron resolution in Andrew's voice.

"It's not possible, not yet Andrew," Mary spoke for the first time.

Andrew got up and wasted no time in storming out.

Mary looked at Boag-Munroe apologetically. "He's upset."

"I know. I'm sure you both are."

There was a momentary silence between the two.

"I know you're trying to help. I'm sorry if I've bitten your head off."

"That's OK. We all go a little crazy sometimes," he smiled.

"Crazy? That's how I feel."

"Well, banish such thoughts right now. You're not crazy, far from it."

They both seemed to hesitate. Mary spoke first: "That poster belongs to Andrew's dad. He was a big fan of Red Leather when Andrew was little. I think that's why Andrew brought it here with him, to remind him of happier days." She paused, "You know him then?" She nodded at the poster.

"I did. But that was a long time ago, a different time, a different life."

"Did he sell his soul for fame and fortune?" She managed a quick smile.

Boag-Munroe couldn't even manage a flicker of a smile. "We both did in a way."

Mary felt herself go very cold.

Somehow Boag-Munroe seemed to read her mind. "Shall we join the others? It's a bit nippy in here." He left. Mary followed.

In the next room things were indeed warmer and were about to heat up even more.

"Where's Andrew?"

There was a chorus of 'don't knows' and shrugs of shoulders.

Mary felt that familiar cold feeling crawling over her again.

CHAPTER TWENTY-EIGHT

Andrew ran. He swallowed air into his already-inflated lungs, thinking that he was going to die from the pain of pushing himself so hard. He was pushing himself to the limit and beyond. He didn't have a clue where he was running; wasn't even sure what he was running from. It was a situation he didn't like and had to escape from by any means necessary. He was sure it was some sort of torture, being made to forfeit sleep by a group of total strangers. He may have been young, but on occasion he'd heard his dad talking about strange cults and what they made people do. He didn't know if this was a cult his mother had fallen prey to, but instinct and his father's voice in his head, pushed him into that pattern of thinking. His father wouldn't have put up with any of this. It must be a cult. Why else would they be so against him seeing his father? His mother had fallen prey to them all right, and if he was to save her, he had to save himself first. He had to find his father.

The pain in his chest became a little more bearable now he knew he had a goal and was not merely running away. The air didn't seem so cold; the streets didn't seem so lonely, now that he could envisage a picture of victory. Although thinking of how to attain that victory knocked him back a little. The way to do it didn't seem so clear, at least not until he saw a phone box and felt the loose change jangling in his pocket. He navigated the busy road carefully. The end was in sight; he wasn't about to fall at the last hurdle. He entered the phone box clutching his change as if they were gold coins, and not shabby twenty-pence pieces. He paused a moment, remembered the number and rang his father.

No answer.

He tried again and again, so much so that he began to feel paranoid at staying in the same phone box. He decided to move on and find another one. He made his way onward. The streets began to get colder and lonelier. Darkness was falling faster than Andrew could possibly hope to run.

"Where is he?" Mary screamed.

Nobody had an answer, so nobody spoke.

"Andrew!" Mary screamed around the flat, praying her son's voice would ring out. But it didn't.

"He can't have gone far," Hannah pushed forward the logical thought.

"He doesn't need to go far. How many kids have been snatched near their homes in the last month?"

Nobody answered.

Mary raced from the flat in search of Andrew. Sue quickly followed.

"Nigel, take the van, and have a look further afield," Boag-Munroe spoke in a tone that was little short of being an order.

"What are you going to do?"

“Follow those two on foot,” Boag-Munroe answered.
“I suppose I’ll be staying here holding the fort,” Hannah shrugged.
Boag-Munroe smiled as he left, “I suppose you will.”

Sam knew someone was watching over him, even before he opened his eyes.
Red, staring down at him, spoke: “We have to go now. We need another.”
“I was just catching up with my sleep. This is more than just a full-time job you’ve got me involved in.”
Red was adamant: “We can’t waste any more time. This is to be the last one. I’m sure of it.”
Sam felt a cold shiver down his spine. He quickly shrugged it off. He’d been used to cold shivers most of his life, and in the last month he’d acquired a taste for the iciness of total fear. He got dressed and followed. He had a job to do, and even if he didn’t like it, he was going to see it through.

Boag-Munroe spied Mary and Sue in the distance. He didn’t feel the need to make up ground on them, so he kept his steady pace. That is, until something caught his eye.
“Hello again.” Eloise was standing, perfect as ever, on a street corner.
Boag-Munroe approached her with tongue in cheek. “Are you getting much trade lately?”
An annoyed look appeared in her eyes. “You’re in danger.”
He shrugged the notion away. “Tell me something I don’t know.”
“Keep away from the Cloud.”
“Ah yes, Congleton’s famed landmark. Or at least famed to people in Congleton.”
“It means death to you.”
“My death, I take it?”
“You’re very perceptive.”
“But not as perceptive as you?”
“I just came to inform you. What you do with the information is up to you.”
“Actually there’s quite a bit of information I think I could gain from you. And I’m not just talking about your psychic powers. I’m more interested in the powers that control you.”
She looked surprised and a little hurt. “They don’t control me.”
“Had a falling-out with them, have we? It doesn’t surprise me. You’re a strong-minded woman. Set-ups like that don’t like strong-minded people, especially women.”
She turned away from him. “I have to go.”
He pulled her back. “Is it so bad that you have to go on the run from them?”

"It's better that way."

"Perhaps you've seen a sticky end in your own future?"

Eloise became as blasé as Boag-Munroe: "Maybe."

Boag-Munroe looked her in the eye. "Why are the Ministry of the Dead so interested in me?"

She matched his level and intensity of eye contact, "Because you're possessed."

He smiled, "Aren't we all?"

"I can't read your mind. You don't make easy reading at the best of times I suspect." She paused, "I don't know what is possessing you, even the Ministry can't answer that, only you can."

Boag-Munroe seemed to be slightly knocked off-guard by this but regained his composure after a few seconds. "What are the Ministry of the Dead doing in Northwich?"

"Waiting for you. And waiting for something big to happen. They've foreseen a chain of events." She stopped abruptly.

"And these events concern me?" He prompted an answer.

"They're not sure. Everything is hazy. But one thing I do know, it involves not just the deaths, but also the souls of others. That's all I know. Goodbye, James. And good luck."

She melted away into the falling darkness.

Boag-Munroe turned around slowly. The shadow of the Cloud was cast over him.

"Oh my God." Mary stopped running and clasped her hand over her mouth.

"What?" Sue, a little out of breath, tried to snap Mary back into some resemblance of reality.

"Mary what's wrong?"

"What's wrong?" Mary looked horrified. "Andrew's gone. They've got him."

"Who's got him?"

Mary didn't dare answer and Sue didn't dare ask the question again.

Mary eyed the phone box Andrew had used minutes earlier. "We have to phone the police." She raced over to the phone box like a woman possessed, almost getting herself run over in the process.

Sue didn't feel anything like possessed. Concerned, yes; but full-on possession or anything like it, no. She made her way stealthily and carefully through the traffic. By the time she'd reached the phone box Mary had already made the phone call and was returning the receiver to its cradle.

"They're coming, the police." She sounded out of breath. "You'll have to go back to the flat, tell them everything."

"What are you going to do?"

A look of craziness flashed into Mary's eyes. "I have to carry on."

John was breaking his promise to himself. He was drinking, and quite heavily at that. Of course he had good reason, sitting all alone, but it was still destructive. He felt so guilty for giving in to it when he'd promised himself that he wouldn't drive himself up the wall; that he would wait and remain calm.

He was thinking about Andrew. He hadn't seen his son for a few days. Absence had not made his heart grow any fonder. He couldn't have possibly loved his son any more than he did already. To say he worshipped him was not too strong a word for his feelings towards Andrew. John would have laid his life down for him. What worried John was the feeling he was getting while he thought of his son. It was more than just unsettling, it was the most frightening feeling he'd ever experienced. For whatever reason, frightening or not, John had the feeling he would never see his son again.

He stood up, grabbing his coat. He didn't know exactly where he was going, but a dark feeling was hanging over him.

Brian was fed up with being a wizard, or rather pretending to be one, even if it was the great Merlin. He'd sat around for days with not much happening. Alderley Edge wasn't the most exciting of places to start with, but sitting around there all day long, dressed as a wizard, just seemed to add insult to injury. Then something happened. As if Merlin himself had performed a miracle, a television crew appeared from out of the woods and into the clearing where Brian was seated. He stood and looked directly into the first of the two cameras.

"I am Merlin." Brian boldly stated the line he'd been practising in his head over and over. Saying it at least, if nothing else, was some form of release from his pent-up tension.

"Good, then we're in the right place," said a man Brian recognised from a local television programme.

Brian paused with stage fright.

The presenter nodded to the cameras. He turned back. "Good evening, Mr Merlin, sir. And how are we keeping?"

"Don't be so smug when you approach the great Merlin."

The presenter grew smugger. "I'm sorry I'm sure." He turned back to the cameras. "Switch it off for a second, lads."

Brian looked surprised. "What are you doing?"

"Conserving energy; mine and the camera's. You see, I'm what you call a serious presenter and journalist. I don't get much satisfaction from joke stories like this, but that's what my superiors, God bless them, have called for to round off the show. Two minutes of fame you'll get and that's it. Play ball with me and I'll bounce it right back into your hand. Don't play ball and I'll bounce it off that brittle-looking head of yours." The presenter took a deep breath. He nodded to the cameras to turn on. "Tell me Merlin, why after all these years have you decided to awaken, and make your presence felt in such a…" the presenter paused, "humble manner?"

Brian had been preparing speeches for this moment over and over. Long speeches and even longer speeches. Then he remembered what the presenter said about him playing ball and having two minutes of fame. He remembered this was just a job and if he did it right, a massive bonus would be his, and he need never venture near Alderley Edge ever again, or dress up as a wizard. Serious drama and Shakespeare awaited.

"I have awakened from my centuries of sleep to save England. But to do that I must find the man known as Professor Boag-Munroe."

It was short and it was sweet. There wasn't any kind of build-up, but he'd imparted the information needed. The job was done or as good as. He'd got television coverage just like his employer had said he would. Now he just had to wait for Boag-Munroe to turn up. The cameras turned away from him. Surely it wouldn't be long.

"Stop!" Red ordered from the backseat of the modest car. "I'll take it from here."

Red alighted from the vehicle, leaving Sam Herbert clutching the steering wheel a little nervously. Of course when they had first started out doing this kind of thing, Sam had been very nervous. But as time went on, to a certain extent that feeling faded, but somehow never completely. How could it? If anything, Sam was feeling the nervousness grow a little again. They were living on borrowed time. Sam felt the large wad of money in his pocket. They were living on borrowed time all right, but living well.

He watched Red, some way off, disappear round an unlit corner. It was always the same. Red would always reappear and with him he would have a new little guest. Red's face was always a picture at this, as was the guest's, so much so that many an unlit corner became alight. Children for the most part loved fame and the famous. People like Red fascinated them even if they weren't fans. What fans he still had. His fans nowadays were few and far between. He still had the money and a hardcore following, but he was becoming more known as a novelty act: an eccentric filling the tabloids, with the little space they'd give him, with daft things he'd done. But recently, even they were losing interest in him. He hadn't been chased by the paparazzi for a good two years. Still, Red would be back on the map soon enough even if he did end up more infamous than famous. And Sam? He had Red's assurances that if anything went wrong he wouldn't implicate him. Although Sam didn't need Red's assurances. He'd be ready to fly the nest soon enough. He had a tidy sum that he'd made out of doing Red's bidding already. The deeper in, the more Red needed him and the more he had to pay. A few more of those big pay days and Sam Herbert would be ready to flee. Mexico sounded good, the kind of place a man like him, with plenty of cash, could set himself up for life without worry. And if Red's plans did go wrong, he'd be long gone and untraceable in Mexico. As long as things didn't go wrong before then, everything was cool.

Red appeared, back from round the corner. The corner was still dark. Red didn't look happy.

"What's up?" Sam asked in a laid-back manner.

"Nothing's up," Red snapped. "Just drive on. We'll have to find somewhere more suitable."

"Nobody about, huh? To be honest what did you expect? The Great British public aren't as dumb as you think."

"I don't think the public are dumb, just that a percentage don't care. And I'm making them care."

"If you say so. But I'll tell you one thing, we're doing too many too close to home."

"One more, that's all I need, just one more I'm sure of it."

Sam started the engine. "If you say so."

They drove off to find more unlit corners where the fishing might be a bit better.

John headed for Congleton. It was instinct really; he didn't even know he was doing it, almost driving blindly. He just wanted to see his son, and even though it hurt to admit it, he wanted to see his wife as well. He wanted to know they were all right. He felt guilty for the feelings he still had for Mary. There were still glimmers of love mixed into the swirl of the hatred that the situation had thrown up, he was sure of it. He looked down at the half-empty whisky bottle by his side. More guilt. He wound his window down and threw the bottle out. He felt a certain satisfaction as he heard the glass smash on the deserted country road behind him. At least he felt that he had exorcised at least one demon tonight. Then the car swerved suddenly. John felt a sudden giddiness overcome him. He didn't know where he was or what he was doing, never mind what had caused him to swerve. He stopped dead in the road, the cold air of the night blasted through the car's open window. He was sure he could still hear the tinkling of the smashed whisky bottle in the distance. Feeling very tired, he managed to pull into a lay-by and fell fast asleep.

"Over there!" Red jolted forward in such excitement that Sam almost lost control of the car. Red carried on with his excitement. "Turn the car round."

Sam did as he was told.

"Now stop."

Sam stopped.

"There! Look!" There was a sickening blast of glee in Red's manner and voice that made even Sam's stomach turn.

Sam saw the solitary young boy. The car door opened and he watched Red walk towards his prey.

CHAPTER TWENTY-NINE

Mary looked like the proverbial headless chicken. For the moment she had stopped calling out Andrew's name, as a sick feeling in the pit of her stomach was threatening to erupt. She held her mouth tightly shut and did her best to push the feeling away. She ventured on, her eyes darting back and forth, desperately looking for him. The streets were empty. Town centres could be lonely at times. This was one of those times. Mary felt very alone. For a second, she thought of her husband John. If she had not done what she had done, if she had tried one more time, then Andrew would be safe, they would all be at home trying to play happy families, perhaps semi-successfully. Andrew would have been happy though, and when it came down to it that was the main thing. The only main thing left now was for Andrew to be found and soon. She couldn't take much more.

"He's OK." Boag-Munroe's voice cut like a sword through the night's shadows.

Mary spun round. "Don't you dare to tell me everything's OK."

The sword-like voice cut her dead: "I never said everything was OK, just Andrew. But he won't stay that way for long. You were thinking something dreadful has already happened to him, but it hasn't. Your son is fine for now, but in great danger, more so than before. He is alone. He must be found as soon as possible. All I'm telling you is that no harm has come to him yet and if you want it to stay that way, I'd ask you to keep calm and stay focussed."

"It's all very easy for you to say."

It may have been easy for him to say, but there was a certain reassurance about his voice that had the strange mixture of calming her, yet keeping her alert to the matter of getting Andrew back safely.

Boag-Munroe moved in closer to her. She felt his presence wrap around her, his aura seemed to mingle into her. It was a pleasant, even reassuring, feeling.

"Come on. Let's go find your son."

John woke up with a start. He was still in the lay-by and still worse for wear due to the drink and worry. He pinched his cheeks in an effort to become fully alert again. He managed to waken up a little, so he started his engine and drove off. This time however he knew his search was futile. There would be no way his son would be out roaming the streets at this time of night, especially with the current child-snatching crisis. Mary may have been a lot of things but she was not a bad mother. John swung the car back home towards Macclesfield, safe in the knowledge that at least tonight his son was safe.

The police had arrived at Mary's flat, a male and female officer. They hadn't taken long to arrive, once Sue had given them the details of what had happened. But what had happened to Andrew? Sue didn't have a clue and the police seemed just as baffled with Andrew's disappearance as all the others were. Still they were keeping an open mind, as was Sue. Andrew had run off to see his father in the first place. He was upset, which was only natural, so the natural thought process was that he might just come back. That was the same thought process Boag-Munroe had hit on, the reason he had directed Mary back to the flat. In his eyes everything returned in the end. Everything came full circle.

"Are you the boy's mother?" the woman officer asked.

"Yes," nodded a jaded Mary.

"We need a few details," the male officer added.

"Details?" shrilled Sue. "I've given you all the details you need. Just go find him."

"If only it were that simple." The male officer sounded and looked harsh. He drew a blaze of harsh looks back.

"We're just making sure we've got all the facts," reasoned the woman officer.

"My son is missing, how many more facts do you need?" Mary trembled with fear, frustration and anger.

"We'll find him, love." The male officer took on a less-harsh approach.

"Like you've found all the others?" Mary wasn't about to be fobbed off.

"We mustn't jump to any conclusions. Your son hasn't been missing for very long. He's obviously confused, maybe because of your marital problems."

"She hasn't got any marital problems. She's separated," Sue rebuffed, in loyalty to her friend.

"Have you come here to find my son or criticise my lifestyle?" At the moment, Mary didn't need her friend's support; instead she had anger, and with that she could more than stick up for herself.

The male officer turned to Boag-Munroe: "We got the name of your friends but not you, sir?"

"Then I congratulate you on a job well done." Boag-Munroe's sarcasm buried in deep and twisted like sharp shards of metal.

The officer again asked Boag-Munroe: "Name, sir?"

Boag-Munroe simply smiled.

"What's wrong now?" Sam asked the returning Red Leather.

"Nothing's wrong." Red slammed the door firmly shut.

"The one that got away, is it?"

"You could say that."

Sam started to drive. "Do you want to try somewhere else?"

"No. I'm tired, just get us home."

A heavy atmosphere descended into the interior of the car.

"So is that it then? Job done?" Sam's words cut the atmosphere like a knife.

"My work is far from finished," Red snapped.

"I thought this one was going to be the last one anyway."

"If it's the money you're worried about, don't. I have another large slice of cash waiting to be served up to you."

"Ah, you're hurting my feelings now; anybody would think I was just in it for the money."

Sam couldn't fail to notice Red's expression of anger in the rear view mirror. Red in turn couldn't fail to spot Sam's satisfied grin.

"So what did happen out there?" Sam asked.

Red paused, obviously mulling over what he should say. After a second or so he decided there would be no harm, and it might even do him some good to get it off his chest. He paid Sam well, so he was always there for his rants and he wouldn't divulge the contents of them to anyone; the money was too good. Not that Red was that bothered. There wasn't anything such as bad publicity in his eyes.

"Adults."

"Pardon?" Sam looked bemused.

"You asked what's wrong, I told you… Adults."

"The kid had someone with him?"

"You could say that. A miserable-looking wretch that smelled of drink, and professed to be the boy's father."

"Did you give them an autograph?" Sam sniggered.

Red was growing dissatisfied with Sam's attitude. He slumped back into his seat, simmering.

"So where did the father turn up from? The boy looked alone."

"The boy was alone, until the so-called adult disembarked from the off license he'd left his son outside." Red was getting fed up now. He only answered the question because of the golden rule. He didn't want Sam to see he that was getting to him. That was the golden rule. The dog might bite the hand that feeds him but only when there is weakness and confusion. The dog will try anything when he knows he stands a good chance of getting away with it. And what better way to do that, than with a weak opponent. Red was not a weak opponent though, nor did he ever intend to be one. People calling him eccentric were fine. Mad he could live with. But weakness? That surely was the end. The end wasn't even in sight for Red as far as he was concerned. He could go on forever, and he would if he wanted. Soon the world would see what Red stood for, call him crank, lunatic or genius, he was ready to stand up and be counted. He was determined to leave his mark on the world, forever.

"I asked your name, sir," the officer grew more insistent.

"Yes." A child-like quality that no one except Nigel knew Boag-Munroe possessed, came floating to the surface.

"I asked you for your name, sir," the officer repeated.
"I know you did," replied Boag-Munroe flippantly.
The male officer grew redder by the second. "Are you hard of hearing, sir?"
"No." Boag-Munroe sounded like a child annoying an adult.
"Are you on any medication, sir?" The officer was willing to make it personal.
"No. Are you?" Boag-Munroe was willing to make it as equally so.
Nigel grew sick of the games: "His name is Boag-Munroe."
Boag-Munroe looked at his friend with some distaste.
"That's a funny name," the officer remarked.
"Is it really?" Boag-Munroe goaded back.
"Unusual like." The officer got the feeling everybody in the room was looking at him, as if he was some kind of an idiot.
"It's double-barrelled," Boag-Munroe added for good measure, to make the officer feel an even bigger idiot.
Mary snapped at the police officers: "I thought you were supposed to be doing something about my son, not playing 'guess the name'. Does it matter who this man is?"
"That depends." The officer's two words sent out a chill.
Nobody asked what it depended on. There followed an uneasy silence.
Boag-Munroe spoke: "Your son will return."
"How do you know that, Mr Boag-Munroe?" enquired the woman officer.
"I just know. Call it a feeling."
"And is that all it is?" followed up the male officer.
"What else could it be?" Boag-Munroe defended himself with a question, a regular habit of his that caught most opponents off-guard.
The police officers looked at each other in a telepathic kind of way. The female officer stepped back, talking on her radio.
Nigel couldn't tell what she was saying, but he had the feeling his friend had dug himself into a hole, which Nigel felt obliged to help him out of. "If James said he's had a feeling, then that's all it is. Whatever he says is good enough for me." All attention turned to Nigel. He fell silent.
The woman officer stopped talking on her radio and rejoined the group. "What was Andrew wearing when he went missing?"
Mary stood back, a little faint. Nigel moved towards her while Hannah grabbed her hand. The fact that the officers had admitted Andrew was missing brought the reality home.
"Why don't you look for yourself?" Sue pointed to the door as Andrew walked in.
Boag-Munroe stood back looking very satisfied.

The officers were gone and the shouting and tears were over for now. The police were informing Social Services in the morning, so even more pressure was piling up for Mary to get her problems sorted pronto. Mary, although still angry with Andrew, sat next to him, sticking to him like glue. Nigel was hammering a board over the smashed window. Hannah and Sue had dozed off in opposite chairs. Boag-Munroe was seated in the corner on an uncomfortable stool, watching everyone and everything like a hawk.

"There. I don't think I've made a bad job of that," said Nigel admiring his handiwork. "It'll keep the draft out at least."

"It's not the draft we're trying to keep out," Boag-Munroe interacted instead of merely being a spectator to proceedings.

Mary looked worried.

Nigel tried to put her mind at rest. "Don't worry about him. He talks in riddles and rhymes."

"But it's all about that though, isn't it?" Boag-Munroe stood. "Not so much rhymes, but riddles. Why are we here in the first place, if not to solve a riddle?"

"Is that all we are? Riddles?" Mary rebuffed.

Boag-Munroe stopped in thought, chewed his lip. "Yes, I suppose we are. All of us." He walked over to inspect Nigel's handiwork with the window. "You've done a good job there, very good. Now me, I'm not too practical…" He cut short his sentence and began to listen intently to the stillness of the air. "Don't go to sleep," his voice boomed out, waking up the dozing Andrew as well as Sue and Hannah in the process.

"What's happened?" Sue was already speaking before fully awake.

"Nothing yet," replied Boag-Munroe.

"What time is it?" enquired Hannah.

"Half three in the morning," Mary replied wearily.

"Sssshh!" Boag-Munroe held his finger to his lip. He listened. They all listened.

The sound of scratching was beginning to fill the empty pockets of silence round the room.

"Mice?" Sue offered.

The scratching grew louder.

"More like rats by the sound of it," Hannah interjected.

Once more Boag-Munroe held his finger to his lips, but this time with a flash of visible anger on his brow because of the lack of co-operation on the part of other people.

Nigel placed his ear close to the wall. "It's coming from behind this wall."

"No, you're wrong. I can hear it behind me here," said Hannah, at the opposite side of the room.

"They're underneath us you mean, over there under the floorboards," Sue added.

Mary was looking up as if she could hear them in the ceiling.

Boag-Munroe moved forward to the middle of the room. "You're all wrong.

They're not in the walls, or the floor, or the ceiling for that matter. They are not rats, or any other kind of rodent. In fact, they are not even a *they,* more of an *it.* And what kind of it I think we are going to determine very soon."

The scratching stopped.

Nigel came up close to Boag-Munroe and whispered as best he could, so as not to alarm the others. "Can it hear what you're saying?"

"I don't know," whispered Boag-Munroe back. "It's possible."

"What is it?" asked Mary in a panic-stricken voice.

"That's what we are going to find out and, with it, the identity of your faceless harasser."

Three knocks rapped on the front door.

"I think we have a guest." Boag-Munroe spoke quite calmly, as everyone around him shook in fright. "It would be impolite to keep whoever it was waiting. I'd better open the door." Before anyone could stop him, Boag-Munroe had reached the door and swung it open, to reveal an empty hallway.

"What is it?" Mary was nearly in tears.

"As I told you – it's a warning that it wants you to see."

"Why doesn't it just let us see what it wants us to see, and then go and leave us in peace?" Mary's statement seemed rational enough.

"How can it go when its work is not done? How can you see if you don't open your eyes?" were the only answers Boag-Munroe gave. He closed the door. "At least we're getting somewhere now."

"Yeah, scared out our wits," chipped in Sue.

Boag-Munroe was honest with her: "You'll excuse me if I don't bring you pleasant news and good tidings, but from hereafter, things get a lot worse."

"Is that possible?" asked Sue.

"You'd be surprised what is possible, maybe even a little horrified."

Three knocks rapped out on the door again.

"Aren't you going to answer it?" asked Hannah.

"Obviously it's not me it wants." Boag-Munroe looked towards Mary.

Mary hesitated. The ghostly knocking echoes were still resounding in her ears. Mary took a final fleeting look at Andrew, before pushing him gently towards the comforting arms of Sue and headed for the front door. She stretched her hand out to open it.

"Wait!" snapped Boag-Munroe.

Mary shut her eyes tight, sweat on her brow.

"Stay perfectly still," Boag-Munroe commanded.

Mary's hand hovered over the door. She stood like a grey stone statue.

"What am I supposed to be doing?" Mary dared to move her lips.

"I don't know. Or at least I don't know for sure," was the only encouragement Boag-Munroe could give.

Again, three raps hit the door.

"Open the door!" Boag-Munroe shouted.

Breathlessly, Mary opened the door on his command.

Everyone stood viewing the open door way.

"There's nothing there." Mary caught her breath.

"It's the same as before," commented Hannah.

Boag-Munroe turned to Hannah: "No, it's not. It's completely different. Consider the knocks as the key. They just needed the right lock to open."

"Mary was that lock," Nigel explained.

Boag-Munroe nodded. "At first it was trying to get Mary's attention. It was trying to find a way in, or rather the right *person* to let it in. In order to receive you have to give. Instead of running away Mary, you've shown it attention by letting it in. You've given. You've said yes to it. Call it contact made. Now you can receive the information it wants to give you."

"Me? I was a lock?" Mary looked bemused.

Boag-Munroe nodded again. "You or Andrew would have sufficed."

"And now it's in?" asked Mary.

"Now we wait," replied Boag-Munroe.

"We've had plenty of practice at that," added Sue.

"How long?" asked Mary.

"Not long. Things are far advanced. To hazard a guess I'd say we were on the last lap." Boag-Munroe sat. "You might as well all relax. The last lap always seems the longest."

Red didn't feel comfortable. The night had been a disaster and he hadn't slept well for days. He was stuck in the never-never land he so often inhabited, between sleep and consciousness. He was restless. He could find solace in nothing. He hadn't bothered with his children tonight. He felt a little guilty about that. After all, that's why he had brought them there in the first place: because they were neglected, left to stray. He wanted to teach their parents a lesson, to make them, the country, and the world sweat. He was doing just as the dreams, the visions, call them what you will, told him to do. Or at least how he interpreted them.

He dreaded feeling the way he did now, it was making him become more and more restless. His body cried out for sleep, but somehow his mind drove him on. Nothing could save him from it, no pills, no treatments, no analysts, nothing; he was at its mercy. The visions would definitely come tonight, they were always more vivid when he felt like this. At first he had blamed it on his lifestyle, the drugs, the drink and women. Then he blamed it on his breakdown, or any of the series of breakdowns he'd suffered over the last ten years since the split from his family. Then as the vision got clearer, more vivid, more violent, he realised he was just passing the buck. The buck had to be stopped, something had to be done.

He felt a sudden jolt of terror. He sat back, covering his eyes, but the sound of screams, of pleading, swirled around him. He had to look, to feast his unwilling eyes on the vision; because the sounds pushed him so unrelentingly they made him a slave to their whim. It was the same as ever: the ground falling beneath people, clutching hands, bodies thrown into the black fiery abyss, and the children, so many children, tossed into the bowels of Hell. How they cried out to him. But he couldn't help them; he couldn't reach them. He breathed a sigh of relief when the visions died out and the sound subsided. The blackness stayed with him for a while but he didn't mind that. He found it quite comforting. What he didn't find so comforting was the latest part to be added to his vision. It wasn't frightening as such, just a new added touch, and something that left him more bewildered than ever. From out of the darkness stepped the figure of a man he hadn't seen in years, nor had he any cause to be thinking about at this present time. The figure emerged from nowhere, stared over at Red and disappeared back, taking the darkness with it. The figure in question was James Boag-Munroe.

CHAPTER THIRTY

Daylight broke, or at least it tried to, through the boarded-up window. Once again, Sue had nodded off, Nigel and Mary were drinking strong coffee, and Hannah was keeping Andrew entertained with stories about when she was a little girl, in the Second World War.

"Would you like a drink?" offered Nigel to Boag-Munroe.

"I'm fine."

"Why don't you get a couple of hours sleep?"

Boag-Munroe repeated his previous answer: "I'm fine."

"It can't be good for you to go all this time without sleep. You've had the least of all of us," Nigel pushed.

Boag-Munroe raised an eyebrow. "Are you questioning my methods?"

Nigel stuttered, "No, I…"

"Good, because as much as I may or may not like it, sleep deprivation is the easiest and quickest way to attain the results we want."

"But is it the safest?" Nigel asked in a concerned manner.

Boag-Munroe didn't answer.

"What was that?" Mary had caught the tail end of the conversation.

A mobile phone rang. Before answering it, Boag-Munroe muttered something under his breath about being saved by the bell. The respite of saviour was short. As short as the phone call. Boag-Munroe's face had turned ashen white.

"James, what's wrong?" Nigel had known his friend too long not to know that something was amiss.

"That was Leyton Blair's daughter."

"What does she want, ringing up so early in a morning? I take it it's not an invite to the funeral?"

"Not quite. It seems bodies go missing in Llangollen, dead ones in particular."

"You mean Leyton?" Now it was Nigel's turn to turn white.

"Yes, missing, but still presumed dead," Boag-Munroe added.

Nigel still looked frightened. "A ghost is one thing, but a walking corpse..."

"Are you guys weird or what?" Mary was so tired she had spoken the words she was thinking, before she could stop them coming out.

Both men turned to her. She fell silent. They were her only hope after all. Only seconds had passed before Mary rediscovered her tongue: "You do realise Social Services could call round at any time and they'll find my son dead tired?"

"He doesn't look like he's doing too badly." Boag-Munroe brought everyone's attention to the fact Andrew was enjoying an action video game, with full sound effects, on his games console, "In fact he looks quite well on it."

"Is that true about Leyton?" Nigel kept his question as quiet as he could.

"I've no reason to lie." Boag-Munroe wasn't so quiet.

"So what's going on there then? And why did his daughter ring you?" Nigel whispered even softer.

"I suppose I'm number one suspect."

"What… body stealing?" Nigel coughed, when he realised his surprised raised tone might cause even more apprehension.

"Body stealing?" Mary was in Boag-Munroe's face before he knew it.

"Yes, but I personally never steal dead ones, live ones are my preference," he was quick to retort.

Before the conversation could go any further, a large cactus plant fell from a shelf, almost hitting Sue, who, however, slept through the whole incident.

"What have you been feeding your plants on?" quipped Boag-Munroe.

"Did I see that?" Mary was unsure of anything now.

A small huddle gathered around the smashed plant pot and crumpled cactus. Even Andrew managed to prize himself away from his beloved console.

"That plant just lifted straight in the air then dropped like a stone," an amazed Hannah added.

"Yes. It did, didn't it?" Boag-Munroe said coolly before sitting back down in the corner.

As the others stood staring in disbelief around the debris of the plant, Boag-Munroe picked up a nearby newspaper, and began reading the advertisements for the best offers on the latest mobile phones.

Carter Whitlowe was not amused. True, his prey was trussed and tied like a turkey to the chair, in the way he'd insisted on, but he still wasn't satisfied. And when Carter wasn't satisfied, he usually had someone on hand to fix it for him. Everyone in New York knew the story of his former business partner and the now-famous industrial meat grinder. And no-one wanted the same fate for themselves. Carter wanted to see his prey suffer. And slowly. In actual fact his prey was already slowly suffering. He had been tied to the chair for the best part of a day and a half. The gag had cut deep into his mouth where it had stifled a thousand cries, the ropes around his arms, wrists and ankles cut even deeper, tearing a bloody path straight to the bone, from all his struggles. He didn't struggle any more though. He knew his fate. He was tired, he didn't want any more pain; he just wanted it over and done with.

Carter grabbed a clump of the prey's greasy, matted hair, and ripped his head back so violently, it almost snapped his neck. Almost. But for Carter that would have definitely been too quick. He was only momentarily satisfied that he'd added whiplash to the growing list of injuries, indignations and tortures his prey had suffered. Moments do not last forever though. After the moment had passed, he felt the need to follow up with a sharp punch to an already cracked rib.

“How does it feel?” Carter asked.

The man couldn’t answer, still choking on the gag.

Carter could now see tears flowing down the man’s cheeks, the fresh urine stains on his trousers were mixing with the already stale ones.

The grotesqueness of the man’s pleading enraged Carter even more. For the second time he let his fists fly, this time into the man’s nose. It broke with a sickening thud, leaving red rivers of blood and flesh hanging from it.

He stood back admiring his handiwork. Another man made his presence felt. He was much taller than Carter, maybe even touching the seven-foot mark. He was thicker set too, muscular and an even more menacing and dangerous presence than the one that was working on the man.

“What are we going to do with him, boss?” the man asked.

“We could feed him to the pigs? After all, he did squeal like one.” Carter paused, thinking. Then he put a name to the other man, “Did you give him a sufficient treatment earlier, Bruno?”

“I’d like to think so,” Bruno replied.

“If you think so, Bruno, that’s good enough for me. After all we’re not savages, are we?”

“I wouldn’t like to think so,” Bruno answered.

“No, I’m sure you wouldn’t, Bruno. Let the pig go, the mess he’s making is polluting my air and stinking the place out.” He knelt down close to the gagged and bound man: “I know this may only be a cellar to you but, to me, it’s a part of one of my properties and all my properties are my home. Would you expect someone who you’d invited into your home, to piss themselves and generally make a mess of the place?”

The man shook his head while the blood from his nose still tainted his gag crimson.

“I thought as much,” said Carter. He backed away. “Untie the pig, Bruno. Let him run home and tell the other little piggies not to mess with me or else.” Carter began to walk away, then stopped and turned back round to see Bruno untie the man, who fell exhausted at his feet.

“Say, you didn’t know Bruno here is a bare knuckle fighter, did you?” Carter asked the wounded man who gurgled something incoherent in return.

“Tell me, Bruno, haven’t you got a fight coming up soon?”

“Yes, tonight.”

Carter put on a look of fake surprise. “That’s right, tonight.” He turned to the blooded man, “Wow, can you believe that? He has a fight tonight.” He turned back to Bruno, “Tell me, Bruno, all the chasing around you’ve had to do to find our friend here must have affected your training, put a dent in your schedule?”

“It has, Boss.”

“Well it hardly seems fair then, does it, that he should just crawl away after all the upset he’s caused? Bruno – I suggest you catch up with your training.

Maybe he can help you? What do you say?"

"No!" the helpless man squealed.

Bruno smiled, and then set about using the man as a living punch bag, until he'd smashed every bone, feature and every last gasp of living breath out of him.

Carter smiled, "Be careful when you dispose of him, Bruno." He walked away and didn't look back.

Jason couldn't believe his eyes or ears. The dinner tray he'd comfortably perched on his knee, unceremoniously ditched itself, and ran the contents down his leg. He had been watching the local news report when a segment had come on, about some lunatic proclaiming to be the wizard Merlin, who had taken up camp in Alderley Edge. This Jason could live with, it didn't cause him any particular surprise or shock. He knew all too well the world was full of nutters, and up to this point, his dinner tray, its contents and his trousers had been quite safe. Then he had heard Merlin speak. He had come in search of the one called Professor Boag-Munroe. That was the moment the tray fell and the segment on Merlin cut off. There was to be an in-depth interview with him televised at six o'clock that night.

Carter Whitlowe wiped the sweat and the blood of another man from his brow, with a pale blue, silk handkerchief. The hankie now thrown to one side, he fell into the arms of a gigantic armchair, clutched a state-of-the-art remote control and turned on an equally state-of-the-art television. A set of double doors to the side of him opened and in walked an attractive, slim, blonde-haired woman, dressed in a nurse's uniform. She was pushing a wheelchair, the inhabitant of which looked to be in his mid-twenties and had a vague handsomeness.

Carter turned to his son in the wheelchair, "How ya doin', Stevie?"

The occupant in the wheelchair didn't speak. In fact there wasn't any emotion or facial movement forthcoming. The occupant just looked straight ahead in a death-like stare, eyes wide open.

"I think he's showing signs of improvement," offered the nurse.

"Do you really?" Carter was sarcastic. "When I want a professional opinion on my son's state I'll ask one of the many doctors and specialists I pay for him to see. You're just the nurse, so nurse him."

The nurse didn't answer back. She wheeled Stevie out of the room, closing the doors behind her.

Carter jabbed angrily at the remote control. He hated the fact he couldn't bear to see his own son, what he was, what he had become. He hated himself, he hated the cruel tricks life could play, but what's more he hated the man who had caused his son's disability. He hated Professor Boag-Munroe. He would make him pay, just like he had the man in his cellar, only Boag-Munroe would have to suffer worse.

A hundred times worse.

Jason stood in pride of place in his living room. Bradley sat slumped back on the sofa with a tired look that betrayed his youthful age. The Gentle brothers sat beside him with the innocent look of children that betrayed their real ages.

"What is all the secrecy? I'm mean you call an emergency meeting, we turn up like good little boys and then you don't even give us a clue what it's all about." A feeling of irritation was emitting from Bradley.

"What time is it?" Jason answered his own question by consulting the clock on the mantlepiece. "Five forty-five. Just wait another fifteen minutes and you'll have your answer."

"I'd like an answer right now," Mrs Ruth barged in without warning. "I hope you realise you interrupted me with your unsolicited phone call. I was in an important meeting. I've just started a new job, love. Can you imagine what it was like for me, sitting there with my new boss and my mobile starts to ring?"

"I can imagine it's annoying," offered Bradley.

"Well, I imagine nothing, I know it was annoying, I was there. And what's more annoying is the fact I don't get any explanation. It was all a case of 'It's a secret, come round to my house by six'."

"I don't think you'll find it a wasted journey." Jason was smug.

"I'll be the judge of that, love."

"Just wait until six, all we be explained." Jason was adamant.

"I need an explanation now. I've got my IBS weekly meeting at seven." Mrs Ruth wasn't backing down.

"What?" Bradley looked perplexed, followed by a rapid look of boredom. If truth were known, everybody was bored by Mrs Ruth's preoccupation with her bowels. Come to think of it, everyone was bored with Mrs Ruth in general.

"IBS weekly – my IBS self-help group. Me and other sufferers meet every other week. It would be every week, but I have such a busy schedule, it would just be impossible."

"Couldn't they meet without you?" Alan Gentle asked quite innocently.

Mrs Ruth looked horrified. "Yes, love, but what would be the point in that?"

Nobody had an answer for her.

Six o'clock came and went. Six fifteen drifted by. They all began to get agitated, not just Mrs Ruth. Jason merely nodded towards the television, which was now on full volume, goading them to wait and see. By the time six twenty-five had come and gone, Jason was beginning to feel a bit nervous.

Those nerves faded though, when a two-and-a-half-minute television slot gave them all the information they needed to know.

They all sat dazed, apart from Jason, as the local news credits rolled by.

"I'm sure you all found it worth the wait," Jason said, a knowing grin plastered across his face.

"Do you think he really *is* Merlin?" asked a still-naïve Alan Gentle.

Jason grinned slyly, "Whoever he is, he knows about our friend Boag-Munroe and, seeing as he is otherwise engaged, I think we should have a little word with Merlin on his behalf."

Mrs Ruth stood up, taking over the situation by clapping her hands. "Does anybody have any questions?"

Alan Gentle put his hand up: "Yes, what does IBS stand for again?"

"It's irritable bowel syndrome, love," replied Mrs Ruth.

"Right," said Alan Gentle, putting his arm down slowly. He turned to his brother Tony, who looked equally as blank.

"It doesn't look like Social Services are coming. That's one good thing," Sue yawned.

"You almost sound disappointed," countered Mary.

"No, I'm just saying it's one thing less."

"They'll turn up all right, sticking their nose in here and there. Bloody social workers never seem to target the guilty; they stick up for them, if anything,. It's the innocent ones they penalise, as if they get some sick pleasure out of it," Mary said angrily.

"It was probably the police just talking big – you know how they are. They were just trying to scare you," was the best Sue could offer.

"I am scared, believe me. What happens if someone does turn up and they see Andrew, two days without sleep? John could have a field day with this one."

"Forget about John and the social workers. Just concentrate on getting through this." Sue was adamant.

"How can I forget about them and concentrate on this, whatever this is?" Mary looked round. Hannah and Nigel were fast asleep; Andrew was fighting tiredness by watching a cartoon on the DVD player. Boag-Munroe was seated in the particular corner he had made his own, scribbling notes into a little black book. He seemed to be in a world of his own. It was not a world Mary particularly wanted to be a part of but, at the moment, it looked like she had no choice.

Andrew began to slump forward, his eyelids drooped as he flitted in and out of unconsciousness. Boag-Munroe lurched forward, gently shaking the boy's shoulder.

"He's had enough," snapped Mary. "We all have. He can't fight to stay awake any longer, he's just a child."

Boag-Munroe produced a fifty-pound note from his pocket. He handed it to a bewildered Andrew. "Here take this, it's yours, and if you stay awake until I tell you, you can have another three more."

Andrew looked bleary eyed at the fifty-pound note he now had in his possession. Suddenly staying awake a bit longer didn't seem all that bad.

"Are you going to keep us all awake like that, with fifty-pound notes? Only I'm feeling a bit heavy-eyed myself?" quipped Sue.

"You've been asleep all morning and most of the afternoon," retorted Boag-Munroe. "Not to mention the forty winks you got last night."

"I'm sorry I spoke." Sue did her best to sound hurt, "I think I'll go for a lie down. Despite what other people might think, I reckon I've done more than my share of hard work." She left the room.

Mary turned to Boag-Munroe: "So have you heard anything more about your friend?"

"My friend?"

"Yes, the missing corpse."

"Oh him, yes I'm sure he'll turn up sooner or later, for better or worse."

"So I take it you're not a particular fan of his, or should I say *weren't* a fan of his?"

"On the contrary, I looked up to him. We were close, very close. Then he betrayed me."

"Why did he mean so much to you?"

"He was, for all intents and purposes, my mentor. He filled a void that was left when my father died. When that happened I still had a lot of questions left unanswered. But Leyton let me down, and I went off on my own to answer those questions myself."

"Did you find your answers?"

"In some cases yes, in others no, and sometimes I got more than I bargained for."

"What did you bargain for in this case? That is how you see us isn't it? Just another case in your search for answers?"

"We all have our own reasons for what we do."

"But yours are a little deeper and darker than others?"

"If you don't want my help I can just walk away, and I could do so with my conscience clear. I don't like to play games, time is too precious to be wasted, mine and other people's."

"What did your friend, mentor, call him what you will, do to you that was so bad?"

Boag-Munroe paused before he spoke, as if to convey that what he was about to say, was of the utmost importance. "He let me down."

"So you've said. Most people do let you down in some way or another, sooner or later. You normally get used to it, or get over it."

"It depends on how badly you get let down."

"And from they way you're talking, I guess you got let down pretty badly."

Boag-Munroe shrugged. "We all have our ups and downs."

"And our crosses to bear. From the look in your eyes I'd say you have a pretty big cross."

"And you can tell all that just by looking in my eyes?" Boag-Munroe didn't sound impressed.

"The eyes are the windows to the soul."

Boag-Munroe looked sad. "Yes, they are."

Mary decided to change the subject. "How long before the waiting is over?"

"Soon."

"How can you tell?"

"I just can. I'm sure that tonight we'll have more answers."

"For you or for me?"

Boag-Munroe evaded her question and carried on with his own propaganda: "By morning we'll have the identity of your bogeyman. Trust me."

"I'm trying to. Let's say I'm just bracing myself."

"What for?"

"A fall maybe?"

Boag-Munroe fell silent. In his eyes he didn't need to defend himself anymore. What would be, would be.

CHAPTER THIRTY-ONE

Navigating round the darkened woodlands of Alderley Edge was not Mrs Ruth's idea of fun, but it was a necessity. She was interested in why this person, who proclaimed to be Merlin, should seek out Boag-Munroe. Of course, she could have taken the easy path and let the others do the work; maybe let them speak to this so-called Merlin, or even bring him back. But Mrs Ruth didn't have much trust or respect for idiots, and although she suspected not all those in the group were idiots, most were halfway there. No, as far as she was concerned, if a job was worth doing it was worth doing well, and to do it well, you had to do it yourself. This was why she was leading the group through the pitch-black woods, with just a fading, battery lighted torch.

"Keep close, keep close to me." Those were the final words Mrs Ruth said before falling headlong into a ditch, which had suddenly appeared. "Agggah!"

"Do you want us to follow you down there?" shouted Alan Gentle, "Only it looks a bit dark, even darker than up here."

Bradley spoke softly: "I can't hear anything."

"Do you think she's dead?" asked Alan Gentle.

"No, I heard her say 'Agggah' after she fell." Bradley spoke even softer, "Or was that as she fell?"

"That might have been the last thing she'll ever say. It might have been her death cry," reasoned Alan Gentle. His brother nodded his agreement, not that it could be seen as they were now in pitch blackness. Mrs Ruth had been the only one with a torch.

"Agggah!" shouted Mrs Ruth.

"If that's her death cry, there it goes again then." Bradley was the voice of reason.

"Mrs Ruth, can you hear me?" shouted Jason, "Are you all right?"

"Of course I'm not all bloody right," an angry disembodied voice shouted back. "You seem to be under the misapprehension that I like falling down dank, dark holes, and landing on my arse in the process."

"Bradley, help Mrs Ruth up." Jason pushed Bradley forward.

"Me?" Bradley looked horrified at the thought of entering the hollow, on a mission to help Mrs Ruth. She wasn't the easiest person to get on with and, because of her large build, she wouldn't be the easiest to pick up.

"Alan! Tony! Help him, would you?" Jason ordered.

Alan Gentle looked at Jason with a horror equal to Bradley's. "Aren't you going to help then?"

"Of course I'm going to help," Jason twittered. "You just pop down there and I'll oversee the rescue from here."

"I bet you will," said Alan Gentle with a certain quality that gave away the fact he wasn't as dumb as he always looked.

"What's that supposed to mean?" Jason snapped, so disturbed that Alan

Gentle would dare challenge him that he fought back straight away. "If you have something so important to say at a time like this, you'd better say it and get it off your chest."

Surprisingly, Alan Gentle was up for the challenge: "Right then," he said, "you asked what I meant, so now I'll tell you."

"Please do." Jason grew even loftier.

"Are you sure you want to know?"

"I'm waiting."

"Right."

"Speak now or forever hold your peace."

"You're all talk and get nothing done, which is why you need someone like me around." In temper, Alan sounded like he'd been inhaling helium; he talked very fast and in a very high-pitched voice.

Jason was sent reeling backward at the outburst: "How dare you."

Mrs Ruth appeared from the darkness on all fours. "Don't worry about me, will you." She then shouted something in a very thick and unrecognisable accent, which luckily no one could decipher.

Brushing herself down seemed to calm her a little. "Now, shall we get on with the job in hand?" She led the way again. They all followed.

Tony Gentle wished she'd fall down a ditch again… the funniest thing he'd seen in a long time.

"There it is." Jason pointed to a tent in a moonlit clearing, "He must be in there."

"It's a tent," said an unimpressed Alan Gentle.

"We can all see that, love," Mrs Ruth added, making sure she wasn't being left out. "I'll approach the camp first. I always think first impressions count." She closed in on the tent before anyone could get a word out. "Hello," she shouted at the tent flap. "I believe you may be the man I'm looking for."

Brian popped his head out through the tent flaps. Feeling vulnerable on his hands and knees, he shivered as he looked up at Mrs Ruth: "What do you want?"

"I want you, love. You are Merlin, I take it?"

Brian noted the others standing by. He had a very bad feeling that a strange cult had come to claim him as a human sacrifice. His whole life flashed before him in a second, and to make matters worse, it wasn't particularly interesting, even in a compact, highlighted format.

"What do you want?" he quivered.

"You want to talk to a friend of ours, a Professor Boag-Munroe. We can take you to him if you would like?"

Merlin nodded, not daring to do or say anything else.

"It's never-ending," Mary sighed.

"You're wrong; everything comes to an end, good and bad," Boag-Munroe argued.

Mary shot him a scolding look. "And you're supposed to be helping?"

"They don't call me England's last hope for nothing," he smiled.

"What are we waiting for?" Sue yawned. "I mean really, what are we waiting for?"

"Whatever," Boag-Munroe answered.

"Whatever?" Sue still impatiently questioned.

"You heard what the man said." Hannah backed up Boag-Munroe, while giving him a crafty wink. He smiled back at her. But for whatever reason, and she couldn't put a finger on it, his smile wasn't like a normal human smile. Instead of comforting her, it did the exact opposite.

"Mum, I'm cold," Andrew whined.

Mary sighed, "No doubt the caretaker from hell has struck again, the heating should be on now." She reached out to touch a radiator, and stopped suddenly. "That's funny – the radiator's boiling hot."

Boag-Munroe stared intently at the empty corner, opposite where he was seated.

"James? What's wrong?" Nigel sounded concerned for his friend.

Boag-Munroe shook his head, and then rubbed his eyes. "Just tiredness. These things have a habit of catching up with you."

"What is there to catch up with you?" Sue asked.

Boag-Munroe didn't answer.

"Perhaps we should call it a night, or rather two nights?" Nigel said in a kind of lukewarm jest, but was really being completely serious.

"No," Boag-Munroe was quick to snap.

"It feels like the heating is warming things up again," Hannah snuck in. "Perhaps that's the end of the cold snap?"

"It is," replied Boag-Munroe, "for now."

The room warmed up, but surprisingly the occupants didn't.

"Don't move a muscle." It was a direct order Mrs Ruth had barked at Brian, plain and simple.

Not wishing to upset the fearsome-looking woman any further than he already had, Brian did as he was told. He couldn't help but feel guilty, such was the measure of her upset. But in all honesty, all he had done was trail a slight trace of mud onto her living room carpet, quite innocently. Without further ado she had ushered him towards a most uncomfortable footstool and ordered him to sit down. Mrs Ruth examined the corresponding carpet area in the living room and the hallway which they'd passed through, eyes alert for the slightest bit of dirt. When she was satisfied she'd cleared everything up, she returned to Merlin who had not dared move, no matter how uncomfortable he was.

Alan Gentle appeared in the living room. "It's only us."

"I thought I told you to wait outside," Mrs Ruth snapped.

"Aye you did, but it's cold, so the others asked me to come in and ask you if you're ready…" he paused, "for whatever it is you were getting ready for in the first place."

"I'm trying to get things in order," Mrs Ruth huffed.

"Oh right, and are they?"

"What?"

"Are they in order now?"

"Order?"

Alan Gentle had managed to do something not many people could even hope to manage: to get Mrs Ruth so completely and utterly confused, that instead of talking about her bowels, she was set about disappearing up them instead.

"Yes, sort things out," Alan continued.

"There's nothing to sort out," she snapped.

"Good. Come on in, lads, it's all clear," Alan shouted out loud.

Tony Gentle appeared first, followed by Bradley and then Jason, before Mrs Ruth could mount any kind of protest.

Brian had still not moved. He was still taking it all in; he had been plucked from one kind of madness, only to be thrown into another.

"What's that smell?" A foreign odour had penetrated Mrs Ruth's bloodhound-like nose. The group looked at one another.

"It smells like..." she paused, choking, "animal faeces!" She gagged, horrified at the thought.

"Aye, it does, doesn't it?" Alan Gentle chipped in merrily, to reinforce the point. "Come on everyone – lift your feet up. Those woods were dark, and someone's obviously trod in something they shouldn't have."

Everybody lifted and examined their feet.

"You as well." Alan Gentle grabbed Mrs Ruth's foot, causing her to fall headlong for the second time that night. "It looks like we've got to the foot of the problem," proclaimed Alan as he held Mrs Ruth's shoe aloft. "Somebody definitely stood in something unpleasant. It must have wafted up when we all came in."

Face down on the floor, Mrs Ruth silently cursed her bad luck, the dog that had caused her bad luck, but most of all she cursed Alan Gentle.

The three rapid knocks on the door echoed events that had happened earlier. As before, the party inside Mary's flat jumped to attention, not quite knowing why.

A bead of sweat appeared on Mary's forehead. She moved to the door.

Boag-Munroe pushed her away. "Stay back!" he ordered, and opened the door himself. As before, there was no one in sight. Cautiously, Boag-Munroe stepped outside. Nigel followed.

"Do you think there's a chance someone might be playing a game?" Nigel asked.

"Games?" Boag-Munroe looked quizzical. "Maybe, and maybe there's more than one game being played."

"What do you mean?"

Boag-Munroe didn't answer. By the time he'd gone back in and Nigel had followed, the knocking repeated itself on the freshly closed door.

Boag-Munroe turned to Mary: "This time it's for you."

Mary didn't even think about her actions, too tired to think clearly anymore, and somehow if she had, she knew it would have clouded her judgement. Now was the time for action while she still had some reserves of energy left. She opened the door. No one. "Now what?" she asked Boag-Munroe.

"As before: we wait. And this time it shouldn't take long."

Mary clicked the door shut behind her. "You said that last time."

"I did, didn't I?" Boag-Munroe didn't seem unduly bothered.

Andrew shivered at the strange events that were surrounding him. His bladder was fit to burst and as much as he didn't want to leave the safety the room offered him, he desperately needed the toilet.

"I need to go to the bathroom."

Mary knew she had to let him go, although worried that he would be out of her sight. He wasn't gone more than thirty seconds when they heard a bloodcurdling scream. Mary raced for the bathroom, quickly followed by Nigel and Sue.

"No!" Boag-Munroe shocked Nigel and Sue both with such a desperate sense of urgency, that it made them both stop in their tracks. "It has to be this way." He waited a second longer, when a second scream that sounded like Mary was heard. Sue broke free as Boag-Munroe's mental grip relaxed. By the time the bathroom door was flung open by Sue, Mary and Andrew were both shaking on the floor.

Boag-Munroe pushed his way in between Sue and Mary. He stood over Mary, who was comforting Andrew.

"You saw him, didn't you? His identity, you know it."

"Yes," sobbed Mary, half in fear and half in relief. "We both saw it. It was the face of the caretaker."

CHAPTER THIRTY-TWO

Brian stood up. Enough was enough. He was supposed to be a master wizard and not suffer fools gladly. If anything, he'd been suffering the fools that surrounded him for a good couple of hours now.

"If you can't bring me Boag-Munroe or tell me where he is, then there's no point in continuing."

"Are you really Merlin?" asked Alan Gentle.

"Yeah, sure he is," said Bradley sarcastically, "and I'm King Arthur."

"Gentlemen, please. We have work to do." Mrs Ruth scolded Alan and Bradley before turning back to Brian. "You, sit back down."

"No, I won't," protested Brian.

"What did you say?" Wizard or no wizard, Mrs Ruth was still taken aback that anyone could possibly disagree with her, and especially to her face.

"I said I'm leaving. I've been brought here on nothing but a wild goose chase, only to be treated like a child, and to be spoken to in the most rude manner by a big mother hen."

Mrs Ruth was taken aback even further. "I have never been so insulted in the whole of my life."

"Really?" said Brian, "Then you mustn't get out much. All I wanted was to find Boag-Munroe."

Mrs Ruth steadied herself. "And I know where he is."

"Well why don't you take me to him, or at least tell me where he is?"

"I won't take you or tell you a thing, not one, you strange little man. Go then, you pathetic creature, off with you. Just look at you, puffing and panting and pushing your weedy little chest out. You might as well get your spidery little legs working, and through my front door," Mrs Ruth barked.

"Fine by me, you truly awful, big fat woman."

Now Mrs Ruth was completely horrified and speechless and there was no way back. Brian left.

Alan Gentle got to thinking he might be the great wizard after all, the way he dared to speak to Mrs Ruth, a feat not taken on by any other human being.

The door slammed shut, but quickly opened again, as Jason followed Brian out.

"Don't worry – I can take you to Boag-Munroe," Jason offered, after he'd made sure that they were alone and the coast was clear.

"Is this another wind-up?"

"No, I know where he lives."

"Will you take me there?"

"Yes."

"Now?"

"Fine with me."

"OK then. But can we stop off at a garage of something to get a packet of biscuits? I'm starving."

"You can have all the biscuits you like, or can eat."

Jason and Merlin left, not exactly holding hands, but definitely as thick as thieves.

"So that's it then?" Mary was still shivering.

"I don't see what else there is to do, you've seen what you needed to see," replied Boag-Munroe.

"So the apparitions will stop now?" she asked.

"In most cases this is just the start."

"The start? I thought this was it; you were supposed to be helping, not making things worse."

"I was merely helping you to help yourself, no more really than your apparition was doing."

"How?"

"Psychic sense, ESP, guardian angels, spirits, or whatever else you want to call it; part of it at least, comes from you. Now you know the person's identity who will do you harm, all you have to do is heed the warning,. It's left to you now; you have to make sure he can't harm you. You have to get away and keep away from him, or keep him away from you."

"But he's just an idiot. I doubt he'd want to harm anyone, or *could* harm anyone, for that matter."

"Even if he didn't want to harm you or anyone else, what's to stop him from blowing this place sky high, with you in it, if he's such an idiot with his not-so-good DIY skills?"

"What?"

"Do I have to keep repeating myself?" Boag-Munroe scowled, "You have to get away from this man. Intentionally or unintentionally, he's going to cause you harm, and in cases where apparitions like this are so strong, so intense, it's often fatal."

He walked towards the door.

"Where are you going?" Mary asked, still somewhat in shock.

"We're done here. There's no more I, or anyone else, can do." Boag-Munroe exited, leaving Nigel and Hannah to quickly say some dumbfounded goodbyes. Sue, Andrew and Mary were left feeling very tired and equally dumbfounded.

"This is where he is, then?" Brian asked.

"It's where he *lives*," Jason corrected him. "Where he is, is a completely different matter. He's the type of person who's very hard to pin down."

"Do you think he's in? Only the lights are off."

"Does that matter? I mean, I took you to where he lives. I kept my end of the bargain."

"Bargain?" Brian looked surprised.

Jason smiled, "What I meant to say is you can trust me. I'm not like those other idiots." He spoke in the sincerest manner possible: "You can tell me as little or as much as you like. But, whichever, I can't help wondering why you're so desperate to contact Boag-Munroe."

"The great Merlin has his reasons," said Brian, in a not-so-great manner.

"And those reasons are…?" asked Jason still digging.

Brian didn't know the reasons; he wasn't even particularly interested in them either. What he was interested in was that his job was nearly finished and a particularly big pay cheque was waiting for him. Jason could dig all he liked, but Jason just wasn't that important.

Jason crossed the road and rapped firmly on Boag-Munroe's front door.

Nigel broke the silence in the van: "Funny way to leave things."

Boag-Munroe didn't answer.

"Very abrupt," added Hannah.

"Things in life have a habit of ending abruptly," answered Boag-Munroe, "including life itself."

A fox darted into the van's headlights causing Nigel to slam on his brakes and causing the van to spin.

Nigel coughed. His heart started to pump again, after momentarily stopping. Hannah groaned softly and pushed her teeth back in, the bottom layer having fallen out, and hoped nobody had noticed.

Boag-Munroe was as unflappable as ever: "See what I mean?"

Nigel straightened the van into something like the right direction, his hands still shaking. "I think we could all do with a good night's sleep."

"Any sleep would do," interjected Hannah, now that her teeth were firmly settled back in. "But what about Mary and Andrew?"

"As I said, we've done all we can."

"Will she still see the apparitions?" asked Hannah.

"If she doesn't take heed," answered Boag-Munroe.

"And then what?" persisted Hannah, pushing the question to new boundaries.

Boag-Munroe didn't seem interested, new boundaries or otherwise.

The rest of the journey was silent until Nigel dropped Hannah home. He knew that, at the best of times, Boag-Munroe was a closed book, so it was hardly likely he was going to open his pages while there was any kind of audience there, no matter how small.

"Do you think this caretaker chap is behind all these kidnappings?"

"Who knows?" Boag-Munroe seemed even more distant than usual.

"Damn it, man! Sometimes you can be so cold."

"I've found it helps to be that way," the Professor shrugged.

"Not with me it doesn't. There's something wrong with you and you're not telling me. In fact, you're not telling me anything and I'm sick and tired of it. You treat me like a stooge, a fool you can talk down to. At best I'm seen as a mere assistant, a lap dog, always there and loyal to the great Boag-Munroe."

"You're tired." Boag-Munroe was still managing to be evasive.

Nigel slammed the brakes on for the second time that evening. He turned to Boag-Munroe, who in turn carried on staring dead ahead.

"Too right I'm tired," Nigel growled.

After a time, Boag-Munroe finally turned to him: "What are you doing?"

"I'm not moving until I get some answers." Nigel was steadfast.

"What answers would you like?"

"Don't play games with me. I'm the first to admit I'm tired, but when it really comes down to it, I'm just not in the mood."

"To get the answers you must first know the question. So what is your question?"

"What did you see in that flat?"

"See?"

"You saw something; something that drained any remaining colour from you. You saw something or thought you saw something and whatever it was, you didn't like it."

Boag-Munroe paused before answering. "It wasn't a case of liking or disliking. It was just something unexpected. An unexpected event that began to lead to other events falling into place."

"What kind of events?"

"If you want to know what I saw, then I'll tell you. I saw people screaming, burning. I saw the ground open up and swallow them all, men, women, and children. The children were the worst part, so many children."

"A premonition?"

"While I've been helping Mary face her demons, I've been facing my own, or at least accidentally unlocking them for me to see clearly enough, instead of the fleeting shadows I would normally catch out of the corner of my eye."

"What's that supposed to mean? People burning, the ground swallowing them up? What's it got to do with you?"

"That's what I'm about to find out. I've only found this out through sleep deprivation. If I can hold out, I should be able find out even more."

"Like when and where these events take place?"

"I already know where."

"You do?"

"I'm hardly not to going recognise my own home town. Especially when half of it's swallowed up in a gigantic black hole."

Jason was glad that on this occasion he had persevered. On catching sight of Nigel's approaching van, it seemed that the torture of staying still in the darkness, with some idiot who professed to be Merlin, might just have paid off. The van came to a halt after struggling into a parking space, and Boag-Munroe emerged, closely followed by Nigel.

Jason was now waiting quite proudly out in the open, on the small pathway to the terraced house with the man he knew as Merlin. As Boag-Munroe got closer he looked straight at them. He reached inside his pocket and pulled out a key. "Good evening," he calmly bid them, before unlocking his door and letting himself in. Nigel as usual, quickly followed. The door slammed shut and Jason and Merlin were left standing out in the cold.

"That was Boag-Munroe," Jason said meekly.

"You don't say?" Brian replied sarcastically.

Jason lightly hammered on the door. "Hello!" he shouted at one of the bay windows before turning back to Brian. "He's a very good friend of mine, Boag-Munroe; it's just that he's a little eccentric. I'm sure you can sympathise with that."

Brian didn't look very sympathetic; just cold and tired. So much so, he almost longed to be back in his tent at Alderley Edge. Nevertheless, he knocked on the door with a sharp rap.

Nigel answered the door: "Yes?"

"Is Professor Boag-Munroe in?" Brian asked in an upbeat manner that simply didn't suit him.

"Yes."

"May I speak with him?"

Nigel disappeared, only to be replaced with a rather disgruntled-looking Boag-Munroe. "Can I help you?"

"You don't know me…" Brian wasted no time before speaking.

"No, I don't," Boag-Munroe barged in before Brian could finish.

"…But I'm Merlin, the wizard."

"Of course you are, but I've had a very busy night."

"Are you Professor James Boag-Munroe?" Brian persisted.

"Yes."

"Then I have something very important to ask of you." Brian reached a hand into one of his robes and pulled out a shabby-looking book: "Could you autograph this for me, please?"

Boag-Munroe looked at the book. "One of my earlier works. I'm told it's quite rare now." He signed the book and closed the door.

"Is that it?" Jason shouted at Brian as he walked off, "Is that all you wanted him for? To autograph a book?"

"Yes. I'm a great fan of his."

Jason was speechless. It was probably just as well.

"Looks like Jason's got a new playmate," said Nigel as he settled down.

"Don't make yourself too comfortable, we're going downstairs."

"To the cellar?"

"Yes. The pool table is still there, a little damper and a little worn, but we can still play a few frames."

They descended down into the cellar. Dusty and confined, here you could really tell the age of the house, as they trod slowly down on cold stone steps.

Boag-Munroe began to rack the balls up on the rickety table.

"I'm surprised you didn't take this with you. You always loved it."

"They do have them in America and it would have been a hell of a thing to fly across the Atlantic on a whim."

They both laughed, and carried on laughing, until Nigel suddenly turned serious, "But you didn't go to America on a whim, did you? And I doubt you came back on one."

Boag-Munroe broke. The clatter of the balls made a comforting clicking sound that he hadn't heard within his cellar for a long time. "I don't know why I came back. I don't even know how I got back. The first thing I remembered was turning up at Marbury. The week before I cant remember a damn thing, although I deduced I'd been staying in the cottage at Llangollen."

"Deduced?"

"Some paper with my handwriting on it in the fire. I came across it when we were in the cottage." He stood back from the table, "That knocking at the door of the cottage, it was meant for me, as were the first ones at Mary's flat. That's why she didn't see her apparition straight away. That wake up call was meant for me only. Only when I opened the door did I let it in for me to get a proper look, and then Mary let hers in. Up to a point it was all crossed wires." Boag-Munroe leaned on his cue, "Something of a coincidence, wouldn't you say? In helping her I helped myself. I was blinded, if you like. I couldn't see the wood for the trees."

"You don't think the strain of things has been getting to you?"

"On the contrary, I think the strain of things is filling in the gaps. Now I just need to fill in a few more gaps. The longer I stay awake, let the sleep deprivation win, the more I'll be susceptible."

"You know I've never agreed with that sleep deprivation lark. It's all a bit too far-fetched."

"We all have to push ourselves, if not we'll never find any truth," Boag-Munroe reasoned.

"How far are you supposed to go?"

"As far as possible."

"And when does the possible become the impossible?"

The professor shrugged, "We don't know until we've tried."

"It's your health I'm thinking of."

"I know, but I also know there's more than physical health at stake here. There's something I'm meant to do, *have* to do even." He paused, "Only I've forgotten what it is. That's if I ever knew it in the first place."

Nigel scratched his head. "So how can a game of pool help?"

"It helps keep me awake. It also stops my mind from playing tricks. If I'm concentrating on the game in hand and not the problem, when a vision or apparition does come along, it will be pure."

Nigel took to the table. He took a shot but missed. Even though Boag-Munroe had not slept for days and Nigel had grabbed sleep here and there, Nigel looked and probably felt the more tired of the two.

Boag-Munroe re-took his place at the table. He potted the ball that he was aiming for straight away.

Five frames later, his face changed from one of idle attention, to utter concentration. As before, his face drained of colour. But this time, whether suffering from the strain of fatigue, or from the horror of what he'd seen, Boag-Munroe slumped forward.

Nigel steadied his friend but Boag-Munroe had rescued himself, pushing himself back up to his full height with the aid of the side of the pool table.

"What did you see?" asked Nigel.

"Surprisingly enough, I saw Red Leather of all people."

Nigel recoiled back, "You really are knackered."

"I also saw the actual start of it."

"The start of what?"

"The collapse of the old mines."

"The old salt mines that run under the town?"

"Yes. The filling-in process. It's too little too late. If we don't intervene everything's going to come crashing down in utter destruction." Boag-Munroe threw his pool cue to one side.

"Where are you going?" asked Nigel.

"To talk to some people."

"It's late."

"But not too late. It's not over, not just yet."

Nigel stood wavering, his pool cue wavering with him: "Where are we going?"

"*We're* going nowhere. I want you to wait here, put some coffee on. I won't be long."

"You're mad."

"Not yet, but I'm getting there."

"It's gone two in the morning."

"I'll be back by half past."

"From where?"

"That would be telling," Boag-Munroe's disembodied voice drifted back down to the cellar.

Nigel placed his cue down on the pool table. "Yes, wouldn't it just."

Miss Cutts entered the nondescript man's office: "He's coming."

Smith was stood beside the nondescript man. "Are you sure? Jones is still trailing him."

"Miss Cutts is always sure and always right," said the nondescript man very seriously.

"It's no wonder this organisation is falling apart," remarked Miss Cutts before leaving and firmly closing the door behind her.

Smith looked annoyed. "What the hell does he want?"

"If you'd been a bit more polite, Miss Cutts might have enlightened us," said the nondescript man. "And after all, that is what we're looking for: enlightenment."

"And politeness." Smith sounded as disgruntled as he sounded sarcastic.

The nondescript man continued: "Besides, I invited him to call back on us, at any time."

Smith looked shocked. "Why?"

"Can you imagine for one second a man like Boag-Munroe being told he can't do something? More than likely he'll automatically do it. If this place is less of a mystery to him, the digging he does will be minimal and our observations of him will be the maximum. That is if we manage to stay with him for once."

"Perhaps the organization is falling apart?" Smith mumbled.

The nondescript man smiled but it didn't last for long. A knock on the front door wiped it away and replaced it with a more bland expression.

Boag-Munroe had entered the building.

"I hope I'm not intruding. Your secretary said to come in. Is that right?"

"Yes," Nondescript answered.

Boag-Munroe pulled up a chair and seated himself. "She said I was expected."

"Smith, we'll finish off this conversation later."

Smith turned to leave, but not before giving Boag-Munroe one of his trademark disgruntled looks.

"He seems an angry young man," Boag-Munroe gave his views on Smith's character, even before he'd left the room properly.

"Now you can see why I was so willing to offer you a position here. We might have the staff but we lack someone with your… shall we say, 'panache'?"

"One does try."

"But try as you might, I take it this isn't a social call?"

Boag-Munroe's expression turned dark. "No, it's not." He paused, "What do you know about mines? Salt mines in particular?"

Nondescript man smiled, "I know there are a series of unfilled salt mines underneath a large part of this town. This, of course, is common knowledge. In the past they've caused subsidence, a considerable amount in fact. Before the Second World War it was not unknown for whole houses to drop into the ground. I think it even happened to a local pub. Measures were taken of course, but over the last few years there has been a fair number of scare stories about how those mines are just waiting to collapse. Hence the Council decided to fill them in; a process that has already started, by pumping brine into them through pipes."

Boag-Munroe leaned forward. "Those scare stories are true."

This time the man's smile was more forced. "If you say so. But only time will tell."

Boag-Munroe's eyes burrowed deep into the nondescript man's soul. "So where do I fit into all this? Where does a town like Northwich fit into all this, into an organisation like yours? You wouldn't be here if there wasn't something in it for you."

"We're not here because there is something in it for us personally. We're here to protect. I will admit we do have an interest in those mines, because of certain information we've gathered."

Boag-Munroe butted in. "You mean information from your mediums, your tarot card readers, your voices from the dead?"

"All methods you and your friends have used on a regular basis to an amateur degree. With our organisation this information can be analysed professionally, by believers, sceptics and those like you that look at both sides of the fence. Only with organisations like ours will we obtain the kind of results attaining anything like the status of truth. The work we do is of great value."

Boag-Munroe butted in again: "To the Government. But when all's said and done, you're just a pile of civil servants."

For the first time the nondescript man seemed riled. "We're so much more than that."

Boag-Munroe had a dark look in his eye: "Enlighten me."

Nondescript calmed himself. Boag-Munroe was getting to him, knocking him off-guard. He had to steady himself. "I take it you would like our help?"

Boag-Munroe paused, "More to the point, would you like *my* help?"

Nondescript didn't answer. It was as if he was afraid of getting dragged into anything else.

Boag-Munroe leaned forward in a highly determined manner. "I need to get into those mines."

Nondescript leaned back. "We are not organisers of potholing expeditions."

"Neither am I," Boag-Munroe retorted, "but I'm willing to try my hand at most things. With or without your help, I'll find a way in. But I'm sure with your help I can do this a lot faster and maybe even a little safer."

Nondescript paused, "Faster maybe. But safer? I doubt it. We've already sent an expedition into the mines, two in fact. They haven't returned yet. The last one went in a year ago."

"An organisation that looks after its workers, I like that." Sarcasm oozed from the professor.

"We do what we have to do. Everybody that works for the Ministry knows the risk."

"What about others that get caught up in your little games? Leyton Blair for instance?"

"A friend of yours I believe? Or at least he was."

"He's gone missing."

"I thought he was dead."

"Like I said, he's gone missing, or at least his body has."

"And you'd like us to find it?"

"To be honest I couldn't care less what you do. As long as you can get me into those mines."

"Go home, get some sleep."

Boag-Munroe didn't budge.

Nondescript conceded: "You're very tired. Tomorrow we go potholing."

Boag-Munroe gave a satisfied nod and left.

CHAPTER THIRTY-THREE

Mary woke with relief. Relief that her son Andrew was still sleeping safely at her side and that the events of last night were over. Additionally, relief that they had not dreamt, or experienced any terrible nightmares during the deep sleep into which they had fallen.

Andrew yawned.

"Everything OK?" she asked.

He nodded. She felt even happier if that was possible. Then she remembered Boag-Munroe's final warning. She looked around the room. It was daylight, a bright winter sun was shining through the gap in her bedroom curtains illuminating the dust particle that swam and drifted about the room.

"You do realise everything's going to be all right now?"

Andrew nodded, still too tired to speak, but this time he did manage a smile that sent Mary's spirits rising even higher. She kissed him on the head. "I'll make your favourite breakfast: bacon and eggs." She grabbed her dressing gown and opened the door.

The caretaker stood before her in the open doorway, his normally dull and vacant eyes now piercing into her. Then he vanished. Mary knew it wasn't her mind playing tricks. From behind her, she heard Andrew's shocked gasp. She turned and faced him. His face was a ghastly shocked white.

"It's OK," she tried to sound calm, "we're going to do as Professor Boag-Munroe says; he hasn't let us down yet. We're leaving right now." She grabbed his hand.

Dexter Pondsdexter was having a sleepless night. Operation Merlin had paid off and Dexter's contact had rung a good four hours ago. Now all Dexter had to do was mull over what he was going to do with the information.

Damn it, he cursed. But what else could he do? It was his neck on the line. Who knows, Carter Whitlowe might have tapped his phone, might have heard everything that had been said, and might be sending someone round to sort him out. But Dexter wasn't completely devoid of humane feelings, there was still some guilt creeping around in his conscience. He had set a trap for his friend, and his friend had been caught in it. OK, Boag-Munroe knew Dexter was spineless and had voiced that opinion more than once. But to set someone up like that, even Boag-Munroe would find that hard to forgive. Then it hit Dexter again: Boag-Munroe wouldn't have to forgive. Not in this life at least.

He rolled onto his side and sighed. He would have to make the phone call. He didn't have any choice. In for a penny, in for a pound, as the English would say. Sometimes it was damn hard being a publishing agent.

He made the phone call.

Carter had been surprised. Not that he wasn't used to getting what he wanted. But the plan which Dexter Pondsdexter had unfolded to him, to get the prey he wanted, had been fanciful at best, ludicrous at worst. Pondsdexter had constructed a scheme to have an out-of-work actor pose as Merlin the magician, in some small town near to where Boag-Munroe was brought up. It seemed the professor had shown a great interest in the legends of the town, about King Arthur and Merlin the wizard in particular. So Dexter had figured that if he got some dispensable loon to pretend to be Merlin and ask to speak to Boag-Munroe, sooner or later Boag-Munroe would find out. The rest would be left to Boag-Munroe's natural curiosity and, hopefully, his love of the legend would finally lead to his whereabouts. It was mad, but after all, Boag-Munroe was English and they liked that kind of eccentric behaviour. The scheme was just mad enough to work. The Merlin figure would automatically be classed as being insane, so when the bodies of both Merlin and Boag-Munroe turned up, it would all fit quite nicely. Merlin would be found having committed suicide, after having murdered Boag-Munroe. 'Crazed-fan syndrome' Dexter had called it. Get the Merlin guy to carry a couple of Boag-Munroe's books, maybe get them autographed when Boag-Munroe turned up. It would be perfect. The way things were panning out, it was beginning to seem that way. Not wishing to count his chickens before they hatched, Carter was quietly pleased with the progress. So much so that he rounded up some belongings, concluded any business he had for the time being, and gave notice for his son, accompanied by his nurse, to fly to England with him in the morning. Later in the evening Carter took a ringside seat for Bruno's bare-knuckle boxing match. It only made the elation of finally tracking Boag-Munroe down even greater, as he watched Bruno pound his opponent into bloody and broken unconsciousness, that could be seen by some as the ultimate submission. But this wasn't the case for Carter. He'd seen the ultimate submission time and time again. He'd made himself a personal promise that when he next saw it, it would be Boag-Munroe who fell to its brute force. Carter congratulated Bruno on a well-fought fight, as well as mentally congratulating himself, on the money he'd earned on the bout. Pin money to him, of course. But it would finance his trip to England, on which they would all be travelling incognito. False passports and identities were nothing to a man of Whitlowe's stature. Everything was now in place. Boag-Munroe was due to pay the price for what he'd done to his son.

"We need to get some sleep," prompted Boag-Munroe to Nigel, on his return to the house.

"That's what I've been saying for the last couple of days."

Boag-Munroe seemed upbeat. "And very good advice it is too." He paused, "Where's the coffee?"

"It went cold," Nigel answered with a deadpan expression.

"Good. I never liked coffee anyway. I'll have a drink of coke."

Nigel shook his head. By the time he'd finished shaking his head; Boag-Munroe had finished his drink and was heading upstairs.

Red Leather felt unbalanced. The feeling caused him concern as, although a lot of people had accused him of being unbalanced in the past, some even to his face, he'd never thought of himself in that way before. The nightmares were now getting worse instead of better. It was getting to the stage where he didn't know which way to turn. Sleep was now a distant memory, and reminded him of the hazy past, when his life had been one long party of drugs and drink. The trouble was: everyone had gone home, the party was now over, and even the drugs and drink seemed consigned to the past. All Red had now, was his own blurred confusion of reality, and he was beginning to wonder what to do with it. Sam was becoming restless, Red was no fool and knew the lure of more money wouldn't be enough for his bodyguard. When the time was right for him, Sam would cut and run. As for the children, the less he thought about them the better. Red had been convinced at all times that he had been doing the right thing, but now… He didn't know anymore. The children were getting just as restless as Sam, some more restless than others. He had the sudden and terrible feeling he had misjudged everything. So where would that leave him in the publics opinion when the game was up? The stakes were high. He'd known that from the start, as he'd equally known things could backfire on him. But what if he wasn't right? What if he was mad? The visions of the poor children being hurt; it may all have been just a part of his madness. Then how would he explain what he'd done? Instead of alerting people as to how precious their offspring are, and how they should look after their children, he would have become what he was warning them about in the first place.

"The natives are restless." Sam entered Red's bedroom unannounced. Red saw this as yet another hammer in the proverbial coffin.

"Do come in," Red said through gritted teeth.

"The Danefields boy: he's a bit too restless for my liking."

"But it's not your liking that counts, is it?" Red tried to win a little ground back.

"You're right, this is your show. If you want me to walk, just say the word and I'll walk. In fact there's nothing that would suit me better right now than a good long walk." Sam's eyes were cold, unmoving. He wasn't bluffing.

"Don't be so pathetic." Red narrowed his own eyes; he had to hold on.

"We'll see who's pathetic," Sam countered, as he turned to leave the room.

"Wait!" Red was trembling. So much for winning ground back.

Sam didn't wait. In fact, it took a Red lunge to bring him to a halt.

"You can't go now. No matter what, we're in this together. If the police…"

Sam cut him off, "If the police catch up with us we've had it. But the thing is, they won't catch up with us. Not me at any rate... So you can forget your petty blackmail. I've got a nice little stash of the money you've paid me ready and, for your information, a quick and safe route out of all this. You see I'm just a nobody. Grow a beard, change my haircut, get a tan, that's me sorted, just another face in the crowd, but you…"

"I'll take you with me." Red sounded as desperate as he was.

"You might try," Sam tapped a patronising finger against Red's temple, "but then again you've had all kinds of crazy ideas up there and they haven't worked up to now, have they?"

"I'll make you a millionaire." It was Red's last throw of the dice.

"You've nearly given me a million already. I'm not greedy."

"I'm talking more… lots more. I'm talking multi-millionaire."

Sam was satisfied. He didn't show it even though it was what he'd been working towards all this time. He wasn't about to take a chance on spoiling things. He'd been with Red for long enough to know, the deeper he got, the more flustered he became and the more erratic and wandering his mind floundered. He would make slip-ups of gigantic proportions; he would be there, more or less for the taking. This was to be the big payday Sam had been waiting for.

"Let's see the money." Sam was definitely going in for the kill.

"Let's see the loyalty."

There was a silence. Red got the feeling he had won some ground back. "We have to look up an old friend of mine," he said.

"Anyone I know?"

"I doubt it. I can't see you being one for reading books."

"No shit," Sam sniped back. "When are you reacquainting yourself with this friend?"

"I think now's as good a time as any."

"Where is he?"

"He was in America, but I've got a funny little feeling he's come back home."

John was speechless. In the doorway stood his wife and child. The expressions on their faces told him that this wasn't just a flying visit, even if there were no signs of suitcases or a bag in sight.

"You don't mind, do you?" Mary looked and sounded like a little girl lost.

John jumped to his feet. "No." It was all he could think of for the moment.

"I suppose I must look a little stupid, coming home with my tail between my legs, but it seemed the right thing to do." She moved a little closer into the living room. Andrew was not afraid however and he rushed to hug his father.

John affectionately patted his son's head and then turned his attention back to his wife. "What do you mean, 'the right thing to do'?"

Mary hesitated.

"Come on, Mary, you can't just expect me to welcome you back, if you won't even say if you *are* back." He paused, "Are you back?"

She shrugged her shoulders and smiled weakly, "I'm back." She wasn't exactly lying either. She had come back, and she did still have some feelings for John.

"I guess that's all there is to it." He patted his son's head again, this time, so hard, with an obvious happiness he couldn't hide, that he almost knocked his son out.

Mary let herself go and reclined back into a chair. "At least you've kept the place somewhat tidy."

"You should have seen it yesterday when I was still cursing you." He stopped; a look of embarrassment crossed his face. He had said too much already. He wasn't about to say any more.

Mary didn't add to his embarrassment. She knew that John was handy enough at throwing objects about the house when things didn't go his way. She could easily make a mental picture of what the house must have looked like: a web of atrocious mess, with John, the spider, seated in the middle.

An awkward silence followed.

"Where are your things? Or is this an excuse to go out and buy all new?" John smiled.

"They're back at the flat." Mary sounded a little afraid. But not so little that John didn't notice.

"Would you like me to pick them up for you?"

Mary nodded, before breaking down in tears. "Sue's there too. We left her asleep." A smile appeared through the quickly subsiding tears.

"We'll go and get your stuff then," he said.

The next thing Mary knew, they were back on the road to her flat in Congleton. She waited in the car with Andrew while John went in to wake Sue, and fetch the few belongings Mary had furnished her temporary home with. From somewhere in the flats, rock music was being played loudly.

It was on Sue's one-hundredth moan, and on John's third trip back to the car, and the fifth time they'd heard *The Ace of Spades*, that Mary saw the face. It had an unfamiliar angry look about it, manic even. John didn't get time to look; he couldn't see over the clothes he'd stacked up in his arms. By the time he'd noticed the speeding vehicle it was not so much too late, more that he'd dived in the wrong direction. The car swerved to take a last-minute detour, but its speed was too fast and the driver, the caretaker, had lost control. The car's new path collided with John's path. John had more or less dived into it. A sickening, indescribable crash, even louder than the rock music, rocked the road. The rock music played on for a couple seconds more and then stopped dead.

The sound of Andrew's screams filled Mary's ears. She pulled her son close to her, away from the disaster that had happened so close.

Finally, Andrew's vocals were drowned out by the wail of an ambulance. It screamed like a howling banshee, swooping down on the scene of devastation.

CHAPTER THIRTY-FOUR

Mary stroked Andrew's hair, but it only served to remind her of the previous hour, when her husband had been patting that same hair affectionately. That affection was dead now, robbed by an idiot who had been speeding in temper. Apparently, the caretaker's son had been playing his music so loudly that the residents in the block of flats had complained. The caretaker, embarrassed and angry that he should be called out to deal with his own son, had driven like a bat out of hell. John hadn't stood a chance. Thankfully they said he wouldn't have felt a thing, but Mary wasn't so sure. She'd felt the impact from where she'd been sitting.

Mary looked around at the hospital room in which she was sitting with Andrew. They were treating Andrew for shock, naturally. The room was private although they could still see the nurses busying themselves outside. The room had that familiar green and white sterile look all hospital rooms seem to have. Mary shuddered, thinking about the mortuary where John must be. At least, what was left of him. The man she had once loved. 'Had' being the appropriate word. A tear welled up in her eye.

Professor Boag-Munroe had been right all along, except for the sickening little twist at the end that nobody could have seen coming. The apparition was warning of the harm that was going to come to both of them, but sometimes harm is as much mental as physical.

Mary rolled her mind back over the last few hours, days, months. If she'd done things differently, maybe none of this would have happened. In a way, she'd had the hindsight, but she hadn't used it, she hadn't been able to use it. Or perhaps she couldn't have stopped it? Perhaps it had all been an unchangeable chain of events, and she was just being allowed a peek at what was to happen, so that she and Andrew could brace themselves for the tragic event. Funnily enough she felt a little easier with this notion. But most of all she felt sorry for Andrew. For John, she felt guilt, grief, that sometimes life can be so cheap, and stolen, without so much as a passing thought.

Standing inside the overgrown front garden belonging to the Ministry of the Dead, Boag-Munroe had the feeling that the bird had already flown the coop. The endless knocking on the front door without an answer more or less confirmed it.

Nigel kicked over a discarded coffee jar; its contents spilled out. He kicked a small dust cloud of the coffee up into the air. He figured kicking coffee grains against the wind made a change from pissing against it.

"What are we doing here? Pretending to be estate agents?" Nigel whined.

Boag-Munroe ignored him, crossed over to a window and peered through. "I can't see anyone about," the professor sighed.

"Perhaps we should have made an appointment?"

"Perhaps," replied Boag-Munroe, before kicking the window through.
"What the hell?" Nigel jumped out of his skin.
Boag-Munroe smiled, "I guess we'll have to add breaking and entering, as well as impersonating estate agents. It's quite a list of crimes we're building up."
The inside of the building was even colder and emptier than before. Boag-Munroe strode confidently and purposely down the creaking wooden corridors. Nigel followed, meekly like a mouse trying not to wander into a trap but feeling he might be drifting aimlessly into one anyway.
Boag-Munroe barged into yet another empty room. "They're gone."
"Just as well really, when you're stamping around kicking in people's windows. People don't take kindly to that type of thing."
"But what kind of people are we dealing with exactly, what are their motives?" the professor asked.
"I'm sorry, I'm lost in all this." Nigel's head was well and truly spinning from the confusion. "Can we go now? And then maybe for once, you can explain to me what's going on. For example, why have we broken into an empty house?"
"We've broken into an empty house because we didn't find an occupied one."
"Oh, at least that clears that up then," Nigel said sarcastically.
"They didn't leave anything behind."
"So this mysterious 'they'… Were you expecting them to leave something behind?"
"No, as a matter of fact I wasn't. But you have to pursue things fully."
"Of course," replied Nigel, deciding now it might be best to humour Boag-Munroe. "At least then, no matter what, if you've done all you can, then you can sleep soundly."
"Exactly," replied Boag-Munroe.
"Can we go home now?"
"In a second, or maybe two. Three at the most."
Nigel sighed wearily, "What are we talking here? Three seconds? Minutes? Or hours?"
Boag-Munroe didn't answer. Instead he began to check the rest of the house. After checking the gardens, he finally found the time to stop and think; an action that enabled Nigel to catch up.
"Do you know I'm fed up of forever asking questions?" Nigel's temper was fraying.
"Don't be. The day we stop asking questions is the day the human race as a whole packs in."
"I'm sorry if I don't seem that interested in the human race at the moment, but to be honest, all I'm interested in is myself."
"You don't say?"

"Yes, I do say. All I want to know..." Nigel paused.

"Is?" Boag-Munroe carried on the sentence, impatient at Nigel's sluggish delivery.

"Is what are we doing here?" A manic expression took over Nigel's face, "How about that then? For a start, just answer me that. Nothing complicated, no mysteries or even long-winded answers needed. Nothing veiled, nothing cryptic, just one honest answer. What are we doing here and now? And don't you dare avoid this question."

"I would never try to avoid a question from you Nigel, dear friend." Boag-Munroe almost seemed happy that Nigel was losing his rag, if not his mind.

"So answer it then," Nigel screamed.

"Of course."

Silence.

"Go on!" Nigel screamed even louder.

"We are here plain and simply," he paused, "to find an entrance."

A horrified silence from Nigel followed.

"Is that it? We've come here, broken in, searched the house and gardens from top to bottom... to find an entrance?"

"You wanted a simple answer, nothing mysterious or baffling, and that's it."

"An entrance?"

"Yes."

The madness of it all acted as a sedative that calmed Nigel down. "But we haven't found one. Have we?"

"No, not here. But it could have been here. It could have been the reason why they set up their temporary base here. What I'd like to know is why they left so quickly. Am I such a threat to them or is there something else?"

"Something else?" Nigel decided to go along with the flow of madness. It was no use fighting it. He hadn't had any success so far.

"I know this was just a temporary base. There was hardly any equipment when they were here."

Nigel's head began to spin so hard it threatened to fly off its axis. "Of course."

"Even so..." Boag-Munroe cut himself off mid-sentence, deep in thought.

The pause enabled Nigel to regain some normal gravity of thought. "Right then, is that it?" Nigel began to stride off.

"Where are you going?" asked Boag-Munroe.

"To find this entrance." Nigel carried on walking while talking. He was making damned sure that for once in his life Boag-Munroe would follow him, even if he didn't know where he was going, or what he was about to do.

"The Ministry always knows what it's doing, Miss Cutts."

"I'm not saying the Ministry doesn't know what it's doing. I'm just saying there are some factions within in it that don't."

The nondescript man sighed, "Your views have been noted and, as always, they are respected but let us not forget, the Ministry is the sum of its parts. All the factions we have gathered, those different view points, is what makes us."

"But what about trust?"

"That's another matter."

"There's too much trust."

Nondescript sighed deeper. "Eloise was monitored to the best of our abilities. We have to accept the consequences of any failure as a whole."

"And what will those consequences be?"

"I don't know."

"For thirty-two years I have served the Ministry."

"I am well aware of your service record, Miss Cutts."

"I warned you over the girl."

"The relevant steps were taken."

"And where did that get us?"

"I'm sure she'll be found."

"I'm sure she already has been found."

Nondescript looked worried: "What do you mean?"

"That was what I needed to see you about so urgently. They've found her."

A bead of sweat appeared on his forehead. "Are you one hundred percent sure?"

Miss Cutts didn't deal in percentages. "I'm sure. But if you'd like one of your foot soldiers to check it out…" She stopped. "Oh I've just remembered, sometimes they're quite ineffective in matters like this," she continued, scornfully.

"Tut tut, Miss Cutts. These are testing times, very testing times. I thought of all the people that surround me, I could count on you most of all."

"And you can count on me. It's because of that I'm not afraid to point out the shortcomings instead of merely being one of these never ending 'yes' men."

"Nobody could ever accuse you of being that, Miss Cutts."

"No they couldn't." The old woman's eyes seemed to turn bright red. It was a side effect of all the bubbling anger that she'd suppressed within the confines of her cold exterior.

"Anyway, shall we get on with the job in hand?" Nondescript was desperate to get onto a new track.

Miss Cutts' eyes cooled down to match the rest of her frosty visage. "The London Road base has been completely evacuated. Boag-Munroe has already been poking his nose around there."

"As we knew he would. What about the other subject who we have our beady eyes, ears and senses on?"

"I sense he's going to be on the move soon. He's still at his mansion for the time being."

"And the children?"

"They're still there, quite safe for the moment."

Nondescript paused. "Do you know, Miss Cutts, it's in situations like this I'm not so sure I like what I do. Do you ever feel that way?"

Miss Cutts answered him as cold as ice: "No I don't feel that way."

Nondescript bit his lip. "It's always a comfort to have someone on board with unflinching views."

"I thought we were getting on with the matters in hand?" She carried on. "There has been no specific movement from Red Leather in the last twenty-four hours. And even Boag-Munroe has been pretty quiet, apart from his trip into our former London Road headquarters." She paused, "I still think we were hasty leaving there."

"It was just a case of moving things on a little. Besides, most of our people were already here."

"But if we hadn't invited Boag-Munroe in, we wouldn't have had to move out."

"He would have found us, Miss Cutts. Of all people I would have thought you would have sensed that."

"If that's the case, what's to stop him from finding us now? We're hardly a million miles away, tucked up in a couple of terraces, twenty doors down from his home."

"At least we might be able to pick up better psychic readings here."

Miss Cutts shook her head. "His mind's a closed book."

"Then it's about time we opened it."

"Wait!" Miss Cutts face took on an even sterner expression than usual, "Something's happening."

The door burst open and a man in a white technician's coat burst in. "Code red! The readings are off the scale!" His message over, his excitement obviously not, he rushed back out.

Nondescript smiled, "You were already on code red, weren't you, Miss Cutts? Apart from your unflinching stance, that's why you're such an asset. Shall we check the readings together?"

"I've no need to," she grimaced.

He smiled at her, "You're invaluable, utterly invaluable."

"It's gone out of the window, hasn't it?"

"Pardon?" Boag-Munroe turned to face Nigel's question head on. The professor stood in a freshly dug hole, a hole he was still digging. He leaned on his spade, looking less like a writer and paranormal investigator and more like a Council worker. "What is the matter with you?" he asked Nigel.

"There's nothing the matter with me."

"It's about this hole, isn't it?"

Nigel turned away.

"It's a scientific fact that digging holes is very therapeutic," Boag-Munroe offered. He started to dig again then stopped. "I'm not quite sure where I heard that, but I'm sure I did."

"And this escape tunnel?"

Boag-Munroe carried on digging, "I told you what it's for. Do I have to explain everything twice, or in some cases three and four times?"

"Ah yes, the way in," Nigel snapped back.

"If I'm keeping you…?" Boag-Munroe shouted up from the ever-deepening hole.

"No, I was just wondering what you're going to say, when the police ask you what you're up to?"

"I'd say I'm about three feet down."

"I'm being serious."

"I could tell them the same as I told you."

"You could. It would certainly be interesting."

"Exactly. Very interesting."

"Anyway, how do you know where to dig?" asked Nigel.

"You know me – I have a nose for these things. Besides, can't you remember where we are?"

"Of course I can remember."

"Then you'll remember what happened to Red and me."

"That wasn't here. It was over there." Nigel pointed to a car park, just past the green area in which they were digging, sheltered by steadfast lines of trees.

Once again Boag-Munroe stopped digging. "Yes, and as you can see, there happens to be a large car park over there – and digging up car parks is definitely not my forte. The Ministry of the Dead must still have a way in to the mines."

"What are you expecting to find in these salt mines, apart from salt? Unless there's some gold down there as well. Is that it? Are you hunting for gold?" Nigel asked.

Boag-Munroe threw his spade to one side. "It's useless." He jumped out from the hole. "They must have a way in, I'm sure of it." Boag-Munroe searched the car park landscape.

"I can't see any entrances to mines there," Nigel said wearily.

"They're hardly going to stick a signpost up." Boag-Munroe held his finger to his lip in thought. "This car park's massive, there are no shops around, no buildings, just cars and vans." He changed the subject abruptly: "How do you fancy a burger?"

"Not really and I wouldn't have one from a mobile burger van; you don't know what you're getting."

"How true. Especially one that's not so mobile."

"You're drifting again."

"Drifting, yes, but to a conclusion."

"Which is?"

"Quite simple. I for one don't think that burger van is all it seems. It's perfect, isn't it?"

"Is it?"

"Of course, nobody would suspect it. Whoever's guarding the entrance could stay there without causing suspicion, merely selling his wares. At night it gets locked up with a guard inside. Perfect!"

"Inspired," said Nigel, in a not-very-convinced way.

"I knew you'd like it."

"Of course. Who wouldn't like chasing an entrance that isn't even there?"

Boag-Munroe gave Nigel the cold shoulder.

Nigel thought he had to try and make him see sense anyway: "The mines are all automatic anyway, just some pipes underground. You couldn't even squeeze a small dog through, never mind us pair."

"Pardon?" Boag-Munroe was only listening half-heartedly, and was getting ready to switch off the remaining half at any second.

"That's the only entrance," explained Nigel. "Some pipes at the back of the library. That's where they're pumping the mixture of brine in, to fill the mines up. It's all done by machinery."

"That's the trouble nowadays. It's all done by machines, there's no room for craftsmen, the personal touch."

Boag-Munroe reached the burger van. "We'll take two of your finest burgers," he said to the man inside the van.

The man was a complete stereotype of how you would envisage such an individual to look: fat, greasy-looking, with an unhealthy fragrance about him. It wasn't a look that went hand-in-hand with the ideals of food or hygiene.

"Well, he definitely looks your man," Nigel whispered as the man went about his business of concocting the worst imaginable. "If I was running a top-secret organisation, he'd be the first person I'd entrust with one of our secrets. It goes without saying."

"Talk louder, he might hear you," Boag-Munroe whispered back sarcastically.

"Not only are you going to get food poisoning, you're going to look stupid, to add insult to injury." Nigel stood back. An action to indicate he was washing his hands of the whole affair.

"Worked here long?" Boag-Munroe asked the burger van man with what almost sounded like a lame chat-up line.

The burger van man looked disturbed. "Long enough," he grunted.

"Still, you have to look on the bright side," Boag-Munroe continued, "at least you get some fresh air while you're serving, although it must get quite stuffy when you're cooking in the back. I bet it's a *mine*field in there; lots of hot fat and stuff. I bet you have to mind what you're doing or you could soon injure yourself. But listen to me waffling on, you're just selling burgers, I should *mine* my business." The '*mines*' Boag-Munroe had peppered his sentencing with were very pronounced.

The burger van man gave nothing away. Boag-Munroe took the burgers and walked away.

Carter didn't like England. He hadn't been before and his first impressions of it weren't good. Dour was the first word that sprang to his mind. Dismal was the second. It was funny what a couple of breaths of Manchester's less-than-finest air could do to a man. At least the hired people-carrier he'd ordered was waiting. Even in England, people jumped for Carter because he followed one rule… money talks. Or, as in Carter's case, money shouts. He'd made sure his group's stay in England would be short if not sweet. It was the way he liked it and he always got what he wanted.

The people-carrier and all its occupants sped away from the airport. They had a meeting to attend. A very strange one, but important nonetheless.

"It's cold," said a shivering Nigel.

"I know," replied Boag-Munroe.

"And it's dark."

Boag-Munroe turned to Nigel: "I know that as well."

Both men fell silent, their gaze concentrating on the burger van.

"He's still in there," said Nigel.

"I know," replied Boag-Munroe.

"It's a bit strange that. I mean... he pulled the shutters down a good two hours ago. When you think about it, there's something definitely not right about all this. It's not exactly a hot spot of activity to run a mobile burger van from, is it? Especially at this time of year."

"He might be trying to attract the Christmas shoppers?" suggested Boag-Munroe.

"No, let's face it, James, you're probably right again, just as you always are and always were."

"Thank you for saying so."

"Don't mention it."

They fell silent.

"Would I sound stupid, after sitting here frozen to death for all these hours and not believing, if I asked what the plan was?"

"Nigel, I never thought for a second that you didn't believe. It was just that you didn't *want* to believe. That's the problem with people: they see and believe what they want. That's why they miss so much."

"You don't have to patronise me. I'm not one of your silly little readers."

The professor raised an eyebrow. "Insults now, is it?"

"Listen, when it comes to people keeping their eyes closed, you're the top of the list."

"Well it's better than being at the bottom," countered Boag-Munroe.

"Either that or you just walk away from the situation," Nigel continued.

"Meaning?"

By the way Boag-Munroe replied, Nigel knew he'd finally struck a nerve. "You know what I mean," Nigel said softly.

"Is that what this is about? Gail? Because you see that I can say her name and speak about her?" asked the professor.

"Partly, but mostly it's because you won't open up," Nigel answered. "Not everyone has let you down or will let you down. I'm not Leyton Blair."

Boag-Munroe looked wounded. "I never said you were. Look, do we have to go into all this now?"

"Yes, we do." Nigel paused, "You're in above your head, aren't you? It's written all over your face. Oh you've still got the familiar swagger and that mysterious veil you hold over yourself, but underneath it all, you're still shooting pot shots into the dark."

"And you're still hanging on to my coat tails watching me do it."

Now it was Nigel's turn to look hurt, and he even went so far as to admit so. "That hurt, that really hurt." He threw his arms up in the air. "But you're right, I'll give you that, once again for the umpteenth time. Basically, that's all I've done with my life: surrounded myself with a bunch of no-hopers, waiting for your return. Tragic isn't it?"

"You do realise we're supposed to be keeping watch and not having a domestic?"

Nigel fell quiet.

Boag-Munroe turned back to his friend, his tone and manner now somewhat softer: "I'm not in it over my head just yet. Just the usual, up to my neck in it." He paused, "Maybe a bit more than that. Let's say up to my eyes."

"And drowning fast?"

Boag-Munroe shrugged, "I have had better times."

"Why did you come home?" Nigel asked.

"Because of my usual problem. The uncanny ability I have of upsetting people. That and the fact I always manage to upset the right or rather wrong people. In this case I upset some city bigwig, the kind with a lot of power. America is a big place but it would seem he had enough clout to bring my book career to a halt. Apparently he blamed me for something that happened to his son when we were working on something together."

"Go on."

"It was for my latest book, this one was about demons and demonic possessions. Carter Whitlowe's son had an unhealthy interest in such things and, seeing as he was a friend of a friend, or rather my publishing agent's friend of a friend, I ended up having him tag along. But Stevie Whitlowe wanted to do more than that, he was gathering his own facts, or rather incantations for summoning demons."

Nigel waited with baited breath. "And did he summon any demons?"

"I'm not particularly sure, but he did end up losing it."

"Losing it?"

"His mind," Boag-Munroe tapped his finger on his head. "Apparently now he's just a vegetable. He needs twenty-four-hour care from a private nurse."

"And you had nothing to do with this?"

"Obviously not," Boag-Munroe did his best to not look hurt.

"Sorry. But I had to ask."

"You've not changed over the years either."

"But why didn't you tell me this in the first place?"

"Before you say it… I wasn't trying to sound mystical or mysterious. I didn't know myself. My mind was a total blank; it was something akin to a barrier being put up."

"Are you sure you didn't get possessed as well?"

"Who knows?" Boag-Munroe joked. But there was an evil-looking glint in his eye that Nigel caught, although didn't comment on.

"So why remember it all now?"

"I got in touch with my agent and he informed me I'd had a breakdown."

"So you are possessed?" Nigel asked half-heartedly.

"No more than usual."

Nigel looked blank.

"All right – the truth is I might be a fraction, shall we say, possessed."

"Oh, that's all right then." The sarcasm dripped from Nigel's words.

"With the aid of my recent sleep deprivation, the barriers came down. I started to remember things, things my mind had blanked out to protect me until the time was right. I'm not joking when I admit to being possessed. And I've been that way a long time. I can see that now. Ever since Red and I fell down that mine shaft when the three of us were kids playing in the rubble where this car park was built. Something hitched a lift with me that day and probably with Red as well."

Nigel looked worried. "What about me? Does that mean…?"

"You didn't fall down the shaft, only Red and me. We were both unconscious for a couple of minutes, until we came round and managed to climb out."

"Neither of you talked about what you saw down there."

"There wasn't a lot to see. Just darkness mostly. But it was the atmosphere that hit you. I'd felt nothing like it before and even though I've felt things akin to it since, it was never in that league."

"You think something came out of that mine shaft with you when you were eight?"

"I'm sure of it now. You see, I did see something when I was down there."

As he told the story, his mind drifted back in time.

Boag-Munroe, Red and Nigel had been playing in a small wood that existed before the car parks took over. The area was at the back of Oak Street where all three boys lived. They were eight years old at the time, it was the school holidays, the sun was beaming down on them and the smell of wild summer grass mingled with the stench of the nearby Northwich tip. The tip always smelt worse on hot days and this was the hottest day for a long time. The area the boys had decided to play in was noted for subsidence. Overnight great craters would appear, and legend said the unfilled and unsafe salt mines that lay beneath caused it. The legend came true for the boys on that hot day. It had all started out innocently at first. The boys were chasing in and out of the wild foliage, as well as jumping in and out of the craters that often unearthed old, interesting glass bottles.

Then it happened. Boag-Munroe jumped into a particular crater where Red was standing and where Nigel was hovering.

The ground fell through and he and Red plummeted downwards. Nigel was thankful he'd heeded his mum's instructions not to get his trousers dirty so had the foresight to stay out of the crater. In the next second, shock followed: the blind horror that his two friends had been swallowed into a black abyss. Nigel, not being the bravest of eight year olds, wasn't able to do anything except stop and stare down at the blackness. He couldn't even find it in himself to scream.

The eight-year-old Boag-Munroe wasn't aware of this. Shaking his head, he tried to get his bearings on what had happened. After the momentary unconsciousness, a groggy feeling followed. In the blackness, he couldn't tell if he was awake, unconscious, or dreaming. As the grogginess subsided, he realised he was lying on some kind of uneven wooden platform, which prevented him from falling even further into blackness. His leg was hanging over into the never-ending dark. It had felt cold, as if the blackness was pulling at his leg, wanting to bring the rest of his body down with it. Boag-Munroe snatched his leg away and scrambled to the higher point of the sloping platform. He heard rotten timber creaking under his frame, and felt pieces of dirt dislodge and tumble down past him and off the tilting platform, down into the nothingness below.

He dragged himself higher towards the light, having a sense of urgency that the platform might not last for much longer. He'd looked up towards the light and was sure he could make it; there were bits of wooden scaffold he could use to climb. If he could reach them in time.

Boag-Munroe felt the platform creak under his weight again. This time he looked down into the darkness. It was then he saw them: people, mostly children, crying. He averted his eyes from them and concentrated on the job in hand.

By this time, his eyes had become accustomed to the darkness. He had found Red unconscious further up the platform. As quickly as possible, he managed to wake him and the two made their way off the platform and onto the scaffold.

As they reached the top of the hole, the platform broke and tumbled away into the blackness. Boag-Munroe, the less unsteady of the two, dragged Red to safety, and allowed himself a glimpse back. The people had gone. Only the dark and the sinister atmosphere remained. The three of them left the hole without telling anyone it was there or what had happened. They didn't even speak of it; more afraid of the trouble they would get into with their respective parents.

A day later and the hole had gone.

"Don't you think I remember all that?" said Nigel, dragging Boag-Munroe back into the future.

"But you don't remember me telling you about the figures, because I didn't."

"Well, no. Why was that then?"

"Because I wasn't sure what I'd seen. I'd been unconscious; I thought it could have been my imagination."

"You said the figures were of people, children mostly?"

"Yes. They were crying, some were even screaming."

"And you saw all this even though it was pitch black?"

"That's it, you see – they glowed, all of them gleaming bright white in the darkness, and then they were gone, just like the hole was gone the next day even though we told no one about it. What does that tell you?"

"That for once the Council did their job and cleared something up?"

"They cleared it up all right, and then the car parks came. It was as if it never happened, but it did."

"Sometimes I wonder myself. It did all seem a bit surreal," Nigel admitted.

"I had nightmares for night after night about what had happened; those people looking up at me crying. Red and I were their only hope. There was no way they were going to let us forget. And they didn't. I can't speak for Red, but as for myself, they've always been with me. The trouble is, as a child, I was so afraid that I pushed them away from my thoughts. Or rather I couldn't push them away, not totally; just into an unused corner. They've stayed in that little dark corner, a corner I avoided so much. I nearly forgot all about them, until the business with Mary and Andrew. What I had seen in the past as fleeting visions, shadows on the wall, became something more. I knew I was a haunted man, but I didn't know what was haunting me, until now."

"You saw something at Mary's, didn't you?"

"Yes, you noticed something was wrong with me. It was them I saw, screaming for help down that mine shaft. You see, now they had a voice. I was a child no more; I couldn't push them to one side and carry on. Their strength and combined power is like nothing I've ever come across before.

They won't let me rest until I put them to rest. Now you can see why I have to get down to those mines."

Nigel looked worried: "Even if that burger van is the entrance, you just can't pop down and have a poke around in something that dangerous. You'll get killed."

"I can assure you I won't. Apparently my death will come about on the Cloud."

"What cloud?"

"The landmark in Congleton. Remember?"

"What are you doing up there?"

"Dying apparently, but that's supposed to be in the future, and I have that from a good source."

"Oh, that's all right then." Nigel's look was of sheer disbelief.

Boag-Munroe slapped him on the shoulder. "I knew you'd help, I knew you'd understand."

"I understand, I think, so what do you expect me to do now?"

"Nothing too complicated. I enjoyed those burgers so much that I'd like another."

"The shutters are down; he's closed for the night."

"He's still in there though."

"Doing who knows what? He could be sharpening his burger carving knife, for all we know," Nigel's face sank. His heart sank along with it. Now it was his time to turn back the clock. He felt like he was once again beside that gaping hole as a timid chubby eight year old, not daring to look down into the dark for what he might see. He'd punished himself for years after; his best friend could have died because of his lack of help. He had branded himself a coward even though Boag-Munroe had not, and had been as understanding as an eight year old as he was now. But he wasn't eight years old anymore. He strode towards the burger van.

"Hello!" shouted Nigel as he hammered on the burger van door.

No answer.

"I said hello," he shouted in a polite voice.

No answer or any movement from inside the van.

"I know you're in there," Nigel shouted. "I'd like a burger. And I'm not leaving until I've been served."

The door suddenly opened outwards, knocking Nigel off his feet. Wheezing, he clambered to his feet as an angry-looking burger man grabbed him by the collar.

"Would you mind putting my friend down?" Boag-Munroe had appeared from nowhere.

The burger man tossed Nigel aside and grunted balefully in Boag-Munroe's direction.

"Now that's better, isn't it?" Boag-Munroe walked slowly towards the burger van. "Now if you'll allow me to explain, I'll tell you why we're here." Before another word could be formed, Boag-Munroe punched the man in his stomach so hard the it brought him down to his knees.

The burger van man vomited onto the tarmac.

"I think he ate something that disagreed with him," quipped Boag-Munroe. "Perhaps it was one of his own burgers?"

This time it was the turn of the burger van man to be helped to his feet… by his collar.

"As you might have guessed by now, we're not the health inspectors," Boag-Munroe added.

"I don't know," coughed the man, "they're a bunch of bastards as well."

Boag-Munroe obviously wasn't in the mood for jokes apart from his own. He squeezed the man's arm making him cry out in pain. "Are there any traps in there?"

"You what?" yelped the burger van man.

"You heard what I said." Boag-Munroe stopped applying pressure and pushed the man to one side. "He's genuine." Boag-Munroe turned to Nigel, "He's not one of them." He entered the burger van and Nigel followed.

"Do you mean to say you've just beaten up a perfectly innocent man?" Nigel asked.

Deadpan Boag-Munroe turned back to him: "No mobile burger vendor is perfectly innocent. Would you eat that food?"

The door slammed shut. A bolt locking from the outside was heard.

"It's locked," said Nigel, checking the door.

Boag-Munroe produced a torch from his pocket.

Nigel panicked. "Now what?"

Boag-Munroe looked around. "At least we won't starve, even if the food isn't up to much."

"I thought you said you wouldn't eat this rubbish?"

"That depends on how long we're going to be in here. There's a first time for everything."

It was Mary's second homecoming in as many days. The hospital was satisfied that Andrew was as well as could be expected. They'd made a fuss at first, but sympathetic though they were, they seemed only too glad to send them home. Not that Mary held this against them; there wasn't exactly much they could do. They were up to the neck in work to start with, they looked short-staffed and overworked, not to mention the fact there were hardly any spare beds. That they had given them a private room for a couple hours was miracle enough.

Andrew curled up into a corner of the chair. It was the chair in which he'd sat on his father's knee, on so many cold winter nights.

Before Andrew had come along, Mary and John had snuggled up on it.

Somehow the chair looked empty now, even though Andrew was still sitting there.

Now she missed him. It was all so different from her leaving him. Now everything was definite, so final. She wondered what to do next. She knew she should be doing something, but wasn't sure what.

She noticed a tear in Andrew's eye. She couldn't tell if it was one of the many he had already shed or if it was a fresh one. She didn't ask. She knew Andrew was like a fragile piece of glass at the moment; one wrong move by her and he might shatter into a million pieces. A million pieces… at the moment, Mary didn't know if she'd have the patience or strength to pick them all up.

She wondered whether she should ring someone. It was what people normally did in a situation like this. But it wasn't a normal situation. How could she play the grieving widow, when she and John had been separated? She could picture the looks people would give her at the funeral. Then she caught sight of Andrew, the one tear still trailing down his face. A sense of selfishness and worthlessness overcame her. She steadied herself, picked up the phone and rang John's parents.

"Can you hear anything?" Boag-Munroe asked Nigel.

"Nothing."

"I thought so." Boag-Munroe carried on searching their cramped, enforced surroundings.

"Do you think he's gone to get the police?"

"Probably not."

"But I thought you said he was genuine?"

"He is, but working for them. He's obviously as thick as two short planks. Not the kind of person to swell the ranks of the Ministry of the Dead, but someone they might use. Let's say they let him keep his trailer here twenty-four hours, all for free, plying his trade. He gets to sell his dubious wares rent-free; maybe they even give him a little bonus in his pocket for not asking questions and being a good boy. All he has to do is keep his eyes open while working and wait until night when the Ministry send one of their own guards. That way the entrance has twenty-four-hour surveillance, with the minimum of manpower and fuss."

"Or it could be that he's just a mobile burger seller, big fat and greasy, and nothing more?" Nigel suggested.

"Well, I'll tell you something for nothing. I, for one, am not waiting to find out." Boag-Munroe motioned for Nigel to move out of his way: "Stand aside!" He kicked the door with all his force and with a hint of professionalism that suggested he'd been in similar situations. But the door didn't budge.

"First we were trying to get in and now we're trying to get out." Nigel still looked panicked.

"I'm trying to let a little air in. I won't be a second. I'll just get the door open and then we can continue with our search." Boag-Munroe kicked out again. Still the door didn't budge.

Nigel turned to the professor, "You were saying?"

"It normally works," Boag-Munroe scowled back.

"So I guess we're stuck here."

"Not for long." Boag-Munroe had heard footsteps. The door was unbolted and swung open. Three uniformed policemen were waiting outside.

CHAPTER THIRTY-FIVE

Mary breathed a sigh of relief that John's parents had taken Andrew for the night. They had been understanding but, then again, like her, they were still in shock. Mary felt guilty again. They had every right to grieve, they were his parents. And what was she? His estranged wife who had only just returned under sufferance. Also, when it came down to it, if she hadn't returned John would still be alive. It would all come out in the end and everybody would know the cold hard facts. Not that it mattered; not when she was already tormented by the truth. It was the truth of a matter she knew all too well, and worse still, so did Andrew. He had been only too willing to go with his grandparents. Mary could not have found it in herself to stop him, even if she'd wanted to. Who could blame him for not wanting to be near her? Who else did he have to turn to but John's parents? It felt as though she was losing a son as well as a husband. She had never felt so lonely. Not even in her darkest hours as a child. This was one situation she knew she couldn't just walk away from. This was forever.

She wavered over the next phone number in her list and found herself doing something she'd sworn she'd never do. She rang a number she'd embedded deep at the back of her mind.

After five rings her mother picked up the phone.

"I'm glad you came."

"You don't sound so sure."

The frail old woman hobbled into Mary's living room. Mary stood back, almost as if she was in awe. There was certainly a presence about the old woman. Frail and hobbling she may have been but her aura was still intact. Mary had the feeling that if she'd have said one thing out of turn to the old woman, and she would have bitten Mary's head off. Indeed from experience Mary knew it to be the case. She had always been an unforgiving, unrelenting woman, and for all intents and purposes, Mary couldn't see any reason why anything should have changed about her.

"Sit down," Mary nervously offered her a chair.

Her mother hovered over the chair, almost deliberately defying the offer of a seat.

Finally and in her own good time she sat.

"John's dead." Mary was surprised how coldly she had made the announcement.

"I'm very sorry to hear that."

There was a silence.

"Why did you come?" Mary asked nervously, feeling like a child all over again.

The old woman paused before she answered: "Because you asked me to."

Mary braced herself. "It was John who asked you first."
"I know. I took the call. That was why I wrote to you."
"You wanted to see me then?"
Once again she paused, "Some answers aren't that clear-cut. But I'm here."
"But do you want to be here?" Now, even Mary's voice grew childlike.
The old woman held her breath for what seemed like an age. "You're my daughter."
"It doesn't seem like that though, does it?" Mary winced.
The old woman's face stayed as unflinching as ever. "No, it doesn't."
"You got here quickly enough."
"A neighbour brought me," the old woman snapped back. "It was an hour's drive exactly." She paused, losing a little of her coldness, "How did John die?"
"An accident." Mary didn't want to elaborate any further.
"Did he suffer?"
Mary shrugged her shoulders. "I don't think so. It was quick."
"These things are never pleasant."
Mary shuffled her feet and bowed her head.
"He's dead," the old woman spoke.
Mary lifted her head, wondering what her mother was talking about.
"Your father. He died ten years ago. A year after we last saw you."
"I know," she replied guiltily.
Mary's mind flashed back to the final argument to which her mother was referring. The argument when she had finally revealed all to her mother.
"I was sorry, believe it or not," Mary jerked herself back into the present.
The old woman brushed a speck of dust from her knee. "These things happen."
"Would you like a drink?" Mary offered, but her heart didn't sound in it.
The old woman took her time considering the offer. "No, thank you. My neighbour is waiting outside. It took an hour to get here, so it's going to take an hour to get back." She stood shakily, but still with presence. "It's been nice seeing you, Mary. I'm sorry to hear about John."

Mary watched at the window as the neighbour helped her mother into the car. Some old wounds could never heal, and some things were obviously best forgotten.

"I suppose they're part of your conspiracy theory too?" Nigel was being sarcastic about the police who had arrested them.
"They might be," replied Boag-Munroe none too convincingly, as they sat handcuffed in the back of a police car.
Outside, the three officers were talking amongst themselves.
"Yes they might," replied Nigel even more sarcastically, showing he too was

not convinced. "You do realise they'll throw the book at us? The list they've got is endless. Aggravated breaking and entering, GBH, not to mention insulting a police officer."

"I only asked if he was a real police officer."

"And he was very insulted. Nobody likes to be questioned if they're real or not. And what did you expect him to say if he was bogus? 'No I'm not'? It would defeat the object of him going to all that trouble in the first place."

"You can normally tell by their eyes when they're lying."

Nigel turned away as best he could while handcuffed. "I don't believe any of this is happening."

"The police have them."

"Yes, I know, Miss Cutts. I've new intelligence coming through this very minute."

"You mean one of your men has rung you up on his mobile phone." Miss Cutts' tone was sharp.

"One of *our* men, Miss Cutts, one of ours." Nondescript repeated the words for added effect stressing the word 'ours'.

"Boag-Munroe found exactly what we didn't want him to."

"Obviously." Nondescript began to sound tired.

"So there was no point in moving our position."

Nondescript almost found himself goaded into replying. He stopped just short of saying what he really wanted to say and smiled, "Our positional move is still equally valid, and as for Boag-Munroe, it seems that he has fallen perfectly into the trap that we had prepared."

"That you had prepared." The way she spat the words, it sounded like she was a little jealous.

"That *we* prepared, Miss Cutts." Pomposity seeped from him.

Whatever Miss Cutts' reply was, it was not audible, as she silently chewed her words, along with her lip.

"The measures have worked perfectly." He grew even more pompous, "and we can let the police handle them for now."

Miss Cutts slinked off. Nondescript might think himself to be her superior but, in her eyes, he was far from it. She also knew Boag-Munroe wouldn't be captive for long. What she hadn't reckoned on was the screaming pain that suddenly entered her head. She fell to the floor in agony.

A man ran towards Miss Cutts in what looked like an effort to help. But proceeded to run past her, so wrapped up in the panic that surrounded him. He ran on and into Nondescript's makeshift office shouting something about the readings going off the scales.

Miss Cutts already knew, as always, even as she writhed around the floor.

An uneasy feeling surrounded Boag-Munroe as they travelled to the police station. It wasn't the feeling connected to the arrest, or the consequences of it, but more of an emotion forewarning that a major catastrophe was about to erupt.

Which indeed it was.

The police car skidded to a barely controlled halt. Boag-Munroe peered through the window as best he could. A massive gaping hole had swallowed up part of the road in front of them. Both Boag-Munroe and Nigel recognised the hole. It was the same type they had encountered as eight year olds.

"What the…?" The officer in the driving seat was about to swear, but found that words now failed him. At first he thought his hands were shaking at the wheel because of his own nervous tremor. When he looked towards his colleague he realised that wasn't true. The whole of the car was shaking.

Both officers jumped from the vehicle.

"Don't tell me this is your doing," Nigel whispered to Boag-Munroe half-heartedly, "because if it is, it's one hell of an escape plot."

"I can't take credit for this but I think if at any time a sharp exit was called for, it's now."

They both turned to catch the officers' horror as they realised that the second police car, which had been travelling ahead of them, carrying the third officer, had now vanished, along with the road.

"It's time to go." Boag-Munroe lashed his foot through the window.

"Hey!" a still-stunned officer shouted, "What do you think you're doing?" He was going to shout again but fell silent, in awe, at the ear-splitting roar of the ground being ripped apart.

A large tremor shook the car, threatening to turn it on its side.

The officer opened the door to release Boag-Munroe and Nigel, but Boag-Munroe had already exited through a window.

"Release us now." Boag-Munroe waved his handcuffs.

The second officer, a younger man, protested: "We can't do that."

The first officer retorted: "Who's going to tell? The only other person who knows we nicked them is the sergeant and he's just driven in his car down that bloody great hole. I don't know about you, but I'm off."

He quickly freed the prisoners from their handcuffs and jumped back into the car. The young officer followed him without further questions. The car sped away.

"Should we be stood here gawping down at this hole?" Nigel asked in a dream-like state.

"To be honest, I don't think it's the best idea in the world." Both men moved back from the edge.

"Still, you did say you wanted to find an entrance," argued Nigel.

The earth buckled again, almost tipping both men over the edge. They fell to their knees, but quickly clambered back up.

The earth stopped grumbling. A strange calm silence descended.

Until the ground roared again. It opened up underneath Boag-Munroe.

The strange calm silence fell again.

Nigel, still dazed, managed to scramble back to his feet. Thirty-five years old, not eight, but it didn't alter the fact that he was peering down a similar mine shaft hole as he had so many years earlier. And as before, Boag-Munroe had vanished into its darkness below.

CHAPTER THIRTY-SIX

"What the hell's happening?" Sam Herbert clutched the steering wheel.

"*It* is happening," Red replied.

"It?" Sam had either done or seen it all before, but even he felt panic in this situation. A chunk of Northwich countryside had been swallowed up, right in front of them.

"My premonitions. This was the reason. This is what it's all been about." The earth bucked again. "God's retribution for mankind's treatment of children. I knew it would happen. I tried to stop it but I failed."

A large tree tumbled down into a fast-appearing crater. Sam spun the car round.

"What are you doing?" shouted Red.

"I'm not about to go on a wild goose chase for a friend you ain't seen in years. No way. I don't know if this is judgement day or not, but shit's happening. Heavy-duty, dangerous shit."

"He's here, I know it. He came in my dream."

"I'm more concerned with reality. Reality as in saving my arse."

Red made an effort to grab the wheel, slamming his foot down on the brake in the process.

The car spun out of control before juddering to a halt.

"Stupid bastard," Sam cursed, before lashing out at Red and pushing him out onto the road.

He sped off, leaving Red wiping blood away from his mouth. He crossed the road and peered down the hole into which the tree had disappeared. The next second, the ground parted where he stood and he followed it.

"Everybody hold your positions," Nondescript ordered, "we're quite safe. The salt mines don't run under here." Nobody looked in a panic. Four people held their positions at their computers.

A youngish woman entered the room, the first person to have an air of panic about her. "The emergency services can't cope. At least ten people up to now are feared dead."

"And what do you suggest we do?" Miss Cutts appeared from behind the girl.

"Miss Cutts – nice to see you've recovered," Nondescript greeted her.

Miss Cutts turned to him. "I apologise for any worry I may have caused. The outpouring of psychic energy was massive. Even I didn't suspect it could ever be so strong or so sudden."

"No need to apologise, Miss Cutts. In fact we won't hear of it," Nondescript tried to smile, "But things are going totally out of control." The girl's panic began to rise, so much so, it seemed to be affecting others in the room, as they now either fidgeted at their computer terminals or stopped worked entirely to watch the scene unfold.

"Information? Is that all this is about – collecting information?" the girl screeched. "People are going to get killed."

Nondescript put a reassuring hand on her shoulder. "And many more people may die if we don't collect the information we need. We have to think long term. The good of the country."

The girl seemed to calm herself. If one could calm oneself when so close to hell that you could hear it breaking loose.

"James?" Nigel's voice echoed downward.

Boag-Munroe could hear his friend's voice. That proved at least one thing: he was alive, even though things did still seem to be left hanging in the balance. For the moment he didn't do or say anything. He moved his right hand slightly, feeling the wire mesh of a lift underneath it. The lift tilted. It wasn't a good feeling.

"James?" Nigel shouted once more.

"It's OK," Boag-Munroe shouted back, "I've landed on some kind of lift." He moved his head slowly to look down. The darkness was complete.

"What is it with me and abandoned mines?" muttered Boag-Munroe under his breath.

"What should we do?" shouted Nigel.

Boag-Munroe felt the rusty chain holding the lift give a little. "Nothing strikes me off-hand, but if you've got any ideas, feel free."

Nigel didn't have any ideas.

With nothing else for it, Boag-Munroe began to shuffle across the lift. With every muscle he moved, the lift swayed further and harder, until by the time he reached the lift cable and began to climb up, the lift was swinging like a pendulum.

"What are you doing down there?" shouted Nigel.

"Doing my best to get out," Boag-Munroe shouted back, losing his temper a little at the ludicrous nature of the question.

His best it may have been, but sometimes the best, no matter how admirable, just isn't good enough. The rusty cable that had already suffered a major blow cushioning his fall, finally gave way. The lift hurtled down with Boag-Munroe clinging to the top for dear life. Finally, after what felt like an eternity, the lift crashed, crumpling like a cross between a concertina and a spring. More than likely it was this spring element that kept Boag-Munroe alive if unconscious.

Nigel stood, silent in horror, his ears ringing from the horrific screeching sound of red-hot metal screaming down the mine walls. Once the screeching had stopped, Nigel felt completely lost.

As lost as Boag-Munroe seventy feet below ground.

Red wasn't sure if he was alive or dead, but then again that wasn't so unusual for him, he hadn't been sure for a long time. After a minute's reflection, he had done enough to convince himself this wasn't another drink-, or drugs-fuelled nightmare. It was still a nightmare, nonetheless, but a real and living one. Reality was so very often the worst nightmare of all for him. He could well do without the cold and total darkness of the reality that surrounded him. He coughed, his lungs felt as though they were full of heavy smoke. He could also taste the vile flavour of his own blood. Then there were the aches, the pain in every bone in his body. He moved; the pain and total darkness dulling his senses so much he couldn't tell if he was seated or standing. He outstretched a hand; it touched nothing. He was in limbo. The only thing Red Leather could now think of, apart from the never-ending pain, was the growing panic. He was injured and alone. The world had caved in and taken him with it.

Desmond spied his chance; the chance was now or never. His initial disillusionment and distrust had grown into something more. He was more than uncomfortable and suspicious –he was now frightened. He knew there would come a time when Red would have to let them go but the term constituting 'letting go' could mean something a lot more sinister than merely setting them free. Desmond didn't think Red and his cohort would let any of them free now. It had gone on for too long. It wasn't so much of a game any more, and if it was, Red had too much to lose. Of course Desmond had not discussed this with any of his fellow, happier captives. Although there had been the odd murmur of unease from a couple of the older kids, it wasn't substantial enough to start a revolt. Besides, Desmond didn't know if he could trust any of them. His father's words rang in his ears: "The only person you can trust is yourself."

Though Desmond wasn't so sure about that. Trusting himself had got him into this state to begin with. He'd been flattered that a singer from the telly should be interested in him, to throw money at him, to invite him to play a harmless game, a trick. Some trick. Desmond had now decided he'd waited long enough to hear the audience applaud this so-called trick. Without telling the others he made his way to the bathroom. Once there, he began to put into action the plan he had been formulating in his brain over the past two days. It seemed about the best and safest bet. He locked the bathroom door behind him, grabbed hold of the loo brush and standing on the sink, set about attacking the ceiling. Any noise he made as he battered the plaster was drowned out by the loud, 5.1 digital sound system, powering out from the DVD player that was entertaining the others in their room. By the time suspicions from the others about what he was doing were aroused, he had nearly made a hole big enough to fit through.

Someone knocked on the door but whoever it was they were too late. He hoisted himself up and into the hole that he'd made in the ceiling, hoping that it would lead him to freedom.

It didn't take much time before he had discovered that his new surroundings was an attic. It was a massive affair but the part he had broken into seemed to contain a collection of junk. Going forward, he found himself in an area that was a cross between a shrine and a personal museum to the disputable talents of Red Leather. Luckily for Red, he wasn't interested in stealing any keepsakes; he was satisfied with the money in his pockets. Finding a skylight, he opened it and left. Unafraid of heights and with the excitement of escape, he scrambled across the roof of Red's mansion until he came to a drainpipe. Within seconds he had shinned down it and was on the final lap for freedom across the mansion's neatly trimmed lawns. He ran as fast as he could, troubled by the feeling of being so exposed. The garden's security fence seemed miles away and there was no foliage or trees to hide in if someone was alerted to his escape bid.

Halfway across the lawn, breathlessness setting in, he got the first signs his escape bid had been noticed.

Three pit bull terrier guard dogs were rapidly gaining ground on him. For all their intensity and viciousness, they might as well have been a pride of lions.

Desmond didn't scream; fear strangled his throat. In one respect it was in his favour. He'd need every bit of energy to reach the fence before they pounced on him.

The fence seemed miles away. He wasn't going to make it.

Even though he was concentrating on the scene ahead, the fence in particular, he couldn't help but imagine the pursuing, baying dogs. He could almost smell their vile breath; sense their putrid evil presence.

Desmond felt his energy sapping, his legs buckling, his pace slowing.

He wasn't going to make it.

Behind him the dogs grew louder, closer.

He didn't make it.

Thrown to the ground by the force of one of the animals, he screamed at the pain of teeth ripping at him from every direction. He threw his arms over his face but it was all to no avail, as the pack ripped at him like a rag doll.

The frenzied dog attack happened straight in front of Sam Herbert. He was still in the distance and helpless to stop it, even though he had put his foot down on the accelerator and blasted his car horn. Swinging the car to a stop, he jumped out. Two of the dogs backed away, the third he dispatched with the baseball bat that always travelled underneath the passenger seat. With horror, Sam looked down at the ripped and bloodied face of the boy. He hadn't meant this to happen, not this.

The boy was still screaming, more so with fear than pain. Sam tried to cradle Desmond's head in his arms but the boy screamed more as pieces of torn flesh slid off or hung precariously from his face.

No matter that Sam hadn't meant for any of this to happen: it had.

But what was he going to do now?

There were two clear-cut options. He could get help for the boy and with that, seal his own fate. Or he could turn his back as if he hadn't seen anything, take his money and anything he could lay his hands on that belonged to Red… and run, never coming back or even looking back.

Two options.

Sam thought for a second. The boy was finally released from his pain now as he slipped into unconsciousness. Sam gently rested his head back on the ground.

His decision was made.

CHAPTER THIRTY-SEVEN

Boag-Munroe was still alive and in one piece, even if he didn't feel like it. He eased himself from the crushed lift and onto uneven rocky ground. He produced a wafer thin-torch from his pocket that illuminated, quite surprisingly, a large area of space. He knelt down to examine a shiny lump of rock.

"Rock salt. It seems Northwich salt mines have managed to get me to visit after all." He tossed the rock aside and continued to examine the thin corridor in which he had landed. The compact space between the walls had slowed the lift down, so impact had not been that hard. He shone his torch up towards the tracks the lift had made on its way down. He could see no daylight and could hear nothing. He looked around him, searching for a way out with the torchlight cutting through the darkness. There was only one way that seemed remotely likely. It was the passage he was in and it was leading further down into the bowels of the earth, to such an impenetrable darkness that even Boag-Munroe's high-powered light stood no chance of illuminating it at that distance. He would have to investigate further.

"The only way is down it seems. Just my luck," he muttered as he made his way down what seemed like an endless tunnel. "Probably a dead end." He stopped talking to himself and halted all movement. For the slightest of seconds he was sure he had glimpsed the same kind of shadowy figures he had seen before in his dark daydream-like states.

The professor had a funny feeling he was here for a purpose, and good or bad, whatever it was, it lay ahead. He moved on. Only to stop again. This time because he heard a sound. He strained his ears. It was a child's sobbing.

The light on his torch wavered, lurching him in and out of darkness. The crying stopped. His torch went dead. Boag-Munroe stood still in the blackness.

"Please help us," an ageless, sexless voice hissed from out of the darkness.

He stood still.

"Help us, please!" the voice drifted away.

Boag-Munroe's torch came back to life.

He moved on towards the end of the tunnel. But another ten strides forward and he stopped in his tracks yet again. At the end of the tunnel a figure was illuminated by his torchlight. Boag-Munroe moved the torch back and forth but the figure didn't move, simply stood still, silhouetted in the darkness.

"Good evening," Boag-Munroe shouted.

At first, silence, then… "I knew you'd come."

Boag-Munroe stepped forward with caution. He found the voice strangely familiar.

"I'm sure you did," replied Boag-Munroe.

"It's good to see you again after all these years."

Boag-Munroe's torchlight fell upon the features of Red Leather.

"I dreamt about you, you see," said Red.

"You don't say?" Boag-Munroe was still weighing the strange situation up, before he'd let himself indulge in any petty pleasantries.

"It's been a long time," Red beamed.

"Time waits for no one, or so they say," Boag-Munroe replied rather standoffishly.

"At least you were prepared." Red nodded to Boag-Munroe's torch, "I've been stumbling about in the dark. In more ways than one."

Boag-Munroe's torch went dead.

"Now what?" Red asked, his voice seeming to take on a new echo in the darkness.

Boag-Munroe didn't answer. Within a few seconds the light came to life again. "New batteries. Like you said, I came prepared."

The sound of a single unseen pickaxe rang out around the passage they were in. Both men looked at one another, startled.

"I take it you can hear that?"

"I can," replied an ashen-faced Red. "What do you think it is?"

"Echoes from the past, trying to catch up with the present."

"Ghosts?" Red's fear was illuminated even in the surrounding darkness.

The sound of the pickaxe stopped.

"Call them what you like. What's down the passage you just came from?"

"Nothing really. I mean I couldn't see anything, until I saw the flicker of your light and I followed it here."

The pickaxe started again.

"There it is again." Red looked even more startled on hearing it a second time.

Boag-Munroe frowned, "Something's trying to get our attention. By the sound of it, I judge the noise is coming from behind where I came in. I think that's probably the best place to start."

"Start to do what though?"

The pickaxe stopped. The silence hung heavily.

"Find a way out. But deep down, something tells me the only way we're going to do that is if we find out why we're here in the first place."

They came to the crumpled lift that had been Boag-Munroe's ride to this strange underground nether world.

Red ignored the shattered lift and surveyed the stack of rocks that were blocking the passage and them from going any further. "It's a dead end."

Boag-Munroe outstretched his hand, touching the cold rock. "The sound came from here."

"How can you be so sure?"

Once more the pickaxe resumed its work, and this time it was obvious its origins came from behind the lump of rocks.

Boag-Munroe turned to Red with a knowing glance but Red backed away from the rocks and the chilling sound that was emitting from behind them, "We're doomed aren't we?"

Boag-Munroe was a little more hopeful, "Not quite."

Red shook with panic, "I don't know what to do."

Once again the sound stopped. The wait for it to start again was filled with tension.

"You don't know what to do? That's simple." Boag-Munroe grabbed a chunk of rock and tossed it to one side, "You help me to dig."

Red stepped back. A mixture of fear and unwillingness to get his hands dirty was the cause of his reluctance.

"We dig as quickly as possible in fact. Come on, dig."

Red dug reluctantly.

The ghostly pickaxe sound drifted up once more from behind the rocks. Red recoiled in horror, his features bathed in sweat.

"No. We're not meant to do this," Red panicked.

"Then what are we supposed to do?" Boag-Munroe calmly asked.

Red backed off even further. "The children. We were supposed to help the children."

"What children?" He surveyed the manic look in Red's eyes. He might not have seen Red for a number of years, but he knew the man was unstable enough as a kid, so heaven knows what a rock'n'roll lifestyle had done to him.

"It was all for the children, you see. That's why I did what I had to do."

"What did you do?"

Red got a hold of himself. "Nothing. I haven't done anything."

"If you've got any information on anything that may have something to do with us being down here, now is the time to tell me, believe it."

"You go on as if we were brought here on purpose. It was an accident." Although Red said it, he didn't sound convinced.

Boag-Munroe hit back, "You mean an accident that happened all those years ago and has been with us ever since, embedded in us, waiting. Waiting until the time was right."

The pickaxe stopped.

"We carry on," Boag-Munroe was adamant.

They both carried on although Red's heart was obviously not in it. After about ten minutes and two torch battery changes later, Boag-Munroe stopped abruptly. Red followed likewise.

"Get back!" Boag-Munroe shouted, pushing Red aside as rocks came tumbling down en masse. The small passage space became engulfed with a mixture of smoky dust and coughing. From the reopened tunnel, the atmosphere that escaped took the breath away. Even Boag-Munroe had to brace himself as he felt the cries of fear, pain and sorrow crash through and around his body.

"I could have been killed," coughed Red, eyeing the rock fall. "You could have been killed."

Boag-Munroe wiped the dust away from his eyes. "No, I couldn't. It isn't my time yet, nor my place."

"What?"

"I won't die here. A friend predicted my death or rather, as I've said before, where it happens… and it wasn't here. So chin up, eh?"

"And this friend is reliable?" Red looked agog.

"She knows her stuff. You can just tell that with some people, can't you?"

"And what about me?"

"What about you?"

"Did anyone mention my death?"

"You weren't even mentioned. So looking on the not-so-bright side, you're right, you could have been killed just then, or any second now for that matter."

The dust cleared quicker than Red could think of a retort. Not that it mattered. Before the dust had settled or cleared, Boag-Munroe had already vanished into what was left of the dusty smoke screen. Red, still coughing, stumbled over the rubble and into the unknown.

Boag-Munroe, as ever, was quite at home in the unknown. He stood in the large cavern area in which they found themselves. Around them at their feet were human skeletons. Of people who looked as though they had died trying to dig their way out.

"A cave-in." Boag-Munroe kneeled beside one of the outstretched skeletons. "They didn't stand a chance."

Red, horrified, looked down at some of the smaller skeletons scattered about. "Children?"

"Don't look so surprised. Child labour would be standard when this was all up and running."

"It was the children I did it for." Red started to babble, "It was meant to make them see what they were doing to children, the neglect, the uncaring nature, the disregard for them in modern society."

"Don't be so hard on yourself. This isn't anything you've caused. Not in this lifetime at any rate."

"This life?"

"Past echoes are all well and good, but you have to wonder why they chose us all those years ago. You see, you can't forget – this has been with us since we were eight, when we had that accident."

What little colour Red had completely vanished. "You mean…" He couldn't bring himself to finish his sentence.

Boag-Munroe finished it for him: "Yes, they've been with us all this time." He pointed to the skeletons.

"What do they want?" Red spluttered.

"To get out, I suppose. They've waited a long time. It had to be now or it would have been never."

Realisation dawned on Red. "The Council… they're filling the mines in."

"Obviously whatever's down here sensed that. They've made their break for freedom just as they tried to all those years ago."

Red surveyed the skeletons with horror. "They must have died suffering."

"Obviously, and it's that fact which has made their presence linger on. So many of them, so much suffering, it's made them strong." Boag-Munroe took a deep breath, "And now it's up to us to end their suffering."

"How?"

"To do what we were brought here to do. Give them one final look of daylight before giving them a proper burial."

"We can't carry all these. There are so many." Red looked forlorn, "So many children."

"They stretched out to us all those years ago. If you remember, that was just as they were building the car park. This had remained festering for all those years, before they disturbed it. So they reached out, and we just happened to be there, or were meant to be there. But we didn't finish the job. We were too young, too scared, we didn't understand. But somehow, a little piece of them escaped and came with us, both of us, just waiting to call us back down when it was disturbed again."

"The filling-in process?"

"Exactly."

Boag-Munroe held a finger to his lips, grabbed Red's arm and ushered them behind an old cart.

"We're not alone," whispered Boag-Munroe, urging Red to stay down and hidden beside him, "and I'm not just talking about ghosts."

Red held his breath, anticipation sweeping over him. "Footsteps?"

Boag-Munroe nodded. He too heard the echo of footsteps. His torch went dead.

"Switch the light off, good idea," whispered Red, trying to sound brave.

"I didn't. The batteries have run down again. And the thing is, I haven't got any more."

"Do you mean we're trapped here in total darkness?"

"Yes. Exciting thought, isn't it?" Boag-Munroe replied.

"Terribly exiting." A bright torch blazed into Red and Boag-Munroe's eyes. "You do realise this is private property?"

Boag-Munroe stood up, brushing himself down. "Posing as miners now, are we?"

Smith's torch stayed trained on Red and the professor, unflinching in its persistence. Beside him stood Jones. Boag-Munroe could just make out past the light that Jones was carrying a handgun.

"Do you have a lot of trouble with the locals, then?" Boag-Munroe pointed in the direction of the gun, and then the skeletons.

"Only the live ones," Smith answered quickly and with a sinister look.

"But what do you lot define as alive or dead?" Boag-Munroe asked the two men.

They didn't attempt an answer.

Boag-Munroe turned his attention to Red. "You've not met the Ministry of the Dead before, I take it?"

Red shook his head, his eyes fixed on the gun. For years he'd had nightmares about a crazed fan shooting him. It was standard rock star territory, but unpleasant and frightening nevertheless.

"So now what do we do?" Boag-Munroe tried for an answer but only an awkward silence came forward. The torchlight flickered away from them, but the gun seemed to move menacingly closer.

"You shouldn't be down here," Jones said.

"None of us should be down here if truth be told. These included." Boag-Munroe pointed to the huddle of skeletons.

"So what do you suggest we do?" Smith asked with a hint of menace.

"I suggest you two give Red and me a hand and we start to take the dead to the surface to get the proper burial they deserve."

"I'm afraid that won't be possible, for the moment at least." Jones spoke softly, and raised the gun to train it on Boag-Munroe more closely.

Red took this movement as his autocue to take action himself. Head down, he ran like a mad man, ducking and diving through the darkness. The torch, however powerful and unflinching, could get no more than a fleeting glance of him. Even the sound of a shot ringing out did nothing to deter Red. By the time Jones and Smith had turned their attention back to Boag-Munroe, he too was gone.

"Bastard!" cursed Smith.

"Stay calm. We've got a job to do," said Jones.

"Don't you think I bloody well know that? It was a job and a half to start with, and now it's just got a damn sight harder."

Jones remained cool, "And how do you make that out?"

"We've got to go running around here trying to find those clowns whilst hoping the damn place doesn't collapse on us."

"If those clowns, as you call them, don't want to be found down here, then they won't. Our orders were not specifically to find them, just to prevent them, or anyone, from removing the skeletons. As far as I'm concerned we've done that."

"That won't be the end of it though," said Smith.

Jones smiled, "If they come back, what does it matter? The filling-in process has already started. We've got the only viable exit under guard. They can hardly fly out. It's only a matter of time."

"You mean leave them in here to get buried alive?" asked Smith.

"We offered them a way out. What do you suggest? Go hunting in these unsafe mines?"

"We were supposed to make sure the skeletons stayed untouched."

"Who's going to know? Even mind readers, the psychics, those supposedly in the know, can't work this place out. As far as I'm concerned, it's time to leave well alone."

"But the skeletons…?"

"What are they going to do with them? They can't make it to the surface, I've told you, we'll be guarding the only exit."

Smith grimaced, "There may be other ways out. It's all going haywire. They made it down here so they may be able to get back to the surface. We have to find them."

The tunnel shook.

"I'm going up top," said Jones

"You can try, but remember – I have the torch." Smith stood firm.

"Yes," replied Jones icily, "but I have the gun."

Smith felt the tremor up his spine. Everywhere shook.

"I tell you what, Smith, I'll leave you to do your job."

"Sometimes finding our way out isn't the easiest of tasks." Boag-Munroe's voice echoed out through the darkness.

Jones' match went out.

"Jones!" Smith shouted.

There was no reply.

"Jones! Answer me!"

More silence.

"Do you think you can find your way out now, without your friend holding your hand?" the unseen Boag-Munroe asked.

"If it's games you want, you've come to the right place," Smith answered with a touch of bravado.

His torchlight began to wane. "Shit!" he whispered, "That wasn't supposed to happen."

The torchlight went out.

"You were saying about games?" Boag-Munroe's voice echoed through the darkness.

Smith couldn't tell if he really had heard or felt a presence come up behind him. It was either that or his imagination. He fired a shot anyway. The resulting fire temporarily lit up the darkness, but gave away nothing of any significance.

"Shit!" Smith muttered again.

"If you know what's good for you you'll stop firing the gun. Things like that have a habit of causing accidents, especially in enclosed spaces like this. Look what happened to your friend."

Smith spun round wildly. He could still not tell where the voice was coming from, and no eyes, never mind his, stood any chance of becoming accustomed to the pitch darkness.

"Jones!" Smith shouted to no avail.

"He can't hear you," replied Boag-Munroe. "I'll give you another twenty seconds to put the gun down."

Smith fired a shot.

Something flew past him. He realised too late that it was a rock and wasted another shot.

"You're wasting time and shots," shouted Boag-Munroe, hammering the point home.

Smith thought he felt Boag-Munroe's closeness. He fired yet again.

"Another one down. There can't be many bullets left. At this rate it'll soon be just you and me left weaponless. Won't that be nice?"

Smith gripped the gun tighter. He steadied his nerves. He'd been in the Paras for ten years, damn it; he'd seen and done it all. He'd done even more when he'd joined the Ministry. A droplet of cold sweat fell from his brow. He couldn't afford to waste any more ammo. He had to hold fire, had to wait until Boag-Munroe made his move.

Boag-Munroe made his move while Smith was toying with these thoughts. Boag-Munroe had deduced that, by this time, Smith would be a bit less trigger-happy and more likely to hang on to his remaining bullets. He'd calculated that now was the time to throw himself at Smith.

Sadly, Smith was quicker than expected.

A shot rang out.

Both men fell to the ground… and only Boag-Munroe got up. He turned his torch back on, dragging out the final drops of the battery power. Smith was lying on his back on the floor, blood oozing from a wound in his shoulder.

"That needs seeing to." Boag-Munroe knelt beside him trying to get a better look at the injury, with his dying torchlight.

"If you hadn't been playing silly bastards…" Smith spat.

"And if you hadn't been trying to shoot me. We could argue all day, but all the time you're losing more blood and this place is becoming even less stable." He dragged Smith to his feet, steadying him as best he could. "Where's the way out?"

Smith wasn't forthcoming.

"Do we have to do it the hard way?" He let Smith fall back onto the hard ground and stood over him. "I don't know if you've noticed or not but I'm getting a little tired of all this."

"And so am I, Professor," Jones' voice whispered in the darkness.

Boag-Munroe felt a piece of cold metal pressed to his forehead. He could imagine Jones' itchy finger, pressing dangerously hard on the trigger.

CHAPTER THIRTY-EIGHT

Nigel ran. He carried on running even though he felt like his innards would burst if he ran anymore. He was definitely running on empty now, but was determined not to give in and let his friend down. After gazing down helplessly into the hole where Boag-Munroe had fallen, he'd finally shaken himself into action to get some help. Though it wasn't going to be easy, especially when all the phone lines seemed to be down. When it had dawned on Nigel to use his mobile, the emergency services had assured him that matters were in hand and that his friend would soon be found. The voice had possessed an air of calmness, which Nigel had found anything but reassuring, more disturbing if anything. More than ever, he felt like a number and an insignificant number at that. So he carried on running towards home, to get the van and get real help. People who would listen to him, people that just might be able to help him find Boag-Munroe. It was a long shot and he didn't know if they'd be up to the job. But, if he was to be completely honest, he really didn't think he was either.

The van now in sight, he spurted forward. Climbing into it, he caught his breath before turning on the engine. Now all he could hope for was that Jason, Bradley and the Gentle brothers could be found and quickly. They weren't much of a hope, but between them, who knows? Only time and desperation would tell.

"They've managed to stop Boag-Munroe," Miss Cutts informed the nondescript man.

"What about Red Leather?" Nondescript enquired.

"Nothing, for the moment. But they'll find him soon enough."

"Are you sure of that?"

"I'm sure."

"Well then, seeing as you're sure, Miss Cutts, far be it from me to question otherwise."

"My record does speak for itself."

"Indeed it does. Still, we both have abundant faith in Jones and Smith to do the job in hand."

"Yes we do," said Miss Cutts, her agreement sounding none too convincing.

"We only have to hope now that things settle down a bit."

"They should in time."

"But do you think they will, Miss Cutts? That's the question."

"It may be the question but I don't have all the answers." She paused. "Just some of them."

"Personally, and I hope you don't think I'm being too blasé, I think we're home and dry. All indications suggest that the danger levels are levelling out."

"I see."

"You don't agree?"

"I think we should send another person down there. Someone more likely to be responsive."

Nondescript laughed. "Miss Cutts, really!" He stopped, then began to realise she was being serious. "You don't need me to inform you of the dangers that could pose to someone responsive."

"It might be the only way."

"Miss Cutts, those mines have already cost the life of one of our own."

"She wasn't powerful enough."

"Maybe she was too powerful, too receptive."

"If she'd been better endowed, she would have been able to protect herself."

"Miss Cutts, out of the five receptive people we've sent down there, one has died, one has gone mad, and although the others have returned to work, albeit at different stations, all reports suggest they haven't been the same since."

"It's all well and good sending the soldier boys down, but what can they do?"

"They're doing their job as instructed."

"I could go down there."

"With respect, Miss Cutts, only a couple of hours ago, you couldn't cope with the higher levels of psychic stress. Or had you forgotten?"

"Send me down to the mine."

"I'm sorry, Miss Cutts, but it's out of the question."

"Then on your head be it."

Miss Cutts silently slipped away. Nondescript knew what she was up to and to the same extent, she knew that Nondescript knew what she was doing. Still, she was doing it anyway and he was quite willing to allow it. Miss Cutts was useful enough, but quite irritating. Whatever would be, would be. What made the situation even better for him was that it was on her head.

Mary was alone. Andrew was still with John's parents. She couldn't even think of looking him or them in the eye. Not yet at least. Sue was a dead loss in this situation. To be honest, Mary couldn't even bear to think about seeing her: her own best friend. Mary would have to cope with being alone, even though it was one of the two things she didn't relish coping with in life. Death was the other thing; it made her think about her own mortality, the time she would be alone, truly, once and for all.

Weighing all this up in her head brought Mary back to square one again. It seemed to be a position she frequented for the greater part of her life.

She flicked on the kettle and opened the fridge. Tea was supposed to have a calming effect on a person, so she decided tea was about as good as she could get. She searched for some milk that hadn't gone bad. There were two cartons, both open, both smelling as sour as each other. It looked like tea was off the menu. She settled for a glass of water, although she wished it had been brandy flowing out of the tap, into her glass and down her throat. Lots of it might have done the trick. But then again, in what state would that have left her? She had to look after herself now, for Andrew's sake. She was just about all he had. He'd lost too much already. She was going to make sure he didn't lose anything else. Even though, for the moment, she felt quite worthless.

She sat for a time, silent. Deep and alone in her thoughts. She thought about John, she thought about her nightmares, the apparition that had haunted her and her son. What Boag-Munroe had predicted had come true. Her mind went back to her childhood and a tale her Scottish grandmother had told her, about the screeching banshees, predicting the deaths of members of old Scottish families. If anything, it looked like her ghost had been her very own family banshee. She couldn't understand why she had worked it all out now, now that it was too late, not that it seemed she could have halted events at any rate.

Boag-Munroe. The name sprang back into her head. She had to tell him – she needed to. She reached for the phone, but stopped. She had to see him face to face. If nothing else it would get her out of the house and away from the shadow of death. She opened the door to her hall, only to be met by the horrific apparition of a familiar, faceless ghost, which was now screaming like a mad ghoul; its smooth, featureless face, no more than a couple of inches away from her own.

She collapsed on the doorstep in a deep faint.

"He's alive. I know he is," Nigel said, more grim-sounding than hopeful… as if he'd said it just for the sake of it.

"Are you sure about that?" Jason challenged.

"If you want to go home, then go," Nigel barked.

Jason fell silent. The hole they were balanced over didn't look safe to say the least, but although he was a coward, first and foremost he was lazy, and he definitely didn't fancy the long walk home.

"So you're going down there?" Jason asked half-heartedly.

Nigel threw him the end of the rope. "Tie this to that pillar box and hold on to it, just in case."

"I'll come down with you," said Bradley with surprisingly heroic resolve. "You don't know what's down there."

"Are you sure?" asked Nigel.

"Of course I'm sure. You might need me," replied Bradley, his resolve now reaching fever pitch.

Alan Gentle popped up: "We might as well pop down and have a gander about as well." Tony Gentle didn't seem as keen, the lack of keenness going so far as to etch itself onto his face. For a good few seconds it looked as if he might speak, but the seconds passed and so did Tony's chance.

"What about me?" Jason seemed a little hurt.

"Make sure nothing happens to that rope," Nigel said, hesitating over the hole.

Mrs Ruth's car came round the bend. Nigel saw it and hesitated no more, quickly disappearing down the hole, and followed by the others in quick succession.

"What's going on here, love?" Mrs Ruth was soon out of her car and ready for action.

"A rescue party," Jason explained.

"I have to say, love, thank goodness for Hannah for taking the time to ring me, to let me know what's happening and where you boys were. On the other hand, very brave and noble that you are, you're also very stupid not waiting for me. Someone could get hurt. Luckily I'm here now, equipped with all my knowledge from my St John Ambulance course, so you can relax, love."

"So what are you going to do?" Jason asked.

"I'm going to navigate things from up here," Mrs Ruth replied.

Jason looked bewildered. "Right," he uttered. It seemed the simplest thing to say.

If anyone thought Brian looked out of place, peering out through the flaps of his tent in the middle of Alderley Edge's winter foliage, then they had experienced nothing. At least not until they had seen the gigantic figure of Bruno, not merely snapping twigs with his size-twelve boots, but smashing down whole tree stalks, as he strode towards the tent like an unstoppable juggernaut. He peered down at the quivering Brian. "I have your money," boomed a voice as deep and as large as the person who owned it.

"And you are?" Brian asked quite bravely, even though he was shaking.

"I have your money," the booming voice repeated.

The giant stalked off and Brian, still dressed as Merlin, followed.

Bruno stopped. He turned back to Brian. "Bring the tent."

Brian didn't question this request. He'd hardly questioned anything in his life, apart from why he couldn't even get a walk-on part in Brookside. The tent was deconstructed in a couple of seconds under Bruno's watchful eye. Everything safely tucked under his arm, Brian followed Bruno out of the woods and to a nearby parked people-carrier. Inside the vehicle was Carter Whitlowe's son Stevie, Stevie's nurse, and Carter Whitlowe himself.

"Say hello to Merlin, everyone." Carter grinned from ear to ear with such a large and vicious-looking mouth; Brian could imagine it biting someone's head off.

He waved his hand in a feeble gesture: "Hi."

Carter put his arm round him. "Say, Merlin, you look a little weedy for such a prestigious legend but I won't hold that against you, because for all intents and purposes, it looks like you've done a fine job for me. I suppose you'll be wanting your cash now?"

Brian smiled, a weak smile. This man's mouth wasn't about to bite anyone's head off.

"I can't say I blame you. But sit tight, the end for you is nearly in sight."

Carter laughed. So did Bruno. Brian couldn't decide which of the two men scared him the most.

Now, more than ever, he wished he'd stuck to trying to get that elusive walk-on part in Brookside.

With the return of consciousness, the fear came rushing back. Mary jumped to her feet gasping for air. Now her quest to escape had taken on a new urgency. With the memory of the returning spectre, now screaming into the part of her brain that held fresh images, she rushed to her car, not even bothering to lock her front door. Thoughts of Andrew crossed her mind. Was he in some kind of danger? Even the same kind of danger as his father had been? She couldn't resist checking, and after spending half an hour in an uneasy atmosphere with her son and his grandparents, she returned to her search. A search for one man. Ringing his mobile phone got no answer but that didn't stop Mary. She blazed into Northwich, her foot firmly pressed on the accelerator.

Boag-Munroe wasn't in. Mary hammered at the front door and even climbed over the rear wall for an assault on the back door. There was nobody at home, and none of the neighbours proved to be any help. Mary settled herself on the wall outside Boag-Munroe's front door. She stayed there for a good hour before she convinced herself to pull herself together. Imagination and stress, she convinced herself, could play havoc with the sanest of minds. Had she seen the faceless man reappear or not? She wasn't so sure, not now that time had settled her nerves a little. She left Boag-Munroe's house and headed home.

A few seconds later, a watching people-carrier followed her.

CHAPTER THIRTY-NINE

Nigel was surprised at how easily he had navigated himself down into the bowels of the earth with just the aid of a rope. It may have had good thickness and sturdiness, but it wasn't the easiest descent, even when putting his torch into a pocket, and clinging on with both hands.

With a thud, Nigel let go of the rope and hit the uneven floor.

"Made it!" Nigel found that he had to speak his triumphant relief out loud to himself.

Bradley quickly followed him down.

"James?" Nigel shouted, "Are you there?"

A different answer came spiralling back as Alan Gentle came tumbling down.

"Ow!" Alan screeched, "I think I've landed a bit funny on my torch."

Thankfully, Tony Gentle descended with a bit more grace.

"We're OK down here," shouted Nigel up to the dwindling skyline.

"I'm glad to hear that, love. I've got everything under control up here."

"I bet you have," uttered Nigel in a manner almost suggesting the sentence was a curse. "We're going to move on." Nigel turned to Tony Gentle, "You sit tight here. If you see anything, just shout."

Tony Gentle looked more lost than ever.

Nigel, Bradley and Alan Gentle ventured further into the all-encompassing darkness, until their very being, torchlights included, were no more. Tony Gentle nervously surveyed his lonely dark surroundings. To his horror his torchlight fell on the huddled figure of Red Leather, rocking back and forth, his eyes closed and a grimace plastered across his face. Tony Gentle stood speechless. Red carried on rocking back and forth, until without warning and with the quickness and cunning of a snake, he sprang up and snatched the torch from Tony Gentle and headed in the direction that Nigel and the others had taken.

For all intents and purposes Boag-Munroe felt like he'd been buried alive. The darkness he'd come round in was as suffocating as the stale atmosphere. He could feel something trickling down the right-hand side of his face. He deduced it must be blood from the blow that had been administered with the butt of the gun. He jerked himself up but found his arms were stretched round his back. He'd been handcuffed to a supporting wooden beam, a beam that obviously wouldn't budge, no matter how hard he tugged at it. He got the sinking sensation that perhaps this was the fate the Ministry of the Dead had planned for him all along, no matter what their motives were. He tugged harder.

"It's no use. You'll only do yourself more harm than good." A female voice cut through the darkness, followed by a torchlight falling on his face.

"You have others down here. They've come in search of you." Miss Cutts produced a key that unlocked the handcuffs.

"It seems like they're not the only ones that have come in search of me." He was glad to be free.

"Don't mistake me. The Ministry means everything to me, but sometimes, even I can find orders a little stifling."

"It sounds to me like you're contemplating retirement?"

"In the Ministry we've had more than our fair share of comings and goings over the years, but we've still withstood anything thrown at us, me included. When this is over I shall face whatever music there is."

Boag-Munroe brushed himself down. "We need to give those bodies a proper burial."

"I sense that now, but it is too late for the others to listen. They fear it is too dangerous. But what they don't realise, is the danger will merely be reburied, like a waiting bomb, ticking until a future event allows it to go off."

"You'll help me then?"

Miss Cutts sounded surprised and hurt: "I already have."

"James?" Nigel's voice cut through the darkness.

Boag-Munroe turned back to Miss Cutts, but she had vanished.

"I'm over here!" Boag-Munroe shouted back.

Nigel and Bradley came into view.

"I bet you didn't expect to see us?" Nigel grinned.

To Nigel and the others' amazement, Red Leather came charging past.

"No more so than you didn't expect to see him," Boag-Munroe coolly replied.

"Where's he going?" asked Alan Gentle.

"Who knows? But we haven't time to dwell on it. We have to dispose of some bodies. Come on."

Between them, Boag-Munroe and the others gathered as many of the skeletons as they could manage.

"Where are you going?" Nigel quizzed Boag-Munroe, "The way out is this way."

"Instinct tells me there is an easier way." Boag-Munroe was determined to have his way.

And have his way he did. They all followed.

They didn't go far before a shaft of light came into vision. They followed it, until they came to a large ladder. Making their way up it, they found themselves in the mobile burger van. Jones and Smith were slumped unconscious in opposite corners of the floor. Placing his load down, Boag-Munroe picked up a cup of half-drunk tea. He sniffed at it. "Obviously you have to be careful what you drink round here."

Nigel placed his load down and rang Jason's mobile from his own.

"But I can't drive!" Jason's panic-stricken voice whined out from the speakerphone on Nigel's mobile.

"Try!" Nigel shouted before cutting his mobile off. He turned to the others: "He should be with us in five minutes."

Mrs Ruth was with them in two minutes. Another five minutes and Boag-Munroe was returning from another trip from down below.

"Is that everything now?" enquired Nigel.

"Just about."

"What about Red?"

"We haven't got time for him at the moment. We have to give these a decent burial, before they catch up with us."

"The Ministry of the Dead?" whispered Nigel.

"Yes. Now come on, carry on loading these bones into the car."

They carried on the gruesome task of loading the skeletons into Mrs Ruth's car.

"I'm sorry, love, but I don't put dead matter on my back seat. I draw the line at that, love, yes I do."

"Draw the line some other time," Boag-Munroe snapped back. "Get in the car," he ordered the Gentle brothers and Bradley. They obeyed. Alan and Bradley squashed into the single passenger seat at the front, and Tony, silent as ever, sat at the back with the equally silent skeletons.

Boag-Munroe got into the driving seat.

Mrs Ruth tried to stop him: "I'm sorry, love, but what do you think you're doing?"

Boag-Munroe pushed her aside. "I'm commandeering this vehicle."

"You can't treat me like this," she gasped.

"I already have." He slammed the door shut, leaving Mrs Ruth red-faced in anger outside.

"If you think that's bad, wait until you see his driving." Nigel made the situation even worse for Mrs Ruth.

"But it's a brand-new company car!" she howled in a panic.

The engine roared into life. Boag-Munroe rolled down the window. "And very nice it is too," he shouted before screeching off.

Boag-Munroe narrowly missed Jason, who was having his own problems driving, or rather swerving from side to side as if he was well over the drink-drive limit.

"You nearly crashed into my lovely car!" screamed Mrs Ruth at Jason, as he managed to stop before mowing her down.

"Don't get at me. That nutter had already scraped it up the side of a lamppost."

"He hasn't passed his test," confessed Nigel to Mrs Ruth, who was looking more tortured with every passing second.

"Neither have I," Jason admitted.

"Ah yes. But as we know, James Boag-Munroe is a little more excitable than you," Nigel pointed out honestly. At the back of his mind though, he had every confidence in his friend. While, at the back of Mrs Ruth's mind, a little silent prayer was said for her car.

"What have you done?" Nondescript was waiting for Miss Cutts as she returned to the Ministry.

"What I considered I needed to do."

"Miss Cutts, I'm not just surprised, I'm stunned. You put your own instinct against the collective wishes of the Ministry. That, Miss Cutts, as we both know, is not what the Ministry is about."

"I know what I have done, and I'm more than willing to take all responsibility for it."

He nodded. "So you shall, Miss Cutts, so you shall."

A hint of anger began to tinge Miss Cutts' voice: "After all, that is what you wanted: for me, and whoever else, to do the dirty work on our own initiative. That way, if it all blows up, your stature and standing should remain intact, apart from it looking like your staff had some disciplinary problems. And , of course, if all goes well, the less said the better and you get the praise."

"How very cold and calculating you make me sound, Miss Cutts."

"It's the way of the world though. Or so I'm told," she hissed.

"Then may I tell you I've already sent all available manpower to stop Boag-Munroe and put things right. That is if they can be put right, Miss Cutts." He moved closer to her, "And I hope they can, for your sake."

"Where are we going?" asked Alan Gentle quite gleefully.

"To find a vicar. We need to give these a proper burial," Boag-Munroe answered as he swung the car into the drive of the churchyard. On the back seat, an assortment of arms, legs and skulls fell onto an ever more nervous Tony.

The car stopped. Boag-Munroe wasted no time in charging to the vicarage and hammering on its door.

"Get some spades," he shouted to the Gentle brothers.

"Where from?" Alan shouted back.

Boag-Munroe shook his head. "This is a graveyard. Just look around; there's bound to be some. Otherwise you'll be using your hands."

"I got one here," shouted a triumphant Bradley.

"That's more like it," Boag-Munroe answered.

Alan set out in search of more spades, while Tony Gentle was still trying to dig his way out of the mound of skeletons that sat on top of him.

"I've found one too," shouted Alan Gentle as if he'd found a winning lottery ticket.

"Good. Find another," Boag-Munroe shouted back, before hammering on the vicarage door again.

The door opened and a frail old gent peered out.

"Are you the vicar?" asked Boag-Munroe.

The bewildered man nodded.

"Excellent," said Boag-Munroe, before clutching the vicar's arm and dragging him out. "We need your help."

"What for?" the frightened-looking man spluttered.

"A funeral. For about twenty. Don't worry, one service should do for all, it's not like we know who they are by name, and if we did, we wouldn't have the time to work out which bit of bone belonged to whom."

"Oh." The vicar looked even more afraid.

"I've found another spade." Alan Gentle was on a roll.

"Good. At the risk of sounding like a foreman or something, you three get digging. Over there should do."

The flustered vicar started to protest, but Boag-Munroe put a hand over his mouth before he could go any further.

"I'm going to have to ring Nigel, let him know where to go." Boag-Munroe produced his mobile and rang his friend.

The vicar shook his head at the Gentle brothers. "You can't do this."

"It's not that difficult,"' Alan Gentle beamed. "Get yourself a spade if you can find one, it's quite enjoyable digging holes. I used to do it all the time as a kid, until the Council sued my mother over it. Some old codger fell down one and broke both legs and a hip." Alan stopped digging, confused, "Or was it both hips and one leg? I can't remember now, but there was a big fuss about it. I was only six." He returned to his digging.

"You're all mad. You're ghouls, the lot of you," the vicar hollered.

"Not quite," Boag-Munroe put what he thought was a reassuring hand on the vicar's shoulder, but which merely served to make the little man jump out of his skin.

"These are human bones," the old man quaked.

"Exactly, and as such they deserve a decent burial. All we need you to do is just say a few words and a prayer."

The old man looked dumbfounded but was helpless to argue.

The Gentle brothers continued to dig. The vicar, under Boag-Munroe's watchful eye, began to say a prayer over the skeletons.

"Maximum force can be used, I repeat, maximum if necessary." Nondescript's voice came through the radio of the car that carried four, unmistakably armed, members of the Ministry of the Dead. Two were male and two female, and all had a cold steely look in their eyes.

"We're approaching Boag-Munroe now. He can't escape." The driver spoke into his mouthpiece, both hands determinedly wrapped around the steering wheel.

"See that he doesn't. Over and out."

Static took over the radio broadcast.

"We'll see to it all right," the driver grinned. "We've as good as got him." The car stopped. "All out."

Everybody tumbled out and set up positions surrounding Nigel, Jason and Mrs Ruth, guns pointing in all directions.

"Where's Boag-Munroe? Tell us now!" ordered the driver.

"Search me?" Nigel found himself in a surprisingly cool mood.

"How dare you point that thing at me!" Mrs Ruth's anger finally erupted. "I've had my car stolen."

The two Ministry females began to search the van. "There's nothing here."

The penny finally dropped.

"Where is he?" the driver screamed, his own anger boiling over.

Nigel replied for the three of them: "Like she said, he stole her car. He didn't think to tell us where he went."

"Come on." The driver ordered the others back to the car.

Mrs Ruth chased after them. "What about my car?" A polite answer was not forthcoming.

Finally, Mrs Ruth ran out of breath quicker than she ran out of insults.

Nigel had a sly smile on his face.

"Job done." Boag-Munroe looked quite pleased with himself, as Bradley and the Gentle brothers finished piling the earth on top of the grave in which they had laid the skeletons to rest. "That was a lovely service, vicar."

The vicar paused, "You do realise you're all mad? Criminally insane?"

"Yes we do, but you must also realise you're one of us now – an accessory."

"But I had no choice," the vicar whimpered.

"Didn't you? I don't remember anyone forcing you. We merely asked for help. And even if we did force you, that's the wonderful thing about human spirit: sooner or later it always has a choice, there's always an opportunity to fight back. It's just a case of waiting for it."

He began to walk away but stopped and turned back to the vicar. "By the way, before you ask, we won't be at church on Sunday, or any other Sunday. You won't see us again; in fact you've never seen us. The less said the better, and that goes for all of us."

He strode off, leaving the others to silently follow him, making him look even more like the Pied Piper.

CHAPTER FORTY

"The danger is over." The relief showed on Miss Cutts' face.

"Indeed it is, Miss Cutts."

Miss Cutts looked the nondescript man in the eye, like a vulture weighing up its next victim.

"It seems Boag-Munroe has solved our problem for us. He's given the skeletons a decent burial."

"Apart from…"

Nondescript cut her off, "Apart from the one that didn't deserve it. It seemed Boag-Munroe knew what he was doing after all, maybe more so than any of us. Unless of course it was pure luck?"

Miss Cutts didn't particularly want to talk about Boag-Munroe. "I sense Red Leather has been found by the police. His bodyguard gave the game away. Apparently he took one of the young boys who'd been injured by Leather's dogs to hospital."

"Then all's well that ends well."

"The boy is severely scarred."

Nondescript didn't seem unduly interested. "That may be the case but we both know we couldn't have intervened. We had to let events play out – it was the only way to bring us to a conclusion."

"Our latest reports confirm that both Boag-Munroe and Red Leather were possessed."

"We never doubted that, did we, Miss Cutts?"

"Possessed with the spirits of the former miners, of course. Luckily the stranded, but decent spirits had managed to temporarily overpower the evil one. Also, the reports suggest that the parts of the mine which the evil spirit still inhabits are being filled in at this very moment. He may never rest in peace, but alone and unable to harness the power of the others, he should be quite helpless."

"Quite so," Nondescript agreed.

"I think our work has come to a satisfactory conclusion."

"So this is the time for goodbyes then."

"It is?" Miss Cutts looked a little surprised.

"I'm moving on, Miss Cutts, as we all are. The psychic energy level in Northwich is now deemed safe."

"What about Boag-Munroe?"

"I'm sure he'll cross the path of the Ministry again, or vice versa."

"I'm not so sure."

"That's the thing though – none of us can be sure, only enlightened, which is why we have the Ministry in the first place."

"I sense death around Boag-Munroe, and soon."

"I hope not. I found him very interesting. Just the type the Ministry needs."

Nondescript paused, "Or maybe not. He does seem a bit of a loose cannon."

Miss Cutts seemed more interested in herself. "When do we leave?"

"I leave straight away I'm afraid. Alone."

"But I've been your second in command for five years."

"Yes, you have, haven't you?" He sounded emotionless, "Still, new people, new horizons and all that. What the Ministry needs, we must try to deliver as best we can."

"You've had a promotion?"

He smiled, the same lame smile he always smiled, "Until we meet again." He held out his hand.

She shook it coldly. "Until we meet again."

"All's well that ends well," Nigel smiled. "The police have caught that idiot Red Leather."

Boag-Munroe nodded, "I know."

"I've never liked him."

"Didn't you?" Boag-Munroe didn't sound surprised.

"Can't you remember how the little bastard used to torment me as a kid?"

"I can recall something."

Nigel was about to say more but he stopped as Mrs Ruth entered the room.

"Help yourself to tea and biscuits everyone," she beamed. "Help yourself to a saucer as well, love." She pulled Tony Gentle up before he could even think of spilling his drink on any of her furniture, fixtures or fittings. "Now… isn't this cosy, all meeting up after a job well done?"

"What exactly did she do?" whispered Hannah sarcastically into Boag-Munroe's ear.

"Not a great deal in particular. She talked a lot. She even shouted at one point, so I'm told," he laughingly whispered back.

Mrs Ruth began to clap. "Attention everyone. I'd like everyone to give our hero and joint founder-member of our group, Professor Boag-Munroe, a warm round of applause."

"Member of our group?" Boag-Munroe whispered to Nigel.

Nigel smiled, "Well, I never tore your membership up."

"Maybe you should have. I hate fusses."

"You shouldn't have come then."

"You made me."

The clapping died down. Every member of the group was present apart from Emily who was off on a jaunt with her new boyfriend, the one who was years older than her and owned a sports car.

Bradley sat smouldering in the corner.

The Gentle brothers looked happy enough, Mrs Ruth was in her element, entertaining and Hannah had her laid-back attitude down to a fine art.

“Ladies and Gentlemen, I think it’s time for our joint leader to speak,” Mrs Ruth beamed.

“Joint leader?” Boag-Munroe growled at Nigel.

“I never revoked your leadership either. I always knew you’d come back.”

“Did you now?”

“Yes. It only seemed good manners to keep things open-ended.”

Boag-Munroe stood as Mrs Ruth asked for another round of applause. “Really there’s no need.”

“There’s every need. You saved the town.” Mrs Ruth carried on the applause, now on her own.

“I wouldn’t say that.”

“In my book, you averted a disaster,” Hannah chipped in. “There was definitely something going on in those mines.”

“There was indeed,” Nigel perked up. “Tell them James.”

Boag-Munroe stuttered with embarrassment, but then decided to give in and go with the flow before Mrs Ruth started applauding again. “The disaster happened years ago. About two hundred years to be exact. A section of the old salt mine caved in and trapped twenty people. A mixture of men, women and children. All peasant workers who toiled down the mine. There was nothing that could be done to save them back then. None of them had enjoyed the best of lives, and sadly, even in death they were restless, wishing for a proper burial, to escape in death the morbid life they had suffered underground. They didn’t want to be trapped there for eternity. So they waited. They tried to make their presence known with various acts of subsidence over the years through the parts of the town running over the mine.”

“How could they do that?” asked Alan Gentle.

“The pain and suffering had given them power in their collective desperation. They lingered on, waiting and suffering. But something else, or rather someone else, was trapped with them. That person it turns out, was who the Ministry of the Dead were interested in, or should I say afraid of.”

“The Ministry of the Dead were those jokers with the fake guns weren’t they, love?” Mrs Ruth seemed quite nonchalant about it all.

Boag-Munroe wasn’t so blasé. “Believe me, anything that an organisation like the Ministry has or gets involved in, is not a fake. Those gunmen were as real as you and I, and if they’d seen fit, they would have used their very-real guns.”

“Cool!” Bradley added in a very naïve way.

“This person they were interested in…?” Hannah asked.

Boag-Munroe was ready with the answers before she’d even finished the question. “He was the owner of the mine. A dubious character who was rumoured to have sold his soul to the devil, to fund his buying of the mine. He didn’t believe in anything but himself, selfish and cruel, a lethal mix at the best of times. It was his own selfishness in the end that brought about his downfall and trapped him in the mine with the others."

"What was he doing down there, love? If he owned the mine he'd obviously got lots of money. He doesn't sound like the kind of person to care about his workforce," Mrs Ruth said.

"You're right," Boag-Munroe answered, "he didn't care about them. But what he did care about was putting on a good show. You see... He used to entertain guests down in the mine. He'd throw extravagant and unusual parties down there, which would amuse his rich friends. So he used to oversee the preparations for these parties. Make sure they were prepared properly. It was during one of those overseeing exercises that the mine caved in, leaving him a rich, but dead man, with the rest all the same."

"But why were these Ministry people so afraid of him?" Hannah asked.

"It was reputed he had some kind of mystic power, probably because of his supposed dealings with the devil. Devil worship, black magic, he was into all kinds. It was even whispered in some circles that he had his own cult that would meet in the mine."

Bradley, who by this point had started to drift off, suddenly woke up. "You mean like human sacrifices?"

Boag-Munroe nodded. "It's a possibility."

"Cool!" said Bradley, heading for new heights of immaturity.

"The Ministry were worried that his evilness had lived on. And that he would be able to harness the power of the other lost souls, and use them to cause destruction. His hatred at his life being cut short, and in such circumstances, was immense. If he could, he would have caused as much chaos as possible."

"So the Ministry wanted the mines filled in for good. And, when they found the skeletons they couldn't tell the good guys from the bad one," Nigel chipped in.

"Exactly. Their psychics were overwhelmed even going within ten feet of the mine. They didn't have a clue as to which was the evil skeleton in question. The mine filling was a slow process, so they set up camp to watch and guard the skeletons, all the time collecting the information for whatever cause they might want to use it for next. Then I came along."

"Not to mention that tit Ian Leather." Nigel was venomous.

"Before Red became a pop star extraordinaire, he was just plain Ian Leather," Boag-Munroe explained.

"Ian?" Bradley laughed.

"Yes, Ian, myself and Nigel were out playing as kids." Boag-Munroe paused, "Do I need to tell this story or has Nigel already filled you in?"

"I've told them some of it."

Boag-Munroe carried on anyway. "The thing was, a little piece of those spirits entered into Red and me all those years ago and stayed there, dormant. Their last throw of the dice was when work was started to fill the mines in.

Somehow they managed to activate that little part they'd left in Red and me and we both returned home, equally confused. Equally we went about things totally differently."

"Yeah, Red went around snatching kids, thinking he was on some mission from God and will probably end up in the nut house," Nigel was only too pleased to state.

"Wouldn't the skeletons have been found when work started on the mine?" Bradley asked quite sensibly for once.

"No, it was all done by machinery. It wasn't deemed safe down there for humans."

"So how did the Ministry get involved in the first place?" Hannah asked.

"Psychics and such like. Them and the usual mumbo jumbo. Apparently someone in the know came across a large amount of psychic energy in the town. The monitoring started from there and just grew and grew," Boag-Munroe answered.

"How did you come by all this information that fits so neatly into place?" Jason asked sourly.

Boag-Munroe smiled, "Let's just say it all came to me, at the last minute, of course."

"Came to you?" Jason pushed.

Push though he might, Boag-Munroe made no attempt to answer Jason in any shape or form.

"And so here we are," Mrs Ruth beamed.

"Yes," Boag-Munroe fidgeted. "But I'm afraid I'll have to love you and leave you. There are a few things I need to attend to." He stood up.

"Oh no, you can't leave just yet!" Mrs Ruth looked hurt.

"I'm afraid I'll have to."

Nigel stood. "I've got a few things to sort out myself."

"Like what?" Jason was as blunt as ever.

"That's for me to know and you to find out. Or not to find out, as the case may be."

The outside air was cold to Nigel and Boag-Munroe, but nevertheless a kind of welcome relief.

"And what things have you got to attend to?" Nigel asked.

"What things have you got to sort out?" Boag-Munroe asked in return.

Both men laughed.

"I had to get out," Boag-Munroe apologised.

"I know, so did I. Which is funny, as I've always liked the group's weekly meetings."

"You can overdo these things you know. Perhaps you should cut it down from once a week, to once a month instead?"

"Or maybe cut it out entirely?"

"Maybe."

Boag-Munroe's mobile phone began to ring.

"I need you to come right now." Mary's mobile phone trembled in her hand, "I can't say over the phone, but I need your help. You must come straight way."

Carter nodded for her to end the call.

She did so.

"That's a good girl," Carter Whitlowe said in the most patronising manner possible. "We should have this situation cleared up in no time."

Mary doubted it. Looking around at her captors, they looked like escapees from a psychotic, circus freak show. Not the type of people to keep promises.

"I take it our mutual friend is interested?" Carter smiled.

Mary nodded.

"Excellent. I think it's only polite then, if we send out a welcoming party. Bruno, would you do the honours?"

Bruno nodded.

As Bruno left, Mary surveyed her remaining captors. Apart from Carter, there was some guy that looked both mentally and physically handicapped, swaying back and forth in his wheelchair, with a great long chain of slobber dribbling from his mouth. Then there was a nurse who looked like she'd walked straight out of an Alice Cooper song. Either that or one of Mary's own nightmares. As if she hadn't had enough of those recently.

When it came to it, her surroundings were just as character-filled as her captors. They had taken her to an unused factory, in a desolate, former industrial area of the town. It was derelict, falling down, and just the type of place that you see people being held captive in, on television shows, she thought. But this wasn't the television, so even though she was being held captive, no television hero was about to kick down the door, in order to save her. Her only hope was the person who had got her into the mess to begin with: Boag-Munroe.

CHAPTER FORTY-ONE

Boag-Munroe put the phone down. "That was Mary."

"What does she want?" Nigel quizzed.

"I'm not quite sure. She was very vague."

"What did she say?"

"Something about needing to see me right away. It's important, apparently."

"Don't you think you've had enough? How about having a rest for a change?"

"Maybe. But something's wrong somewhere. It feels too much like unfinished business to me. Could you drive me there?"

"Now? Half the town's on emergency alert, plus all the roads are closed to cars."

"That's OK. I've had an idea, and it doesn't involve a car."

"We could just ring her back and ask what's wrong?" Nigel suggested.

"We could… But why waste time? Besides, I've thought of another mode of transport we could use, courtesy of the Gentle brothers."

It wasn't so much the fact that he was riding a bicycle that embarrassed Nigel; it was more that the ones Boag-Munroe and he had borrowed belonged to the Gentle brothers. Although they were racers, they were both bright yellow and covered in babyish slogan stickers, which made matters a lot worse. The fact that they had to cover a good twenty-plus miles to their destination and were already dropping before they started out, only served to rub more salt in the wounds.

"At least this is keeping you fit," Boag-Munroe shouted at the flagging Nigel.

Nigel didn't have a clue from where Boag-Munroe got his energy. Although Nigel had noted that the professor was at least beginning to slow down a little and show some signs of wear and tear from his recent adventures. Nigel gave silent thanks that they'd declined the bright yellow safety hats the Gentle brothers had offered with the bikes. Yellow hats, with the Gentle brothers' trademark aerials jutting from the side. Now that really would have been the icing on the cake.

Surprisingly it didn't take them very long to get to Mary's flat and also surprisingly, when they pressed the flat's intercom there was no reply.

"Still no answer?" Nigel sounded cross, "Have we biked all this way for nothing?"

"We'll soon find out. The door's open. You watch the bikes and I'll nip upstairs to her flat. She might not have heard."

"Right, she might be in the shower or something," Nigel murmured under his breath as his friend disappeared upstairs. "You get all the glamorous jobs."

As feelings go, it wasn't the worst foreboding Boag-Munroe had encountered but it was heavy enough for him to approach the flat's open door with caution. But caution only got you so far. Finally, after some thought, Boag-Munroe threw caution to the wind and pushed the door wide.

Bruno was seated there. All gold teeth and steroid-fed muscles, waiting.

"Professor, I think you know the score. Don't try anything clever." Bruno was polite in his tone. The fact that he was there at all was enough of a threat. There was no need for him to do anything else.

"You seem to have mislaid a friend of mine." Boag-Munroe entered, his eyes peeled for any other surprises. It was an action not lost on Bruno.

"It's OK, Professor. It's just you and me for the moment."

"Don't tell me we're expecting guests? I've not forgotten my own birthday, have I?"

"Nope, Professor. You're the special guest and the party should just be getting warmed up by the time we arrive."

Both men stood their ground in silence.

Bruno smiled, a gold-toothed smile. "Now this is the part where you're supposed to say 'If you've harmed a hair on her head…', or if you're a bit of a coward, 'Please don't kill me'."

"I'm sorry if I don't fall into either of your categories."

"Oh, you will. You see... There is a third category for the ones like yourself who play their cards close to their chest. But it doesn't matter, in the end they all come down to one category – the coward, begging for mercy."

"Studied psychology, have we? Or just watched some very bad, gangster B-movies? Personally, I'm a bit of a fan of B-movies. Not gangster films so much, more science fiction. What is it they say when they land on an alien planet? 'Take me to your leader'. Yes, that's it."

The gold teeth in Bruno's mouth gleamed all the more as he hissed: "It will be my pleasure." Bruno plucked a small handgun from his pocket.

Boag-Munroe looked at it with distaste. "Do you know, for such a big man you've only got a small weapon?"

Bruno laughed, and with a snort, aimed the gun at Boag-Munroe's head. "Yes, but it's not the size, it's what I do with it that counts."

"Shall we go then?"

"No time like the present, is there? And by the way, if you try to escape and if by some miracle you manage to, the girl, Mary, we'll cut her skin off strip by strip."

"After me then, is it?" Boag-Munroe led the way. "It's nice to see a better class of henchman. One that actually likes his job."

"And I do enjoy mine. I put it down to a repressed childhood," Bruno replied.

They made their way down the stairs, Boag-Munroe continuing the conversation. "There you go again with that psychology. If you ever think about getting out of the butchering and maiming lark, you should seriously think of taking counselling up at a professional level. I'm sure you'd find a niche for yourself in the market. There can't be many seven-foot-tall, golden-toothed psychos in the business?"

"You'd be surprised."

But not as surprised as Nigel was as they exited the building. He was crouched down pumping up a bike tyre. He stopped what he was doing when he saw the gun.

"Would you care to join us?" Bruno asked casually.

Nigel was at a loss for words.

Bruno shepherded them to the people-carrier.

"What about the bikes? They'll get nicked," Nigel flustered.

"They'll be fine," hissed Boag-Munroe through clenched teeth.

Nigel followed the professor into the back of the vehicle, still moaning: "They're not even ours."

"Do you know, Nigel – sometimes you just have no sense of occasion," snapped Boag-Munroe.

Sense of the occasion or not, Nigel managed to keep tight-lipped for the short journey to the disused factory.

"Gentlemen. If you would care to make your way into the building." Bruno motioned Boag-Munroe and Nigel inside, still under gunpoint.

Mary, Carter, Stevie and his nurse were waiting inside.

"Say, Bruno, it looks like you've got two for the price of one," Carter mocked.

"It seemed a shame to break them up," Bruno played along.

"I know what you mean. It's going to be an even bigger shame breaking them up into little pieces," Carter laughed and slapped his thigh. "Still, it has to be done." In an instant, his expression changed into a look of pure evil. "But what didn't have to be done was what you did to my son."

Boag-Munroe sighed. "Are you all right, Mary?"

"Oh, I'm just bloody wonderful!" Mary tried not to sound hysterical but it seemed she at least had more sense of occasion than Nigel.

"Look at my son!" Now it was Carter Whitlowe's turn to become hysterical, together with a frightening tinge of psychotic rage.

"I've seen him," said Boag-Munroe with an air of the unimpressed about him.

Carter laughed. "You really take the biscuit. You know that don't you?"

Boag-Munroe shrugged. "One tries."

Carter nodded to Bruno who handed the gun to him. Bruno began to take off his shirt, showing his raging muscles.

"An impromptu strip show? How quaint," chided Boag-Munroe.

"A bare knuckle fight." Carter smiled his biggest murderous smile, "It's called pay back, you see. So let the sport begin."

Boag-Munroe readied himself for the first blow as Mary and Nigel looked on. Bruno turned as if to swing one of his almighty fists into Boag-Munroe's face. He wasn't to be the target though. Nigel fell to his knees breathless as he felt the pain from what he guessed to be at least two broken ribs.

Bruno stood goading Boag-Munroe, as if to say, Look what I'm doing to your friend, what are you going to do about it? Boag-Munroe stood like a block of ice. Bruno grabbed Nigel's hair, snapping his neck back so everyone could see his pain. The block of ice melted and Boag-Munroe shoulder-barged into Bruno, hitting him underneath the ribcage, and sending him spiralling backwards. Bruno was up in an instant. Now it was Boag-Munroe's turn to recoil back as a flurry of punches hit his own ribcage. For a second it seemed as if he was done for, as all he could do was block the head and body shots as best he could. Some of the punches landed with such force, a lesser man would have curled up and died. Boag-Munroe however dropped to the floor, kicking out in an attempt at a leg sweep to bring Bruno down. It failed but the follow-up, a punch to Bruno's nether regions worked. The big man could not contain his gasp of pain. Now it was Boag-Munroe on top with a series of heavy right hooks to Bruno's head. Bruno swayed, but regained his balance with an intensity that suggested he'd found hidden strength from within. A left upper-cut sent Boag-Munroe off balance, slashing his bottom lip with its fierceness. Huge arms wrapped round him in his dazed state. Bruno hoisted him up in a bear hug and squeezed with all his might.

"Squeeze the life out of him!" Carter shouted in an ecstatic frenzy. Carried away in this excitement, he pointed the gun at Nigel's head. "I reckon your friend's got another twenty seconds before all the life is crushed out of him. I'm gonna do the decent thing and give you the same amount before I blow your brains out. One, two…"

Boag-Munroe continued to struggle but it looked to be in vain.

"Three, four…"

Both men were completely trapped.

"Five, six…"

Mary spied her chance; they were all going to die by the looks of it. She bolted for the exit.

"Seven… Get her!" Carter screamed at the nurse as he saw Mary's escape attempt.

Mary nearly made it before she felt herself being dragged back by the hair.

Carter pulled the gun away from Nigel's head and trained it on Mary. "One more trick like that and it'll be your brains that get blown out."

The word 'brains' reverberated round Boag-Munroe's head, as he felt himself passing out while the python-like arms crushed him. One last throw of the dice led him to one last powerful struggle, but Bruno's arms held him too tightly. His struggling however did cause Bruno to lose some of his balance, causing him to almost fling Boag-Munroe's head into a large stone support pillar in the centre of the room. With a last-gasp move, Boag-Munroe lashed both feet out and off the pillar, powering himself and Bruno back. Bruno landed on his back with Boag-Munroe still in his grip, having the life crushed out of him.

"The entertainment goes on," Carter applauded.

But it had become less of an entertaining show for Bruno. The vicious façade of his face had dropped. A temporary look of shock replaced it, soon followed by pain. The floor of the abandoned factory was littered with debris, some more dangerous than others. A shard of glass had embedded itself into Bruno's shoulder. With a yelp he pushed Boag-Munroe to one side, dragging himself to his feet as he tried to pull it out.

"Bruno?" Carter's voice wavered, obviously worried.

"I'm fine," The deep voice reverberated as he plucked out the bloodied glass and tossed it aside.

"Bruno?" Carter shouted again in a panic.

"I said don't worry. I've had worse. And now this little bastard is going to have worse." He closed in on Boag-Munroe, who had fallen underneath a huddle of cardboard boxes, the discarded home of a tramp who had frequented the depressing building some weeks earlier. Bruno had little regard for it as he waded into the boxes to finish Boag-Munroe off. But what had, at first, been determination, turned to wonderment and embarrassment. A battered and bloodied Boag-Munroe had made his way out unseen from the boxes and was catching his breath behind another supporting pillar.

"I thought you were fine?" There was a mixture of a disappointment, anger and fear in Carter's voice.

"I *am* fine," Bruno bellowed back, his eyes now narrowing on Carter. "He's a dead man."

"Dead man, am I?" Boag-Munroe's voice echoed seemingly from every direction, but nowhere in particular around the room.

Bruno and Carter both spun round wildly.

"I don't feel particularly like a dead man, or a beaten one for that matter." The hidden Boag-Munroe spoke out again.

"Come out and fight or your friends won't see tomorrow," Carter screamed in frustration.

"The way I figure, it's a pretty uneven fight. If I do put down Goliath out there, I get shot any way and so will my friends. This way, I'll miss my friends of course, but at least I'll get to fight another day."

Bruno searched like a mad man to no avail.

"Find him!" screamed Carter, "Before he escapes."

"Escape? I don't intend to escape. I think I'll just wait around until Goliath runs out of blood, it can't be that long now and then what are you going to do? You'll be all alone then. With my friends gone and your henchman gone, it'll just be me, you, the cabbage and the wacky nurse."

"I'll fucking kill him!" Carter waved his gun about.

"You just tried that a minute ago and failed. Say tough guy, how's that wound going on? You're looking a bit bloody."

Bruno looked down; he was indeed stained in blood, more so than a few seconds ago. He peered deeply into his hands, now covered in his own blood. "Fuck!" he hissed.

A brick sailed out through the air, smashing Carter on the forehead.

A shot rang out. Carter grabbed his cut head. The gun fell to the ground.

"Bastard!" Carter screamed, blood pouring from the wound in his head, down into his eyes. He lurched blindly for the fallen gun, but Nigel was already onto it. More was the pity that the nurse was nearer and, for the second time that night, Nigel found himself looking down the barrel of a gun.

"Kill all the bastards!" Carter shouted to the nurse.

The nurse stood looking befuddled. On first holding the gun she had looked the real deal but now, ordered to use it, she looked anything but. She seemed shaky; a cold sweat visible on her face.

"Do it!" screamed Carter.

Bruno was still looking down at his hands when Boag-Munroe appeared from behind the pillar.

"Boo!" He sent his fist into Bruno's face. Somehow the bloodied giant still stood, even though Boag-Munroe followed it up with a mixture of hooks and uppercuts that even the best prize fighter would have been proud of.

"The gun!" Carter lunged at the nurse, grabbing the weapon from her grasp. He aimed it in the direction of Boag-Munroe and Bruno. The two fighting figures fell to the floor once more. Carter wasn't able to get a clear shot. He aimed the gun at Nigel one more time and pressed the trigger.

"Oh my God!" Nigel had said the words thinking he was about to meet his maker. He wasn't though. Carter pulled the trigger again. The gun continued to jam.

"Get to the car," Carter ordered the nurse. She quickly pushed Stevie outside in his wheelchair. Carter was following when Nigel stopped him in his tracks. It had just dawned on Nigel that Carter no longer had his gun to rely on. The trouble was that, by the time he reached Carter with both fists clenched, he paused, wondering what to do next. Whitlowe, hard-nosed business man and part-time mobster that he was, didn't need to pause to think what he was going to do next. He just did it. Carter hit Nigel over the head with the butt of his gun.

Nigel fell to the floor unconscious while Boag-Munroe and Bruno battled on, seemingly locked in eternal conflict. Until Bruno dealt a staggering blow to the other's ribs. Boag-Munroe staggered back in pain. Bruno tried to hide the fact that he was still hurt, keeping his distance so that no-one could see. He looked tired and glad of the break in hostilities.

Mary decided now was the time to make her second break. Too late. Carter grabbed her arm, spun her round and punched her on the chin, knocking her unconscious. He headed to the door with her under his arm.

Making his way back onto his feet, clutching his side, Boag-Munroe spotted his friend's silent and still body. "Nigel!" he screamed, the scream causing him to wince from the pain in his ribcage.

The sound of an engine roared into life outside. "Bruno! Come on," Carter shouted unseen over it.

Bruno hesitated. It wasn't in his character to leave unfinished business. But then again, neither was it in Whitlowe's. It wasn't in either's make-up.

Bruno felt his back. He was still bleeding badly. They needed to regroup. He stumbled out into the fresh air and clambered into the vehicle that was raring to go. Which it did as soon as he was aboard.

"You should have let me finish him," Bruno spat through the blood dripping from his mouth. Brian, still hunched up in the back, recoiled at the sight of Bruno's injuries.

"And he might have finished you," Carter replied, brushing his own blood away from his brow, as he drove.

Bruno's face now contorted with not just pain, but anger as well. Carter picked up on this and chose his next words carefully. "He got lucky. You fell on some glass, it was a freak accident, but it happened nevertheless. We've got to patch you up."

"You mean you're going to let him get away?"

Now it was Carter's turn to look angrily at Bruno. "When I want a job doing, I get it done no matter what's thrown at me. In this case, it was you deciding to impale yourself and being careless by getting me a dud gun."

"What about the girl? Do we kill her before she wakes up?" Bruno snarled.

"No. Boag-Munroe knows we won't kill her, not unless we have to. He'll come to the rescue when we let him know the time and the place."

"What time and what place? We're fucking lost, driving round in circles."

"That should do for now – that big hill thing, up there in the countryside. Places like that are always deserted, with plenty of places to hide in. Let's head for the hills," he smiled, as they headed towards the Cloud.

CHAPTER FORTY-TWO

Boag-Munroe helped Nigel to his feet. "You're alive then."

"Shouldn't someone who's been injured be left unmoved until medical help comes?" Nigel groaned.

"Probably," agreed the professor. "But in this case the bad guys might come back and this time they might have working guns." He helped Nigel out of the dreary building and into the fresh air. It was only now he succumbed slightly to the pain he was in, grabbing his side.

"What's the matter with you?" Nigel asked.

"At a guess I'd say a couple of my ribs are broken," Boag-Munroe replied.

"Only a couple? I feel like all of mine have been trashed."

"Well, now we've finished feeling sorry for ourselves, we'd better get on with matters in hand."

"Ringing the police and getting to hospital?"

"I think you're jumping the gun a bit there."

"Don't talk to me about guns," Nigel shuddered.

"The police will want to talk to both of us, if you start mentioning guns."

"What about the mentioning kidnapping?"

"If we call the police now, it'll be a murder case."

"It's an attempted one as it is."

"Mary won't stand a chance if we bring in the police."

"We can't just do *nothing*."

"We won't. We're going to find them."

"You what?" Nigel looked incredulous.

Boag-Munroe smiled. "How do you feel about playing hero?"

"Sick to my stomach."

"At least we know your stomach's working then."

Nigel stopped. "Where are we going?"

"To where they're holding Mary."

"But you don't know where they're holding her."

"I've got an idea though."

"Great." Nigel didn't sound enthusiastic.

"If you're nervous, just think of it as an adventure, like in the movies."

"That's as may be, but if we are going to do it, the way they do it in the movies, shouldn't we wait by the phone at home for the kidnappers to get in touch?"

"We'll do that if my hunch is wrong. But then again, when have I ever been wrong?"

Nigel sighed, "So where are we heading?"

Boag-Munroe pointed, "There… To the Cloud."

"Why there?"

"They'll have to go somewhere close by. The Cloud stands out, and it's desolate. It seems as good as any place for a hideout, or an ambush."

"I don't like any of this," Nigel frowned.

"You don't? What about me? It's been predicted that the Cloud means death for me."

"Then heed the prediction. Let's let the police handle this."

"And spoil my appointment with destiny? Never."

They began their trek through the edge of the town towards the Cloud, drawing suspicious glances at every turn. It looked desolate. A cloud bleaker and darker than ever as they drew nearer.

The trek to the top of the Cloud was long and taxing. The people-carrier was parked as discreetly as possible at the foot of it while the strange group headed towards its peak, staying away from its dangerous edges and cutting through the wooded area in the middle of it.

Mary was now more convinced than ever that she was going to die; Brian was also facing up to the fact that there might be something unpleasant in store for him.

The nurse put her back into pushing Stevie Whitlowe in his wheelchair, every muscle in her body aching as she ploughed the chair and its occupant forward over the rough uneven dirt track that weaved through the woods. Bruno's bleeding seemed to have been stemmed, although he didn't look half the man he had, still a giant of staggering proportions and viciousness, but weaker nevertheless. Carter, on the other hand, had grown in stature. He had managed to miraculously fix his gun. He let a shot fly. A flock of birds screeched, and then once more, the wood fell silent.

"Doesn't it just feel great to be alive?" Carter enthused.

Nobody answered him. They were all silent until they left the woods and came to the rocky peak of the Cloud.

Carter seated himself, gun in hand, on a large smooth rock. "How's the wound?"

"It's stopped bleeding," Bruno answered.

"And how do you feel?"

"I just need some rest."

Brian put his hand up, timidly. "Excuse me, but am I really needed now?"

Carter turned. "It's a long way down, isn't it?"

Brian gulped and said no more.

Bruno found himself a flat piece of rock to sprawl over. "It's going to take them some time to get up here, if they manage it."

"You do realise they'll just go to the police?" Mary had said it before she'd even thought about it.

"And you must realise that if they do you'll die, slowly?" Carter scowled.

Mary recoiled. Carter had been mad enough so far. She didn't have to question if he'd go all the way, she just knew it.

The nurse sat beside Stevie who was now rocking back and forward in his chair.

"Make him stop that," Carter shouted at the nurse.

"Ssssh!" she whispered into Stevie's ear as she stroked his hair, but still he persisted.

Carter's rage grew. "I said make him stop!"

"I can't," the nurse replied meekly.

"You can't?" Carter laughed sarcastically. He sat back with a tear in his eye, looking somewhat lost. "No you can't, can you? Nobody can stop him rocking like an idiot, sitting like a zombie for hours on end, or drooling into his food. All that we can do is pay back those who did this." He sent a shot ringing out in anger, "And pay them back we will."

Nigel was dropping. In fact he wished he could drop into a blissful oblivion and then his part in the proceedings would be over. But it wasn't going to be like that.

"Do you really expect us to climb that thing in the state we're in?"

Boag-Munroe eyed the foot of the Cloud. "We've made it this far."

"That doesn't mean to say we'll make it any further."

"Ever the positive thinker," the professor commented sarcastically.

"I'm sorry if I don't share your optimism for any of this," Nigel retorted.

"Never mind, there's still time for you to find a bit of optimism. It's a long climb ahead."

"Excuse me? Climb?"

"Did you really think we could just take the main path and waltz up there?"

"No, I was thinking we could just hang-glide in."

"It might not be a bad idea, but seeing as neither of us has a hang-glider about our person. It'll have to be done the hard way: up the side of the Cloud."

"Now he tells me."

"You'll be safe enough here."

"Meaning?"

"One of us needs to stay here in case anything does go wrong. And if it does go wrong, there's no point in there being any more corpses up there than need be. Plus, with you alive, you'd be able to inform the police of what happened." Boag-Munroe paused, "Of course that's if I fail."

Nigel showed his nerves. "And you think you might? You believe there could be some truth in these predictions?"

"They're just precautions. Give me an hour. If I'm not back in that time... Well, you know what to do."

"I've come this far I might as well finish it." Nigel moved to follow him.

"No." Boag-Munroe was adamant. He patted Nigel on the shoulder, "You've always been a good friend, Nigel."

It seemed like a final goodbye.

Nigel stood firm. "And good friends don't leave their friends in a crisis."

"They also respect each other's wishes."

"I'm coming with you."

"No." Boag-Munroe blocked his path; a cold steel in his eyes clearly portraying the fact that he would not be swayed. "Give me an hour."

Nigel backed away and prepared for the longest hour of his life.

Boag-Munroe began to crawl up the side of the Cloud as if it was a mountain and he an expert rock climber. It looked every inch the scene from an action film, the lone hero off to confront the bad men who outnumbered him completely. But this wasn't a mountain, Boag-Munroe wasn't an expert climber, and it wasn't a film. Nigel stood back. In his eyes, for all intents and purposes, his friend was a hero; he couldn't have been more so, even if he'd have rode up the unforgiving terrain on a white charger. Nigel couldn't help but feel a little jealousy that he couldn't be like that, but most of all he felt great pride in being associated with such a figure, and an undying honour that he was his friend.

"He's here." Carter stood, "I can smell him."

Bruno sat up, now looking a little better for his rest. Bruno may have been an animal at the best of times, but Carter was a businessman, and a very successful one: a man who had used his common sense and a good dose of instinct to get to the very top. Bruno took anything that Carter said very seriously.

Carter spun round to look down into the woods.

"Can you see anything?" asked Bruno, now standing to his full height and ready for action.

Carter spun back round. Slowly he crept to a vantage point, close to the edge of the Cloud. He looked down gingerly, at the sheer drop and the various rocks and brambles jutting out.

Boag-Munroe was close, very close; flattening his body against the rock, fighting the winds that were threatening to rip him off the Cloud's surface. Hidden underneath the jutting rocks that Carter was trying to peer over, Boag-Munroe waited, holding his breath. He could sense Carter, just as much as Carter could sense him.

Carter moved even closer to the edge. "Merlin, my friend. Come here."

Brian hesitated, his nerves shrieking out.

"Take a look at this," Carter insisted.

He scuttled over to look beyond the edge, at Carter's insistence.

"Quite a view of your quaint English countryside, ain't it?" Carter patted him on the back.

"It is, but I'm not really one for heights," Brian quivered.

“Shame. Then all this is wasted on you.” He grinned, “Say, it sounds to me like you’ve got a phobia. You know what you should do if you have a phobia?” He put his arm round Brian, “You should face it.”

One violent push later and Brian was indeed facing his phobia as he went straight over the edge.

Carter turned back to the onlooking group. “He’ll feel a lot better for coming to terms with his fear.”

The ripping wind drowned Brian’s screams.

Almost.

It was now or never as far as Mary was concerned. She closed her eyes and bolted for the woods.

“It looks like the party’s falling apart,” said Carter, casually levelling his gun in the direction of Mary’s sprinting figure. “She’ll never make it of course.”

A shot whistled so close to Mary’s head that she dived to the floor, a crumpled figure.

“See what I mean,” Carter sneered.

The sneer was lost on Boag-Munroe but the emergency of the situation wasn’t. Climbing unseen over the edge from which Brian/Merlin had plummeted, Boag-Munroe pounced on Carter with all the grace, silence and power of a tiger. Both men fell to the ground with Bruno quickly joining the fray. Mary brought herself up to her knees, ready for another escape attempt. Carter however had escaped the tussle and was now closer than ever with his gun positioned on her.

Boag-Munroe and Bruno were once again locked in one of their power struggles as they brawled wildly to the edge of the Cloud. Mary knew that this battle would inevitably end in death. There could be no other way.

The two bodies, now locked in combat, fell to the ground on an edge that led to a sheer drop. Closer they rolled, before Bruno seemed to get the upper hand, managing to nearly throw Boag-Munroe over the edge with his brute force. Perilously close to the edge now, Boag-Munroe managed to get back up on his feet, unsteady though he was.

Bruno charged, hoping to finish him off.

Boag-Munroe slipped back into the grip of the wind that was trying to feverishly pluck him from the Cloud.

The storm clouds descended further.

Boag-Munroe toppled over the edge, grabbing at Bruno’s arm, taking him over the edge with him.

The wind raged louder as the rain began to pelt down on the now-empty edge.

“Move and you join your boyfriend!” Carter barked at Mary. She stood shivering in the rain.

All hope was now lost.

Carter shuffled cautiously to the edge. His face lit up with delight when he realised the game wasn't entirely over and that he would get to make Boag-Munroe suffer after all.

Boag-Munroe was gripping the edge of a jagged rock, his whole body dangling, helpless, over the drop that had claimed Brian and now Bruno.

Stevie began to rock in his chair again.

"Keep still!" Carter shouted to his son.

Stevie continued to rock.

Carter pointed his gun down at the helplessly hanging figure of Boag-Munroe. "So how does it end? Do you let go first? Or do I shoot?"

Boag-Munroe struggled, but there seemed to be no foothold and no hope. His arms felt as though they were ripping out of their sockets.

"How does it feel for you now? To feel as helpless as I feel towards that thing that used to be my son?"

"It wasn't my fault, you fool." Boag-Munroe felt his grip slipping.

"Me the fool? I'm not the one hanging from a piece of rock about to die."

Stevie began to murmur while he rocked back and forth.

"I said shut up!" Carter shouted again at his son.

"Killing me won't solve anything."

"That's what they all say." Carter crunched his foot on one of Boag-Munroe's hands leaving him gripping on for life, one-handed.

"It's you that's the fool. A fool for blindly seeking revenge, and your son for tampering in things he shouldn't. Hard drugs and black magic is a lethal concoction for the best of us. Even more so for some brat who was obviously unstable in the first place."

"You did this!" Carter screamed against Boag-Munroe, above the raging elements.

"He was a rich boy playing games. I warned him."

"You can plead all you like."

"I'm telling the truth, but the truth isn't something you want to hear."

"Bastard!" Carter brought his foot down on Boag-Munroe's remaining hand. Boag-Munroe slipped some more, his grip lessening, but still somehow managing hang by a thread.

Stevie Whitlowe began to rock more violently back in his chair.

"Shut up!" Carter slapped his son hard across his face. Stevie stopped rocking.

Carter turned his attention back to Boag-Munroe. "Look at me. I want to see the fear in your eyes as I send you to your death."

Stevie's face began to contort into what looked like anger.

Boag-Munroe gasped, his hold now faltering. "Then I'm afraid you're going to be disappointed. The only fear you're going to see is your own."

Stevie clenched the sides of his chair, his knuckles white.

Boag-Munroe's grip loosened more, the pain showing on his face, the wind now tugging heavily at his legs.

"Are you sure about that?" Carter spat at Boag-Munroe.

Stevie lurched from his chair.

"What?" Carter Whitlowe managed the one word of surprise… before his son sent him sailing over the edge with a solitary push.

Carter's scream was the loudest Mary had ever heard.

Boag-Munroe saw the terror in his eyes as Carter plunged past him to his death. Even so, this action had no effect on Boag-Munroe. He was still swaying high above what could soon be his own demise. Above him, Stevie was now rocking back and forth on the floor, mumbling something about the voices in his head making him do it.

Mary stood speechless and motionless. The nurse simply turned as if in a trance and walked away, obviously washing her hands of it all. The way she did so, so coldly, left Mary wondering if she wasn't as mad as the loon she was supposed to be caring for.

More or less alone now, Mary carefully approached the edge of the Cloud, past the gibbering Stevie. Boag-Munroe was trying to haul himself up with his last bit of strength. She outstretched her hand. He caught hold, but the weight of him almost dragged her down.

"Go get help," he ordered her.

"You'll never make it." A tear welled up in her eye. She'd seen too much of death.

"Just go. Nigel's at the foot of the Cloud."

"You won't be able to hang on." Panic overcame her. "You're falling."

She was right; he couldn't hang on, not that he'd admit it. Perhaps it was as Eloise had predicted, and was meant to be.

"Just do your best to get Nigel here," he said, seemingly resigned to his fate.

"Nigel's here already." He stretched a hand to Boag-Munroe, "Better late than never." He helped Boag-Munroe up who, with his aid, scrambled to safety.

Boag-Munroe looked at his watch. "You're not late, you're early."

"If you'd like me to come back later?"

Both men laughed.

"I saw the figure again … the apparition." Mary spoke.

The laughter stopped.

Boag-Munroe could see more than Mary's discomfort; he could sense it all around her. He put a comforting arm round her.

"John's dead," she sobbed.

"I'm sorry to hear that."

"I thought it would be all over. That was the warning fulfilled." She choked on her tears. "I couldn't save him. I must be cursed."

"You're not cursed." Boag-Munroe forced her to look him in the eye, "It just feels like that. It's something you're going to have to live with. It might get easier, it might not. I'm not the one to say."

"Then who is?" There was a hint of anger in between her tears.

"You are."

Everything fell silent apart from the haunting sound of the wind.

"The apparition came back though… after John's death."

"Just another warning."

"Of what?" The tears had stopped. She stamped her foot.

"Of this. This could very easily have ended very differently."

Mary felt obliged to turn her gaze to the edge of the Cloud, and thought about those that had so recently fallen from it.

She turned back to Boag-Munroe. "So I have to live my life under the fear that Mr Faceless could turn up at anytime? And when he does, something terrible is going to happen?"

"It sounds about the sum of it."

"And you say I'm not cursed?"

"Not cursed. Just scarred. Just like the rest of us."

Boag-Munroe began to walk away.

"What about him?" Nigel nodded in the direction of Stevie Whitlowe.

"We'll take care of him," an unfamiliar voice spoke.

More people appeared.

"The police?" exclaimed Mary quizzically.

"I never called them," mumbled Nigel. "I stayed true to my word in that sense."

A familiar figure now emerged from the woods. A female figure.

"I said the Cloud meant death for you," said Eloise coolly.

"Not mine though."

"We can't hit the bullseye all the time." She tossed her hair back, "Maybe next time."

"I see you've made some new friends," remarked Boag-Munroe.

Eloise smiled, "We'll clean this mess up. You'd better get yourself some medical treatment."

"I'll live."

"This time."

Boag-Munroe brushed passed her.

"Is that it?" screamed Mary.

Boag-Munroe turned. "What more do you want?"

"Who are these people?"

Boag-Munroe shook his head.

Eloise pushed an envelope into Boag-Munroe's hand. "Take this. Read it when you get to the foot of the Cloud, then don't look back."

He took the envelope, and staggered away, battered and bloodied from his battles.

At the foot of the Cloud Boag-Munroe opened the envelope.

"What does it say?" asked Nigel.

"It says '*From a haunted man, to a haunted man. This time I didn't let you down*'."

Boag-Munroe studied it for a moment longer before throwing the letter and the envelope to the ground.

A strong gust of wind carried the crumbled paper away into the heart of an endlessly green, English country field.

EPILOGUE

Dusk. The cool air was kissing a breeze, softly, around Marbury Park.

Two figures strolled along the lonely country road keeping in synchronised time with one another's footsteps.

"You never did get round to telling me exactly how you managed to be so precise with your information on the mines." Nigel spoke so softly, that his voice was almost cancelled out by the crunching sound of the gravel underneath his feet.

"Didn't I?" Boag-Munroe's playful sarcasm was obvious.

"There's nothing to back up your claims about what happened down there all those years ago."

"I hope you're not accusing me of making it up?" Once again Boag-Munroe sounded playful, if a little hurt.

"Would I dare do that?"

A grey squirrel darted out in front of them, stopped, and then scurried back to the safety of the undergrowth.

"I think it's past his bedtime," Boag-Munroe commented.

"Perhaps he's like you and never sleeps?" Nigel smiled.

Boag-Munroe stopped. He looked hurt. "I do sleep."

Nigel's grin grew broader. "Yes, but with one eye open."

They continued their walk, through the park gates and beyond.

"It's quite mild for this time of year," Nigel said.

"Yes it is," Boag-Munroe blindly replied.

"Are you still hoping to see her?" Nigel asked.

"I'm not sure I want to now."

"Nobody's reported seeing her for years. Perhaps it was all nonsense? Local girl loses her life at beauty spot that has a history of previous hauntings. It's too good to be true for some sick bastards," Nigel scowled.

"Whatever the case, I can feel her here."

"You mean she does haunt?"

"Only me." Boag-Munroe drew a deep breath, "Not so long ago a certain person accused me of being possessed, and they were right. Gail has possessed me. She's been in my mind and thoughts ever since she died, ever since I met her in fact."

Nigel looked down at the floor.

Boag-Munroe looked a little guilty. "I'm sorry. I've spoken out of turn."

Nigel looked up and smiled, easing the situation somewhat. "When did you do otherwise?" His face saddened, "She may have been my girlfriend, but she loved you." He paused, "And you loved her. You were meant to be together, and would have been, if not for events."

Now it was time for Boag-Munroe to look sad. "Events eh? We all have them don't we? Some good, some bad, some completely soul-destroying."

"I stopped blaming myself years ago and so should you."

"I don't believe you."

"You don't have to." Nigel paused, "We weren't to know."

The evening suddenly grew colder with Boag-Munroe's mood change. "Weren't to know? Every day she told us how she'd seen a vision of a boy in forties dress style, in her bedroom."

"And what was that supposed to signify to us then?"

"It was a warning. One we didn't heed."

"And what good did the warning do for Mary's husband?"

"Some you win, some you lose." Boag-Munroe sounded distant.

"And we both lost Gail."

They continued to walk solemnly.

"I wonder what Mary will do now," Nigel pondered out loud.

"Pick her life up I should imagine."

"You mean move on?"

"If you like. What else is there to do?"

"It's not that easy for some of us though, is it? Some of us move on, some just stay and sit dormant."

"And do you think that's all you've done?" Boag-Munroe asked.

Nigel stopped. "Look at me. Are you going to tell me otherwise?"

"So what do you think is the worse then: staying dormant or coming back full circle?"

"You mean to say you're staying for good?"

"Who knows?"

"There you go again – never a straight answer."

They carried on walking.

"There's never a straight question; not any interesting ones at least. But let's just say I have a few interesting unanswered questions around here to keep me occupied for the time being."

"Such as?"

"Now that would be telling, wouldn't it?" Boag-Munroe allowed a smile. "You didn't expect a straight answer, did you?"